MW00622248

BOYS IN THE VALLEY

ALSO BY PHILIP FRACASSI

NOVELS

Gothic

A Child Alone with Strangers

Don't Let Them Get You Down

STORY COLLECTIONS

Beneath a Pale Sky

Behold the Void

NOVELLAS

Commodore

Shiloh

Sacculina

FOR CHILDREN

The Boy with the Blue Rose Heart

POEMS

Tomorrow's Gone

BOYS
IN THE
VALLEY

PHILIP
FRACASSI

NIGHTFIRE

TOR PUBLISHING GROUP
NEW YORK

This is a work of fiction. All of the characters, organizations, and events portrayed in this novel are either products of the author's imagination or are used fictitiously.

BOYS IN THE VALLEY

Copyright © 2021 by Philip Fracassi

Introduction copyright © 2021 by Andy Davidson

All rights reserved.

A Nightfire Book
Published by Tom Doherty Associates / Tor Publishing Group
120 Broadway
New York, NY 10271

www.tornightfire.com

Nightfire™ is a trademark of Macmillan Publishing Group, LLC.

Library of Congress Cataloging-in-Publication Data

Names: Fracassi, Philip, 1970– author.
Title: Boys in the valley / Philip Fracassi.
Description: First Nightfire edition. | New York : Nightfire, Tor
    Publishing Group, 2023.
Identifiers: LCCN 2023007584 (print) | LCCN 2023007585
    (ebook) | ISBN 9781250879035 (hardcover) | ISBN
    9781250879042 (ebook)
Subjects: LCGFT: Gothic fiction. | Horror fiction. | Occult fiction. |
    Novels.
Classification: LCC PS3556.R24 B69 2023 (print) | LCC PS3556.
    R24 (ebook) | DDC 813/.54—dc23/eng/20230303
LC record available at https://lccn.loc.gov/2023007584
LC ebook record available at https://lccn.loc.gov/2023007585

Our books may be purchased in bulk for promotional, educational, or
business use. Please contact your local bookseller or the Macmillan
Corporate and Premium Sales Department at 1-800-221-7945, extension 5442, or by email at MacmillanSpecialMarkets@macmillan.com.

First Nightfire Edition: 2023

Printed in the United States of America

0 9 8 7 6 5 4 3 2 1

For Dominic

INTRODUCTION

Let me begin by saying this: I've never actually met Philip Fracassi, but I've known him forever.

It's hard to explain, how a couple of phone conversations or a story exchange can engender such a sense of another person: their talent, their work ethic, their ambition. Thousands of miles may separate us, but somehow, despite all the reasons it's absurd to claim so, I think of Philip as kin. Read his blog and you'll see: his struggles are every writer's struggle, his dreams every writer's dream, and his victories, yes, are every writer's victory.

Because, let's face it, we're all of us richer for his work.

Take *Boys in the Valley*. The set-up is pure horror: an unknown evil infests a group of young boys in an isolated orphanage in rural Pennsylvania. In lesser hands, this could easily be an off-putting tale of exploitative violence. But Philip's is a sure and steady hand, and his execution of that premise is extraordinary. Think Jack Ketchum's *The Girl Next Door*. Here is a book that confronts our worst cruelties, without flinching, and demands answers to the great questions that plague our spirits. What is evil? Is it benign neglect, malicious intent? Some deeper, more incomprehensible darkness? Do we, as humans, possess a light strong enough to overcome such darkness? Where is God in all this? For us, against us?

It's a book that puts me in mind of two other great works: William Golding's *Lord of the Flies* and Michael Powell and Emeric Pressburger's *Black Narcissus*. In Golding's novel, a group of boys stranded on a deserted island fashion their own doomed civilization and sink quickly into depravity. In Powell and Pressburger's film, a group of nuns are stationed high in the Himalayas and find themselves haunted by their own earthbound desires. Both works suggest that our environment has a hand in driving us crazy, but also that our own doom is somehow inherent to "some final, rebellious act of the haunted flesh," to borrow a phrase from *Boys in the Valley*.

And yet: Philip's book offers as much hope as despair. In my favorite passage in the novel, Father Andrew tells our hero, Peter, a young candidate for the priesthood, that "the discovery of Christ is not found in a darkened room . . . It's found in the light. God is not found through escape from a distant place, but through the arrival of where you already are." (Sometimes, as a writer, you read a passage in a book so achingly beautiful and perfect you wish you'd written it. Other times, you surrender to the realization that you're not even capable of writing something that good. So it goes here.)

I could go on about *Boys in the Valley*—its language, its humanity, its compassion—but that would only delay your experience of reading it, which will be, by turns, gut-wrenching, terrifying, heartbreaking, and sublime.

In many ways, it feels like Philip Fracassi has always been here, working quietly among us, book after book, story after story. I hope he always is—in part because, one day, I hope to meet the guy out in sunny Los Angeles and buy him a beer, to tell him what his work has meant to me these last few years. But mostly because, these days, our world needs all the hope it can get, and as long as there are writers like Philip Fracassi toiling in the light, the darkness cannot overcome us.

Andy Davidson
Cochran, Georgia
February 10, 2021

When I am asked how many demons there are, I answer with the words that the demon himself spoke through a demonic:

"We are so many that, if we were visible, we would darken the sun."

—Father Gabriele Amorth,
Chief Exorcist of the Vatican

I'm just a man, not a hero
Just a boy, who had to sing this song.

—My Chemical Romance

BOYS IN THE VALLEY

The muted thunder of wagon wheels wakes me from shallow sleep.

Outside my darkened window, the clop and hard breath of horses. A rattling wagon pulls close to the house, then slows, then stops. Men's raised voices group together then fall apart. Disappointment veiled by revelry and drink. I hear Mother in the kitchen, dividing my attention. I throw off the blanket and run barefoot to the window. Cold air pushes through thin glass and I shiver. Father's inky silhouette stands in the narrow lane, one arm raised. He cries out and now-distant voices reply. His arm drops to his side. He turns toward the house and appears to stumble then catch himself. The long black line of the rifle cradled in his arms points skyward. Pots clatter from the kitchen and I run to the door that separates my room from the living area—this includes a sitting space, a dining area, and kitchen. Our whole world is but three rooms and a pair of outhouses, a world held together by warped wooden planks and warmed by a rusted black stove that eats coal faster than we can fill it.

I am lucky to have my own room, even if it's small. Though I'm little, I'm not able to take three large steps in any direction. Father says I'm a *runt* but Mother says a nine-year-old boy has room to grow. I hope to get big, but not so big I can't fit in my room. I like it too much.

I see more clearly now because Mother has lit the kitchen lanterns. There's enough space between my bedroom door and the frame to stick a finger, so light comes through easy, coats the dark walls and disrupts the shadows in the corners and beneath my bed. I step softly to the door—it wouldn't do for them to know I'm up—and put an eye to the gap. If I swivel my head, I can see the entire kitchen and the dining table, but not much else. I'm cold in nothing but long johns but want to hear about the trip. Mother has the stove going and I smell the warming onion soup she'd taken from the icebox. She puts on a kettle for coffee. Father slams the door and the house rattles. Mother wipes her hands on her apron in a way she does when she's upset, like she's wringing it dry.

Father enters my field of vision, all beard and worn leather. A beat-to-hell Stetson wedged over black hair. He pulls out a chair, sits heavily. The rifle butt clunks against the floor and he looks at the old Winchester as if willing it to speak.

"Nothing?" Mother says. "Nothing at all?"

Father waits for the gun to answer but it stays silent.

"I'll have what's in that pot, Sissy. And some coffee."

"It's heatin'," she says, stirring. She keeps her eye on the stove, off my father. "You've been drinking."

I inspect him more closely for signs of drunkenness—wondering what my mother sees that makes it apparent—but nothing stands out. He looks tired and wronged, but that's his natural state.

"Sheriff is shooting poachers. Land's dry." Father shakes his head. He takes off the Stetson, sets it on the table. He still holds the rifle.

I want to open the door and go to him. Sit with him and talk like men about the Sheriff and the land.

The kettle starts to whistle.

"What are we gonna do, Jack? The garden can provide some, but we need meat. Winter's coming."

Father runs a hand through his long hair. "Please . . ." he says, and I tremble at his voice as well as the cold. "Shut up, Sissy. Just shut up and bring me some coffee."

I will my mother to stop. To leave him be. She knows what he's like. I close my eyes for a moment and silently pray. Then I watch.

The kettle is screaming, and I know if I hadn't been awake already, I would be now. The house is filled with the high-pitched shriek of rushing steam. "I see . . . I see . . ." Mother says. "You go out with the boys for two days, drinking and who knows what else. Leave me and Peter here to starve. To starve!" She screams this last at him and I see my Father's face redden. His eyes close tight, then open wide.

"Shut your goddamned mouth!" he yells, spit flying in the lantern light like mist. "Shut it. Shut it. Shut it!"

"You're horrible, Jack! You'll wake Peter . . ."

Father slams his hand on the table and Mother, realizing she's gone too far, pushed him too hard, quickly removes the kettle and pours coffee into a cup next to the stove. The reprieve of the kettle's whistle is luxurious. "You're a disappointment," she says as she pours. "How dare you swear in my house. Use the Lord's name in vain . . ."

He mumbles something. It sounds like "that's enough," but I'm not certain of the words. I just know he's upset. I've never seen him in such a state. His downcast face is stone, his eyes black pearls.

Mother brings the coffee cup to the table. Lips tight as a pulled drawstring. "You aren't no husband," she says. "You aren't even a man!"

He turns to retort just as she arrives with the cup. His elbow knocks it from her hand and the hot coffee drops into his lap.

Father screams in pain, leaps up. The chair clatters to the floor and Mother backs away, hands raised in supplication. Apologies and terror spill from her mouth.

"Enough," he says.

I watch as Father, with a practiced and casual movement, raises the barrel of the rifle and cocks the lever with a hideous smoothness.

Mother holds up her hands. "Oh Lord Jesus!"

The eruption of the gun shatters the air.

Mother jerks backward as if tugged by the hand of God. She hits the stove with such force that the door pops open and coals fly out in a shower of sparks like burning souls. A lantern on a nearby hook crashes to the ground and fiery oil splatters the floor and wall. Frail curtains catch the hot spray and burn.

There's a moment where time stands still, and then Father is howling.

"Oh, Sissy!" He puts a dirty hand over his mouth as the room brightens. "Oh damn it, Sissy!" He kneels beside her and sobs.

Wet heat runs down my leg and I look down to see a puddle forming around my foot. When I raise my eyes, Father is once more seating himself at the table.

One wall crawls with flame. Dark smoke rides the low ceiling like storm clouds.

Father turns his head toward my door and for a moment our eyes meet. I imagine how I must look to him. A sliver of son. A bright probing eye in the dark, watching his sins.

Father holds his eyes on me. I make a study of him. Wet eyes and mussed hair. Straggled beard. A sweat-sheened face smeared in prancing red flames. He looks away, back to my mother.

He doesn't turn toward me again.

I want to cry out, to scream. To run to him.

My teeth chatter. I begin to moan and can't stop.

I can't move. I can't breathe.

All I can do is watch.

He slowly cocks the lever of the Winchester—the very one he'd taught me to shoot with that past summer—puts the grip between his knees and the barrel's lusterless tip beneath his chin.

Something inside me comes awake and at the last second I shut my eyes.

This shot is duller than the first.

Breathing fast and heavy, I pull open the door and stare boldly at the scene.

For a moment, I see myself as a spectator—a thin shadow shaking before a fiery dragon—crotch-stained and whimpering.

Before me is nothing but death and blood and smoke and flame.

My whole world is fire.

PART ONE
WE ARE MANY

1

"Peter, wake up."

I open my eyes to the familiar.

White walls. Two rows of metal-framed beds. Bleached pine floor. Bright pale light bursting from large, uncovered windows that line the east-facing wall. Two large, arched oak doors at the far end of the long room are closed. The winking glimmer of the polished iron cross that hangs above them a constant sentinel. Always watching.

Simon pokes me in the shoulder. "Wake up. You're having a nightmare."

I sit up, rub my eyes. Most of the kids are still asleep, so it must be early. Not yet six.

"I'm up," I say, and shove Simon gently back toward his cot. He laughs and sits down on his mattress, looking out the large window between our beds.

"Might snow today," he says excitedly, as if that's a good thing.

"Too soon." I yawn and stretch. It's icy cold in the dorm. My thin robe is balled up at my feet and I pull it on over my wool pajamas, which I've long grown out of, annoyingly exposing my ankles and wrists. I slip my feet into shoes and follow Simon's stare through the glass.

The sky outside is white as bone and just as hard. I stand up to get a better look at the grounds.

The surrounding trees are leafless and gray. They look dead and withered. The earth is a wealth of weedy grass that, in the

dim light, looks as gray as the trees. Colorless. The barn that
holds our horses, sheep, and goats sits to the south. Ahead is the
field we'll be working that morning, pulling what we can from
the earth and storing it for the winter, which I've heard will be
long and harsh. I wonder if any of the boys will die before spring
shows its face again, and say a silent prayer for all of them.

I glance at the metal wind-up clock on my dresser—the only
furniture we're allowed—and see it's a few minutes before six.
I'm the only one who has a personal clock, and it's the only thing
I have left from my childhood, my prior life; the only thing I
saved when I fled the burning house.

I push in the knob on the clock's alarm, disabling it. No
need to hear the shrill bell to wake me. My memories serve well
enough to break my sleep.

"Go wash, Simon. And take Basil with you."

Basil, a small, sickly, black-haired English boy not even ten
years old, watches me and Simon from across the room with
wide owl-eyes. He is already fully dressed.

"Oh, why, Peter?"

"Because he's up and ready."

I watch them as they trudge out the dorm toward the washroom. I study the others in the early-morning light, curious if
anyone else has woken.

It seems my nightmare didn't disturb the others, and I feel badly
for rousing Simon. But it's near dawn now, and Poole will be ringing first bell shortly, expecting us to be dressed and ready before the
subsequent bell ten minutes after.

I shed my robe and pajamas, begin pulling on the heavy
shirt and pants folded neatly inside my dresser. It will be cold
today, and the idea of winter's arrival worries me for reasons I
don't fully understand. I've been through many winters here at
St. Vincent's and they're all the same. A seemingly eternal purgatory of cold and dark.

And yet, as I look through the window at the dreary landscape, I find myself frowning with worry.

My melancholy breaks when the first bell brays its command from the foyer. I turn to the room and see the lumps beneath the sheets begin to stir and groan.

The boys are waking.

2

I step outside and see Father Andrew waiting by the gate which leads to the crops. He waves and I wave back. Boys clamor past me with a divided urgency: excited to be outdoors, but wary of the labor ahead. Aaron, a pink-cheeked boy with blond hair so fair it looks white in the morning sun, falls in next to me. He's only thirteen but tall, if skinny, and one of a few orphans who almost matches my height.

"Fields again?" he whines. "We've stored enough food for an army."

"You'll be thanking the priests a few weeks from now, when the storm has us snowed in, trapped like rats. Remember last year?"

He groans dramatically and I laugh, patting his shoulder. "Get the boys divided, will you? Help Father Andrew."

Aaron nods and begins pulling at coats, shoving the little ones lightly. "You lot who were in the field yesterday are with the animals today. You others, in the field. Come on, ya rascals."

The other priest in residence, ancient Father White, emerges from the large front doors of the orphanage and begins sorting the remaining children. The ones destined for the barn head off in a tightknit horde to tend the animals and squeeze what milk can be had from the goats. More cow milk will need to be purchased, along with our meat and bulk items, from the Hill farm a couple hours' ride to the east.

The Hill farm is the furthest I've ever traveled from the orphanage since the day I arrived. The city of Chester is yet another three hours past the farm, and that by horse. The valley is remote, and the priests like it that way. One road in and one road out, a brown ribbon flowing like a reverse stream up the green hills to the east, seeming to vanish at the crest of the swell into crisp blue sky. Heavy forest rises to the north and west; a barren plain lies to the south, a sea of heather that ultimately rides upward, a heaving wave.

For better or worse, our home is a reclusive haven, settled deeply in the hollow of the valley's throat.

I take a moment to look over the children—a habit of mine in recent months—to make sure everyone is accounted for. It can be tricky since the boys, with their short haircuts and matching pale blue coats, are almost indistinguishable from one another. Almost, but not completely.

I note Bartholomew—a quiet, sulky teenager who arrived two years ago—standing alone alongside the barn, kicking at something in the grass. He's a dreamer, easily distracted, but I'm not sure I like him. He seems to always be alone . . . but watching, as if studying the others. I dislike myself for thinking it, but I find him a touch peculiar.

Finnegan and Jonathan, or the "twins" as we call them, are of course side-by-side. Their dirty blond hair and pale skin, equal height and build, along with their harmonizing personalities, makes them seem brothers instead of who they really are: two boys brought together in the same month—a stormy December three years past—who bonded so quickly and effortlessly that it seemed destined. Now they're inseparable and charming. Both laugh easily, and if one is punished the other cries. Even Father Poole seems taken with them, often letting them get away with more than he might the other kids. It says something about their charm that nobody really minds.

I glance around for Simon and see him talking, in an animated fashion, with Byron, a tough kid from the city who, frankly, was a considerable problem when he first arrived, often getting in fights and bullying the younger ones. A trip to the hole settled the first concern, and I like to think I helped with the second.

One afternoon I sat him down and explained the importance of sticking together, especially here. I explained what it meant to be one of the older boys (although him being only eleven hardly qualified, but we say what we must). He appreciated my candor and my treating him, I think, with respect. The only issue I've suffered since that warm afternoon chat is his ensuing, and unforeseen, overprotectiveness of my person. Which is kind, if sometimes embarrassing. But at least his bullying days are behind him.

I turn back to see if any of the boys are straggling. Father Poole stands directly behind me, filling the open doors of the orphanage, watching all of us. Just past him are David, Ben, and Timothy, all carrying buckets and brushes. I can almost feel David's rebellious smirk as he makes ready for a long day of scrubbing floors. He and I are the same age—both sixteen years—and the de facto big brothers of this strange clan, even if he doesn't see it that way. He pretends to not notice, or care to notice, how the younger ones look up to him. Regardless, he and those other two will be scrubbing floors until lunch, a light punishment for failing to learn the Bible verses they'd been assigned . . .

Caught in my inner thoughts, I'm startled to notice Poole's cold blue eyes locked onto me. I turn away and head for the shed.

A rough line has formed at the shed door. The structure stands amidst high grass near the barn, clustered with two large outhouses and a dilapidated, older structure now used for little but housing mice and spiders. The large shed primarily holds farming tools, and although newer and sturdier than the older buildings, still has a slight lean. Father Andrew says the shed and the other structure will likely be torn down next summer, the tools transported to the larger, and much newer, barn.

Standing at the shed's open door, like a bulwark, is the massive brute Brother Johnson. He hands each boy a field tool—rake, scythe, shovel, etc.—as they approach.

Johnson is a hateful man. A towering giant with long, dingy

hair, brown teeth. Heavy eyebrows shade dull brown eyes. He's never clean-shaven like the priests, and although he wears a cassock it's unadorned and coarse, heavy as a saddle blanket. All the boys know the rumors of how Brother Johnson came to be with us, a sentence of servitude to Poole for crimes committed in the city. What kind of crimes, and the specific horror of them, are rumors and no more, but I have my suspicion it is no mere thievery for which Johnson serves a life of penitence. Whatever he did was far worse than stealing, and oft repeated. I'd stake my life on it.

Even now, I feel Johnson's dark eyes glower at me at the rear of the line. I refuse to meet his eye and wait patiently as the last few boys are given their tools for the morning's work.

"It's too heavy, Johnson!"

I step to the side and see Basil at the head of the line, a tall shovel with a heavy iron spade gripped in his pale hands.

"You can't work, you don't eat." Johnson's voice is guttural and flat. "That's the rule."

"But I *can* work," Basil says, trying to balance the unwieldly thing in his arms. His roughened English accent always a strange, rogue sound coming from his slight frame. "Just not with this bloody shovel!"

Whatever amusement had been playing on Johnson's face vanishes. "You watch your mouth, boy, or you'll spend the day in the hole," he growls, then leans down to poke Basil in the chest with a gnarled finger. "Now get!"

"Ow!"

A sudden anger fills me. I leave my place and walk past the few remaining boys to the front of the line. Blood rushes in my ears, and my face feels hot, but I focus on keeping my mind calm, my breathing steady.

"I'll take it, Brother Johnson," I say. "Give him one of the hoes. He can manage that much." I point to a slim-handled hoe resting against the shed.

Johnson stands up straight, looming over us. He looks back at the hoe, grips it, and tosses it at me. I catch it reflexively.

"You take the hoe. Basil has his tool."

Without thought, without hesitation, I take the shovel from Basil's hands and thrust the hoe into them. I push him away roughly, wanting him out of it. He stumbles in the direction of Father Andrew, who I notice is watching. I turn back to Johnson.

"Thank you, Brother Johnson, for your charity."

I turn to walk away, heart racing, when a bear-sized palm clamps painfully onto my shoulder and spins me around. Johnson's face is inches from my own. I can see the light scar running the breadth of one brow, the coarse hairs of his chin, cheeks and nostrils. The maniacal fire in his depthless eyes.

"Fuck your charity," he hisses into my face, his breath hot and sour. "We all work for what we reap here, boy. I'll be damned if..."

"Brother Johnson, if you're done with the boys, we need to get a move on!"

Both Johnson and I turn to see Father Andrew, closer now, eyes fixed on us. He's smiling, and his tone is light, but there is a hardness there. I feel it, and I know Johnson does, as well.

Johnson breathes out heavily, squeezing my shoulder so tightly I'll see bruises there in the afternoon. He talks into my ear. "Watch your step, Peter. I ain't no priest, remember that. Hell, I ain't even been baptized."

"Maybe that's why you have devils inside you," I snap, surprised by my insolence.

Johnson stares hard at me, his mouth working. But his eyes lose their fire, shift away. He shoves me hard, but I don't fall.

"Fuck off," he grumbles, and turns to fetch tools for the remaining boys, who stare at me wide-eyed.

I turn on my heel and walk steadily toward the waiting group of boys and Father Andrew, whose eyes remain fixed over my shoulder on Johnson. There's a warning in his glare, and I'm thankful not to be on the receiving end of it.

Johnson watches the last of the boys run off toward the field along with that dandy of a priest, Andrew Francis. What Poole sees in the man is beyond him. He's too tolerant of the boys. Lacks discipline.

Still, Johnson has no interest in crossing him. The young priest could make things unpleasant if he chose to, so for now Johnson keeps his head down and mouth shut when it comes to *Father Andrew*, as the boys call him. Shameful letting them use his Christian name. Poole's too easy on the newest addition to the clergy staff. Too easy by far. Andrew spoils the boys. Gives them rebellious thoughts. More and more they talk back. Disobey. Give him shit.

Ah! If only these little men knew the things I've done, he thinks, watching Peter fall into step with Andrew as they all march through the gate and into the field to pull peppers, corn, cabbage, tomatoes, spuds, and whatever else is harvestable before the frost kills it all. *The things I've done to men, women . . . to children younger than the youngest of them . . . they'd shit their little britches.*

Johnson huffs a misty breath and closes the shed door. A rush of shame heats his face at the thought of his violent past and he mumbles a half-hearted prayer of contrition. Besides, he has his own chores to do before the snow comes. There's wood to cut, enough to feed the furnace for a long winter, and he can't dawdle worrying about a couple smart-mouth brats.

But if Peter thinks being a priest-in-waiting will save him from retribution, he couldn't be more wrong.

"I'll see you soon, boy, yes I will," he grumbles, stomping through the wild, dewy grass toward the barn.

Someone needs to make sure the little bastards aren't making a mess of the place.

3

From his hands and knees on the rough stone floor, wet scrub brush in hand, David keeps one eye on Poole and the other on Ben.

Ben had gotten him a good one, and David is eager to repay it. While Poole had been ogling the expanse of his domain, Ben had doused his brush in soapy water and flicked it at David's face, catching him perfectly—mouth and eyes wide. He's almost proud of the little shit. But he'll be getting him back, all right. If not now, then later. They have all day, after all—he, Ben, and poor Timothy, who had nearly shat himself when Poole handed out the punishment for not learning the stupid Bible verses. Ben couldn't remember the day of the week, but Timothy was smart, and David knew the kid could memorize the entire Bible if it was asked of him.

But Timothy also stuttered, and Father White was feeble-minded as a wingless bird who'd fallen on its head too many times trying to fly. It had been painful to watch the pale-faced ginger try to stammer his way through the words of John the Baptist. Old man White assumed it was because Timothy didn't *know* the words, not that he couldn't *say* the words. Timothy was in tears when dismissed, and despite Peter sticking up for him—*because that's what Saint Peter does*—he'd caught the same punishment as the others. A morning of scrubbing floors.

Checking to make sure Poole's back is still turned, David flips Ben a middle finger and mouths words of revenge. Ben laughs carelessly and continues slopping water over the floor.

Without warning, Poole glances back toward the foyer, and David quickly goes back to scrubbing, eyes down. He hears

Timothy's ragged breathing and figures the poor kid is really putting some muscle into it.

After a few moments, badly wanting to get revenge on Ben, David risks another glance in Poole's direction.

The tall priest stands silently in the open doorway, looking skyward, as if considering a great question. With his thick white hair, long nose, and icy eyes, his appearance is that of a regal king in their court (albeit one who wears a beggar's clothes); a royal personage who does not deign to look down at the peasants beneath their feet. Instead, chin up and jutting, Poole leaves the entry doors and walks crisply across the foyer, boot heels clicking, toward the chapel at the far end.

"Hey," Ben whispers, and David turns.

Like an idiot.

A cold, soapy splatter hits him in the face, and Ben laughs again. Furious, David dips his brush in the bucket. Enough is enough.

"Mr. Mason."

David freezes. Ben's smile vanishes, his face drains of color, and he turns his attention to the floor, increases his scrubbing speed. From nearby, Timothy groans.

Damn it to hell.

With an inward sigh, David sets down the brush and stands, hands at his sides.

He is afraid, and he hates himself for it.

"Yes, Father."

Poole holds open one of the chapel doors, his back to David and the others, but his head is turned—just enough—so one cool blue eye can target him.

"Everything you do," Poole says, quietly but evenly, each word soaked in threat, "every breath you take, every thought in your head, exists only to bring glory to the Lord God and his son Jesus Christ. Do you agree?"

David swallows. Beneath the priest's gaze, he pulls up

memories of being called into Poole's chamber as a child. Poole ordering him to lay his hands flat on the writing table. The leather strap crossing his knuckles again, and again.

The pain. The blood.

"Yes, Father."

"Remember, children," Poole says more loudly, his voice a dusty echo in the high-ceilinged foyer, "the Lord's eyes are always upon you. Always."

This time all three boys murmur the desired reply: a meek, feeble chorus. "Yes, Father," they say (except for Timothy, which comes out as *Fa-Fa-Father*).

Without another word Poole disappears into the chapel, the heavy door closes behind him. David drops to his knees, grabs the brush, and scrubs, all thoughts of retribution wiped away.

As he works, tile-to-tile, his mind wanders. A familiar, haunting thought tickles his brain as he leans into the brush, pushes the bristles harder into the stone.

What if?

What if he hadn't been abandoned? Left in an alley by a mother and father he'd never met. Dumped in the gutter like old meat. Like trash.

What if he hadn't been brought here?

Raised here?

A servant. A prisoner.

What if he'd been loved? If he'd been cared for? Educated. Given a chance to do something good with his life . . .

David is surprised to see tears spot the stone where he works. He sniffs and wipes his eyes with the sleeve of the same dull shirt he's worn a hundred times in twice as many days. He glances over at Ben, who works quietly, not meeting David's eyes. Knowing better.

"You all right?" Timothy asks. "Ca-Ca-Ca . . ."

"Just fuck off," David grunts, not wanting to hear whatever

follow-up question the kid was working at. Scowling, he me-
chanically moves the brush, thinking only one thing with each
rotation of the bristles as they scrape rhythmically over and over
atop the hard, cold stone:

What if ... What if ... What if ...

4

Andrew takes in a deep breath of chilled, hay-scented morning air, lets it out. It feels like a *good* day. A beautiful, God-blessed day.

He watches Peter walking with the rest of the boys. Sees him say a few words to Basil and nudge him good-naturedly. Sees the rare sparkle of a smile on the small, sickly boy's face. Andrew also notices how old Peter looks compared with the others in the group, how *adult*. He's delighted he's been able to convince the boy to follow him into priesthood, and secretly harbors a wish that Peter remain at the orphanage; not as an orphan, but as a priest. As a father to these poor, beaten-down children who come to them injured, forgotten, abused, disposed.

Andrew knows, however, that there are two roadblocks to Peter's path as a priest: his stubbornness, which he feels can be curtailed and constructively directed.

And Grace Hill.

A much bigger problem.

But, all things considered, Andrew would be just as pleased to see Peter become a farmer, if that's what made him truly happy. He would make sure, as well, that the boy got every chance to consider *all* the possibilities of his future, then make his own decisions. After all, one cannot be forced into sacrifice. One must choose it.

The boys, laughing and jostling, reach the gate. Andrew joins them as they head through, young legs tromping down the narrow dusty path toward the large garden. He falls in beside Peter, lowers his voice.

"That was a nice thing you did, Peter. But I'd be mindful of Brother Johnson. He has a colorful history, you know."

Peter shrugs in the way of all teenagers, lowers his head in modest rebellion against the modest retribution of his actions. "I guess."

"Anyway, on to important things. Tell me, do you feel ready for today's lesson? Have you been studying the Latin I assigned?" Andrew keeps his tone light, not wanting to pressure the boy. It's a delicate time for Peter, and the next few days will be a struggle, a wrestling match between his human desires and God's will. Andrew thinks about the trip he has planned for them, but keeps it to himself for the moment. He's not going to make the boy's decision easy, and that's the way it should be. The way it was for him. The harder you fight to join the path of your choosing, the more the decision will resonate within you.

"You're going to make a fine priest, Peter. You don't need to worry."

For a few shuffling steps, Peter doesn't reply. Then, "I don't know, Father."

Andrew frowns. "What is it? Tell me what bothers you."

Peter's face reddens, and he looks left, right, everywhere but at Andrew. As if trapped and seeking escape. "To be honest? I worry about the strength of my faith."

Andrew lets this sink in, knowing *exactly* what the boy struggles with, but wanting to choose his words carefully. "You have doubts."

Peter nods, eyeing the dirt path.

"Would these doubts have something to do with a certain young woman?" He doesn't wait for Peter's reply, or denial, but pushes onward. "Of course, you cannot be a priest and be intimate with a woman. And, as you know, you can never be married. Further, you cannot be with a woman prior to marriage. It's a sin."

Peter kicks at a stone, looks over the field toward the rising sun. "I suppose God's covered all the angles, hasn't he?"

Andrew laughs, unable to contain himself. "Yes, I suppose He has. Sometimes, my boy, you make me think that the first step to saintliness must truly be scorn." Andrew grabs his arm lightly, stops them, looks to make sure the other boys are out of hearing. "The priesthood is not for everyone, Peter. The choice must be yours. However, I'd ask you to consider who you are, what kind of man you want to be in this world."

For the first time, Peter meets his eyes. "I want to be like you. You're . . ." He looks skyward, then back to Andrew. "You're the only good man I've ever known. But when I see Grace . . ."

"It's okay. Be honest."

"When I see her . . . my thoughts are not always pure."

Now it's Andrew who looks away. Playing the role of spiritual Father and paternal father to Peter these last five years hasn't always been easy. He has no experience guiding a boy to adulthood in the way a parent could, and discussing sexuality is certainly not in his purview. Still, God gives everyone their burdens to bear, and he will not turn his back on the young man. Honesty, he knows, is the easiest and most correct course.

"You're sixteen years old, Peter. Thinking otherwise would be . . . unnatural. We're all human. Yes, even priests. Look, *you* must decide which life is more important to you. This life, of the flesh, which is over in the blink of an eye, or your eternal life with God."

Peter nods, seemingly unmoved. Andrew grips him lightly by the shoulders. "Peter, there is one truth you must know. Please, look at me."

Peter does, his young face contorted with indecision. Around them, the warming sun ignites the tips of the tall grass, waving in the chill breeze. The gray sky has turned a bluish hue.

"If you can sacrifice this life for the other, you will know more joy than you can possibly imagine. A joy that will last for eternity."

Peter kicks his shoe into the dirt, eyes cast downward. "This life would not be much of a sacrifice."

Andrew turns the boy and they continue walking. "All of life is a great gift," he says. "Not because of what it gives us, but because of what it allows us to give others."

They walk in silence until they reach the crops. The other boys are already dividing up, well-versed in their jobs. The ground is brittle with cold.

Peter sticks the heavy shovel into the dirt, studies the other kids, watches their work. "Father," he says, his tone simultaneously whimsical and urgent. "Will Grace be in heaven? I mean, could we be together in eternity? You know, if not on earth?"

Andrew blows out a breath, rubs his hands together for warmth, hoping Peter doesn't notice his shocked amusement. "I think we best leave the intricacies of that question for another day, my son."

5

As I watch the others wash up after a hard day of working the fields, I find myself reflecting on the orphanage, on this strange place we call home. The stone floors in the washroom seem almost new compared with the rest of the orphanage, the draining system almost modern. In many ways, the rooms we inhabit feel like a different world, which in some ways they are. Since the boys' dormitory was built long after the original structure, which was made up of the chapel, the dining hall, and the private rooms (only a handful intended for priests), the addition carries the odd feeling of an architectural afterthought.

The original structure was intended as nothing more than a home for traveling missionaries and a seminary for priests-in-training. When money ran thin, the church converted St. Vincent's into an orphanage for boys, using the influx of church funds to build an addition atop the dining hall. A large washroom was added, complete with its own pump, long troughs for handwashing, and metal bathtubs that drain through a pipeline and into the fields. Three additional rooms were constructed—currently used as classrooms, a massive cloakroom, and storage. The dormitory itself, where the boys sleep and spend a majority of their time, was built at the south end of the revised structure. It is a broad, long room big enough to house thirty-two children, and is currently at capacity. A narrow crawlspace extends along the top of the addition, built primarily to ventilate heat in the summer and insulate heat during the long, harsh winters. Where the attic crawlspace meets the foyer, it connects seamlessly with the pre-existing, broader attic space, which is wide enough to be used for storage, and rests directly above the priests' rooms on the north side.

To complete the addition, a wide staircase was constructed to reach the new upper level, the banister of which was spindled with thick oak dowels, terminating in a buttressed balcony that overlooks the building's entrance and the wide, stone-floored foyer.

In the two decades since construction was completed, St. Vincent's has housed hundreds of boys, and secured a sharp increase of annual funding from the church by doing so.

When I think about all the souls who occupied these rooms and hallways, it makes me feel as if I'm part of something larger—more than just the kids who have come and gone since I arrived, but the community of a thousand spirits that continue to linger here, even after their departure. Or perhaps St. Vincent's is simply the place where orphan souls return. A beacon for wayward spirits traversing cities and farms and open lands, finding this place once more, the home with which they most readily identify.

A purgatory.

It's quite easy to imagine the orphanage as a holding area where all the past orphan souls linger, shadowy and hostile, until called forward into the afterlife, or left behind for eternity.

As I pump water into the washroom trough, and the others bristle the dirt from the morning's work off their fingers and from beneath their nails, I think about all those lost souls. I can almost *feel* them pressing around the living, urgent for touch, for warmth. But this is our time now, and as I visualize all the labor-tinted water running back into the crops we grow as food, the recycling of sweat and dirt and energy, I consider these boys—these children—who occupy the tacked-on building space. I scan their small faces, their fragile bodies, their clean, flesh-housed spirits. We are the ones who occupy St. Vincent's. We are its lifeblood, its energy. We sanctify and secure this prison of restless souls. It's we who work the land, who clean and maintain the structure, who provide pleasure and pain to the cycle of growth that is as visible in the bodies of the growing children as it is in the sky-reaching crops of the field.

Without us, I wonder, would the lingering spirits be freed, or damned?

"Peter! Pump harder!"

I push away my wandering thoughts and double my efforts as water sluices toward the faucets where soapy hands wait for rinsing. As eager as they are for lunch, they also know the importance of clean hands, of passing inspection.

Between cranks of the pump's handle, I pick up a withered block of soap and clean my own hands, careful to get the dirt from the fingernails, the palms. I've only failed inspection once, many years ago, and the unpleasant memory of going all day without food is a constant motivation to never let it happen again.

Soon the boys filter out, make their way down the hallway toward the stairs. I give a cursory glance toward the open doors of the dorm but see no one. All the boys should be accounted for.

It wouldn't do to be late.

I hustle down the stairs and across the foyer, past the chapel doors and the hallway entrance leading to the priest's rooms, and through the wide-open doors of the dining hall.

Six equally long tables in two neat rows fill the room. Five boys sit at each one, save two near the back that seat half a dozen. No one wants these tables of six, because the food allotment is the same per table, so it simply means each boy gets a lesser portion. I've had to stop many an argument when a late-coming sixth member tries to find a seat, the others knowing it means food out of their mouths.

The places aren't dictated, but the seating arrangement rarely changes. Groups form naturally in the orphanage, even with the frequent turnover we experience. Friendships form, similar personalities congregate. As the oldest and longest-tenured, David and I are the only ones who tend to move around, choosing the seats we want, moving a younger boy if needed. We are monitors of a sort. David, of course, would never admit to being in any kind of leadership role, but neither of us wants to see a child punished. There has been too much of that over the years. It makes one queasy just to think on it.

Today, I'm the last to enter. All the boys are standing, backs to the tabletops, as our two kitchen servants drop plates of bread, meat in a light gravy, and pitchers of water (milk is reserved for dinner exclusively). Everyone's sleeves are pulled up past their wrists. Everyone's arms are fully extended so that the tips of one boy's fingers could easily brush the tips of another at the table adjacent. The boys will stay this way, holding their arms out, palms turned upward, until inspection is finished.

I make my way to the nearest table, stand next to the twins, who both look at me smiling, and I assume they're pleased I've joined them for this meal. I nod back, then jerk my sleeves high and hold out my arms.

Palms up.

And wait.

I sigh inwardly, tired of playing my part for another of Poole's tiresome rules.

Staring directly at me is Simon, who has stationed himself at the next table over. He rolls his eyes at me and I smile back, both of us hoping this part of the meal tradition moves quickly, as we're all hungrier than usual after a tough morning's labor.

Brother Johnson and Father Andrew do the inspections to-day. Andrew, thankfully, is on my side of the room. Johnson the other. Johnson glances my way wearing a significant frown, but I ignore him. The priests sit at their own long table at the front of the hall, which is slightly raised on a dais. All the seats face forward, face the children. Poole and White sit placidly, hands in laps, watching the inspection. Plates and bowls filled with food are dropped at the table behind me and Finnegan emits a weak groan of hunger. I feel the same way but try not to think about it. Not yet.

Andrew walks past pale hands, some fingers still wet enough to drip. He smiles and nods, says a kind word or two, giving the upraised hands the most cursory inspection. I look over and see Johnson grabbing wrists, turning hands over, studying fingernails. When a boy puts his arms down after he passes by, he turns back and rumbles something that makes the boy lift his arms once again. They shake discernably.

Andrew finishes his loop and approaches the head table. Johnson still hovers at the next table over, just a few feet away, seemingly frustrated. We're all getting anxious to eat the food we can, for now, only smell, and my stomach rumbles loudly as I imagine the stew and bread cooling behind my back. I keep an impatient eye on Johnson as he stalks past the last boy, rounds their table, and finally begins to head back toward the front of the hall.

His eyes meet mine for a moment as he is about to pass by, and I gaze back coolly. After a moment, his attention diverts away from me.

I'm about to breathe a sigh of relief, when he stops.

He stands in front of Simon, whose arms are still extended. I can't see Johnson's expression, as his hulking back blocks my view, but I hear him clearly enough.

"Your hands are filthy."

"What?" Simon replies, and I wince. "They're not! Brother Johnson, where . . ."

"You talking back to me, boy?" Johnson says, loudly enough that the full attention of the hall narrows in on him and Simon.

Please don't talk back anymore, please . . . I think, both out of concern for Simon and, being honest, my own gnawing hunger.

"No, sir," Simon mumbles, defeated.

"Then go wash 'em. And be quick about it."

Simon runs from the table, darts along the rear wall and out through the doors. I imagine him at a dead sprint for the washroom. He knows, as well as anyone, that the others won't wait. Food is too precious, and they starve us. Water and a biscuit in the morning, a lunch of stew or soup, and a light dinner where we can share full pitchers of milk. When food is scarce it can be worse. Much worse. As it is the boys—me included—grab what we can, when we can. When you're hungry, goodness is forgotten until you're not, and the guilt lives in your stomach along with the meat and bread.

You get used to it.

Johnson turns to watch Simon go. As he does, he catches my eye again, a smirk on his lips. "All done here, Father," he bellows across the small hall, and Poole raises his hand. The boys, on cue, drop their arms and bow their heads. Poole offers a brief blessing. When the word *Amen* passes his lips the boys fall silently, and diligently, to their task.

I sit quickly and begin moving food from platter-to-plate. As he sets up his own portion, Byron makes fun of Basil, who always does a personal set of prayers once his own plate is secured. An impressive feat.

"Who you always praying for, Bas?"

"My mother told me to always pray to the Saints," he answers.

The others laugh between mouthfuls, but Basil only shrugs, stuffs a torn piece of bread and gravy into his mouth.

Byron raises his head and winks at me, greasy stew on his lips. "What? All of 'em? There's thousands."

"Nah," says Basil. "Just the ones that matter."

Soft-spoken Terrence takes the bait. "Which ones are those?"

Basil's smile grows. It brings me joy to see it. "The English ones, o' course!"

The twins burst out in laughter, as does Byron, which is rare for him.

I smile gamely and make short work of my plate.

No more than a few minutes have gone by when Simon runs back into the hall, lands with a huff at his table. I turn to watch as he sits slack-faced, studying the empty platters, the full plates of the other boys. None of them look at him. None of them speak.

I turn back to my own food. My hunger is an animal in my belly, clawing to escape, biting and chewing at my insides until I feed it what it wants. It will continue to make me suffer until I quell its need. In my suffering, and to my shame, my charity empties like water from a cup.

"Please," Simon pleads. "I'm starving."

I hardly listen. There's a rushing sound in my head, filling my ears. I can't think clearly, and I can't help Simon. It's beyond me. I'm smearing thin gravy off my plate with a knuckle-size piece of bread—the last of it—when an unfamiliar voice speaks up.

"Here."

The voice is small, and I don't recognize it because the word is rushed and whispered. I twist my head around, trying not to draw attention.

Bartholomew. Quiet, reclusive, dark-eyed Bartholomew. The studious dreamer with thin black hair and large, glassy brown eyes. From my angle, I can only study his face in profile, his eyebrow a slash across a pale forehead, as he reaches a hand across the table toward Simon. "Take it."

I can't help myself. I watch openly as Simon reaches, hoping it's not a cruel joke. Bartholomew is handing him treasure, an offering of pure gold in the digestible form of a hunk of bread topped lazily with a portion of meat not big enough to fill the belly of a mouse. Simon's face lights up as he reaches for it.

CLAP.

The loud, abrupt sound of someone slapping their hand against a table fills the room.

"Stop!"

The children fall silent, and all heads turn toward Poole, who is glaring directly at the table adjacent to our own. Staring, I know, at Simon and Bartholomew.

I notice that all the priests are watching the table now, most likely wondering what's happened. Johnson is already on his feet.

After a moment, Poole speaks. Calmly, assuredly. "Something wrong with your food, Bartholomew?"

Poole is only asking a question, but everyone hears it for the threat it is. I pop the last bit of bread into my mouth and force myself to swallow it down as I watch.

Bartholomew, as if frozen, still has one hand extended. Simon, who looks visibly frightened, has pulled his own hand back. It sits in his lap, hidden beneath the table.

"No, Father." Bartholomew's voice sounds unexpectedly strong in the large, high-ceilinged room.

If I didn't know better, I'd call it defiant.

That would be a mistake.

"Don't worry about it, mate," Simon whispers. "Please, it's fine."

Only a few of us are close enough to hear this. Bartholomew, however, acts as if he's heard nothing.

Poole remains seated, but now he leans forward, elbows on the table, as if studying a chess board. "Are you not hungry? Or perhaps you are ill, Bartholomew?"

"I feel fine, Father." Bartholomew's tone sounds less certain now. He's pulled back the offering of meat and bread, but continues to hold it awkwardly, as if unsure what to do with it. I watch a thin brown line of watery gravy run down his thumb and drip onto the tabletop.

I look toward the priests. Poole's face flattens, a blank slate, but I notice Andrew's brow is creased in worry. White appears his usual befuddled self. Johnson, of course, is eager.

Meanwhile, none of the boys in the dining hall have so much as twitched. All of us simply stare, transfixed. Helpless.

"Then," Poole says mildly, silky as a cat inviting a mouse to dinner, "eat your food."

It's truly a chess match now, everyone watching each move, all of us wondering how bad it's going to get.

Simon shakes his head at Bartholomew in warning.

Don't do it.

I pray Bartholomew heeds his advice.

Andrew feels sick to his stomach.

The boy is not someone he's especially close to, but he has never seemed obstinate. Now, however, Andrew sees plainly the defiance in his face, sees it and prays for it to disappear into servitude, for the child's own sake.

He has no wish to see anyone else get hurt.

Against his better judgment, he turns to Poole seated next to him, and speaks softly. "Father, perhaps we could let the boy have the food. He's guilty of nothing but dirty fingernails, after all."

Poole turns to Andrew as if bored. He replies loudly, as if wanting the boys to hear the rebuke. The lecture spills from his lips, easy as a recitation. "It's a matter of discipline, Father Francis. Today it's dirty hands, tomorrow they're oversleeping. Next, they're talking back, not following instruction. Sound structure needs sound discipline. Rebellion needs to be completely, and totally, dominated by those in charge. Without it, the structure will topple like a house built on sand."

Andrew forces down his bitterness at being lectured like a child, knowing it's exactly the tone Poole is aiming for—he doesn't want to rebuke Andrew; he wants to humiliate him.

"Do you understand?"

Andrew nods, unable to keep the heat from his cheeks.

Poole gives him a final glance, then turns back to the matter at hand. "Bartholomew, please stand."

At the rear of the room, Bartholomew swings his legs over the bench and stands, one arm held aloft, the food resting in a trembling hand.

"The rules of the orphanage are simple, and direct," Poole continues. "If your hands are not clean for meals, you must wash them again until they *are* clean. If this means you miss the meal, then you go without and you do better the next time. Tell me, do you understand why we have these rules?"

Bartholomew thinks for a moment, although his look of defiance does not waver. "For order, Father Poole."

Andrew sits back, wipes a hand across his face. He silently prays for God to give the boy wisdom. There's a look in the child's eyes that worries Andrew greatly.

He looks *angry*.

"That's correct. Next time, you see, Simon will make sure that his hands are properly washed, thus ensuring good hygiene, which in turn keeps everyone healthy. This is how we *learn*. Now, by sharing with him, you are taking away this important lesson. You're actually *hurting* him."

Poole reclines, and Andrew struggles with the dark, wormy feeling that the priest is enjoying this. "And now," Poole says, voice dripping with politic sorrow. "I need to teach *you* a lesson. A lesson about remembering the rules."

Bartholomew trembles, as if a chill wind has blown past him, but says nothing. Andrew wonders how cold the meat in his hand has gotten; how all of the remaining, uneaten food must have cooled during Poole's lecture.

"Since you want to take away Simon's lesson . . ." Poole puts a finger to his chin, as if debating the proper outcome, one Andrew knows he's already secured in his mind. "Then Simon will take away your food." Poole leans forward. "*All* of your food. Both what is left on your plate, as well as what you would have received at dinner tonight."

Bartholomew doesn't move. The room is deadly silent.

"Give him your plate, Bartholomew."

Andrew wants to turn away, to stand up and leave. To walk out of the dining hall and back to his room, where he can get on his knees and pray and forget the boys and the other priests and all of the pain he's witnessed over the years.

He notices, for the first time, that Peter is sitting at the table next to the one where Bartholomew stands, and fights not to meet his eye. He doesn't want the boy to see his shame.

"Now!" Poole roars in a sudden, vehement burst. He slams his palm onto the table with such force the plates jump and rattle. Andrew jumps as well, nerves burning, as if he's the boy under Poole's glare.

Bartholomew stands still for a moment . . . and then does something horrible.

He smiles.

No, son, Andrew thinks in a panic. *Please don't.*

Poole must see that smile as well. Andrew knows it's fueling the fire, stirring the man's prideful conviction of authority. "This is your last warning, Bartholomew."

Still smiling, Bartholomew lifts the hard bread, still topped by a tiny chunk of cold meat, to his mouth. Then he stuffs it in, chewing greedily.

The hall buzzes as boys begin to whisper. Andrew can't help notice a thin line of browned drool leak from the corner of Bartholomew's mouth.

Poole stands.

"This is your last warning! Give Simon your plate and all . . ."

Bartholomew reaches for the table. He grabs his plate, lifts it to his face and begins grabbing food in his fingers. He pushes potatoes and meat and bread into his mouth with abandon, hardly chewing. His cheeks bulge. Bits of meat and crumbs spill down his chin onto his shirt, the floor.

Through it all, he grins.

Poole looks down at the table, as if pained. Andrew wants to reach out, put a hand on the older man's sleeve, beg forgiveness for the boy. He stays still.

Poole lifts his face to the ceiling, his hands lift from his sides, as if giving a benediction.

"Arise, O LORD." Poole's heightened voice fills the room.

From the corner of his eye, Andrew sees that Johnson is already moving.

"Save me, Oh my God! For thou has smitten all mine enemies upon the cheekbone, thou hast broken the teeth of the ungodly."

As Poole bellows his prayer, Johnson knocks the plate from Bartholomew's hands. Bartholomew yelps and cowers as Johnson roughly grips his arms, twists them around the boy's back, and thrusts him forward, face contorted with fresh pain, toward Poole.

As if the child is a shield. Or a sacrifice.

Andrew forces himself to study Bartholomew's features, to feel the pain and emotion there as his own. The child's eyes are wide, black, terrified. His mussed inky hair, too long, clings to his sweat-moistened face. The smear of food across his lips—crumbs of the wasted remnants he couldn't physically swallow—cling to his clothes, shoes. The mess on the floor.

Somehow, through the mess, through the pain and the fear, he still grins.

Poole rests his fingertips on the table and lets out a long sigh. His words are spoken softly, but carry well.

"Put him in the hole."

In a heartbeat, Bartholomew's defiance vanishes. His wide, hard eyes melt in fear. "What?"

It is Johnson who wears the grin now. He begins to drag the child out of the hall.

The panic on Bartholomew's face twists it into something inhuman, turning a child's innocent visage into a mask of animal terror, a cognizant beast being readied for slaughter.

"Father!" he screams, and Andrew winces at the sound of broken youth. In that moment, he craves the defiant boy once more, hopes for the look of rebellion. Anything but this raw fear. It pains him to see it stripped away in the blink of an eye, as if the child's very soul has been snatched by the devil and consumed. "Father, no! I'm sorry!"

But Poole's eyes are closed, just as, Andrew knows, his mind is closed to the consequences and ugliness of his discipline. "Rules will be followed . . ." he says, sitting down, hands knitted together beneath his chin. His voice is lower now, a soliloquy for himself alone. "We survive because of *rules*. Without them, we are no more than lost sheep."

"FATHER!" The boy kicks and twists. Andrew is surprised to see Brother Johnson, big as an ox, struggling to keep the thin child from tearing free.

Fear gives strength, he thinks. *My lesson for this day.*

Having had enough, Johnson lifts the boy off the floor and carries him, as he might carry a giant fish plucked from ocean waters—wiggling, fighting, desperate to breathe.

"Please don't do this!" Bartholomew shrieks, tears wetting his face, his fear palpable.

Andrew hears his own name like an electric shock.

"Father Francis, please!"

For a moment, he debates. He begins to stand. Perhaps this is too far. Perhaps now is the time to . . .

A hand falls on his shoulder, and Poole leans close, his mouth an inch from Andrew's ear. "Don't ever question me in front of the boys again. Do you understand?"

Andrew, all thoughts of rebellion quelled, simply nods. His weight drops into the chair, his eyes lower to the table. "Yes, Father."

The entire room waits in silence as Bartholomew's heaving cries for help, for mercy, finally leave the hall. The screams continue, for a few more moments, to echo from the foyer, before they finally disappear into the afternoon light, his voice cut off sharply by the closing of the orphanage doors, as if sliced with a knife.

6

"Please, Brother Johnson!"

Johnson carries the small boy, who's stronger than he looks, by God. A real pain in the ass is what he is. But he doesn't take pleasure from this kind of punishment, not for the young ones, especially. Still, without order this place would have fallen apart years ago, and Johnson would have been without a benefactor, left to rot away in a damp, rat-infested prison cell.

He would do what Poole asked of him. Without question, without complaint.

Outside the orphanage, the air is cold, the sky slate. The ground is hard and unyielding beneath his feet as he walks toward a patch of weedy grass between the barn and the narrow dirt lane leading east. Johnson is well aware that the location is strategic—Poole wanted the hole easily viewable from the boys' dormitory windows. A reminder of what happens if discipline breaks down.

"Please . . ."

The boy's begging grates on his nerves. He wrenches the child higher, tightens his grip on the thin body flailing against his chest.

"Ow . . ."

Don't you dare start crying little whelp, or I'll give you a taste of real pain.

"Brother Johnson, you can't do this. It's too cold, Brother Johnson. It's too cold! I'll die out here, please. I'll die!"

Nestled into the ground a few feet ahead lies a broad wooden platform. Built into the platform is a liftable hatch, its opening large enough for a full-sized man. A knotted rope rests coiled like a snake in the weeds beside it. The platform itself is crafted from heavy oak planks. The handle coarse iron.

It had been Johnson, nearly ten years ago now, who had brought the idea—albeit inadvertently—to Poole's attention. There had been a similar concept at the prison he'd been plucked from, a form of punishment by solitary confinement. Only instead of a cell, the prisoner was taken outside.

And buried.

It had only happened to Johnson once, and once had been enough. Stuck in a pine box, nailed shut while you screamed for mercy, settled three feet beneath the ground. The guards would laugh while they threw dirt over the makeshift coffin. Joked about their questionable memory, hope that they'd "remember where they put ya," and mockingly hoped that the "air wouldn't run out before they returned."

Johnson hadn't done well in the coffin. Thanks to an overbearing mother, his childhood had carved a deep-rooted fear of enclosed spaces into his psychological makeup, one that had triggered—*panic roaring like thunder in his brain, a nerve-frying terror racing through him, a rabid lion broken loose from its cage*—when they'd nailed the box shut.

When Johnson told Poole about this particular form of torture handed out to unruly prisoners, the old priest had suggested a similar—though not as psychologically traumatizing—punishment for the children.

Over the next couple weeks, Johnson, along with a few older boys living at St. Vincent's at the time, dug a trench into the earth the size of two graves side by side. When completed, the hole was eight feet deep, six feet long, and four feet wide. They'd packed the dirt below until their hands bled, making sure there was no risk of the walls caving inward. Johnson himself built the platform that serves as the roof, the planks now rooted into the earth so fast he doubts they could be removed without first being torn apart with an axe.

The hole served its purpose over the years. And—so far—had been the cause of only one fatality. A young, sickly boy who'd taken ill after a full day and night underground. He died shortly thereafter; his brain boiled by a fever so hot it warmed the room in which they quarantined him. Personally, Johnson hates the damn thing, and rues the day he gave Poole the notion. Being trapped in the dark, in the earth, is a fate much worse than death.

A fact with which he is intimately familiar.

Thankfully, the hole has been used sparingly, transforming into the psychological deterrent it was designed for.

Lately, however, its more practical application has been coming back into regular use.

A shame, he thinks, and drops Bartholomew to his feet, gripping his narrow bicep so tightly that the boy begins whimpering and tugging away from him. No matter, it is almost done.

With his free hand, Johnson kneels and grips the iron handle of the hatch, then yanks upward. The door squeals open on old hinges—*need to replace those soon*, he thinks—and drops heavily with a CLAP as it falls back and away, slapping against the platform.

Johnson gives Bartholomew a hard shake, glares into his face. "You gonna do this easy, or you gonna make it hard?"

Bartholomew stares back at him, eyes wide and full of fear. "I'll die, Johnson," he mumbles, as if knowing the words are useless but feeling the need to say them regardless. "Tonight will be the first night of the storm. I'll die from the cold."

Johnson tightly squeezes the boy's arms and drags him toward the opening.

Below lays nothing but dark and cold, the insects who live in the dirt to offer welcome. Johnson kicks the coiled rope through the opening. It unwinds then snags, the top tied off in a heavy, frayed knot to one of the planks. He leans down so his eyes meet the boy's.

"If I were you, I'd stay on my feet. Keeps the blood flowing."

He shoves the boy to his knees atop the platform.

He doesn't move.

"Grab the rope! Get down there, damn you!"

Bartholomew shakes his head. "Please, have mercy," he says, weeping. "I'm so afraid."

"Fine," Johnson says, huffing out a breath, ignoring the cloud of mist it becomes in the cold air. "Hard way it is." He bends over, grabs the screaming child by a leg and an arm, and pushes him roughly into the hole.

The boy shrieks as if he's being stabbed, then goes quiet—in the space of a heartbeat and the *thump* of meat smacking dirt—when he hits the bottom eight feet below.

Johnson quickly grips the heavy rope and pulls it back up. He tosses the loose coils into the grass, then steps onto the creaky platform and lifts the door.

He gives a last glance into the dark.

He hears nothing and sees less.

Johnson lets the door drop. It lands in place with a heavy *whump.*

He waits for the screams, the crying, the begging.

He hears nothing.

"Boy?" he says, hating the tremor of anxiety in his voice. "Boy!"

Johnson grimaces sourly. It wouldn't do for the boy's neck to be broken. Poole would not be pleased.

Then, like a miracle, he hears a shuffling sound from below, followed by the jagged sounds of a child crying.

"Keep your feet moving," Johnson says loudly, not knowing if the brat can hear him or not. "Keep the blood flowing and you'll be fine." He waits for a response, gets none, and shrugs.

He begins trudging his way back toward the orphanage, praying his interrupted meal will be there waiting.

If not, there'll be hell to pay.

7

THUMP THUMP THUMP THUMP THUMP!

Andrew stirs. The black veil of sleep rips, then pulls apart like cobwebs.

THUMP THUMP THUMP THUMP THUMP!

A man is yelling. Outside the doors. Echoing down the hall to his chamber.

Yelling?

Andrew sits up in darkness, breathing fast.

Footsteps move quickly past his door, the pulse of a held lantern ignites the space beneath, then vanishes.

Poole.

Andrew fumbles for his own bedside lantern and ignites it. He lifts his watch. Half-past three in the morning. Despite the oddness and urgency, he takes a moment to wrap his robe over his undergarment and buckle on his shoes.

He freezes a moment at his door, holding his breath, listening. The pounding has stopped. He assumes Poole has opened the door for whomever was attempting to gain entry.

There are voices now. Men's voices.

They are heated.

Rushing, Andrew plucks the lantern from the bedside table and hurries for the door. He pulls it open, runs into the hall. Ahead, there are lights in the foyer. Bobbing lanterns held by shadows. The sound of two men, now three. Poole among them.

What's going on?

He enters the foyer and sees that one of the large double-doors is open wide. A frigid wind blows inward and covers him in chilled night air. Goosebumps riddle his exposed flesh. A large man is talking with Poole, who stands stoic in nothing but an undershirt, feet bare atop the stone floor, which Andrew knows from experience must be freezing. The older priest turns briefly when he hears Andrew approach, then turns his attention back to the man, who is pointing animatedly out the door. Pointing to something in the night.

As he gets closer, Andrew sees more men standing just outside. They appear anxious, as if waiting to be allowed entry.

They all carry guns on their hips.

"Father?" Andrew says, arriving to stand beside Poole. He speaks too loudly, trying to sound forceful instead of fearful, which is how he truly feels. He doesn't know what's happening, and the men don't seem to be an immediate threat, but there's something here he doesn't like.

Many things he doesn't like.

Poole ignores him for now, and Andrew strains to hear snatches of the conversation: "Help . . . lost . . . no time . . ."

"Father Poole?" Andrew says, again too loudly, his emotions less fearful now and truer to his tone. He wants to know what's going on. Both men turn to face him. Poole's face is alive and anxious, brewing with thought. The stranger is worry-creased, sweat-dampened and wild-eyed.

This close, Andrew recognizes him immediately.

The sheriff.

The only major township within twenty miles of the orphanage is Chester, an industrial river-town straddling the Delaware River, where the priests travel twice a year to trade agricultural stockpile for certain hard-to-get supplies and, more often than not, pick up one or two new orphans—the ones waiting in hospitals or jail cells, biding their time until they are shown what will become of their lives.

Andrew has dealt with the sheriff many times over the years, and overall thinks him a fair and Christian man. A *good* man. He's never mistreated a boy in his care and has worked hard over the years to help find placement for those he could, whether it be in workhouses or homes.

"Sheriff Baker," Andrew says, putting out his hand.

"Father," the sheriff says, gripping Andrew's hand firmly. His skin is ice cold and rough as bark. "I'm sorry about all this. As I was telling Father Poole, I've got nowhere else to go."

Poole turns to Andrew, almost distractedly. "He has a sick prisoner, one who needs immediate care."

Andrew turns from Poole to the sheriff with a look of surprise. "We are not a hospital, Sheriff. We have few supplies and no medical personnel, as you must know," he says, not unkindly. "Certainly Chester . . ."

"He'll die long 'fore we get there," Baker says, his fingers anxiously working the brim of his hat that he removed upon entering. "I'd say he's got minutes to live, not hours, and it's a three-hour ride to town. My next stop would be the Hill farm, but I don't even know if he'd make it that far, and John doesn't have any experience . . . well, with this kind of thing."

Poole nods sagaciously, his eyes bright now, alert.

Andrew feels there's something happening here other than a sick man, something being held back from him. He's well aware of Poole's time as a young hospital steward during the war, having heard countless retellings of battlefield horrors, terrifying deaths. Poole has done his share of surgery on dire men, but it was the priesthood—not the world of medicine or the field of battle—which called him home once the war ended. Andrew doesn't know what ails the man the sheriff spoke of, but he must be desperate indeed to call upon a priest who last practiced medicine forty years in the past.

But he also has the feeling it's not just medical treatment—not *exactly*—that the sheriff is referring to.

What is this man bringing to our door? Andrew thinks worriedly, but his thoughts are interrupted by an urgent-sounding Poole.

"Start at the beginning for Andrew, Sheriff. I must put on a garment."

"Father, we don't have much time," the sheriff says as Poole shuffles away into the dark.

He does not stop, but only throws up a hand, his voice vacuous in the large room. "Then speak quickly! I'll be no good to you frozen."

Andrew rests a hand on Baker's arm, hoping to calm the man. He only now notices how fervent he appears—his constantly-shifting eyes, the sweat running from his beaded brow, the hunched posture of someone being beaten, or hunted. Andrew forces himself to speak calmly, soothingly. "Just tell me what happened, Sheriff. Speak generally, if you must."

The Sheriff sighs, eyes downcast, and Andrew once more notices the men standing past the open doorway beyond him, frowning and shuffling their feet like fearful children. *They're as skittish as the sheriff*, he thinks. *And is that mud that spatters their faces, or blood?*

"We've come from the hills. From the forest," Baker begins, drawing Andrew's attention back to him. "Full bore the whole way back, but now the horses are run out and, as I said, we have a dying man in our care."

Andrew nods for the sheriff to continue.

"Well, we went out there in the late evening looking for a young girl who'd been taken from a home just outside town." Baker looks up, and Andrew is shocked to see tears in the grizzled man's eyes. "She was only three years old, Father."

Andrew swallows and spares a glance back to the darkened hallway, hoping for Poole's expeditious return. He chooses, for now, not to comment on the sheriff's use of the past tense as it pertains to the girl.

"Anyway, a farmer out that way sent his son to me with word. He'd seen some odd things in the trees near their home. Men and women ... fires ... screams. *Strange* things. So, me and three other men rode out there ..."

Baker shakes his head, takes in a breath. Andrew waits, his serene face belying his quickening pulse.

"It was awful, Father." Baker's voice cracks, turns pleading. "Hellish. There ... there was a group of 'em. They'd ... oh sweet Jesus, Father ... they'd *sacrificed* her."

Andrew's blood turns to ice water, a spider-like chill crawls up the knobs of his spine. He swallows hard, thinks of reaching out a hand, to comfort the distraught man, but refrains. Part of him fears that his own hand would be shaking. "You say sacrificed?" he asks, trying to stay resolute. "Not murdered?"

Baker wipes his nose, taps his hat against his hip. "She was stripped naked, Father. And bound with straps to a flat stone. Tied down. And ..." Baker pauses, lets out a breath, then rushes on. "They'd been cutting her, Andrew. The cuts were ... patterns, I guess. Symbols of some sort. Deviltry. It was Satan's work; I'd swear on it. Anyway ... the man we've brought here? He was drinking her blood."

Andrew tries to reply, to think of something—anything—to say, but his thoughts are a maelstrom, his head numb with the horror of what he's being told. "Sheriff ... I ..."

But the sheriff plows forward, as if needing to get through the story, to purge the memory from his mind one last time. "We killed them all." Baker's eyes, which were widened and distant during his retelling, now go hard as flint. "We slaughtered the bastards where they stood. I never gave the order ... hell, I hardly remember ... we all just started firing. No one thought about it, no one questioned it. That girl was opened up, Father. I could see her heart."

Footsteps behind him. Andrew turns to see Poole hurrying back. *Thank heaven.*

Behind him another, larger shadow emerges. Johnson. Sheriff

Baker turns and motions to the men outside, and they disappear into the dark.

"This man you've brought," Andrew says, eyeing Poole as he arrives. "The one you spoke of. He survived?"

Baker starts to reply, then stops as loud grunts and curses carry from outside, loud enough to be heard over the wind, which has elevated to a whining howl. Andrew hears the anxious whinny of a horse, the blown lips and foot stomps of another. Suddenly, three shadow-faced men block out the doorframe. Andrew raises his lantern, and his eyes widen in shock.

Two of the men, he realizes, are deputies. They both wear guns, and one has a dull silver star on his leather coat.

They hold a man between them. The prisoner.

A coarse grain sack covers his head, darkened in places by what Andrew assumes is blood, or perhaps sweat. The man is tall and skinny. His clothes are torn. He's shoeless, and his feet are blackened.

In the air above them, lit silver by a heavy moon, snowflakes dance.

Baker nods to the men, then looks back at Andrew, who is surprised to see tears running through the dirt and stubble on the sheriff's cheeks. "He's my brother, Father. His name is Paul. I spared my little brother, and now I'm hoping you can save his life." He pauses, as if debating internally, then says, "Or if not that, then his soul."

Poole, now in a cassock and carrying a bright lantern, motions to the men. "Bring him," he snaps, already turning on his heel to head back to the priest's chambers. "Quickly! To my room."

Andrew and the sheriff step aside as the two deputies drag the tall man between them, across the threshold of the orphanage, and into its depths. A third deputy comes in from the dark, looking sheepish as a guilty schoolboy, and closes the door behind him. The three of them trail behind the others.

"I couldn't kill him," Baker says quietly, as if ashamed. "Not my own flesh. But now I realize, he's not my brother any longer. You'll see. There's something *wrong* with him, Father. Horribly wrong."

As they follow, Andrew notes the long lines of wet blood running from the dragged man's black, naked feet; the flow of blood inking a wavery line across the stone, as if it were paint, and the sheriff's brother the dampened brush. "I would say so," Andrew says, careful not to step in the dark lines being drawn across the foyer. "He is badly wounded . . ."

The sheriff's strong hand grips his elbow, and he winces from the pain of it. Baker's feverish eyes stare into his, pleading. "Not the flesh, Father," he whispers, eyes raised as if to make sure neither God or the Devil are hovering above, listening. "Something else. Something has *overtaken* him."

Poole's voice cuts through the dark. "Andrew!"

"Come," Andrew says to the despairing man, hurrying along toward Poole's chamber. "We'll do what we can."

Andrew walks past Johnson, who stands at the end of the hall lighting a wall sconce. He turns as Andrew approaches, his face ghastly white, his tone surprisingly nervous. "Andrew, is this safe?"

Taken aback by the large man's obvious fear, Andrew breaks stride to study Johnson, wondering if he knows something Andrew does not.

"I don't like this, Andrew," Johnson says shakily, and crosses himself.

He doesn't look afraid . . . he looks terrified.

"It'll be okay," he says, then continues down the hallway. There are lights and voices emanating from the open door of Poole's chamber. The sheriff is now a step ahead. All the deputies, along with Paul Baker and Father Poole, are tucked away inside the room.

Before they enter, Andrew finally formulates the question that's been nagging at him. "Sheriff?"

Baker turns, a dark shadow, waiting.

"Why the sack?"

Baker's mouth tightens, but he doesn't answer. Instead, he turns and disappears into the glow of Poole's chamber.

A harsh, barking sound comes from the room. At first, it sounds to Andrew like the loud, rapid barks of a dog. But then it evens out, lengthens and repeats, and he recognizes it for what it is:

Laughter.

8

Something is wrong.

I huddle by the dormitory doors, ear pressed to the wood, hoping for a clue to what's happening.

Minutes ago, I'd been asleep, woken by the sound of horse hooves beating the earth. Not, in itself, an unusual sound at the orphanage. But in the middle of the night?

Worried, I climbed out of bed and looked out the window. At first, my attention was caught by the thick snow flurries—the first of the year and a sign of things to come—but then I saw movement below, near the entrance. I could make out several men on horseback. One large horse pulled a crude wagon. I couldn't see, with any clarity, what lay inside. But I would have sworn it was a man.

When the knocking and shouting came, I ran to the doors and listened, but haven't dared open them. Not yet. Being caught out of the dorm after lights-out is a significant offense, which is why we are given bedpans, something none of us like to use, and fewer to *have* used, as the stench always filters throughout the room. Besides, I can hear well enough. The pounding echoes from the foyer that filter down the hallway are clear and unrestrained.

"Peter?"

I turn and see a couple of the boys are awake, standing like ghosts in the night's bright moonlight. All around the cots, the walls of the dorm flicker with tiny shadows—black, whirling confetti. A trick of the snow.

Simon is one of those standing, watching me from the middle of the room. David is sitting up, and others are stirring. It is

Simon who spoke my name, and I put a finger to my lips. "Someone is here," I whisper. "Men from town, I think. They're upset. Poole is there now, talking with them."

"Maybe they've come for Johnson," a voice says from deeper in the room. I don't know who spoke, but it's not a crazy thought. Johnson getting his due is something many of the boys fantasize about. I nod, unsure what else to say.

Simon seems to lose interest and walks to one of the windows, stares outside. I wait for him to comment on the snow, but he surprises me. "I hope Bartholomew is okay," he says, standing so close to the window that the breath of his words fogs the glass.

At the thought, shame fills me. In truth, I'd forgotten about him. I'm equally sure that, with the ruckus of whatever is happening below, the priests have likely forgotten about him as well. I doubt if it would matter. After all, part of the punishment of the hole is dealing with the elements, hot or cold.

Bartholomew's luck is simply worse than most.

Still, others have pulled similar short straws. I recall David once spending the night in the hole during the heart of a brutal winter. Johnson had to shovel two feet of snow off the door just to get him out again. He'd laughed about it later, said the insulation of the snow and earth had kept him warmer than he would have been in the dorm. But the next morning I'd seen his blackened toenails, heard him weeping in the washroom when he thought himself alone.

Of course, I'd said nothing, only praised his strength and resilience to nature's foils. They'd already taken his boyhood, I wasn't going to let them take his pride, as well.

"I'm sure he's fine," I say, hoping I don't sound uncertain. Hoping it's the truth.

"What's going on?" David is fully awake now, feet on the floor, eyes alert.

I shake my head, wanting them all to be quiet so I can listen.

The voices are in the foyer now; the words grow louder, crescendo, then lessen to foggy murmurs.

David moves in next to me, his own ear to the opposite door. "Sounds like they're going to the chapel, or the priests' rooms."

The heavy, hurried footsteps fade. After another moment, there is nothing left but silence.

A few more boys are out of their cots, standing, whispering, excited for anything out of the ordinary to be happening. Byron kneels close by, looking eager, relishing the disruption. Some others have shuffled close as well, sitting cross-legged, or resting apprehensively on their knees, as if I'm about to tell them all a story. Others are up and strolling the room like sleepwalkers, mystified to be seeing their world this late at night. They stare out the windows at the falling snow with a look of awe on their faces. Surprisingly, more than half the boys are still asleep in their cots, buried in dreams, oblivious to the night's excitement.

"I don't . . ." David starts, then stops. His brow furrows, and his eyes take on a sheen of fear.

"What?" I say.

But then I hear it.

Behind me, another boy must hear what we do. He groans in despair, as if he might start crying. I feel like joining him.

Instead, I lock eyes with David. We both listen to this new sound flowing through the orphanage, filling the air like smoke.

Someone is laughing.

But not *cheerful* laughter. There's certainly nothing casual, or remotely uplifting, in the sound. It's horrible. It sounds deep and ragged. Hysterical. Like listening to a madman lose what remains of his mind.

David leans back and pulls on the iron handle, opening the door a few inches.

"What are you doing?" I hiss.

"I can't hear . . ." he starts, then just listens. We both do. The sound is twice as loud with the door open, and I suddenly realize what he's trying to understand. "The laughing . . ." he says, and I already know what he's going to ask, because I'm wondering the same thing. He closes his eyes in concentration. "Is that one man?"

When his eyes open, they are wide. Frightened.

I shake my head, wondering if I look as afraid as he does. Icy fingers brush the back of my neck, raising the hairs on my skin.

"I can't tell," I say.

9

Andrew enters Poole's bedroom—the largest of all the priests' quarters—and almost reels in horror.

I've entered hell.

He can't help the thought. It comes unbidden. Multiple lanterns are alight, including two wall sconces, and the room is doused in the orange glow of dancing fire, as if the crowded space has been somehow detached from the world and submerged within the burning lake itself. Paul Baker lies flat on Poole's narrow bed. The deputies have removed the ropes from his hands and legs, but are now re-tying them—one to each wrist and ankle, pulling the limbs taut—securing the man to the bedframe's speared posts.

The bound man does not struggle, but simply continues to laugh—heavy, deep-throated bellows, guttural and sonorous, that emanate from beneath the soiled sack covering his face. Andrew wonders if the man's intent is to show the others that he isn't afraid; or perhaps to indicate that *he* is the one in charge of the drama taking place here, the sole writer of the horrific play being performed before Andrew's eyes.

Once the knots are secure, Poole, looking stricken but determined, notices Andrew and points toward the door. "Go to the chapel. Bring me the Rituale Romanum and holy water. My vial if you can find it, otherwise grab a cup and fill it to the rim."

"Father Poole . . ."

"Go! It is more than disease or wound of the flesh that sickens this man," Poole says, then turns to the sheriff. "Remove the hood."

"Father, he's already bitten one man. I don't think it's a good idea."

Poole waits, stone-faced. "The hood."

Andrew stops at the doorway, his curiosity getting the best of him. *I must see his face,* he thinks, then watches as Sheriff Baker grips the top of the soiled sack.

Baker pauses. Uncertain. Afraid.

The laughter stops.

The room goes still.

"Go on," Poole says.

In one quick jerk, Baker yanks upward. The hood comes free. He tosses the sackcloth away, disgusted.

Unseen by anyone in the room, the hood slides into a corner and settles beneath a wooden chair, lost in shadow.

All eyes—including Andrew's—are on Paul Baker's face.

Andrew gasps despite himself.

It is a nightmare.

That is no man. The force of this sudden belief—a staggering awareness—is stronger than anything he's felt in his lifetime. *That is a demon.*

Paul Baker's pale skin is deeply wrinkled, as if pruned, and tinted an unnatural dark, ashen gray. The eyes are jaundiced, wild and ferocious as a jackal. The hair—a coarse, brittle blond— has fallen out in places, giving the skull a splotchy, misshapen look. The teeth are rotten and black—and quite evident—as Paul Baker stretches back his pale, wormy lips in an effort to fully expose them in a fiendish rictus. A devil's grin. The pupils in his yellow, milky eyes are black and misshapen as drops of ink on wet parchment. They dart rapidly between his brother and the other deputies. Then settle on Poole.

The grin vanishes, his eyes sink in a supplication so devious as to be mocking.

"Father," he rasps, his quiet, tortured voice filling the room. "Wilt thou save me?"

Poole begins to answer when the ghoulish creature jerks his head back, exposing a bony throat, and screams with such force that a deputy covers his ears. His back arches impossibly, and Andrew hears the tap-dance clicking of bones, the strained creaking of bedposts as their strength is tested.

Poole turns, eyes flashing. "Andrew!" he screams. "Go, damn you!"

David slips through the door first.

Once they heard the scream, he and Peter shared a look. A silent agreement. Peter had turned back to address the other awakened boys, told them to stay put.

Now, halfway down the dark hallway, they hear raised voices. The sounds of a struggle? There's a *crack* and a man shrieks in pain. David is sweating, terrified, but it helps to have Peter with him. He mocks Peter enough, more than he deserves, and enjoys rubbing his nose in all that blue-eyed *goodness* he exudes, but the truth is that David respects Peter, even if he doesn't necessarily *like* him all that much. He assumes it's a similar feeling to what one might feel for a sibling. A brother. The feeling where you hate having to be in the same room with a fella for more than ten minutes, but if push came to shove, you'd give your life for him.

Peter tugs at his sleeve as they approach the stairs. "Stay down," he whispers, and David nods. Once they make it to the banister, they'll be easy to spot for anyone gazing upward from the foyer below.

Side by side, they crawl onto the balcony, stopping short of the dark oak spindles riddled before them like prison bars, each attached to a slanted shadow, flattened by the muted moonlight coming through the foyer's solitary round window. Cautiously, they glance downward in hopes of seeing the cause of this incredible, late-night disruption.

The foyer is poorly lit. More dark than light. From the hallway leading to the priests' rooms, an orange glow spreads outward across the floor like spilled paint. Multiple voices can be heard coming from that same direction, and David assumes that whoever was laughing—then *screaming*—resides somewhere down that hall.

"Look," Peter whispers.

David leans forward in time to see the chapel door open. A shadowy figure hurries out, then walks into the glow of the orange light before disappearing down the corridor.

"Andrew," Peter murmurs, and David nods.

"What do you think?" David says quietly.

Peter opens his mouth to answer when another scream shatters the air.

This scream sounds much different. And David realizes, with a sour twist of his stomach, that it did not come from the same man as the first.

10

"Be still!"

Andrew re-enters the room to see the bound man writhing like an angry eel atop the bed, his mouth stretched impossibly wide in some unfathomable torment. Wide enough that Andrew notices that it's not just his teeth that are black, but his tongue and mouth, as well.

Like he's been drinking ink.

Poole is tearing at the man's shirt, ripping it off his bleeding torso. The mattress is already heavy with blood. Red tendrils trickle to the floor like ivy.

"Hold him!" Poole yells, and two deputies grab Paul Baker's arms, careful to keep their hands away from his snapping jaws. He intermittently laughs, cries, or wails, with seemingly no reason for the rapid changes in response to whatever darkness boils within him.

Andrew rushes over to stand behind Poole, placing the surgery kit, book, and vial of holy water on his dresser. "Father, how can I help?"

"Hand me scissors, the large ones."

Andrew pulls open the bag, sees the array of field surgery instruments neatly displayed, and pulls a pair of hand-sized scissors from a leather loop. "Here!"

Poole reaches behind, grabs them, and begins cutting the shirt off Baker's contorting, convulsing body. "Hold him steady, please! I don't want to stab the man."

Sheriff Baker enters the fray, pushes down on his brother's narrow hips as Poole cuts.

Andrew leans over Poole's shoulder to study the man's exposed flesh, and recoils. "Oh God," he says in disgust, then clamps a hand over his mouth in an effort to keep further words from spilling out.

The flesh of the man's chest is partially torn away, exposing red meat and white rib beneath blood-slicked skin. His entire torso, from neck to waist—on what skin remains—is covered in symbols. Occult and blasphemous. Some designs appear to be roughly tattooed into the skin, others seemingly *burned* into the flesh, as if drawn with heated steel.

"What happened to him?" Poole asks the sheriff, shocked at the severity of the wound.

The sheriff releases his brother, stares down into his twisting gray face with a pain so profound it breaks Andrew's heart. "He came running at me, screaming and covered in blood . . . I brought up the shotgun, told him to stop. He flashed a knife, kept coming. I shot him." The sheriff wipes tears and sweat from his face, takes a breath. "At first I thought I'd missed. He didn't even *slow down*. Then I saw the blood, and my men were shooting at the others, putting them down. I didn't want to see my brother die, so I tackled him, held him to the ground. I had no idea he was so badly injured until we tied him up. My God, Father . . . how is he *alive*?"

"We'll need to get the metal out of him . . ." Poole mumbles uncertainly, ignoring the sheriff's question.

A voice comes from the bed, interrupting Poole. It's a new voice, a different one than what they've heard since the sheriff's arrival. Andrew assumes it's as close as they've heard to Paul Baker's *true* voice, and the sound of it—the innocence of it—is chilling.

"I'm scared, Father," Paul says weakly. "Don't let me die. I'm so sorry . . ."

He shifts his head to his brother, who takes a step backward, his face ashen and slick with sweat. "I'm sorry about what I did to that little girl, Teddy. I don't know what's happening to me . . ." Paul begins to cry, but he continues speaking through his choked tears. "I'm sorry I drank her blood," he says, black tongue running over his top lip, as if reliving the memory of it. He begins weeping, shaking his head side to side, his sobs deep and wet.

Andrew, feeling empathy for the poor, foul man, steps forward with thoughts of offering what comfort he's able.

But then the sobbing grows louder . . . *twists* into something different; contorts into sounds of hacking, ghastly laughter. When he speaks, the voice is deep, grating. Inhuman.

"But it tasted so *fucking* good."

"Jesus Christ," a deputy whispers, and crosses himself, momentarily releasing his hold on the man's arm.

Andrews jerks backward as Paul Baker begins to bellow, howling out a chilling chorus of deep, hollow laughter. The sound fills the room like poison. All the men take a step backward, away from the bed. Following his deputy's lead, the sheriff also crosses himself. Andrew follows suit, whispering a Hail Mary for good measure.

Poole turns to Andrew, eyes unfocused. The old priest appears lost. Confused. He starts to ask Andrew something, then stops, shakes his head. He looks back at the man on the bed, who is now breathing heavily, his lungs filling and emptying in rapid, hiccupping swallows. His black-dotted eyes are wide and vacant, and the fine, crisscrossing veins have burst, filling the whites—previously the color of curdled milk—with dark, splotchy blood.

He's a monster, Andrew thinks. He's ashamed of himself for the thought, for letting fear overtake his duties, but can think of no other description. *A monster.*

"Andrew, I need . . ." Poole starts, and then the words run off. Instead, he closes his eyes, mumbles a silent prayer. After a moment, his eyes open once more, the prayer complete. When he looks toward Andrew again, he seems resolute. Ready to do what needs to be done. "Holy water. Yes, give me the holy water, please," he says crisply. "And open the Ritual. Begin reading the ritual of exorcism. You know the section?"

Andrew nods numbly, reeling inside.

Poole offers him a small, encouraging smile. "It will be okay, Father. Just read it, please."

Andrew nods, opens the book to a passage near the back.

He reads.

"I, therefore, enjoin every unclean spirit, each devil, each part of Satan . . ."

As Andrew reads, monotone and timed, Poole begins praying over his words. Quietly at first, but with building strength.

He removes the stopper on the vial of holy water, and tips it over onto Paul's flesh.

11

"What the hell are you two doing?"

Both boys turn toward the voice.

Johnson glares up at them from the base of the stairs, his eyes dark hollows in the shadowy silver light of the moonlit foyer. His face is a pale sliver above the collar of his black cassock, his long, unkempt hair slashed across his ghostly visage like a scythe.

He takes two aggressive steps up the stairs, and both boys stand, rigid. Snared.

Knowing how much Johnson hates Peter, David steps forward, hoping to soften the inevitable blow to come. "We're sorry, Brother Johnson. We just . . . well, we heard the yelling. We were concerned someone might need help."

Johnson huffs a breath. "Curious, more like it. Gossipy hens, the lot of you. Now, listen. Get back to the dormitory. Close the doors. I want every boy in his bed. The next boy I see out of that room goes straight to the hole to keep young Bartholomew warm. Understood?"

David knows this is no bluff, and nods briskly. "Yes, of course. We'll make sure. Thank you, Brother Johnson."

Johnson, looking mollified in the dim light, begins to turn, then stops. "It's nothing to worry about. It's nothing . . ." he says, in a tone less aggressive than the boys are used to.

Is he speaking to us or himself? David thinks. The thought redoubles his anxiety about what might be happening in Poole's bedroom.

Neither David nor Peter move or speak, but stand frozen, waiting. With a huff, Johnson goes on, as if questioned. "An injured man was brought to us for medical care, that's all. Father

Poole is trying to help him." He turns his face up to them, his expression no longer placid. "There. You have your answers. Now go before I come up there and drag you back by your necks."

Without a word, Peter and David turn on their heels and walk briskly back to the dorm. Once inside, they shut both doors and whisper to those who are awake and waiting.

"It's nothing . . ."

"A sick man, that's all . . ."

"Back to bed now . . ."

When the others are settled, David lays in his cot, eyes and ears open and attentive. He knows Peter is doing the same.

Johnson's lying.

He turns onto his side, eyes glued to the dim outline of the double-doors, the heavy metal cross hanging above. There's a tightness in his belly, one that has little to do with the constant bite of hunger. He knows whoever is down there is more than simply injured.

Injured men don't laugh, he thinks.

Despite his worry, his disquiet at the night's events, the dark settles heavy on his head. His thoughts slow, the sharp edges of his fears dulled by exhaustion.

Finally, unable to keep vigil, he gives in to the night, and closes his eyes.

The reaction to the holy water is immediate, and savage.

Paul's body buckles and bucks, slamming up and down, over and over, against the mattress. His eyes roll up into his head, showing full whites. Dark red foam pours from the corner of his mouth.

"Sheriff!" Poole yells, taking a half-step back so the men can move in.

Baker and the two deputies lunge at Paul, grab his arms and legs. The sheriff grunts with the effort of restraining his brother.

His hat falls clumsily to the floor, his long unwashed hair hangs in his face, catches in his beard. Pleading eyes look at Poole. "Father, please help him! Help my brother!"

Poole hisses at Andrew. "Keep going!"

Andrew does, raising his voice. "Shake with fear, not at the human fragility of a miserable man, but at the image of the all-powerful God . . ."

Poole pulls a silver cross, bound to a leather strap around his neck, from beneath his robe, lifts it over his head and holds it close to Paul's face.

"What is your name, demon? Tell us your name!"

There's a loud *snap*.

Andrew stops his reading. There's a momentary stillness to the room, as if time has been sucked away, a split second of purgatory.

Paul's arm is free, and his freed hand now holds the splintered top of a broken bedpost.

Impossible, Andrew thinks.

Poole shouts a warning. "Sheriff!"

Time resumes—seemingly at double speed—as the mad play proceeds with terrible, unstoppable rapidity, as if time were a great spool of thread, knocked rolling downhill.

Snarling, Paul thrusts the splintered post like a sword into the neck of the deputy nearest the bed. The tip sinks deep into flesh as the man's scream is cut with his throat. Snarling like a rabid dog, Paul jerks the makeshift weapon free. Blood sprays from the wound in a wild arc as the man spins away, knees buckling, and collapses to the floor.

Paul kicks wildly with one bared, blackened foot. Another post cracks free. He swings the bloodied post in his hand at the sheriff, who falls backward to avoid the blow. Andrew sees another deputy pull the gun from its holster. Paul kicks again, now at the post binding his opposite leg, his body all jerking spasms and rapid movements—inhuman motion, impossible strength. The post stays whole but the rope snaps, freeing his legs. In a blink, he flips onto his knees, grips the final post with both hands, and breaks it off the bedframe, effortlessly, as if he were snapping a dried twig in two. The wood slides through the looped knot and clatters to the floor. His eyes roving everywhere, Paul slowly rises up.

As one of the deputies lies motionless in a growing pool of his own blood on the floor, Paul stands atop the bed. He is a horrible sight. His bared torso, flesh torn and bloodied, covered in inked symbols; the gray, wrinkled face; the deep-set, rheumy eyes. He is tall and thin—the top of his head nearly brushes the low ceiling—but strong. Taut muscles flex beneath his skin like snakes.

For a few heavy heartbeats, they all watch as he surveys the room.

His eyes momentarily meet Andrew's, and he shudders at the contact. Terrified, he steps backward, flattens himself against a wall. The book of prayers drops from his hand and lands splayed, useless, on the floor.

Paul's eyes shift to Poole, who still holds his small silver cross aloft. Mumbled prayers pour from his lips. From his lofty height, Paul looks down at him and grins, exposing those blackened teeth.

"You cannot count my names, Father," Paul says, his voice deep and resonant. A chorus. He steps down off the bed and toward Poole, who quickly steps backward. Paul looms over him, easily a head taller than the weathered priest. His shredded torso bleeds more freely with the movement, running in rivulets down his chest, dripping onto the tops of his bare feet, spotting the floor. Ropes dangle from his wrists, snake away from his ankles. He still holds the bloodied wooden spike. Foam and drool soak his unshaven chin, saliva hangs like a string from his bottom lip. His eyes are blisters, his face that of an aged corpse. He bows slightly, meeting Poole's eyes, and whispers.

"For we are many."

Andrew catches movement from his left as Sheriff Baker steps around the bed, unhurried, grim-faced. He raises his pistol, presses it against the bony hinge of his brother's jaw, just below the temple, and pulls the trigger.

The gunshot is deafening in the small room. Andrew screams and covers his ears. A spray of Paul's head bursts away and finds a wall. He slumps backward, landing awkwardly atop the bed. A broken doll. A mewling sound escapes his lips, a long moan that is part vocal, part the finite hiss of escaping life.

Andrew pushes away from the wall, puts a hand on Poole's shoulder. "Are you all right?"

Poole nods and they both step forward, look down at what remains of Paul Baker. "We should pray for his soul," Poole says, but without energy.

Andrew says nothing, can only stare at the man dying on the blood-soaked bed.

He watches, solemnly, as Paul Baker's head twitches once before his jaw falls open, the black tongue lolls out, and his body goes still.

12

I hear the gunshot and think, at first, it's my recurring dream. The memory of my father. But sitting up in bed, I know it's not. After finally getting everyone back to sleep, some are stirring once more, whispering in urgent tones to neighboring beds.

I consider getting up again, finding out what happened. But I fear Johnson's warning. I lay here struggling with my thoughts, conflicted as to what to do ... what if there's danger? I need to protect the others. If the men brought guns ...

My thoughts are shattered by the crashing sound of the dormitory doors blasting inward, blown open with such force that they smash against the walls. A few boys scream and now everyone's awake, or so I assume. I leap from the bed, standing to face whatever comes to us from the dark with such strength. Such anger.

But there is nothing.

There is no one.

The hallway beyond the open doors is dark and empty. It seems to stretch forever, an otherworldly corridor, ending in oblivion.

I turn to notice David also standing and, like me, staring dumbly at the open doors, the empty hall. I try to think of what to say, but cannot formulate the words, or come up with any answers.

I have no idea what's happened.

Only now do I realize that I'm shaking uncontrollably.

Before I can think further, I watch in disbelief as the heavy iron cross hanging above the doors—the one I have seen every morning, noon, and night for the last ten years of my life, seemingly unmovable—dislodges from its mount and falls, clattering like a broken bell against the floor, where it rests.

I turn, dazed, and see many of the other boys are now out of their beds, standing and staring. Someone is crying. Another boy moans in his sleep, as if fighting his own nightmare.

For a few minutes, no one moves. There is no more sound.

Outside, the snow falls heavily past the windows.

I notice Simon, a silver-trimmed shadow. He stands with his back to me, facing out the large window between our beds, framed within black sky, gusting flakes of snow.

I start to ask if he's okay, but decide not to.

He seems transfixed by the night.

PART TWO
SIDES

13

I wake up.

The room is filled with brilliant daylight.

About half the boys are already awake, a few even dressed, which is odd. I haven't heard Poole ringing the morning bell, and it appears others haven't, as well.

I look at the clock on my bedside table. My waking brain is slow to understand what I'm seeing. It reads just past six-thirty, and the memories of last night come back to me. At first, I wonder if any of it was real, or only a dream.

Screaming men? A gunshot?

Did David and I really sneak out to the foyer? It's all . . . muddled.

And the doors. And the cross.

I sit up and look at the doors, which are closed.

The cross, however, is leaned against a wall. I remember now. That's right where I'd set it after I finally mustered the courage to get out of bed and close the doors, seal off the dormitory from whatever was happening in the rest of the building. That done, I went around to a few of the cots, tried to comfort the younger kids. Poor Michael was beside himself. Sobbing hard. Asking for his dead mother again and again. Finnegan and Jonathan, the inseparables, were found hiding together under a cot. It took David nearly ten minutes to talk them out and back into their beds.

Some of the boys, strangely, hadn't even stirred.

They'd slept through it all, apparently. I envied them. Especially now, with my eyes heavy and my head throbbing.

I sit up, look across the room. David is still asleep, and I decide to let him be. Simon, in the next bunk, is also still lying down. But I can tell he's awake.

Because his eyes are open.

He's staring right at me.

"Simon," I ask, rubbing my tired eyelids. "You okay?"

He doesn't answer, but continues to watch me closely, the sheet pulled up past his mouth. I know it seems odd, but it almost looks as if he's smiling.

"Do you know what time it is?" I ask. "We should be up. My alarm . . ."

He doesn't answer, but (thankfully) closes his eyes, apparently finished with the conversation. I wonder why one of the priests hasn't come to wake us. Today was to be another day in the fields, pulling whatever crop we could from the hard ground before the snow . . .

The snow.

I jump out of bed, stand on the cold floor, and look out the window. The sky is a sheet of white, the sun pale as a blind eye. I step close to the window, turn my gaze downward, and gasp.

The ground is covered in snow. The fresh layer appears to be at least a couple inches deep, maybe more.

In the near distance, the large, black-cloaked form of Brother Johnson catches my eye, a blank space against the white. He walks into the gap between the barn and the narrow road, and I realize he's going to get Bartholomew. I can't help but wonder if the boy is still alive.

My peripheral vision flitters. I hear windswept voices. I press my forehead against the cold, wet glass, and look down to my left. What I see there explains why we haven't been disturbed. I assume the priests most likely hoped we'd all sleep through the morning.

This is not something they'd want the children to see.

Poole, Andrew, and Father White stand outside our graveyard, which is nothing but a small patch of crudely fenced-in ground dotted with crosses, the tapered points rammed into the earth near the heads of dead boys. To my knowledge, at least one priest sleeps in the earth with the orphans, a man named Gideon who died the year I arrived, having succumbed to a strain of flu that also claimed the lives of several children.

Standing with the priests are three other men, and I assume they're the ones who arrived in the night. Closer to the road is a horse-pulled wagon. Three more horses are tied to a nearby gate, stomping the thin layer of snow to mud.

On the ground at the men's feet, wrapped head-to-toe in brown sackcloth, are two bodies. I can't tell if the men are preparing to bury them or take them away. I assume one of the bodies is the injured man Johnson spoke of. I have no idea who the other might be.

I try to recall the sounds from the night's chaos: the horrible laughter, the screams, the loud voices . . . the pistol shot.

Was a man murdered here? I wonder, and decide I'll need to pry the entire story out of Andrew as soon as the right moment allows.

"What's all this, then?"

I turn to my left, toward the voice. David has woken, standing on the other side of my cot, staring out the next window. His head is tilted toward the graveyard, and I assume he's seeing the same things I am, but I have no answer.

"Hey!" Another voice calls out to my right. "It's Bartholomew!"

A small group of boys have grouped against the window to my right, all of them staring outward, gawping and excited. More boys leave their beds and jostle past me for position, relieving me of my view of the graveyard.

Distracted as I was by the strange men and the bodies, I had forgotten about seeing Johnson stalking out for Bartholomew. I look that way now and understand why it's gotten the others so worked up.

Bartholomew stands in the snow, still as a statue. The gaping mouth of the hole's hatch still open behind him, Johnson ready-ing to drop it back into place. I study the thin boy as he walks, seemingly unbothered, through the blanket of snow toward the orphanage. Johnson, seemingly surprised to be left behind, hur-ries to catch up, walking in stride with the boy. He asks him something, but Bartholomew doesn't respond.

As they get closer, Bartholomew tilts his head upward, to-ward the dorm windows.

I try to imagine what he's seeing: pale faces through distorted glass, hands pressed in curiosity and greeting, all eyes following his crossing back to us, to warmth and comfort. To reality.

I get jostled again but hold my place. Something about what I'm seeing strikes me as odd, but I can't put my finger on it. I rub a sleeve across the glass, wiping clear a patch fogged by a thin film of condensation.

Bartholomew is close now, almost beneath us. He still stares upward, and for a moment it feels like he's not only studying the windows, but looking at *me* directly. I can't help the sensation that he's meeting my eye.

I realize then what's off about him—something I've never seen from a boy who just spent a long, cold night in the hole.

He's smiling.

14

Andrew watches Poole and the sheriff with a dreamlike disconnect.

He's exhausted, emotionally and physically trampled, and still reeling in partial disbelief over the events he witnessed only hours ago.

The deputy Paul Baker had stabbed in the neck was dead. Paul Baker, also, was dead. The sheriff and his two remaining deputies had apologized to Father Poole, and to Andrew, for bringing horror to their doorstep. It was obvious they'd had no idea what they'd been up against.

Andrew is convinced Paul Baker had been possessed, which was implausible but—as he'd been taught many times over, with acute examples and firsthand accounts—nowhere near impossible. Demons were out there, an infestation among the people on the planet, the remnants of a battle fought since before the existence of man, a war that raged on every day. In Andrew's mind, there was simply no logic, no hidden rationale, that accounted for the injured man's strength, or his ability to continue living and breathing despite brutal physical damage. His strange vocal emanations and his violent, painful reaction to Poole's attack, fueled by nothing more than prayer and blessed water, were inexplicable.

The discussion now, in the early morning light, is about burial. Sheriff Baker wants to bury his brother at the orphanage, and return the body of the deputy to his family in Chester.

"No one but me is gonna mourn him," Baker says, nodding toward the graveyard. "Rather he be buried out here, in the open, near a holy place. Maybe his soul will find rest."

Finally, Poole agrees, albeit reluctantly.

Meanwhile, Andrew grows more anxious about the children. It's getting late in the morning and he knows they'll be waking up, expecting to be told the day's responsibilities, to be fed a meager breakfast.

But it had taken hours to clean up the mess. The kitchen staff had been woken by Johnson, and despite being horrified by the scene, they had nonetheless proceeded to sponge blood from the walls and floors. With Johnson and Andrew's help, they wrapped the bodies and brought them outside. Poole's mattress and bedding had been dumped behind the orphanage with other trash meant for burning, replaced by a mattress from the spare guestroom.

The bedframe, and its broken, jagged bedposts, remained.

Poole had insisted upon it.

"Let it serve as a reminder of the work we have left to do in this world," he'd said. "A reminder of the strength of the evil we fight against."

As Poole agrees to bury the diseased man in the orphanage graveyard, Andrew holds back a shudder. He has no wish to be reminded of last night's battle, of the poor man's mutilated body, that sonorous voice betraying the hidden voices within, the pure evil of his enraged face, those blood-splotched eyes.

Regardless, it is Poole's decision to make, and he will abide by it.

The two remaining deputies load their murdered associate into the wagon, gently lay him down where the sheriff's brother recently lay, bound and hooded. When Sheriff Baker isn't looking their way, Andrew sees one of the men spit on Paul Baker's corpse.

He can't say that he blames him.

Sheriff Baker shakes Poole's hand, tips his worn, brimmed hat toward Andrew, and gives orders to what remains of his posse.

As the riders and wagon pull away, the dead deputy's horse tethered behind, Paul Baker's body lies on the ground where they'd left it. A parting gift from their late-night visit.

"I'll have Johnson and the kitchen man Stewart bury him this morning. No need for the children to see a body lying around," Poole says wearily, exhaustion etched deeply into his face. "A horrible thing," he says, as he and Andrew watch the sheriff and his men ride off. The wagon rattles and bumps over the snow-covered road, the wrapped body rolling and swaying in the rear.

"Should we ready the children, Father?" Andrew isn't sure what the day will look like. Everything feels out of sorts, and although he's too tired to analyze the true events of what occurred during the night, he feels it's important the children not be affected.

"No," Poole says, staring at the distant horizon, Baker and his men already small shadows pushing up the gentle slope of the valley road. "I think we all need a day to recover, including the children."

Andrew looks at him questioningly, and Poole chuckles softly.

"I've been doing this a few decades longer than you, my son. I guarantee you those kids heard a good amount of what went on last night. Johnson told me this morning he'd spotted the two oldest boys spying from the top of the stairs."

"Peter?"

"Yes, and David. An unlikely pairing, those two. But good boys."

Andrew nods. "Peter will make a fine priest. It's my hope he'll stay on. He's good with the young ones."

Poole nods but says nothing. After a moment, he turns back toward the orphanage. "I must rest, Andrew. I think you should, as well. Neither of us have slept, and tomorrow will be a big day."

Andrew turns away from the horizon to follow Poole's departure, and sees Bartholomew and Johnson are stepping inside. Somewhat surprisingly, Andrew notices that Bartholomew looks none the worse for wear. Still, maybe Poole is correct. They could all use a day to rest and reflect. Tomorrow, after Mass, he'll be going to the Hill farm for supplies, and for that journey he'll need to be refreshed. Even if he is planning on enlisting help.

Andrew calls after Poole. "I'll see the boys get breakfast."

Poole lifts a hand and waves without looking back.

Andrew's eyes travel up toward the dorm windows. He sees the faces of many of the boys peering out, some looking down his way, most likely having noticed the sheriff and his men.

Which means they've seen the bodies, he thinks, and sighs deeply.

He wonders how he'll explain it all to Peter. He suppresses a smile at the thought of him and David sneaking out last night. Poole was right about them, they *are* an unlikely pairing, but Andrew has a suspicion they are also more tightly knit than even Poole realizes. Perhaps more than they fully realize themselves.

He sighs once more, feeling the weariness from lack of sleep infiltrating his mind and body. He stares down blankly at the wrapped corpse of Paul Baker. Something tells him that whatever evil, whatever *power*, had been locked inside Baker's body has since been released. Unbidden, he recalls the story of Jesus and the wild man who lived in the tombs.

We are many.

"My name is Legion," Andrew mutters, quoting the passage from the Book of Mark. "For we are many."

In the story, Jesus commanded the demons out of the man and cast them into a herd of two thousand pigs. Driven mad, the pigs rush into a nearby lake and drown.

Staring at the body, Andrew gloomily considers the story, then debates bestowing a final blessing on the man before he is buried. After a moment's thought, he decides against it. Deep down in the darkest parts of his mind, where the evils of the world are caged away for inspection, he finds fresh fear. Fear that blessing this man may cause some sort of a *response*; some final, rebellious act of the haunted flesh.

Andrew grimaces, turns away quickly, and follows Poole's path to the orphanage.

He has no desire to see the corpse protest its soiled bindings.

15

I leave the window and sit down on my cot, unsure what to do next. It's highly unusual to be allotted extra free time in the mornings and, like most of the boys, I'm not sure what to do with myself. I'm hoping the kitchen is preparing breakfast, even if it is just biscuits, because my stomach is filled with needles, sharp stabs of hunger piercing me every few seconds.

I don't notice David until he sits at the foot of my cot. The springs creak beneath the weight of two of us, and I look at him in surprise. It's unlike him to be this familiar.

Looking at him now, I find it's strange to think that I've known David nearly my whole life. He came to St. Vincent's about a year after I did, and at the time we were two of the younger boys, both still reeling from our abrupt change of scenery, the disruption of our childhoods. We didn't hit it off like many others in similar situations, certainly nothing like Jonathan and Finnegan, our notorious "twins" (despite being born on completely different continents). Instead, he and I sort of gravitated around each other, neither friends nor foes, like the moons of a planet we had no interest in observing, but whose orbit we were forced to nonetheless reside within. Now, years later, we are the oldest of the boys. Those ahead of us having gone off to workshops or military. Many died. At least one ran away.

Being the oldest (we're both at least two years older than any of the current orphans) has always borne for me the weight of additional responsibility, an albatross my training for priesthood has only added to. I never thought David felt similarly. I'm beginning to think I was wrong.

"Weird, right?" he says quietly. I study him, not understanding.

He nods his head toward the north end of the dormitory, and I look over.

Most of the boys are awake now. It would have been impossible to sleep given the excitement and activity of the others. Many sit on their bunks, as if unable to function without instruction. A couple have slipped on shoes and coats and hurried to visit the outhouse.

What David is indicating, however, is something else entirely. Something I can't explain.

At the far end of the room a group of boys are sitting on the floor, cross-legged, forming a rough circle. This in itself isn't totally strange, although certainly not common.

It's the *combination* of boys that makes it bizarre.

I easily spot Simon among the group, along with Terrence, Samuel, and Jonah. A few younger boys have joined them as well, including Frankie, who boasts the olive-toned skin of an Italian immigrant, and Auguste, a tall fourteen-year-old whose only claim to individuality is that he is French. (He always made a point to say he isn't French, but French-*Canadian*. To kids from Pennsylvania who've lived on the streets most their lives, the distinction is slight.)

Samuel and Jonah are tight friends, have been since they arrived several years back. Samuel is short, but strong as an ox. A farmer's boy whose parents were robbed and murdered in their home, their only child somehow being the only one to avoid their horrid fate. As for Jonah, he never speaks of his past, but it is clear that he is rotten to the core. Always wearing a chiseled smirk on his waxen face, and often brushing a fingertip along a puckered scar that splits his cheek, a marker of his violent history. As far as I know, Samuel is his only true friend, so there is nothing odd about them huddling together. But they're also tyrants, those two, and have a well-worn history of teasing Simon and Terrence mercilessly.

But now, as if their pasts were forgiven—or forgotten—they

all sit together, whispering to each other like conspirators. As if they're suddenly best of friends.

As if they all share a secret.

"Since when is your pet so tight with those little assholes, eh? Samuel and Jonah? Come on, they hate Simon."

I concede with a shrug, even though I know he's right. Still, I hate it when he calls Simon my pet, a nickname he came up with when I took the poor kid under my wing upon his arrival. He'd been badly abused by his parents for years and was free of them only when they'd both succumbed to influenza, a fate he miraculously avoided. He was so helpless, so shy, and I could see how hard it was for him to not be afraid of the others, of the priests, of his own shadow. I befriended him and he, subsequently, looked up to me, as one might a big brother.

Ironically, since he likes to wear such a callous emotional front, I think it annoys David how many of the boys gravitate toward me. But it's only because I treat them with kindness. Because I feel a protective responsibility, an inherent defensiveness for them that triggers when the situation calls for it. I know that if David ever gave the younger boys even the tiniest bit of sponsorship, they'd flock to him as equally.

This outer shell he wears leads many—priests and boys alike—to misunderstand David. They don't see the kindness in him that I do. He has a big heart, bold as a rose in full bloom, even if it is surrounded by protective thorns. In addition to this, there's one other misperception about my friend that his cool demeanor often suggests. Most, I think, assume that he's not very intelligent. Not perceptive. I know from experience that neither is true. In fact, he beats me on both counts. Still, I don't think he wants the responsibilities, or the attention, so playing the careless dullard keeps him out of that particular light.

In times like these, however, I welcome both his keen perception and his amity. I'm grateful that, if push comes to shove, I won't be standing alone.

"I'm going to go over there," I say.

David scoffs, but wears a concerned look. "Your funeral," he says, and shoves off my cot to return to his own bed. He pulls a magazine from under the mattress, the same well-worn POPULAR SCIENCE magazine he's owned for months, lies back and opens it wide, effectively cutting himself off from the goings-on.

Wonderful.

I take a moment to muster my nerve, then stand and walk toward the circle of boys. I get the sense, as I move toward the back of the room, that many eyes are on me. When I'm near enough to the circle of would-be conspirators, I count heads.

There are nine of them.

I glance around as I pass the cots of the others, all of whom are either lost in their own thoughts, enjoying a few more minutes of sleep, or simply waiting, perhaps furtively, for something to happen. I find it curious no one else has intruded on the circle's makeshift assembly. Either the other boys don't notice, don't care, or, like David, distrust the strangeness of it.

I smile as I step up to them, hoping to project friendly nonchalance, even if it's not exactly how I feel. Not even close.

Although Terrence is the first to notice me, it's Simon who raises his head and addresses me directly.

The rest of the boys go quiet.

"Hello, Peter."

"Hi, Simon. What are you lot up to?"

Simon smiles broadly, and I fight a queasy feeling in my gut as the rest of them turn their heads, address me with blank stares.

"Oh, nothing. Enjoying the free morning, I suppose."

From a nearby cot behind me, Jonathan pipes up. "It's like a holiday!"

He and Finnegan giggle, and I realize that whatever's happening here, the others are at the very least watching, if not listening, from a distance.

It's all very odd.

"Right," I say, trying to sound cheerful, although I don't know why I feel the need to put on that sort of front. I suppose it's to settle my own nerves from what feels, frankly, *wrong*. Out of character, at the least. For all of them. "Well, hopefully we'll get breakfast soon enough," I say. "I know I'm starved."

When none of them respond, when they do nothing but stare at me with those blank expressions, I turn away, flushed with embarrassment. I begin the journey back toward my own bed, but after a few steps, I pause. I'm not often at the end of the room, and I find myself studying the length of the dormitory: the double-doors at the far end, the two long rows of symmetrical beds, the makeshift placement of the orphans.

Something in my vision feels off. It's like I'm standing on a gently rocking boat (having never actually been on a boat, it's at least how I would imagine it to be). The entire room seems to sway or, perhaps a better description, *pulse*. As if the walls are sucking in and out like lungs, the air itself a thumping heart, pulsing in steady, repetitive movements, as if pumping blood.

I rub my eyes, force myself to study the room anew. I inspect for other things that might qualify as strange or out of sorts, which might lend a clue to how and why I'm feeling like this, offer some rationale to the attitudes of the circle of boys gathered behind me. Enemies who are now friends. Wolves communing with sheep.

But I can find nothing else that strikes me as odd, other than, perhaps, the fallen cross. It still rests, solemn and undignified, against the far wall.

Otherwise, everything is as it always is. Sane and, frankly, dull.

I decide the best thing to do is get dressed, make a much-needed visit to the privy, and try to find out what the plan is to feed everyone. Some semblance of normalcy, focusing on points of action, will go a long way to calming my nerves.

Feeling better, I start back toward my bed and my bureau,

slightly annoyed with myself for allowing David to get my anxiety stirred up . . .

When the dormitory doors open.

Johnson stands there, looking sullen.

Bartholomew stands next to him.

Up close, I realize that Bartholomew is in far worse shape than he appeared through the window. He's pale as a ghost, for one, and noticeably shivering. His clothes are muddy. The cuffs of his trousers are wet from the snow and blackened with mud, and I'm sure his shoes and socks are in an equally bad state.

At their arrival, the room goes quiet, as if holding its collective breath.

Johnson gives Bartholomew a light shove into the room, then turns away with a grimace, pulling the doors closed. Bartholomew's eyes roam the room briefly, then, without a word, he walks straight to his cot, pulls back the coverings, and tucks himself in—still wearing his muddy shoes and dirty, wet clothes. He raises the sheet and blanket over his head, then lies motionless.

After a few heartbeats, children begin moving and talking again. Time resumes.

"It just gets better and better," David says.

I turn toward him, but he's hidden behind his magazine. For the first time, I notice the detail of the cover, a painting which depicts a man in a metal shield, photographing the flaming heart of a live volcano, the spewing lava bright red and cut with dark shadow, the shielded man small and overwhelmed.

It appears to me as an image of hell.

16

God, I hate Mass, David thinks, sitting near the back of the small chapel, eyes heavy with boredom, desperately waiting for the sermon to be over.

All the boys are present, squirming and elbowing and pulling at their ears, picking their noses and shifting their asses on the hardwood benches they're forced to sit on. Poole drones on as usual, and it's all David can do not to lie down on the bench and close his eyes.

The oddness of the previous day, and the night which preceded it, seems to have thrown everybody out of sorts. Including the priests. As it turned out, none of the orphans were put to work in the fields yesterday, nor did they go to any classes. David can't remember the last time he had a free day—was able to do nothing but lounge around the dorm, read his magazine, take a mid-afternoon nap. It was wonderful, but at the same time disorienting. The schedule was thrown and it was like a cracked gear in a motor, screwing up the timing of the machine and making everything seem just a little bit . . . *broken.*

It doesn't help that half the boys are acting like lunatics. The way some of their personalities have seemingly changed overnight makes no sense to him at all, and trying to talk to Peter about it, on-and-off-again all day yesterday, didn't get him far. The poor sap keeps looking for rational explanations—even after David told him about the grave.

David had gone for a stroll in the early afternoon, relishing the freedom to do so, and decided to have a look at—somewhat morbidly, he'd admit—the freshly-dug grave of the mysterious dead man. The recent snowfall had mostly melted, and the cemetery was, for the most part, uncovered. The fresh sod which had been lain over the new grave was easy to spot.

The sight of it made David's breath catch in his throat.

"What about it?" Peter asked, the two of them sitting at the dinner table, when David brought it up.

"The grass, where they buried him? It's *dead*, Peter. Not withered, not browned from the cold . . . but dead. Like, crispy and black." He paused, hunting for the right word. "Burned."

Peter scoffed, as did the other boys around the table. Despite his annoyance at their disbelief, he was comforted sitting with boys he still trusted. Boys who didn't have their heads up their asses, who still acted like their normal selves. Basil, for one. The little shitter was a nuisance, but David liked him okay. He was a helpless little guy and, probably, wouldn't survive if David didn't come to his aid now and then. Too sickly, too skinny. Smart, though. He showed promise as a future ne'er-do-well, and David figured the old henhouse needed another fox or two.

Also seated with them were fragile Ben, soft as bread dough, seemingly always on the verge of tears about something or other. James, who was a good kid, loyal, and always willing to pitch in. And Timothy of course, who David thought was a nuisance, but the kid kept his stuttering mouth shut most of the time, which he appreciated.

For some reason, he felt it was important to keep his thoughts confined to a small, reliable group. Byron, seated at the next table over, was obviously trying to listen in, but David didn't mind that. The rough-edged kid was as stalwart a protector of Saint Peter as you could ask for.

He probably wants to be sure nobody is upsetting his holiness.

"I'm telling you," David continued, "I was out there this afternoon while you lot were wanking in the privy." Peter gave him a glare, which he ignored. "I wanted to, you know, *see* it."

"Who'd want to look at a dirt-bath?" Basil said, giggling at his turn of phrase.

"What do you mean, burned?" Ben asked, ignoring Basil's comment, eyes wide.

David told them what he'd seen. "It was easy to see the sod they cut and removed, then laid back over the grave. Black as oil, I'm telling you. Like it had been poisoned." When he finished, the table grew quiet, each of them lost in their own nervous thoughts.

After dinner, things didn't get much better. Once Bartholomew got himself cleaned up and had a long nap, he started acting even stranger than the rest of them put together. Out of nowhere he was talking to the other boys as if he were the newly appointed mayor of St. Vincent's, all smiles and handshakes. A child politician if there ever was one.

But he'd *never* been that way. Not in all the years since he'd arrived. He'd been quiet, reclusive. David had always thought of him as distant and, quite frankly, strange. Consciously or unconsciously, he'd kept a wide berth of the boy, as had most of the others. A wallflower, yeah, but poisonous to the touch.

Now, however, he'd apparently come out of his shell.

At one point, during a game of after-dinner cards, even Basil had noticed. "What's he so happy about, anyway?" he asked, shooting careful glances past David's shoulder at the group gathered in the rear of the dorm, Bartholomew right in the middle of them, as if holding court. David didn't have a good answer then, and doesn't have one now.

Maybe a night in the hole did the boy some good.

Still, David can't help but find the whole thing bizarre. Unnerving. Boys are chumming together who had always kept their distance. Even at supper, David noted that Bartholomew's table was filled to capacity.

But the strangest thing of all is Simon's newfound affinity for the oily-haired ghoul. Suddenly the two kids are inseparable, when only a couple days ago you'd have needed a sharp knife to remove Simon from Peter's hip.

David knows that Peter also noticed. And looked, if not worried, at least confused.

Once they'd finally doused the lights and gone to bed, David made a point to keep an eye and an ear open well into the night, making sure no one was doing anything untoward. Unable to explain his own trepidation, his own *fear*, he nonetheless wanted to make sure no boys were moving about, sneaking between cots. The last thing he wanted was to wake up and have someone's wide-eyed face inches from his own. Even worse, waking up to a group of smiling faces, surrounding his bed, hands ready to clamp down . . .

No, he doesn't trust this new normal, and he likes the timing even less. As he lay in bed, the same recurring question popped into his brain for the hundredth time. Unbidden, nonsensical. Burrowing into his thoughts like a rat, gnawing at his brain like cheese.

What had *been wrong with that man?*

Now, however, between the late night, the lack of sleep, and Poole's droning sermon, he isn't able to properly focus on his nagging concerns. Besides, the old bastard is finally at the wine-and-crackers part of the program.

David spruces up. Food is food, after all. Even if the "wine" is just grape juice and the piece of cracker isn't enough to satisfy a baby bird's hungry guts, he'll take it gladly.

They all will.

As they stand for communion, David keeps his eyes moving to catch anything that seems out of place. He's morbidly curious to see if the kids' strange behavior will permeate the service.

He doesn't have to wait long.

In the front row, two boys sit side by side at the end of a long bench. They are, at this point, the only ones still sitting. The rest are lined up like sheep waiting to be clubbed on the brain and sold for wool. All but the two.

Bartholomew and Simon.

David huffs a breath and looks around for Peter, wondering if he also noticed the odd stragglers. Before he can locate him amongst the others, however, he notices rickety old Father White shuffle over to the two seated boys, the ancient priest apparently winding himself up for a rare reprimand. As David steps closer to the front, he tries his best to listen to their conversation, difficult as it might be to hear anything clearly over Poole's mumbling prayers as he thumbs stale wafers onto sprung, eager tongues.

"But I can't, Father," Bartholomew says, face earnest. "I haven't confessed."

"Neither have I, Father," Simon repeats, looking decidedly less innocent. David thinks his expression is more amused than anything. "I missed confession yesterday, so I can't possibly take communion. There's mortal sin in me, Father White. Mortal sin."

Bartholomew nods along, and Father White alternates between looking apoplectic and totally befuddled.

"You saw it yourself, Father White," Bartholomew adds. "In the dining hall on Friday. The sin of pride."

"And my sin was sloth, Father," Simon says merrily. "Oh, and envy."

"But, but . . . boys," Father White stammers, "those aren't mortal sins."

Both boys sit up straight at this, their eyes widening as they fervently shake their heads in disagreement. David can't help but smile at the temerity of their off-stage play, even though he knows it will be called out soon enough, that they'll pay dearly for it.

"Well, we will certainly discuss this with Father Poole after the service," White says finally, shaking his head in annoyance as he waddles his bag of bones back to his chair.

For a moment, David stands even with the two boys. Bartholomew—as if sensing his attention—turns his black eyes to focus on him. David gives a light nod, and Bartholomew smiles in return with pale, wormy lips, hiding his teeth.

A wash of queasiness floods his stomach, and David turns quickly away, skin prickling. He swallows a rush of bitter acid rising in his throat, then steps shakily forward and into the extended hand of mumbling Father Poole, whose sticky thumb waits impatiently with the body of Christ.

17

Andrew is more rested from a day of recuperation after the incidents of Friday night, but he still feels his eyes grow heavy during Poole's ponderous sermon. He keeps himself alert by focusing on the children, making sure *they* aren't nodding off, or creating mischief, during the service. He knows it's hard for many of them—especially given how little they generally get to eat and the lack of daily exercise—to stay alert during the long Sunday morning Mass. Still, he will do his part to make sure they remain at least relatively focused.

Once the boys finish taking communion and Poole dismisses them for their hour of reflection, Andrew makes sure to catch Peter before he goes upstairs to the dorm where, like most of the others, he'll likely take a late morning nap, something Andrew himself would very much like to do.

Alas, that will not happen today.

"Peter!"

A head taller than most of the others, Peter is easy to spot in the crowd of children exiting the chapel. He turns back toward Andrew—who points meaningfully to the foyer—and nods in acknowledgment. Andrew gathers his things and hastens out, meeting up with Peter outside the doors.

"Good morning, Father," Peter says, suppressing a yawn.

"Good morning. Tired?"

Peter shakes his head, but his heavy eyes counter the lie. "I'm okay. The last couple days have been . . . odd."

Andrew understands why Peter would think that about Friday night, but is confused as to why he'd mention the last "couple days." Did something occur yesterday Andrew isn't aware of? He decides to dig deeper on the subject.

Later, when there's more time.

"I see," he says, letting it go for the moment. "Listen, I hate to ask, but the weather is turning against us more quickly than we expected, and I'm afraid I can't wait another day to make a run for supplies."

Andrew tries not to smile as Peter's face lights up, his tired eyes suddenly wide and alert. Even his pale cheeks flush, albeit slightly. "So," Andrew continues, "I need to go this afternoon. Or, rather, this morning . . . to put a finer point on it, I need to go *now*. The snow is only going to fall harder, and by this time tomorrow we might be looking at a foot or more, double or triple the day after that." He puts a hand on Peter's shoulder, winces inwardly at how frail it is, at the feel of jutting bone through the thin shirt.

We must find a way to feed the boys better, he thinks, for what is probably the thousandth time. Peter waits silently, expectantly, for the question he wants to hear, and Andrew can't suppress a small sigh. *Boys will be boys.*

"If you're able, I'd like you to come with me. I can always use the help."

Peter is already nodding. "To the Hill farm."

"That's right." Andrew tilts his head, gives Peter a wary look. "But Peter, you will be *helping* me, you understand? We'll need to hurry. I've no desire to push through heavy snow with a wagon filled with supplies. It's not a social visit."

"Of course, Father. Should I get my things?"

Andrew pauses a moment, weighing whether the boy needs more recrimination, then nods. "Yes. Bring your coat, and a hat. It'll be cold on the road."

Peter is already backing away, eager to turn and run up the stairs to the cloak room.

Andrew knows Peter is excited for the trip and, hopefully, the boy is looking forward to some quality time with his teacher (or so he'd like to imagine).

But mostly, Andrew knows, he's eager to see Grace Hill.

"Go on," he says, waving a hand. "Fifteen minutes, out front."

Peter walks briskly toward the stairs, and Andrew admires his restraint at not breaking into a gallop. Andrew is not a stupid man, and he realizes the dangers of putting coal too near an open fire, but he also doesn't want to hide the boy from the world only to have it revealed to him later, when he's already a priest and his life decisions, forever finalized, are based on limited experiences.

If Peter is to become a priest, Andrew wants him to make that decision with eyes wide open. Being a priest is a calling, but it's also a choice. And, in Andrew's mind anyway, it should be an *educated* decision. If you choose the priesthood, the knowledge of what you are sacrificing should not be something ethereal, something told to you or that you read from a book, but something you've *experienced*. Perhaps even loved.

Loved . . . and then purposely let go of.

Only then would the decision be whole; strong enough to withstand the many years, the countless temptations. Still, he hopes Peter *will* make the choice to be a priest, to forego so much of what the world offers in order to be a pure vessel of the Lord.

And if he doesn't—if he chooses the love of worldly things over the love of the Lord, if he accepts earthly treasures instead of heavenly rewards—then Andrew will support him. He loves the boy, after all, like he would his own son, and his happiness is paramount.

Pondering all these thoughts, and worried about the oncoming weather, Andrew slips through the large double-doors and into the whispering cold. He walks brusquely toward the barn to ready the wagon. Light snow flutters around him, but the ground is still easily passable. He smiles to himself as he thinks of Peter, of the grand decision which lies ahead of him.

Yes, he'll let the boy make up his own mind.

But he doesn't plan to make the decision an easy one.

18

Grace!

I try to temper my excitement. I haven't been to the farm in several months, and my anxiety is surpassed only by my desire to see Grace once again.

Andrew took me to the Hill farm for the first time when I was only twelve. He'd already taken me under his wing by then, begun my early lessons that would eventually lead to the path of priesthood, especially once he saw my affinity for scripture, for the spiritual. That first trip to the Hill farm was—and still is—one of the greatest days of my life. Most certainly since the death of my parents and my bequeathal to the orphanage. It was exhilarating. It was an adventure.

The farm is owned by John Hill, a man Father Andrew already knew well by the time I was introduced, and had been supplying the orphanage with supplies even prior to Andrew's arrival. There are other farms, of course, but none as close as Hill farm, and none as well-stocked with the necessities of feeding and housing thirty-two growing boys. The city of Chester was forbidden to any of the children, including me, so the Hill farm was as close to the real world as I would likely ever get, at least until I turned eighteen and was able to leave the orphanage as an adult (or hired out to a needy workhouse or factory, the fate of many of the children, especially the more unruly ones).

Being so young and sheltered at the time, I was eagerly looking forward to meeting Mr. Hill, to seeing animals I'd only read about, to exploring a new world.

And then, something incredible happened.

I met Grace.

Being a single child from a reclusive family, I'd never interacted with a female other than my own mother. And, as an orphan in an all-boys home, the opportunity was even more implausible. But fate intervened, and at the age of twelve years, there I was, meeting my first real *girl*.

John and Andrew were openly amused by my response to Grace Hill, herself only ten years old at the time. I recall being tongue-tied, and shy at first. But she was kind, and funny, and wasn't put off by my sullen, confused demeanor. Looking back on it, I wonder if John and Andrew had perhaps discussed it with Grace, meeting one of the orphans, and if John prepped his daughter not to take offense if we acted, well, peculiar.

Or maybe it was just the way Grace was—forthright, open, energized. Blazing.

That first magical afternoon, while Andrew and John discussed matters of no interest to children, Grace took my hand and pulled me, without preamble, toward the farmhouse for a tour. She showed me their neat, modest home, all of which was amazing to my naïve eyes. *They had so many things!* I wanted to pick up every item and study it! Lamps and vases and painted bowls, a carved wooden pipe, an entire stack of magazines. And toys! It was dizzying. When she led me into her room I gasped, dumbstruck.

"Is this whole room for you?" I asked, beside myself with shock (along with a shameful, painful stab of envy).

She nodded, unaware or unconcerned by my gawping expression. She generously showed each of her toys, done in a way that was the opposite of conceited or snobbish. She proudly presented her colorful drawings, her colored pencils and paints.

Finally, she showed me her books.

I remember staring, with a sort of reverence, at that orderly, purple-painted bookcase, delicately decorated with oil-based white flowers. Shelves packed with rows of bright-colored spines.

"Do you like it?" she said, catching me studying the painted flowers along the sides. "My papa made it himself."

I thought of John Hill, tall and bearded, broad-shouldered and muscled, gently painting each of the fine petals for his daughter. The thought made me want to weep with bitter resentment and self-pity, but my mind was too overwhelmed to dwell on those raw emotions. My thoughts were racing in a different direction.

I was giddy with curiosity. With blatant *wonder*.

Obviously, the orphanage had books. Bibles, mostly. And there was a broad selection of volumes on history and grammar, biographies of great men. In other words, schoolbooks.

But *this* . . . this was something else altogether. Titles I'd never heard of, pages filled with images and stories I couldn't believe.

"What are they?" I asked, not knowing how else to phrase the question in my eagerness, my wonderment.

"They're books, obviously," she answered. Not cruelly, but factually, with a smidge of confusion and a larger dose of pride. "Have you read any of these?"

"I mean, I've seen books," I answered shyly, and somewhat defensively. "Father Francis says I read quite well. For my age, anyway . . ."

"Oh, yes, I'm sure," she said, nodding along as I stammered.

"Father Francis, that is, Andrew, has me study many subjects. We're all taught to read by the priests, of course . . ." I caught my tumble of words, looked once more at the bookcase, the spines bursting with colors, each one tugging at my imagination. "But these . . ." I shook my head, awestruck. "I've never even heard of them. Of *any* of them."

Without preamble, she reached out and pulled one from a shelf, turned it to face me.

"What about this one?"

On the cover was a young girl in a blue dress. In the image, the girl was talking to a large rabbit, one that wore a suit and top hat.

"*Alice's Adventures in Wonderland* . . ." I said slowly, wanting nothing more in that moment of time than to take the book from her hands, find a well-lit corner, and study each page until my eyes could stay open no more.

"It's my favorite," she said, and then her cherubic face lit up. "Hey! Do you want to borrow it? You can bring it back the next time you visit."

She pushed it into my hands, would hear no argument.

And so, my friendship with Grace Hill began.

On that long-ago day, Andrew had kindly extended our stay to last the entire afternoon. A one-time luxury he has rarely repeated since. But back then, while he and John loaded supplies and spoke of adult, worldly things, Grace and I let our imaginations travel through her purple-cased library, me in amazement and she amused, happily giving me summations of each and every story (while being careful not to spoil the endings). The more she showed me, the more my veneration for the books grew, until it felt as if an entire new realm of existence had opened inside my mind, a million worlds all aching for me to visit, to meet each and every one of their fantastical inhabitants.

After the tour was over, we were finally put to work. John put us to gathering eggs and milking the cows—the bounty of which was all destined for the orphanage—along with sacks of wheat and flour, crates of vegetables, jars of preserves, cans of fruits in sauce, dried meats; plus an entire side of beef and a sleeve of steaks, near frozen after being stored in the Hills' gas-powered icebox.

After a few hours of work and quick escapes of play, the wagon was full. By the time it came to say our goodbyes, Grace had shown me every inch of the farm—the massive barn, the pigs and goats and cows and horses, and even their two large mastiffs (it was during an ensuing trip she informed me her father purchased the massive dogs from an Englishman selling a recent litter; having bought two because he feared that the man might kill the ones he didn't sell, wanting to save those he could).

As I climbed atop the wagon, Grace's eyes popped open wide and she yelled at her father to make sure we didn't drive away. She turned and ran for the house in a dead sprint.

That *might* have been the moment I fell in love with her. Hard to say.

John and Andrew, amused, had a good laugh at our expense, but I didn't much mind, and I know Grace certainly didn't.

When she came back, she held a small package wrapped in brown paper and tied with string. I looked over to Andrew for approval, and although his brows were furrowed—whether in confusion or disapproval I didn't know—he nodded.

"Just to borrow," she said, holding my eyes with her own; a sparkling, brilliant green. "You need to bring it back, you understand? I expect you will comply, Peter Barlow."

The wording was so odd and her gaze so strong I was momentarily flummoxed. Girls certainly were peculiar, I realized. But I nodded and said, "Of course" and "Thank you."

Minutes later, we were back on the road and I was waving behind us at Grace and John, the former running after the wagon for a few yards. As she ran out of breath, she yelled out: "Don't forget!"

Once they were out of sight, I could wait no longer.

I opened up the package.

It was *Alice*.

I showed it to Andrew, who raised his eyebrows, but smiled. "I suppose that's all right."

I stared at the book, mesmerized. "Have you read it?"

"I have. It's a strange story, but not a harmful one."

Gratefulness and relief swept through me, and I thanked him repeatedly for letting me hold onto the prize.

He nodded and waved his hand at me, charmed at my exuberance. "Yes, all right." He gave me a serious look then. "Still, it might be best if you didn't let the others see it, Peter. Not that I want you to be selfish, but if it causes a stir, Poole might take it away. And we want to make sure Grace gets her book back, don't we?"

I looked at him and nodded, hoping the inference meant what I hoped it did.

That I'd return with him. That I'd see Grace Hill again.

It wasn't until I was alone in the chapel later that evening, having escaped from the others under the pretense of a tutoring session with Andrew, that I finally realized what Grace was implying with her odd behavior while giving me the book.

Stuck within the pages, neatly folded, was a handwritten letter.

Dearest Peter,

I'm writing this quickly while you and Papa load the wagon, so my apologies for being brief, or for any misspellings.

It was nice meeting you today. I already know we are going to be best friends. I'm glad you liked my house and my books. It made me happy to share them with you. I'm also glad you liked my papa, who is a wonderful person. I'm sorry, though, that our dog drooled on your shirt and got it muddy. Those dogs are messy creatures. I hope you enjoy reading the book. As I said, it's probably my favorite, though there are others I enjoy equally. When you return, I will give you another to borrow, if it's okay with Father Francis.

It would make me very happy if you could write me back. I never get letters and have always wanted a Pen Pal. I want to hear more about Saint Vincent's, and about your life. I've enclosed another page of paper, in case you don't have any at the orphanage.

Let's keep it a secret, okay? Our secret. It will be more fun that way.

I look forward to seeing you again, Peter Barlow. I'm glad we met.

God Bless You,
Grace

I read the letter over and over. Read it through so many times I almost completely forgot to use some of that rare solitude to read the book itself.

Over the weeks and months, however, I did find the time. Andrew allowed me a portion of our tutoring sessions to read a book of my choosing, and I was able to read by candlelight at night, when the others were asleep.

The letters remained our secret, one we would keep for many years, and after many return visits to the farm.

As the years passed, the letters between Grace and I became more eager, more *open*. I suppose an outsider might call them love letters, although they were less about passion, and more about our respective thoughts of an uncertain future.

I never told her, or anyone, about my other, darker thoughts. As open as I became with Grace, I worried those parts of me would alarm her, perhaps cause her to question her feelings toward me. So, even with my secret letters, I stayed silent about my greatest fear: the knowledge that something dark and *alive* lived deep inside of me. Hidden in the folded shadows of my soul. A poisonous barb stuck through my heart that tainted my thoughts, turned my dreams into terror-strewn nightmares.

This hidden part of who I am will sometimes make me see things that don't exist, think things no priest-bound young man should think. It is a black seed waiting to take root, twine itself into my bones, my flesh, my mind. It is my constant, silent adversary. A slow poison that I feel will forever be my secret burden, and one that I would never inflict upon another.

So, instead, we discussed different things . . . more *pleasant* considerations. My decision to train for priesthood, for example. Or Grace's desire to travel, to have a family. Neither of us broached the parallel nature of these respective paths, the impossibility of our exclusive journeys intersecting.

What was left unspoken, however, was that we *would* discuss such things one day.

But not yet.

For now, we would wait. There was time.

"Hey, Peter!"

I'm about to enter the dorm when I hear the voice. I turn around, startled from my thoughts. Behind me, standing shoulder to shoulder at the open doorway of the cloakroom, are Simon and Bartholomew.

"What is it?" I say, stepping no closer.

"Can we talk to you a minute?" Simon asks, smiling like he always does. Cheerful. Innocent. Next to him, Bartholomew does not smile, and watches me closely. It makes me uncomfortable, that studious stare.

"Not now," I say. "I'm in a hurry."

Bartholomew takes a jerky step forward; his face catches a shadow and dissolves. "Why so eager, Peter?" And now he does smile, but his grin contains no cheer, no innocence. It's somehow too wide, as if his lips are stretched, his teeth crowded. "What's the rush, little rabbit?"

I start to reply, then stop. My blood chills, my face goes numb.

Little rabbit?

"So talk," I say, infusing the words with whatever meager bravado I can muster.

"Not here," Simon says, looking up and down the hallway, as if wary of hidden conspirators. He points into the cloakroom. "In private."

"Please," Bartholomew adds, stepping aside to let me through, as if it's all well-and-done.

"Can't," I say, swallowing hard. I know my coat and hat are in that room, but I've already decided to forgo them. I'll add a second shirt if I must, but right now, with these two at my heels? No, I wouldn't step foot into that cloakroom if all the devils of hell were chasing me. I can't say why. Just something I know. Something I feel. A warning. "Look, I'm heading to get supplies with Father Andrew. Maybe later, okay? He's waiting for me."

Simon starts to say something—his smile now wiped away—but Bartholomew touches his sleeve, and my old friend pulls the words back.

"Sure, Peter," Bartholomew says. "Later."

I nod and, without another word, turn away and push through the dormitory doors. I walk quickly to my bed, sit down and slip off my shoes. I quickly pull on the stocky leather boots we use for field work, then kneel on the floor to lace them.

I take a look around to make sure no one is paying close attention, then slide my leather book satchel from beneath the bed, the one which contains my tutoring books and my Bible. As I do, I slip my other hand beneath my mattress and pull free another book—one that has a letter inside—and slip it into the satchel.

"Where you going?"

I turn my head, breath caught in my chest, to see little Basil standing at the foot of my bed. I exhale heavily, my tense muscles relaxing.

"You scared me, Bas," I say, and stand up, hoisting the bag onto my shoulder. I motion as if to depart, but Basil doesn't move. He continues to stand beside my bed, effectively blocking my exit. It's unlike him, and it unsettles me.

"Strange, isn't it?" he says.

"What's that, Basil?" I ask, impatience boiling inside me like water over fire. The run-in with Simon and Bartholomew has already unnerved me but, more than that, I'm anxious to be on the road, to see Grace.

"Oh, I dunno . . ." he says airily, glancing around the room. I follow suit but see nothing extraordinary. Most of the kids are napping, and those few still awake are paying us no mind. "It's hard to explain," he says, rubbing the rough tousle of black hair atop his head, as if trying to work out a riddle. "It's like . . ."

I take a deep breath and let it out. I will myself to be patient. Basil is a sensitive kid, and he needs me more than most; needs to feel he's protected, that he's *cared* for. I take a knee, put a hand on his thin shoulder, and look him in the eye. "Like what? What is it, Basil?"

He leans in close, his mouth only inches from my ear, and whispers.

"It's like everyone is taking sides."

For the second time in as many minutes, my blood turns icy in my veins. Something in his words strikes me as truth, but I don't understand why, or how, that could be. I don't know what's happening, but I would be lying if I didn't believe that *something* is off about the way everyone has been acting the last couple days.

Since the doors blew open and the cross fell.

Since the men came.

But then I think of Grace, and of Andrew waiting for me at the wagon, and of the letter, ink-scratched with my handwriting, tucked inside *The Wonderful Wizard of Oz*, the book I've been harboring beneath my mattress.

Basil leans back, his face still close, eyes searching mine. But I don't know what to tell him, what it all means. If anything at all. I try to smile, give his shoulder a reassuring squeeze.

I must leave!

"Sides for what, Basil? What are you saying?"

Basil shrugs in a way that seems indifferent to the world, to himself, to me.

It's the saddest thing I've ever seen.

"I dunno," he says with a sigh. "No one's asked me."

"Asked you what?"

He shakes his head. "I don't think I'm included."

I remove my hand from his shoulder, try to keep the hurry out of my voice. "Basil, I'm sure . . . whatever you think is happening, it's nothing to worry about, okay? You're just upsetting yourself. We've had a rough couple days, and you should probably lie down, get some rest. Whatever you're thinking, or whatever you think is going on . . . it's all in your head."

Basil nods, but still doesn't make to move. He sniffles, then runs a finger absently along the steel bar at the foot of my bed-frame. "A lot of them are waiting, I think."

I stand, knowing my time is up. I know I shouldn't be impatient, but I am, and I can't help myself. My words to him are curt, almost cruel. "Waiting for what? Enough mystery. Just tell me so I can be off."

Basil looks up, his large brown eyes still locked on mine. He has a rare look of annoyance on his face, as if I'm too thickheaded to understand what he's saying.

"To see which side you take, of course."

I hold Basil's eyes another moment, not knowing how to respond. He's shaken me, and part of me is angry at him for it. Finally, I simply shake my head and ruffle his hair. "Get some sleep, Basil."

I blow by him, all of my focus now on getting outside to meet up with Andrew.

I hardly hear Basil's quiet reply as I pass.

"Sure, Peter," he says to my back. "I'll see ya."

19

By the time I arrive outside the wagon is fully loaded, wall-to-wall with empty crates, barrels, and heavy sacks that will soon be filled with food and stores for the priests, the children, and even the animals. Everything our own meager crops don't provide or, at least, provide in abundance.

Andrew notes my lack of hat and jacket, raises an eyebrow, but says nothing. At the sight of the book bag slung over my shoulder, he sighs dramatically but, thankfully, does not lecture. I climb up onto the front and sit next to him as he plucks up the reins. The horses stamp impatiently. Snow floats on the air all around us—fat, lazy flakes that foretell a heavy fall.

We must hurry.

"You all right?" Andrew asks.

I glance at him, confused.

"You look worried."

I shake my head. "Nothing. It's nothing."

"Okay, then."

He flicks the reins. As we jolt forward, I unconsciously lick my fingers and press my hair down across my scalp, hoping the wind doesn't make a complete mess of it. I curse myself for being too cowardly to grab a hat and, as the wind picks up, a jacket.

Andrew is smiling.

"What?"

"Don't worry, Peter. You look fine. I'm sure Grace will think so, as well."

I shrug, frowning. "I'm only as God made me, Father."

To my surprise, Andrew bursts out laughing. "That He did," he says, challenging the frigid wind with the warmth of his amusement. After we make the bend—despite being uncertain that it's not at my own expense—I can no longer help myself.

I begin laughing as well.

David watches from the dormitory window as the wagon pulls out of sight. He doesn't begrudge Peter his friendship with Father Andrew, and the last thing he'd want is to spend any of his free time hanging around a priest, even someone as kind as Andrew.

Still, he'd have liked a trip to the farm. Maybe he'd mention it to Peter, see if he could go with them next time. Just once. Anything to break up the monotony of his pathetic, entrapped life.

David knows about Grace, of course. They *all* know. Even though Peter thinks he's been clever about hiding the books, the letters. Hell, he and half the boys have read the things when Peter wasn't around to catch them. They were boring as sin.

He's about to leave the window, find someone to play cards with, when his eye catches movement from directly below. He leans in for a clearer view and sees Basil walking toward the privy. He looks tiny and thin from this high angle, a small figurine surrounded by open land: the vast, pewter sky hanging above like a weight about to drop, the air around his shadowed form alive with whirling snowfall. David watches as, for only a moment, Basil stops. He looks left and right, then turns his face to the sky. He holds out a pale hand, as if to catch a snowflake. David feels a sudden, powerful wave of protectiveness for the boy, and glances around the rest of the yard to make sure no other kids are outside who might make trouble. When he first arrived, Basil was a magnet for bullies, but it has gotten better since David befriended him. The others now aware that if they mess with Basil, he'll set them straight right quick.

But the yard is empty, and after another dozen paces, Basil disappears into the outhouse.

For a few moments, perhaps inspired by seeing that small hand catching snowflakes, David watches the snow drift past the window, lets himself daydream; he stares blankly at the hazy, gray ridge of the horizon. He imagines a life beyond that coarsely drawn line separating brown earth and bone-white sky. Imagines a future. He tries to picture himself as an adult— married, perhaps, with kids of his own. A *real* family. He'd be working on a farm somewhere, or in a factory, or at a market. Content. Maybe even happy.

Stricken by a sudden melancholy, David leaves the window, shoves away the whispering thoughts of an illusory, uncertain future. He finds his cot, lays on his back, and studies the blank ceiling, lets emptiness fill his mind.

Eventually, he closes his eyes.

Outside the thin window, the wind whistles carelessly as two shadows cross the open land, their minds filled with death.

20

Basil *hates* the privy. He hates it in summer, when it's hot and the air is thick and foul and filled with flies. He hates it in winter— like now—when it's bitter cold on his legs and bottom, the weak walls buffeted by cold winds startling him at the most inconvenient of moments. Slick icy fingers slip through the cracks, climb up from the ditch dug beneath, and it's all he can do to hurry as best he's able to get it over with. One time he got so scared (it was dark, the wind was howling something awful, causing the boards of the structure to shake and rattle as if being rammed by wild beasts) that he pulled up too fast and shat into his pants. He'd stunk so bad Peter had made him take a bath while he scrubbed the stained trousers with soap and water. He's never lived that one down, even though it was almost two whole years ago.

All the boys tease him anyway, so what did it matter.

Lately, though, it hasn't been too bad. He's made a few friends this past year. It helps not being the newest arrival anymore, and he is a bit older. Plus, the oldest boys stand by him, keep things from getting out of hand from some of the others. Because of that, he loves Peter and David like big brothers. Peter is almost like a *father*. It feels strange to think that, but it's true. Besides, Peter would be a priest one day, and then he would be a Father.

Basil giggles at his own internal play on words, finishes his business, and rises off the wooden plank and its smooth, shit-stained opening, a dark portal to the trench below. Humming a tuneless song, he grabs a fresh cob from the bucket, wipes, and tosses it through the plank hole. He ties his trousers and stamps his feet—one, two—to get the blood going. He's glad to be done with the chore, feels lucky to have been left alone this time. There are two other seats on the bench, but he hates to share. Plus, it's disgusting, especially if he happens to get caught going the same time as Finnegan, who farts a lot, or Jonah, who likes to make fun of him while he tries to do his business. He makes vulgar jokes and laughs about his *size*.

He hates Jonah. And he hates being teased.

And these last couple days, things have gotten even worse.

It's almost as if it's no longer *teasing*. As if it's meaner than that. Dangerous, even.

The previous night, when most of the kids were asleep, a few boys got together at the end of the room and huddled there, talking quietly. They sat only a few feet from his bed, and even though he heard their whispers, he pretended to be asleep.

They discussed horrible things.

Unholy things.

Eventually, they must have realized he was faking, because Samuel started talking more loudly, as if wanting Basil to hear every word.

"When we're done with the others, I say we get little Basil next. I'd like to kill that little shit. Strangle him to death."

The others laughed, and Basil was terrified, but kept his eyes shut *hard*. They couldn't know he was awake, not for certain. They were just hoping to scare him, make him open his eyes so they could get him—attack him in the dark.

Another voice had followed Samuel's, and Basil wasn't sure whose it was. He thought maybe it was Simon, but he hoped not. Simon had always been nice to him, and he was good friends with Peter. He prayed it wasn't him.

"I'd like to cut him open," the voice said. "Cut him open and play with his guts."

There was a murmur of agreement at this, but Basil said nothing. He forced himself to focus on breathing steady, on keeping his eyes closed.

After that, they stopped, maybe believing him, maybe not caring anymore. They continued talking deep into the night, but their whispers grew quiet again, so he couldn't hear what they were saying. At some point, he drifted off for real.

When he woke the next morning, with the sun shining and all the boys acting normal, he wondered if perhaps he'd dreamed it all. But he doubted it.

After he spoke with Peter—well, *tried* to speak to Peter, before he left for Hill farm—he noticed a few of the boys watching him. He ignored them, like he always did nowadays. He was tired of being picked on. Tired of being scared. And if they wanted to tease him, or attack him, he'd be ready. He'd give them as good as he got.

As Basil exits, the outhouse door is yanked hard by the wind, as if a giant hand has jerked it out of his grip. The icy wind has picked up something fierce. It whips against his face again and again, and it feels as though he's being slapped. He's pushed off balance, knocked back a step before he finally pushes outside the small building. He starts to close the door but the wind rips it from his hand again, this time slamming it so hard against the outhouse wall that it makes him jump.

"Jesus, Mary and Joseph . . ." he mutters, his heart thumping hard in his chest. He's anxious to be back inside, maybe find a deck of cards and play Patience. Perhaps Timothy would play a game with him; Timothy is always pretty nice. Potentially a friend even.

Basil stops at the pump, cranks it until icy water flows over his hands. He soaps them on what's left of the bar sitting in the mud, then rinses as best he can before drying them off on the cold, filthy rag hanging from the pump's neck.

His ears and cheeks are prickling from the frigid air, and he shivers beneath his thin clothes.

Damn, it's cold.

Stuffing hands in pockets, he pushes on beneath the dismal sky, through the chill wind. Despite it being the early afternoon, it's almost dark. Or, at least dim. A large, silver-tinted sun hides behind a slate of piled clouds. The surrounding trees are all leafless, their branches naked and twisted, as if screaming prayers to God. Growing uncomfortable (maybe even frightened), he strives forward, distracting himself with planning the rest of his day. He debates whether he should go to the dining hall before heading up to the dorm, maybe convince one of the kitchen staff to fix him a cup of tea . . .

"Basil!"

With a gasp, Basil spins around. Darting snowflakes blur past his vision.

Someone is standing outside the toolshed. They raise their hand and wave at him.

"Simon? That you?"

Simon, bundled in a coat and hat, nods and smiles.

Basil hears a random *thump thump thump* sound, and he realizes it's the shed door, off its clasp, beating against the frame as the wind tugs at it.

"What d'you want?" he yells, not wanting to move any closer, something deep inside him telling him to stay right where he is.

Thump . . . thump thump . . . thump thump thump . . .

Simon turns around to study the beating door a moment, then turns back toward Basil. He motions at him. "Come here, dummy, I want to show you something."

Basil doesn't move, but he also doesn't run. The orphanage doors are close, less than twenty steps, give or take. But despite himself, he's curious. Were it anyone but Simon, he would have told them to toss off and then run like hell for the building.

But Simon has never been cruel to him, never even teased him. Not once.

"What is it?"

Simon's smile broadens. "It's a garter snake! At least three feet long. We've trapped it in a corner of the shed. Come take a look at . . ."

"Who's *we?*" Basil interrupts. He takes a couple steps toward the shed, without even realizing he's done it. He loves snakes, something everyone knows about him. Mainly because it's weird, seeing as how he is such a scaredy-cat about so many other things (the dark, Father Poole, loud noises, the wind, Father White, being alone . . .) and yet simply adores snakes. Even the snake in the Garden of Eden—Satan in disguise—is Basil's favorite character in the Bible. Not that he'd tell the priests that . . .

"It's just me and Terrence. Come on, you like Terrence, right? He's trapped the thing, and I came out to find a sack or something to put it in and saw you there. Figured you could help us. So come on! You've got to see it before it gets away."

Basil continues walking slowly toward Simon as he speaks, his interest in seeing the snake outweighing his innate radar for danger. And besides, so what if he's being fooled? He's been fooled lots of time. But if they *aren't* fooling, then there really might be a three-foot-long garter snake in there. And boy, he'd love to see it. Maybe even keep it, like a pet.

"What's it look like?"

Simon's eyes brighten, and he puts a hand on the door. "He's black, with a white stripe going all the way down his side. He's quite something. Come on."

Basil's only a few feet away. He tries to see through the thin opening, where the door thumps against the rotted frame.

Without another word, Simon opens the door and steps inside. Into the dark.

Basil stands still for a moment, debating; staring at the door as if all of life's answers are carved into its stripped, faded wood. A sudden, strong gust of wind blows through his thin clothes. He shivers.

Thump thump . . . thump . . . thump . . .

He takes two more steps, puts a hand on the door. It stops beating against the shed, its broken pattern temporarily halted.

"No tricks," he says, not knowing if they can hear him.

He hears someone giggle, and is about to let go of the door, to turn away and run, when Simon's voice comes once more, now from inside. "Come on, Basil. It's really neat. Maybe we'll let you name it. Would you like to name it?"

Basil pulls open the door. The interior is pitch dark. He can't see Simon, or Terrence, and certainly not any snake.

"Where are you?"

"Get inside!" a voice says urgently. Terrence? "You want it to escape? Close the door!"

The urgency of the voice prompts Basil into action. He steps inside quickly. The wind slams the door shut behind him. He reaches out one arm toward the dark, then steps cautiously forward, moving deeper into the large shed. It's so dark he can hardly see his hand in front of him, and he's afraid of running into something sharp.

"I don't see you!" Basil nearly yells, and—as if he's only now realizing what he's done, what kind of *situation* he's put himself into, as if waking up to find you've been sleepwalking—turns to leave.

Idiot!

Once outside, he's going to run hard and fast as he can, back to the orphanage and up to the dorm. To the safety of his warm bed. He'll wait there until Peter comes back, and then he'll *make* him listen. Make him understand what's going on. What he can't see for himself.

"I'm leaving!" Basil yells into the dark, surprised to feel tears running down his face.

"Basil! Wait!"

Basil turns back, flustered and scared and angry. "What!"

A warm hand closes over his and pulls him hard into a world of living shadows and shuffling feet. The air is heavy with the weight of others.

Now more hands are on him, gripping him, tugging him, shoving him down.

He grunts and struggles. All around him is hard breathing

and laughter. He's about to scream when something coarse wraps around his neck—and now he can't scream.

He can't even breathe.

"Stop . . ." he croaks.

Oh please stop it hurts!

There's a heavy, painful pressure on his arms, as if someone is driving their knees into his wrists. He can't move. His throat is on fire.

He feels his clothes being ripped from his body. The air clings to him like ice.

Something sharp pierces his skin . . .

He wants to beg. Wants to tell them he's sorry, to ask them not to tease him any further, to please *stop*, to stop and leave him alone.

I won't tell. I promise I won't tell. Just please stop now please please . . .

But he can't speak, so he can't beg.

And he can't cry out.

And they don't stop.

21

Johnson sits at his table, of which he is the lone member. Away from the raised table of the priests. Away from the children. Every once in a blue moon he'll be joined for a meal by Carl, the head cook who lives in a cabin to the west. He'll talk Johnson's ear off about hunting, about how to properly cut and smoke a wide range of animals, none of which Johnson could give two shits about. But, for the most part, he sits alone. Tucked into the corner like a dog. But watchful, always watchful. Ready to heed his master's call.

Even now he watches as that doddering old fool, Father White, handles inspection. Ridiculous. White couldn't see dirt under fingernails if you gave him a magnifying glass. The old man is nearly blind in one eye and can't see the side of a barn from ten paces with the other.

Johnson scoffs. What does he care? Let the boys eat with filthy palms. Get disease. They could use a good culling, anyway. There are too damn many of them. Too many mouths to feed. A few years ago, they were down to twenty boys. It was glorious. Lots of room, plenty of food. But now, with this overcrowded, slack-mouthed lot of pissants? There is never enough. Not enough to eat. Not enough discipline. Not enough priests to school and care for them all.

And now, to make things even worse, with a hard winter coming down on their heads, they'll be lucky if . . .

"Father Poole?" White's shaky voice carries from the middle of the dining hall, where he stands, agitatedly working his hands together. "It seems we have a boy missing."

Johnson rises to his feet. His eyes fall on a gap between

children next to the old, feeble priest. White simply stands there, hunched and uncomfortable, offering a watered-down smile. As if a tardy boy is some sort of a joke.

Already doing his own count of heads, Johnson begins turning over possibilities. The boy isn't asleep; the others would have roused him. He could be hurt somewhere—always a chance—but an unlikely one. Again, someone would have noticed, or seen him.

A runaway?

Johnson almost salivates at the idea. In his mind he's already saddling up one of the horses. There is only one direction they'd run, and that's west, toward town. Any other direction in this weather is a death sentence. He looks over at Poole, waiting on the order.

Before Poole can respond, White's smile becomes a frown. He begins muttering nervously. "Oh, wait, wait . . . hold on a moment . . ." Father White glances around the room, mouth moving in silent calculations. The boys all stare back at him, innocent and curious. When he speaks once more, his quivering voice is a whining wind, whistling through the cracks. "I fear my count is actually *two* short."

Johnson's nerves twitch, his mind racing.

Two boys?

Together then! Yes, that makes sense. But who? Johnson resumes his scanning of heads and faces. But then he remembers: Peter is with Andrew, of course. He feels his energy sour, his apprehension lose steam like a slowing train. That stupid fool must not have been told that Peter had left. As for the other, the old priest probably miscounted . . .

"Who?" Poole is standing, his voice iron.

"Benjamin is one . . ." White looks around, confusion wilting his face. A boy whispers at White, but Johnson can't see who. The priest nods, grateful. "Ah, yes. And Basil."

Ben and Basil? Running away together? Not completely unlikely.

They are both part of the little clique who follows Peter around like orphan disciples.

It's now Poole who scans the room, his face turning a dark shade of red. "Does anyone have information about Ben or Basil? I demand to know or there will be punishment!"

None of the boys answer. Most look into their laps. Some keep their eyes raised, faces masked with feigned innocence.

"Father?" Johnson says, fingers tightening into eager fists.

Poole turns to him from the raised table.

He nods.

Unleashes his dog.

Good, Johnson thinks, jaws clenched, already striding past the scared faces of the children. *Wait until I catch up with them.*

I'll bite those little brats.

Knowing it's useless, but wanting to be thorough, Johnson begins by checking the dormitory. If the kids aren't there, he'll check the other rooms, the chapel, then the barn. He doesn't expect to find them in the dorm, but he's rushing through options in his mind so he can quickly cross them each off the list. Then he'll return to Poole for permission to pursue on horseback.

They won't make it a mile, he thinks, but hurries nonetheless. No sense in giving them too much of a head start. Not in this weather.

The dorm, as he expected, is empty. He gets on his knees and looks beneath the beds, walks all the way to the far end, just to be sure no one is lying on the ground or hiding behind a blanket.

Nothing.

He grunts and begins to head out, ticking the next places from the list in his head: cloakroom, classroom, washroom, chap . . .

THUMP.

Johnson freezes.

He turns toward the windows, takes a step in that direction.

THUMP.

THUMP THUMP.

Johnson spins. It's coming from behind him? Impossible.

THUMP!

Above!

He looks up toward the low ceiling. Then he sees it: the hatch leading to the attic.

The pounding comes from the hatch door.

Someone's in the attic.

"Hello!" he yells, moving to stand directly below it. He spots a knotted rope hanging from a hole drilled in the hatch. He can easily reach it, but . . . not yet.

"Hello!" he yells again.

"Brother Johnson?" A muffled voice. A boy's voice. By the sound of it, a very panicked boy. "Help me!"

Johnson grunts and frowns. Damn kids and their damned hijinks. He reaches up, grabs the coarse knot of the rope, and pulls.

The hatch swings down smoothly, and a ladder unfolds, dropping to the floor and nearly catching him on the head as it does. He curses under his breath.

He looks up at the open square of darkness and sees a boy with no face staring back. Johnson flinches at the sight, momentarily terrified, before realizing it's nothing but a damned feed sack stretched over his face. "Jesus," he murmurs, his fear turning quickly to ire.

"Take that thing off your head!"

"They said not to! They said . . ."

"Do it! Or I'll rip it off you."

The boy grips the corners atop his head, pulls the sack free. Beneath, his face is crumpled and red. Slick with snot, sweat, and tears. He starts weeping once more, and Johnson feels the anger inside him abate, albeit slightly. "What the hell are you doing, Benjamin?"

Ben shakes his head, wipes his face with a sleeve. "Can I come down?"

"What? Yes goddammit, and make it quick! What's all this about?"

Ben reaches the bottom of the ladder, his words coming in spurts between hiccups and sobs. Johnson is taken aback by the child's despair and forces himself to calm.

Damn boy is scared half out of his wits.

Johnson takes a breath, does his best to speak gently. "Okay, lad. Enough of that. Tell me what happened."

Ben nods, takes a deep breath. "I was here alone. Or thought I was . . . everyone else was washing up, getting ready for lunch. I was getting something from my nightstand, when someone put a hood over my face. I couldn't see, and I was scared. Then . . ."

Johnson grips Ben by the arms and leads him to sit on a nearby cot. *A hood? What madness is this? Is the boy lying? No, no . . . he can't be. Look at the poor bastard.*

"Then?"

"Then I felt something sharp jab my back. Like a knife. They told me not to move, not to speak, or . . . or they'd stab me."

"My God," Johnson says, knowing this is beyond a prank. The consequences will be dire.

"I heard the ladder drop, and they pushed me over to it, made me climb. Then, I don't know, something happened. There were voices in the hall, and they told me not to move, or take off the sack, or they'd come back and finish me. Then the hatch closed . . . and I was trapped. I was so scared, Johnson!"

Ben starts crying again, and Johnson puts a hand on his shoulder. "All right, all right. Enough of that. Just a couple boys pulling a trick. Nothing to sob like a baby about."

Ben nods, tries to hold it back. "It didn't seem like a trick, though. I mean . . . they sounded . . . I don't know. They sounded *serious.* They weren't laughing or anything."

Johnson frowns. This isn't good. No, this isn't good at all.

And one boy still missing.

What the hell is going on?

"All right. Well, let's get you cleaned up and down to the dining hall."

"Poole's gonna be furious!"

"Don't worry, lad. I'll talk to him. You're the victim here, that's my position. He'll listen to me."

For the first time, Ben looks mildly relieved. "Thank you, Brother Johnson."

"And for the record," Johnson says, standing up. "That hatch will come down if you push on the ladder. Just need to put some weight into it."

Ben nods, wipes away the last of the tears. "I don't ever want to go up there again. It's dark, and I felt things crawling on me. I hate it up there."

Johnson thinks of the hole for a moment, wonders how Ben would fare if forced into that situation. Not well. Not well at all.

Ah, he's a good boy, not as bad as the others.

Best not think of it.

22

Johnson waits while Ben cleans himself in the washroom. He's antsy to get going but wants to make sure the boy gets to the dining hall with no further problems. He's already second-guessing where to look for Basil. The fact that he's not with Ben is . . . troubling. The scenarios he'd previously considered have shrunken.

He can't see Basil running away. Not by himself. Boy's too small. Too weak. Maybe he figured he could make it to the Hill farm? Catch up with Peter? Even so, that's a three-hour walk for a small child, in the cold. No. Chances are he's holed up somewhere, like Ben. Perhaps outside; in the barn, or locked in the privy.

Johnson grits his teeth. Nothing like this has ever happened at St. Vincent's. A boy—or, as Ben tells it, *boys*—threatening another with a knife? Unthinkable.

He almost feels sorry for what Poole will do to the culprit, or culprits, when found out.

He wonders if they'll survive.

"Ready, Brother Johnson."

Johnson is tugged from his thoughts and looks down at Ben, whose face is scrubbed and blessedly snot-free. "Let's go, then."

Together, they walk down the length of the hall and down the stairs.

They are crossing the foyer toward the dining hall when Johnson notices one of the chapel doors is open. Wide open. Wedged at the bottom with what looks like a shoe.

He stops, glances down at Ben, who has stopped alongside him, looking up at him with apparent confusion. "Stay here," he says. "Wait for me. I don't want Poole seeing you without me next to you, understand?"

"Where are you going?" Ben says, but then he also notices the chapel's open door, his eyes curious.

"Just stay here," Johnson repeats, and walks toward the chapel.

He approaches the open door cautiously.

Go on, you nit. What are you worried about? That some little brat will jump from the shadows and scream BOO!

If Johnson is honest with himself—beneath the shaggy black beard, the wicked scar, the six-plus feet of height and broad bulky frame—he truly is a coward at heart. Most lifelong criminals are. Vicious, yes. Like dogs. But when confronted they balk, they cower, they flee. Also, like dogs. Yes, he'd done horrible things. Terrible things. But those are things done from the shadows. In darkened alleys. To turned backs. He never walks *toward* danger, not if he can help it.

It's a damned chapel, Teddy, not a warehouse on the docks. What are you scared of?

As the chapel interior comes into view through the open door, he leans cautiously to look inside. The large room is dim. All the candles are extinguished. But gray daylight seeps through the single stained-glass window, offering a rusty duotone image of the room's innards. He pushes in, closer, and sees the backs of the benches, the matching curtains that bookend the raised stage from which Poole gives his sermons, upon which the deacons—Father Francis and Father White—sit during ceremonies.

Licking his lips, he steps fully into the doorway, the entire room now visible . . .

And stops, frozen. Eyes transfixed. His mind swirls like black smoke, trying to make sense of what he's seeing.

My God, what in hell is that?

Numbly, he stares at the pulpit, and then the altar nestled behind it, which is nothing more than a broad, mahogany table crudely etched with Christian symbols. On either side of the altar stand two massive, unlit candelabras. A large, bare wooden cross—nearly six feet in height—hangs against worn brick above and behind it.

He takes a step closer, squinting. It's deathly quiet. The air is thick, muffling his senses.

As he studies the cross, his face twists in disgust. In naked horror.

Soft footsteps approach from behind, but he can't turn, he can't speak, he can't look away. What he's seeing is impossible. It's a nightmare.

"Brother Joh . . ."

He comes alert, his wits finally breaking free from the trap of shock. He spins around, eyes frantic and wide. "No, boy! Don't look!"

But Johnson is too late.

Regardless, Ben pays him no attention. His eyes are fixed on the frail, naked body hung from the cross; the stretched, bared arms sliced open across each wrist; the dripping blood pooling atop the altar.

And then Ben screams.

23

By the time we reach the farm I'm shivering. The road, along with the surrounding hills, is now coated a thick white with fallen snow. It's beautiful and expansive. The sky is the color of stone, flat and hard in appearance, but brittle, as if it would crack like an eggshell—revealing black seams of the universe beyond—if struck hard enough. The surrounding horizon rolls gently, disrupted by waves of white knolls. The barren, uneven land gives the world an ethereal, almost heavenly, feel.

If I wasn't so cold I'd almost be enjoying it.

The Hill farm, as always, is a welcome sight. The house is sturdy and well-kept, sided with brown panels and stamped with navy shutters. A comforting curl of smoke drifts from a red-brick chimney. I imagine the warmth of being inside, and the imagined contrast to the cold wagon makes me shiver again.

The massive red barn is settled further back, and the doors are closed to keep the snow out and the animals warm. Past the barn are the fields, the snow-dusted acres of crops.

John Hill steps out the front door, likely having seen our approach. He's lightly bundled in a flannel shirt and knit cap. There's a pipe in his mouth, per usual, curling smoke to match the chimney's. It makes me think that he and his home have melded certain characteristics, like an old married couple.

I wait for Grace to appear, looking from the barn to the house, not certain from where she'll emerge. Moments later, however, she hurries through the same door as her father. A deep green dress flowers from beneath a toughened, wool-lined canvas jacket. Like her father, she also wears a knit cap, a green that matches her skirts, and her eyes.

Andrew waves an arm as we approach, and John lifts a hand in return. I can see Grace's face in more detail now, and the bright smile she wears gives me all the warmth I'll ever need. A long blond curl has fallen loose from her hat and rests aside her face. I wave as well, unable to hold back my eagerness.

We settle the wagon near the barn as John and Grace walk over to greet us. John speaks to Grace in the fashion of instruction, likely giving her a list of things to start acquiring. Andrew and I disembark from the wagon, and I'm thankful for my boots; the snow is already a few inches deep, and my feet would have been quickly frozen if I'd worn only my brogues.

Grace is smiling broadly but the first words from her mouth are a rebuke. "Peter Barlow, where are your coat and hat? Can you not see winter all around you?"

I start to respond, then close my mouth. Unsure of a reasonable excuse.

"Go fetch the boy one of my coats. And a cap, please," John says to Grace, and I nod to him in appreciation as she runs off. John puffs his pipe, turns his attention to Andrew. "You fellas going to need a good bit of supply, Father. This storm is going to block you in for two, maybe three weeks."

"Yes, that's our thinking as well. It's been a decent season of harvest for us, and the animals have remained healthy, thank goodness. But we'll take our usual supplies . . . plus, oh, fifty percent more, I'd think."

"I figured." John points his pipe to the barn. "I've got most of your goods set aside in there, with a few things more to gather. I waited on the eggs. No good to you frozen."

Grace returns with a pea coat draped over an arm and a black cap clutched in one hand. "Here, Peter. Papa's coat will hang on you a bit," she says with a critical eye, "but at least you'll be warm."

I put on the coat and instantly feel better. It does indeed hang on me, almost to my knees, and my thin frame swims in the coarse fabric, but I'm warm as a bug in July, and that's what matters. I pull on the cap and Grace flashes another smile that makes blood rush to my face.

"Papa, Peter and I will gather the eggs, if you'd like."

"In a moment," John says absently, his sharp eyes—gray and intelligent beneath heavy brows—never leaving Andrew. "Heard you, uh, had some trouble at the orphanage the other night."

I startle at the words, glance toward Andrew to see his response. Despite my prodding, he wouldn't tell me all of what he knows, but seemed deeply bothered by it. I tried to bring it up again on the ride over, but he would say nothing he hadn't previously said, which amounted to: the man was injured, and then he passed. I didn't want to press him on the other details, such as the dead deputy and the strange laughter. The gunshot. The screams.

I'm hoping that, since there's an adult inquiring, he may reveal more.

"Trouble?" he says, and I almost laugh at the feigned innocence on his face. Andrew is many things, most of them good, but a liar he is not.

"Well, now, I don't mean to pry." John scuffs his boot into the snow, revealing frosted strands of grass and packed dirt beneath. I feel Grace's fingers clutch my elbow, as if she too had heard rumors, and is anxious to hear Andrew's reply. "Anyway," John continues, "Sheriff Baker came through here the other morning. Had a dead deputy in his wagon. They stopped for some food to take with them, stayed long enough for a cup of hot coffee, and we got to chatting. Heard some strange things."

"Strange?" Andrew says, looking considerably more uncomfortable.

"What they did to that little girl, for one."

"Papa," Grace says, her voice small but filled with warning.

John, to his credit, looks properly abashed.

"Just rumors, I suppose," John finishes lamely.

"Yes, well," Andrew says, his face now having lost its mask of innocence, replaced with a hardening of his features I've seen many times. Mostly when I'm asking for something he knows I shouldn't be. "It's in man's nature to seek knowledge."

Hill seems to think a moment, then nods. "And Proverbs says a man who whispers separates close friends. So how about I shut my trap and get you stocked up?"

Andrew chuckles, but his features do not soften. "Fair enough."

"Good, good. Let's have the kids work a bit while you and I have a chat in the house, settle on numbers. I have some brandy that will put some color in those pale cheeks."

Andrew turns to me before heading off. "Don't load anything into the wagon just yet. Gather together what you can. We'll want a count before we put everything in crates."

"Yes, Father," I say. I feel the weight of my leather satchel beneath the coat and against my hip, and I'm anxious to give Grace back her book, along with the letter tucked inside.

He gives me one last glance, one that is more worry than warning, but Grace is already taking my cold hand in her astonishingly warm one, pulling me toward the barn. "I'll keep a close eye on him, Father Francis, don't worry."

Andrew scoffs once as I'm led away, as if pulled by a rope.

At the barn, Grace pulls open one of the large doors, which glides easily outward, shoveling snow away before it. She slips into the musty darkness, and I follow.

The barn interior is dim, lit only by the light coming through the bright seams of the walls and ceiling. It's cold inside, but there's no motion to the air so it's less bitter. Grace pulls the door closed behind me, pulls a lantern off a peg and a tin of matches from a pocket.

"I think one light will be enough, don't you?" she says, moving deeper into the barn.

I can smell the animals, hear the rustling cluck of the chickens, the whinny of horses. The cows, silent and stagnant, have been brought in for milking. Most of the other horses, goats, and cows remain in the pasture. A pigpen resides behind the structure, and I can hear their honking snorts. The entire barn is ripe with the smells of manure, hay, and beast.

"Where are the pups?" I ask, my nickname for the Hills' two massive dogs.

"Sleeping inside the house," she says. "They don't like the cold, I guess." We reach the main hen coop, which extends the length of the barn's interior and is protected with heavy chicken wire to keep out predators. There are more than two hundred hens here and gathering the eggs will be no small task. By the end, my hand will be well-pecked, I know, but I love doing it nonetheless. We have only twenty chickens at St. Vincent's, and none of them broilers; the meager egg supply barely enough for the many who need to eat, so the Hill eggs are always an essential item. Aside from the egg-layers, the farm boasts another fifty or so chickens that peck around in a separate pen, hand-picked to be sold for meat.

"Grace," I say, bursting to speak with her before we get deep into the work. "I brought your book back. I read it three times through. It was wonderful, and even a bit frightening at times."

She gives me a sidelong glance that brings fresh heat to my cheeks. "Is that all?"

"No, of course not," I say, both nervous and excited. "I wrote you something, as well."

She stops walking and turns. Steps toward me. "A nice long letter, I hope."

I swallow. She's very close. The lantern light flickers warmly on her soft features. My thoughts jumble like tossed jacks. "I hear . . ." I turn my head, cough into my hand, which I notice is trembling. "I hear that the winter will be harsh."

Grace tilts her head, her lips curling into a smile. Her green eyes glitter like jewels. "I'm sure you'll manage."

Before I can respond, Grace has hooked the lantern and slid her arms beneath my coat and around my waist. Her face looks up at mine steadily, studying. My whole world is green eyes and golden hair.

I'm too frozen to react, but she does fine for both of us, and gently pushes her warm, moist lips against mine. I close my eyes and kiss her, knowing full well that I'm lost in love.

And that my days of craving priesthood are behind me.

24

They must have heard the scream.

It's the first thought Johnson has when he enters the dining hall. All the boys stare anxiously at the doors when he comes through. There's no chatter of thin voices, no clatter of flatware, only a sea of wide-eyed faces boring into him. An infested wave of curiosity.

Johnson takes long, brisk strides between the tables toward the dais, where Fathers White and Poole sit rapt, faces eager for information.

White's expression is one of mild confusion and worry; Poole's a boil of swelling anger.

Johnson tries to ignore the oddness of what his peripheral vision caught on a few faces as he walked through the boys. He could have sworn he saw a few of them *smiling*. Not friendly smiles, either. Cunning. Cats with sealed lips, their mouths filled with canaries.

Now face-to-face with Poole, close enough that he notices the crooked red veins in the man's eyes, he whispers: "Father, we have a problem."

Poole and Johnson stand in the middle of the chapel.

Johnson notices, with a repressed wave of revulsion, that the dripping has stopped.

All is complete silence, as if the two men stand inside a sealed tomb. Ben has been ordered back to the dormitory, instructed to stay there until further notice. Under *no* circumstance is he to interact with the other boys or tell anyone what he's seen.

White, meanwhile, was appointed the duty of making sure none of the other children left the dining hall. When Johnson first asked for Poole to come with him, he asked why, of course. Asked what happened. *Demanded* answers.

But Johnson refused to say anything other than: *Please come.*

The last thing he wanted was a reaction from Poole, or White, that would transform the boys' stirring breeze of peaking curiosity into a whirlwind.

Now, they stand before the hung body, a flesh-and-blood mockery of Christ's crucified form, the doors of the chapel sealed shut behind them. Nearly a minute has passed, and Poole has yet to say a word. Johnson is sweating, his nerves burning hot as red coals.

Finally, Poole breaks the dreadful, heavy silence.

"Take the boy down," Poole says, his tone stoic. "He is desecrating a house of God."

Johnson flinches at the priest's tone, his demeanor at such a horrific sight as this . . . this poor child. He sulks forward, warily eyeing the large pool of brilliant red shimmering in the dim sunlight atop the bleached wood of the altar. Thin tendrils of red hang like string between the altar's surface and the oak-planked hardwood of the floor. The boy's life flowing away.

Flown away, now. Flown, flown away . . . he thinks, feeling jittery. Feeling unmoored.

He grips one of the deacon chairs, moves it close to the body. Standing upon it, he can easily reach the top of the hung cross, the loop of coarse, frayed rope. The rope's other end is similarly looped, tight against the boy's purple, swollen neck.

Is this the same chair they used when they hanged him? When they hooked his body on a peg like a fucking ornament? Did they stand upon the altar while they cut his arms, opening the veins?

Johnson figures, based on his limited experience with such things, that Basil must have been alive when they cut him. There is too much blood for it to be otherwise. His mind conjures up images of them holding the rope tight to his neck ... somehow, someway, dragging him through the front doors and into the chapel, where they stripped him, hanged him, and butchered him.

Must have been at least ... three boys that done it. A lookout, for sure. At least two to strangle him, catch him unaware, force the rope around his throat. A scout to run ahead, checking there was no one to see them when they towed the body through ...

"Brother Johnson, if you please."

Johnson's thoughts snap like kindling at Poole's sharp command. Without further delay, he grips Basil around the waist with one arm, lifts the loop over the top of the cross with the other, and pulls the limp body to his chest. He steps carefully, gently, down from the chair.

"He's so light ..." Johnson says, feeling strangely outside of himself, as if he's watching the scene play out from afar. His shoe squelches into a pool of blood settled on the floor, and he winces in disgust. He puts his other arm under the boy's legs, lays him down on the clean side of the altar like a sacrifice.

"I'm going to go check on the others, make sure Father White has them well secured in the dining hall. Please take the body to my chamber." Poole shakes his head, sighs. "We'll need you to build a casket, it seems."

Poole turns to leave. Johnson looks at the body, the blood.

So much blood.

"Father?"

Poole turns, a questioning look on his face.

"I'm sorry, Father, but shouldn't you at least look at the boy?"

Poole's face is still as deep water. "I have looked, Brother Johnson. I've looked, and I've seen. Now take the body to my chamber. Use a blanket from the linens if you must, to cover him." He starts to turn, then adds: "Please make it an old linen."

Johnson's face gets hot. His mind clouded and riled as a thunderstorm.

It's not right, this isn't right!

"Father Poole," he says, surprised at the pleading in his voice. "At least give him last rites."

Poole's eyes flicker like sapphires, hard and cold and impenetrable. "Last rites? For someone who took his own life?"

"I'm sorry?" Johnson stammers, confusion and shock and anger conflicting within him like a storm. "Father, you think he did this to *himself*?"

"I do." Poole's stoic face remains unmoved. "And suicide is a mortal sin, Brother Johnson. Now . . ."

"He's just a child . . ."

"He's a sinner!" Poole screams, the serenity of his face coming apart like a shattered mask, revealing a boiling rage. "A blaspheming sinner who has desecrated my chapel!"

Johnson bows his head, the words hitting him like blows. Poole takes a moment to cool down, wipes his mouth, and turns his back to the scene. "Make sure no one sees you." With that, Poole strides quickly from the chapel, leaving Johnson alone with Basil's body.

He looks up at the cross, then down at the boy laid on the altar, thinking. Calculating probability. He searches the floor around the table, seeking the knife the boy must have used on his wrists . . . but finds nothing.

This is no suicide, you cold bastard.

"Who hung you up there, son?" Johnson says softly, studying the child's puffy face. He lifts the frail, empty body, pulls it to his chest, not minding the blood which stains his black cassock, nor the tear that drains down his cheek. "Who would do such a foul thing?"

Basil, his face slack, his limbs limp and lifeless, does not answer.

25

We drop over the crest and the farm disappears, swallowed by white horizon.

For two hours, we stay mostly silent. Both of us enjoying the fresh air, the winding road, the hills and valleys of our trek.

As we go on, I'm increasingly thankful that John and Grace insisted on me keeping the cap and old pea coat. John told me, with a final pat on the shoulder, that the coat served him well during the Civil War, when he wore it aboard the ironclad steamer USS *Philadelphia*. Grace gave me the history of her father over the course of previous visits, how the Navy had retired him after the war ended, along with nearly everyone else serving at the time. She told me, without meeting my eye, how they bought the farm and moved out of the city when her mother grew ill, how John hoped the clean air and country life would revive her.

When Grace was six, they buried her mother in a small plot behind their house.

So yes, it felt good to have the coat, even if I felt a stab of guilt at accepting it. I felt like I was wearing a small part of John Hill's history. A small part of his grief.

"Don't worry, you'll grow into it," John said, and knuckled my hair affectionately. Tears stung my eyes when he'd done that. It was a fatherly thing to do. A kind of affection I've craved my whole life, a type of love that was taken away from me by the blast of a gun and a flame-soaked cabin.

It also makes me wonder, somewhat anxiously, if John knows my intentions with his daughter. This is both a sobering and . . . *complicated* thought. I also wonder if Andrew has the same inkling. A look of sadness passed over his face in that moment of fatherly warmth with John. It was fleeting, but it was there, nonetheless. It was the look of a child whose toy is being taken away. Or, more fairly, a father realizing his son is preparing to leave. Perhaps to never return.

My bookbag lies heavy beneath the coat, now holding a brand new volume from Grace's library, along with a thick sheaf of handwritten pages. Our letters to each other have grown progressively longer over the years, become harder to hide amongst the pages. It's a wonder Andrew hasn't caught on to our secret correspondence . . .

And now a thought hits me.

I look across the rickety bench at him as he guides the horses, and for the first time in my life I realize something so large, so moving, that it swells inside my mind, then bursts into enlightenment. I think—no, *acknowledge*—a fact I think I've always known. A fact that I, perhaps, didn't want to admit to myself.

Andrew *does* think of me as a son.

In that light, secrets and loss take on a different hue, a more significant weight.

What will he do when I tell him I've decided to abandon the priesthood? What will he do when, one day—one day soon, I hope—I leave the orphanage forever?

These thoughts trouble me, and the letter in my bookbag no longer feels like a thing to be proud of, or thrilled by. It doesn't seem to me a wholesome thing, tucked away in its shroud of privacy, its secrecy. It feels shameful.

As if sensing my thoughts, Andrew gives me a sidelong stare. "What?"

I shake my head and study the passing landscape, keeping my thoughts to myself for the moment.

We say nothing as the wagon creaks onward beneath the weight of the supplies, now tarped over and tied down for the return trip. The sound of the horses' footfalls is padded by the cushion of new snow, their breath steaming billows in the frigid air.

I must get tangled in a daydream, because I only hear Andrew's question when he raises his voice to ask a second time. "The book, Peter?" he says. "Which book did she give you?"

I recall the forest-green cover, the shimmer of gold accents, Grace telling me that this one was somewhat new to her, having received it only a few years earlier. A birthday gift from her father, purchased for her during a trip to the city.

"*Huckleberry Finn*," I say. "By a man named Twain."

Andrew gives me a wary look. "Oh, that's wonderful. A book about a rebellious, precocious boy. Just what the doctor ordered."

He laughs and I chuckle along, the idea of reading about the adventures of a rebellious boy exciting me almost as much as the clandestine contents of Grace's letter.

Almost.

"To be honest, Peter, I've not read it. Only heard the usual condemnations."

"If you think it's not appropriate, Andrew, I won't read it. I swear." I mean this. I don't want to upset Andrew, and I don't wish to go so far against decorum as to seem ungrateful. Or worse, defiant.

But he waves a hand at me. "It's fine." He seems to think for a moment, and I wait for what comes next. He looks pained, a sickly smile on his wind-reddened face. "Truth be told, it's the letter inside the book I worry about."

I feel myself blush and look away. My cheeks are tingling, whether from the rush of blood to my cold face or the briskness of the icy wind I don't know. My mind untethers, and there comes a not wholly unpleasant feeling of floating.

In an effort to focus my thoughts and emotions, I fix my sight on a faraway tree, leafless and black against the pale canvas of snow and sky. At first, I consider ignoring his remark, but something in my heart tells me that now might be the right time to bring it all into the open. To bring Andrew into my secret. We are not far from St. Vincent's, so I decide to pursue the topic.

Or, at least, shed the guilt of keeping my correspondence, and feelings, of Grace from him.

"Are you angry?"

Andrew sighs. "No, of course not. Those are your private affairs and no business of mine."

I turn to him, surprised. "Really? I think Poole would feel different."

A small smile—a genuine smile—lifts Andrew's features. "I am not Father Poole," he says forcefully, but I can see he immediately regrets making such a bald statement. "For better or worse."

I don't respond. Nothing I can say in answer to that will make him feel less guilty. I look for the tree again, but it seems to have disappeared. All I see now is endless sky of unbroken gray, a floor of white.

"Peter, I bring you with me to the farm for your companionship, and so we can discuss, one-on-one, the matters of your training . . ."

I swallow what feels like a stone in my throat at the mention of my training, but stay silent. I'm interested in what he has to say on the matter of my visits to the farm. We've never discussed it, and it's the first time I've even wondered at his motivations.

"But I also bring you because of Grace. Don't misunderstand . . . I'm not pushing you two . . ."

He's stumbling and I can't help but smile at him. "Go on," I say, teasingly.

He looks at me, startled, then laughs. "Okay, thank you. What I'm trying to say is I *first* brought you because I thought it would be fun for you to see another child, someone outside the orphanage."

"A girl, you mean."

His brow furrows at that. "No, not exactly. But yes, after a few years, both John and I could see that you two were growing fond of each other, in a most natural and innocent way. It's a beautiful thing to witness, honestly. God's greatest gift to us is our ability to love others, and to see it happening before your eyes . . . it's like watching a garden grow."

I'm confused at his tone, his words. "But it's not allowed."

"For *priests*, Peter. But you're not a priest yet, are you? Besides, we can have friends who are women. It's not forbidden. But, look son, what I'm saying is . . . or trying to say . . . is that I know about your feelings for Grace, and you should not feel bad, or guilty, or in any way ashamed of those feelings."

I'm stunned at this message, feel myself reeling. I clutch the coat in tight fists, as if trying to hold onto an old world that seems to be turning over, twisting, unraveling. It's both heartbreaking and thrilling.

Before I can think of a response, Andrew continues. "Frederick Douglass once wrote, 'The soul that is within me no man can degrade.' Now, I'm shifting the context a bit. He wasn't referring to a life in Christ, but he *was* talking about the power of humanity, about rising above the oppression of those who had forced him into slavery. And he was talking, I believe, about being true to himself, to the man he was at his core." Andrew pauses a moment. When he speaks again, there's a weary sadness in his tone that hurts my heart. "I'd like to think his statement applies here, as well. What I'm trying to express, Peter, is that whatever you decide to do with your life, you must have faith that your soul will always remain your own. It cannot be degraded, not if you stay true to yourself."

I think about this for a moment, my mind flooding with ideas, with visions of the future, with strange ideas of my eternal soul. Of what it means to control my own destiny.

"Peter, the . . ."

Abruptly, Andrew stops talking, as if the very words catch in his throat. He turns his head away from me, studies the horizon. I can sense his tension, his inability to continue.

As if what he wants to say is physically impossible.

I almost don't want to hear it. It's as if I've waited my whole life to be let go of, but then, when the time comes, I'm stood on a ledge, and no one is there holding me back, and the world is calling from far below. All my hopes and dreams lie down there, hidden by a distant mist. But it's a long fall. A lonely, terrifying drop into the mystery of an unknowable future.

I pretend not to notice when Andrew wipes a tear from his eye. After a moment, he clears his throat and continues, his voice a bit bolder, more confident.

"The discovery of Christ is not found in a darkened room, Peter," he says solemnly. "It's found in the light. God is not found through escape from a distant place, but through the arrival of where you already are. Hiding you from Grace, hiding the world from you, will not help you decide your life's ultimate path. You must be fully aware of all aspects of each decision you make in this world. All sides. Only then can you be certain that the choice you make is the correct one."

"I understand, Father."

"Do you?" he says, sounding pleasantly surprised. Then he nods to himself, blows out a large breath. "Good."

"Thank you, Andrew."

His smile comes back, and he flicks the reins to speed up the horses. "Of course, Peter. Of course."

Familiar landmarks begin to emerge. I recognize an approaching swell of land that, past its crest, will dip us into the valley. Our valley. We are very close to home.

"Besides," he says, his tone light once more. "We are friends, correct? And I would not lose your trust over a few novels and a young woman's letters of . . . well, let's just call them letters of friendship."

I laugh at this. I'm oddly elated, embarrassed, and somehow more confused than I've ever been in my life.

"Just be careful, Peter," he says. "Guard your feelings like gold coins from those who would steal them, or pick them from your pocket."

"I'll be careful."

"Good, good. You know, I remember when I was your age, I . . ." Andrew's voice trails off, and I follow his eyes to look straight ahead. "Oh no . . ."

Andrew's eyes are focused on the orphanage, which has now come into full view.

"Oh Jesus, no . . ."

The first thing I see is that the front doors of St. Vincent's stand wide open.

The second is Brother Johnson walking from the shed, a rectangular pine box hefted upon one shoulder. Recent events aside, it's obvious to both of us what it is.

A coffin.

He carries it toward the orphanage.

Andrew yells at the horses and cracks the reins. The wagon speeds up, all but charging down a final descent of the narrow, snow-covered road.

Another sick man?

But I know in my heart it's the wrong answer. It makes no sense.

It can't be a man, because the coffin is so very small.

It's the size of a boy.

26

Things are getting strange.

David sits on his bunk, cross-legged, scanning the dormitory from one end to the other. The windows on the opposite wall are dimming into late afternoon, and all the kids have been cooped up now for hours. Ever since lunch.

Boys who went to the privy were closely watched from the orphanage doors by Father White, told to do their business and return straightaway or there'd be punishment. David makes a lot of fun of old man White, but the way his eyes blazed giving those orders, even he didn't have the temerity to push him on it.

Everyone else went straight to the dorm. Where they remain.

Everyone but Peter, that is.

And Basil.

"This is horrible," Finnegan moans, sounding every bit like the child he is. He and Jonathan sit on the next cot over, legs dangling over the edge, staring at David as if he's got some sort of answer to what this *new* thing is that's happening.

"It'll be dark soon," adds Jonathan, mimicking his best friend's whiny tone. "We won't get recreation time outside at this rate."

"We want to play in the snow," Finnegan adds, the two of them running their thoughts so close together David can't help but feel he's listening to the whine and moan of a single voice. A madly *annoying* voice, at that.

Flustered, he reaches into the top drawer of his dresser and pulls out his deck of cards. He almost smiles when he sees their eyes widen. He sighs, hands them the deck.

"You know any games?"

They both nod. Finnegan starts: "Sure, I know War."

Jonathan plucks the deck neatly from David's fingers, the well-worn cards secured neatly with a frayed piece of string.

"You lose even one card . . ."

They nod again. In unison.

David stands and leaves the twins to it, starts pacing the room, studying faces.

Most of the kids are lying down, reading pamphlets the priests give them or studying one of the boring books from the small library. He notices that the cadre of kids around Bartholomew hasn't grown, but the faces have changed. They whisper in the corner like conniving mice, figuring out how they're gonna skin the farmer's cat.

He stops in front of Ben's cot. So far, everyone who has approached Ben for information about what made him scream like a stuck goat has walked away disappointed. David, however, thinks it's time to get some answers.

Ben's been hiding under his blanket since the rest of them arrived, walking like prisoners from the dining hall to the dormitory. At first, kids seemed eager to try and coerce the shrouded form to speak, but after a while they lost interest. Ben isn't the most popular kid to begin with, and when Peter is absent, he tends to climb into a shell. Now he is doing it literally.

Regardless, David sits down on the next bed, currently empty. For a moment he tries to remember whose cot he's sitting on, then shoves the question aside, focusing his attention on Ben. *Most likely another Bartholomew disciple*, he thinks.

"Ben." He gives Ben's cot a soft kick.

To his surprise, the blanket covering the small head slides downward, revealing dark eyes, red with tears and strain.

"Hey there," he says.

Ben looks at David a moment, then the eyes duck beneath the blanket once more, like scared rabbits. "Go away," he moans.

David looks around to see if anyone is listening in or even

paying attention. But Ben is near the end of the line, closest to the doors, and David sees no other kids trying to eavesdrop.

"I want to know why you were screaming your lungs out earlier," David starts. At first he thought it was Basil who'd been screaming, but now the math is easy. Only three boys were missing at lunch: Ben, Peter, and Basil, and only one has returned. David has the bad feeling that something has happened to Basil, and can only hope he's found safely, wherever he is. But that leaves only Ben for interrogation. "I'm sorry you missed a meal. Listen, at dinner? I'll give you half my portion, okay? You sit with me and I'll take care of you."

Ben sniffs and the blanket slides down to his nose. The dead eyes come alive a bit, focus a bit more assuredly on David.

Nothing like offering food to a starving child to get what you want, he thinks sadly, but smiles at Ben in a way he hopes projects kindness. Sincerity. He leans in close, drops his voice to a whisper. "But you got to tell me what you saw."

Ben's eyes sink into his head again, his brow furrows. "Can't . . ." he says. "Won't."

David puts a hand on the boy's shoulder. His body feels hot under the blanket. "Okay, okay. Don't tell me. How about I tell you, and you just say where I got it wrong."

David gives it a moment, but Ben doesn't reply. Reading his silence as acquiescence, he continues. "I know you saw what happened to Basil."

Ben's face goes soft, as if remembering something terrible. *Haunted,* David thinks. He looks like a boy who has seen something unbelievable. Shocking. Something that might stay with him the rest of his life.

It's that bad?

"He was hurt, I guess?" David says, trying to sound light. Casual. Even though inside his stomach is churning. He watches Ben's eyes for clues, for confirmation. "Someone did something awful to him? Beat him up?"

Ben stares at David with those haunted eyes and, despite himself, David's heart breaks for the kid. Ben gives his head a little shake. Fresh tears slip down his cheeks to wet his thin pillow. "Worse," he whispers, like a curse.

David sits up straight, mind racing, nerves strained.

Worse?

He leans in again, his voice still low, but now more urgent. "What do you mean? Ben? What do you mean . . . worse?"

Ben is weeping. His stifled sobs beneath the blanket are filled with despair and horror. Finally, he lets go of what he knows. "He was *hanged*."

David's skin tingles from head to toe. The nape of his neck flowers with icy tendrils that ride up behind his ears, down his arms. He's stopped breathing.

"I don't understand," he says, dreamlike. Then refocuses, knowing it's impossible. "What are you saying, Ben? What? That he killed himself? Hanged himself?"

Ben shakes his head again, and those icy tendrils grow faster, wrap around David's body more tightly. They grip his legs, his stomach, his chest, his heart. He's numb. He's frozen.

"He was up real high," Ben says through choked sobs, the words barely audible. "On the cross, in the chapel. He had no clothes on, David, and . . . he'd been cut up."

David is leaning so close to Ben he can smell his sour breath, the sharp tang of his terror stinging his nostrils. He stays close, not believing what he's being told but, at the same time, believing every word.

A new feeling creeps into David's mind. One that feels almost familiar. It is similar to what he once felt, when he was very young, and being hit with the strap by Poole. He remembers thinking that it was different this time, because this time Poole wasn't stopping. He was hitting him again and again, more than he ever had, cursing and praying and swinging the strap down . . . and David thought he was going to die. Thought this would be the time when the old man would finally do it. Finally murder him. He'd been so small. Too small to defend himself. Too small to fight back.

Swallowing hard, he pushes the memory away, forces himself to meet Ben's frightened, tired eyes. "Go on, Ben. But no lies now, only the truth."

Ben says nothing, offers only an almost imperceptible nod.

"You're saying someone did that to him? Ben, are you saying someone *killed* Basil?"

Ben doesn't answer. His eyes lose focus, go distant, as if his mind has made the decision to shut him down for protection. A defense mechanism to keep the boy's sanity intact . . .

There's a cough.

David raises his head, looks over Ben's burrowed shoulder to the far end of the room, where Bartholomew's group of seven or eight boys sit together in their mismatched clothes, their wild hair.

They're all looking right at him.

David stands, and now he feels the icy tendrils slip away, fall to the floor and shatter like shards of glass. His distant, painful memories catch fire like dry paper put to flame; they turn to ash and blow away, out of his mind.

New feelings flood his body now. New emotions take root in his mind and grow.

Anger. Violence. Hate.

He thinks of little Basil, laughing, joking. The most helpless kid there was.

And then another emotion sparks deep behind his eyes, tightens his throat, causes his fingers to curl into fists. *Retribution.*

He leaves Ben where he wallows, begins walking between bunks toward the far end of the dorm. Toward the circle of boys. Toward those faces that are watching him. Some faces wear cocky smirks. Some frown. Bartholomew, in the middle of them all, looks placid. Almost bored.

As he nears, it's Simon who stands first. Gentle Simon . . .

"Hello, David," he says calmly, but the eyes say different. The eyes say GO AWAY.

David ignores him, keeps his focus on Bartholomew. "You fellas know something about all this? About Basil?"

Simon takes a step toward him. David is breathing fast, his heart races. He turns to face Simon, takes a step forward of his own, looks down at the younger boy. "What are you gonna do, ya fucking bootlicker?" Simon flinches, but doesn't move.

David shifts his eyes back to Bartholomew. "I asked you a question, goddammit. Answer me."

Simon turns to look at Bartholomew, then back at David. "You should watch yourself, David. There are things happening here you don't understand." Then Simon smiles. "But you will."

"Is that right?" David says, and he can feel the tightness of his fists, the vibrating energy of his muscles. Without turning to look behind him, he can tell by the sudden silence that the whole room is now watching.

Simon takes a half-step to his left, forcing David to look at him instead of Bartholomew.

David glares at him hotly. "Tell me what you know. Tell me now."

Simon's face turns quizzical, his eyes trail away from David, toward something else in the room. Toward Ben. "What did he tell you, exactly?"

Now it's David who steps to the side, blocking Simon's view of anything but his own rage. "Look at *me*, you ginger prick. I asked you a question." Simon's eyes flick up, but there is no fear there. No concern. In fact, it's David's will that begins to falter.

Simon looks somehow . . . *older*. And there's something else.

The eyes are wrong, he thinks.

"Simon, please." Bartholomew says, standing. He steps forward, puts a hand on Simon's shoulder. Simon smiles at David, all innocence again, shrugs, and sits down.

"I'm sorry, David. Look, why don't you sit with us? We can all talk about it."

But David feels his fire flickering out. The heat of his resolve turns cool and slippery. He can't cling to it, can't find the pulse of his righteous anger. Something about all this is wrong. Something about these boys is *wrong*.

"I'm okay, thanks," he says curtly.

When Bartholomew takes a step forward, David surprises himself by stepping back.

"You sure?" he says, the dark eyes widening, thin red lips curling at the corners. David thinks he looks like a fox who just burrowed his way into a henhouse.

A sly, hungry, sharp-toothed fox.

Bartholomew leans closer. He whispers, "I have something I'd like to tell you."

David looks around, sees other kids watching. Frightened, confused. "Maybe later," he says, hoping to sound indifferent, but fighting off a deep tendril of growing fear. To his shame, he finds himself taking another step away from the smaller boy.

Bartholomew's smile shows teeth. "Later it is."

He turns away from David, walks back to the others, who are all talking between each other, laughing and casual, as if David never existed.

As if murder is the last thing on their minds.

Trembling, David goes back to his own bed.

In the cot next to his, he hears fervent, continuous mumbles of prayer coming from Michael. "Hey Michael," he says loudly, a ragged attempt to settle his own nerves. "Say one for me, will ya, pal?"

Michael doesn't reply, and David can't see his face because the boy's pulled his bedding up and over his head. *Everyone's hiding,* he thinks. *Maybe I should hide, too.*

"Ah, never mind, I guess." He lets out an exasperated sigh,

tries to get his head around what, exactly, is happening at St. Vincent's. "Carry on as you were," he says.

Lost in his own thoughts, David doesn't notice the growing spots of blood soaking through Michael's white blanket. He can't see the younger boy's strained face, or his wide, crazed eyes, and he's spared the horror of seeing Michael's bloodied fingers, the result of him having chewed away the tops, nearly to the bone.

27

The wagon comes to a halt in front of St. Vincent's.

Andrew and I watch Johnson, who does not turn to watch our approach, disappear inside the building, the coffin cradled in his arms.

"Andrew . . ."

But Andrew sharply raises a hand toward me, halting my thought. His eyes are focused on the area Johnson walked from the shed to the entrance, the large man's footsteps a blackened path in the new-fallen snow. "Hold on, Peter. I . . . I have to think."

I sit quiet for a moment, wanting out of the wagon, needing information on what's happened. But I wait patiently, willing to let Andrew figure out what's best.

Finally, he turns to me, his face a mask of worry. He speaks in a quiet rush. Something in his demeanor sends a flutter of panic through my gut. "Go find the other boys. See what . . . no, sorry, go see if anyone is missing. I'm going to speak with Brother Johnson."

"The supplies . . ."

"Don't worry about the supplies. I'll handle it. I'll get Brother Johnson to help, and the kitchen staff. Just . . . it's better if you go. I'll find you later, all right? Let me know what you find out."

I nod and hurry down from the wagon. I know better than Andrew that the answers don't lie with Johnson, but on the tongues of my brothers. The priests underestimate us orphans, discount our ability to find the truth of things they think hidden.

I step through the open doors of the orphanage, walk quickly through the foyer and up the stairs. I enter the cloakroom only after checking to make sure it's empty. Annoyed at myself for being fearful, I hang John Hill's peacoat on a wooden peg, put the wool hat on the shelf with my other one.

When I arrive in the dormitory, I'm taken aback at the demeanor of the others. I expected turmoil, loud voices, gossip, and excitement.

What I find is like the inside of a tomb.

It's quiet. Much too quiet.

Like the day before, a group of boys are clustered at the far end of the long room. I notice David sitting up on his bunk, watching me. His eyes are both eager and frightened . . . and something else. A warning?

I drop my satchel next to my bed and examine the room. I try to count heads, faces, but the boys are scattered about, not in their usual places. I sit on my bed to remove my boots, eager to put on dry shoes again. David comes over, stands restlessly at the edge of my cot. His hands are clenching and unclenching, his mouth set in a grim line. He's not himself, and that, almost more than the sight of the coffin, worries me greatly.

David is not easily knocked off his course. He has walls within walls to keep himself insulated from things of the world, from the needs and feelings of those around him. I've never thought less of him for it. We all do what we must to get by. But I can't recall ever seeing him anything other than sardonic. Any emotions he may or may not feel at certain events, or punishments, or curiosities, are buried deep within him, visible only by his inner self. Which, I know, is exactly the way he likes it.

To see him so visibly, dramatically shaken is like seeing an adult cry for the first time. Seeing someone—someone you had thought unbreakable—splinter and crack. I still recall the first time I saw my mother cry. It was the first time in my life I felt truly exposed. Truly at risk. Because if our parents can be hurt, or shaken, or brought down by despair, what hope have we?

I feel a similar way seeing David in his current state. I didn't realize, until this moment, how much I rely on his solidity, his composure. In a way, it allows me to be more open and vulnerable for the other children. We balance each other that way.

Now it is I who must be strong, and stoic.

I steel myself to be so.

"What is it?" I say, pleased at how level my voice sounds, and pray it has a settling effect on him. "Tell me everything."

David lets out a deep sigh; his hands unclench, his features soften. He sits on the foot of my bed, eyes darting around the room as if expecting a sudden attack from all quarters. "It's not good, Peter."

"Okay," I say.

He turns and meets my eye, lowers his voice. "It's Basil," he says.

I think of that small coffin, and my stomach hollows.

No. Impossible.

"What about him?"

"Peter," he says, and swallows hard. He looks around once more, nervous and edgy, as if wary of eavesdroppers. He tries to act casually, but I can tell he's only pretending, as if not wanting to show his fear, his pain. But why? And for whom?

After a moment of furtive movements, he looks at me squarely, lowers his voice. "They killed him, Peter."

My mind goes blank at the words. I don't understand what he's saying, can't conceive of a reply. I shake my head, scoffing. "You're not making sense," I say.

He nods, as if expecting my response. "I know, it's crazy. But it's true. Basil's dead, Pete. Murdered."

His words linger in the air between us like butterflies my rational mind tries to catch with slow fingers. He exhales and slumps over, head bowed, hands knotted between his knees. We both sit silent for a moment. Finally, I'm unable to help myself, and I look around the room, searching for Basil's face.

He must have it wrong. There must be a mistake.

"I'm sorry, I know how much you liked him," he's saying. "It was Ben who saw the body. Whoever did it, they hung him, cut him open. Insanity."

I can only nod, allow myself to take it all in, ignore the growing void in my stomach. When I've gathered myself enough to speak, I manage to whisper: "Who?"

But David only shrugs. "The others," he says.

As if this explains everything.

Or anything at all.

Before I can question him further, the dormitory doors burst open. Most of the boys lying down sit up. Some stand. The boys huddled at the end of the room also stand—albeit casually, carelessly—before facing, as a group, our visitors.

David and I turn our heads toward the doors.

Father Poole, his face ashen and worn, stands at the entrance. Directly behind him are Brother Johnson, Father White, and Andrew.

Poole does not wait for questions.

"Basil is dead," he says loudly.

A few children start crying, but most stay silent.

The brutality of the words is a shock, but it also erases any doubt. I close my eyes in disbelief, mumble a prayer for his soul.

"There will be a service tomorrow morning," he continues, his bellowing voice stampeding my sorrow. "Nine A.M. sharp, in the chapel. I will ring the bell ten minutes prior. You will all attend . . ."

Some of the kids begin whispering to each other now, and the dorm takes on the din of unruliness.

"Quiet!"

Poole's voice is like the crack of a whip, and just like that, the room is his once more. For a moment, he looks almost smug. The thought sickens me.

"I understand many of you have questions. I understand this

is a shock to us all. I feel the best thing is to simply be forthright and honest now, right now, and get it all out. I think you boys can handle it, don't you?"

There's a general murmuring, a few shaking heads. The whimpers of little ones.

Andrew steps forward, whispers something into Poole's ear. I can't hear him, but I know he's asking Poole to take some of the younger children out of the room. It's what Andrew would do. What I would do.

Poole shakes his head, irritated, and waves Andrew away. As if swatting a fly.

"So, let's do this once, and then we don't need to have a house filled with whispers and gossip and half-truths." Poole clears his throat. To his credit, he looks somewhat stricken, but quickly buries whatever emotion he may be feeling beneath his well-practiced veneer of impassiveness. "Basil hanged himself in the chapel. He stood on the altar, tied a rope around his neck, and looped the other end over our sacred cross. He stepped off the altar and hanged by the neck until he suffocated and died."

Andrew steps forward, grabs Poole's sleeve. This time, I hear him clearly. "Father Poole, please."

More children are crying.

Poole turns and physically shoves Andrew away from him. The scene is surreal.

"Quiet, damn you!" Poole shouts, spinning back toward the children. "Or you will have no dinner tonight!"

Sobs turn to sniffles, then silence. Some boys, I notice, hold their breath.

"Better. Between now and dinner, you will remain confined to the dormitory, where will you spend the next hour in prayer and reflection. That's all. Are there any questions?"

For a moment, no one speaks. The room is stifled by shock and hostility.

Then a voice comes from behind me.

"I have a question, Father Poole."

David curses under his breath. "Bloody hell."

I turn to see Bartholomew approaching from the far end of the room, walking down the wide row between the cots like a duelist approaching a saber-wielding combatant. Poole draws himself up, sniffing loudly. He likely didn't think anyone would have the nerve to ask anything, but now he is stuck with it.

Good. Let him answer.

"What is it, Bartholomew?"

Bartholomew stops a few paces from Poole. He speaks loudly, clearly.

Because he wants everyone to hear.

"I would like to know if Basil will be buried in the St. Vincent's cemetery. In consecrated ground, I mean."

From beside Poole, Andrew's eyes find mine, his face a question: *What is this?*

I shrug.

"Yes, after the memorial, we will bury him in the cemetery," Poole replies. "No one needs attend. Now, if that's . . ."

"But he killed himself," Bartholomew says sharply, interrupting Poole's dismissal. "*Thou shalt not kill.* It's a mortal sin, Father Poole. He can't be buried in consecrated ground. He simply can't."

Poole looks at Bartholomew with wary, narrowing eyes. "That decision is not for you children . . ."

"But if it's a sin, he can't . . ."

"It is up to the priests to commune with God on how . . ."

". . . against God's divine will, is it not?"

". . . to proceed with the burial. Now, if that is all. Goodnight."

As Poole turns, I feel a draft of air on my face. I don't know where it could have come from. All the windows are sealed tight.

Suddenly, the dormitory doors—open as bird wings—*slam* shut with such violence that the metal cross leaning against the wall drops on its face with an audible *clunk.*

Startled, Andrew jumps backward, bumping hard into Father White, who falls to the floor with an anguished cry. Johnson crosses himself, and Poole spins back around, face red, eyes bulging. His mouth is a snarl.

"*Who did that?*"

There's laughter from somewhere in the room. All heads are turning to see who it is, including my own. I notice Bartholomew hasn't moved. His posture hasn't changed. His eyes are still on Poole, calm and wide and innocent. As if nothing at all strange had occurred.

"You didn't answer my question, Father."

Poole steps toward Bartholomew. I've never seen him this angry. I wonder if his vitriol is driven by fear. He points an accusing finger at the skinny, unwavering child.

"Insolence! Insolence!"

As Poole takes a step forward, another voice enters the fray. "It wasn't suicide!"

All heads turn to a cot near the doors, right next to where Poole and the other priests are standing. My mouth drops open, and David cusses under his breath a second time. I don't know if it's from surprise or worry.

I put a hand on David's arm and squeeze. I share his sentiment.

This is going to end badly.

Ben stands atop his cot, one finger pointed directly at the head priest. His face is red as Poole's, but tear streaked. His hair is matted with sweat. He looks like an avenging spirit, singling out Poole for damnation.

Andrew, having helped White up from the floor, approaches Ben, hands raised. I know he's trying to save him, to intercede, but I also know it's too late.

"It was murder!" Ben shrieks, his voice grating and broken. "I seen him! He was hung, all right, but not by his own hand. And he was cut open! Cut up like a pig!"

Ben turns his accusing finger away from Poole, points it at the boys in the room.

"It was some of you who did it! It was some of you murdering bastards!"

Now many things happen at once.

Johnson, appearing like a phantom at Ben's side, plucks the boy neatly from his cot and pushes him to the floor. The giant drops on top of him, swings a fist downward. Ben screams in pain. Andrew leaps forward, grips Johnson's arm, tries desperately to pull him off Ben. Poole is screaming at Andrew, at Bartholomew, at everyone.

"Enough! Insolence! Lies!" He bellows each word like a command, like a condemnation from God Himself.

Astonishingly, Bartholomew is laughing. "You fool!"

Poole lunges forward. He grabs Bartholomew by the collar, pulls his body toward him with a jerk. Bartholomew's head snaps back, but he does not resist.

Poole turns to Johnson, now facing off with Andrew, who stands, iron-spined, fists clenched, between the large man and a cowering, hunched-over Ben.

Johnson looks ready for murder.

Father Poole shoves Bartholomew toward Johnson, who grips him by the arm. "Take this one to the hole, see he goes without a blanket."

I study Bartholomew's face, looking for signs of fear, of protest, of pain.

But he only smiles. It's as if . . . as if he *knew* this would happen. As if he *wanted* chaos. As if it was all planned.

Poole stabs a finger at Ben, still huddled on the floor, sniveling against the wall, all his temerity and anger emptied like an overturned cup. "Take that one, as well."

Ben leaps to his feet, eyes wide as saucers, and runs to the corner of the room. I've never seen such pure terror in a human face. "NO!"

Johnson, still gripping Bartholomew in one hand, stares at Andrew. "You heard him," he says. Reluctantly, painfully, Andrew steps aside.

Johnson doesn't wait. He reaches for Ben, tugs him from the corner so hard it's a wonder his arm doesn't come off. The boy's legs collapse and he drops to the floor. Johnson drags him like a mop as he screams.

"No! No, Father, please! Oh God, oh God no, not with *him*, Father! Not with him!"

Andrew's face is in his hands. White is shaking badly but manages to open one of the dormitory doors.

Ben fights with such fervor that Johnson is forced to let go of Bartholomew, who, in a last bit of strangeness, begins walking ahead, through the open door, into the hallway. His chin is held high, his strides are easy, relaxed. He turns toward Johnson and speaks evenly, as if describing the weather.

"I'll walk, Brother Johnson. You won't get trouble from me."

Johnson grunts as he yanks Ben again. The boy is screaming as if he's being murdered before our very eyes, burned by flames we cannot see.

I'm standing, as is David. As are all the boys, I think. I have no recollection of getting up, but I am. I badly want to do something, anything. I feel helpless. I can only watch in horror.

"Father Poole! I swear on my soul I'll be good! Oh Father, please! Don't put me in the hole with him. He ain't right, Father. He ain't . . ." He's wailing now, inconsolable. Broken. He points at Bartholomew, leading the way, already disappearing into the gloom of the hall. "Oh, please. Not with *HIM!*"

And then he's gone. Through the doorway, dragged into the dark. His screaming and begging grow echoey and distant, as if he's not being pulled down a hallway but through a portal to hell itself. It's the only sound I can equate it to. The whole thing is a nightmare.

Poole turns back toward the room almost wearily. His face,

though deeply lined with exhaustion and slick with sweat, is composed once more. The room is deathly quiet.

"You children *will* learn to listen and obey," he says slowly, breathing heavy. "If you don't, you'll end up in the hole like the two boys who just left us." His eyes turn hard. "Either that, or in a pine box. Like your friend Basil."

No one moves. No one breathes.

I look to Andrew, but he avoids my eyes. He covers his mouth with a shaky hand.

Poole smiles. It curdles like bad milk.

"Now, we will see you all in the dining hall in one hour, cleaned up and ready for dinner. Remember, memorial service in the morning. Do not be late."

Poole leaves in a flurry of black robe and ill will. White follows, as does Andrew, who closes the door behind him. None of them look back.

"Fuck him."

I spin and see Simon, strong and confident. His eyes are on the doors, his face set in an expression I've never seen on him.

Pure hate.

No one else says a word.

28

The wind grows fiercer by the second.

As soon as they step out the front doors, Johnson's hood is whipped off his head, his mangy hair blowing, over his face, into his eyes: long unwashed strands flicking at the sky like frog tongues in search of flies.

Bartholomew walks steadily, five paces ahead, seemingly unbothered by the drop in temperature and skin-grating gusts. Johnson is waiting for him to burst into a sprint, run away toward the horizon, where gray snow-covered earth meets up with the dim red twilight of a hellish sunset.

Meanwhile, Ben has thankfully slowed his struggling, like a fighting fish finally succumbing to the poisonous atmosphere above the water.

He's mostly crying now. And shaking.

"You can't do this, Brother Johnson," he whimpers, the boy's words nearly lost to the howling wind filling his ears. "Please, you know I'm right!"

Johnson grunts, continues pushing the boy in front of him. "Right about what?"

Ben tilts his head upward to look at Johnson. His eyes are wet and red. His face sallow. Stray snowflakes stick to the moisture on his cheeks and eyelashes. He lowers his voice, barely audible even inches away. "There's something *wrong* with him."

"Nonsense," Johnson grumbles, but deep down, he *is* concerned. He's not sure the boy will survive the night in the hole, not if the temperature continues to drop.

Well, at least there's two of 'em. That'll knock the temperature up a couple degrees, anyway. Little bastards are like hot coals.

They reach the sunken square in the yard where the wooden ceiling of the hole is stamped into the frosted ground. Bartholomew, having reached it before Johnson, stops and turns to him, an inquisitive look on his face.

"Shall I dust the snow from the door, Brother Johnson?"

The hell is wrong with that boy? He seems almost eager. His brain must be broken. Yes, I've seen it before. Boys whose minds have gone rotten under Poole's care, like apples browning in the sun, infested with worms.

"If you want," Johnson replies loudly, and stands in awe while Bartholomew kneels and brushes snow from the trap, as if he's smoothing bedsheets.

Rotten . . . Johnson thinks, knowing for certain now, in his heart, that the boy is mad. Which explains what Ben is caterwauling about. Doesn't want to spend the night trapped with a madman.

Can't say I blame him. That child gives me the willies.

With a speed and strength Johnson thought long-sapped, Ben twists violently beneath his hands and begins to run. "No!" he yells, reaching for the boy. Although caught momentarily off guard, he's dealt with these brats enough over the last decade to have developed certain reflexes, his long arms already reaching well before his mind even registers the boy's escape. He feels one hand snag a head of hair, the other a worn shirt collar. He grips and pulls. Ben yelps in surprise and then drops to the ground, writhing and screeching like a banshee.

Johnson drops to his knees as the boy convulses beneath his hands, sobbing hysterically, wide, terrified eyes bulging from his head. Ben actually begins *crawling* through snow and earth to pull free of Johnson's grip, as if he can somehow scratch and claw his way to freedom.

This one's mad as well! he thinks. *But enough is enough.*

Johnson's mouth tightens as he grips one of the child's thin arms with both hands, gets back up onto his feet, and drags Ben toward the now-open hatch. The boy's legs kick wildly and slide in the snow, his breathing fast and harsh.

"No no no no no no no no . . . please God, please Jesus . . . oh Lord, oh Johnson, please, I pray to thee . . ."

"Shut up!" Johnson roars, exasperated and disturbed by the protestations. Part of him wants to punch the boy's skull, stun him and toss his body into the pit. The other wants to pick the poor bastard up and hold him tight, tell him it's over, that it was a joke, that he can go back inside now and play with the others, have a warm supper.

Instead he continues to pull the boy backward, a hunched demon dragging a soul into the lake of fire. "Damn you," he grunts, fighting the boy every inch of the way.

"I'm scared!" Ben screams. "Don't do this! Brother Johnson, he ain't right!"

Johnson looks down into the opening, sees Bartholomew already below. His serene, pale face gazes upward.

That mad little fucker looks almost happy.

"Enough! Climb down that rope or I'll throw you down. And it's a long drop, boy. You hear me?"

With a lurch, Johnson swings Ben's body over the opening. Ben's legs slide into the open trap, dangle in mid-air. He's breathing fast as a hare, face white with fear and shock, hands clutching at Johnson—small fingers scrabble at the sleeves of his garments, rake his beard, paw his face.

He shrieks and wails. Begs.

"Fine, we do it your way!" Johnson yells. He grips Ben's arms and holds him over the opening, his feet kicking at the darkness, eyes desperate for salvation.

Johnson lets go.

He hears the *thud* of Ben's body hitting the dirt below. Not wanting to listen to any further protestations, he yanks the rope upward, hand-over-hand, then grips the icy-cold door and slams it shut, hot breath puffing out in crystallized clouds. He waits for more screams, more tears . . . but hears nothing.

Although he'd never admit such a thing, perhaps not even to himself, he does feel badly for the child. He's never seen a boy so terrified. Yeah, sure, many of those he carried out here fought. Some more than others. And many of them cried.

But this was something else.

This was a boy fighting an executioner.

Johnson's had enough. His troubled mind pulses with emotions, fills with thoughts that make him sick and uncomfortable. He shuts them all out, begins his trek back to the orphanage. He'll find the kitchen and demand some soup. Something to warm him, settle his nerves.

By God, what I'd do for a drink.

He's twenty paces away from the hole when he hears a harsh, wailing scream.

He spins, goes still.

Listens.

The snow-filled wind whistles in his ears.

A distant tree branch snaps.

It's just the wind, Teddy. Just the cursed wind. Nothing more.

He pulls the hood tight over his head and continues on his way, eager to be out of the cold.

29

There are no voices at dinner.

For the second time in as many days, David sits at my table. Right now, he's across from me, and I'm glad. He and I need to be unified if we're going to get through this and, more importantly, help the *others* get through this.

I look down at my plate and nearly weep as my stomach wheezes in despair.

Two pieces of watery cabbage. A potato so small and knotted it takes all my willpower not to put the whole thing in my mouth at once for the fulfillment of having, temporarily, the wonderful feeling of being full. That, and so I won't have to look at the ugly, misshapen thing another second.

"Did you hear about Michael?" David asks.

Oh no.

"Tell me."

David takes a moment to see who is within earshot, and it strikes me again how paranoid all the kids are acting now. As if everyone is wary of everyone else.

"James went to the outhouse after Poole's big speech, saw Michael wandering around outside, along the fence by the road. He called out to him but got no answer. When he went close to check on him . . ."

"What?"

David swallows hard, takes a moment, then continues. "He was all bloody. James said his hands were like raw meat." David shakes his head. "He'd chewed off his own fingers."

"David . . ."

"It's true, Pete."

I'm disgusted, and more than a little skeptical. This must be exaggeration. The rumors now will be far worse than any truth, but this seems a step too far. "Sorry, I don't believe it."

David shrugs. "I checked his bed before dinner. It's soaked in blood. One of the staff was up there with an armful of sheets just as I was leaving."

"Then it was an accident. Got his hand caught in something."

David stabs at a leaf of soggy cabbage with his fork. "Maybe. But James says his mouth was dripping blood, and that he was laughing like a fool." David drops his fork on the table, rubs his face. "God, I can't eat this shit anymore." He looks at me, almost accusatory. "I thought you brought back supplies."

"We did. A wagonful," I say, as if it serves as an explanation for being forced to eat scraps. "There are many of us," I add lamely.

David grumbles and sighs, picks up the fork and stabs again, lifts the dull green cabbage into his mouth, chewing slowly. He takes a small sip of milk, most likely wanting to make it last. "Anyway, he's in the infirmary."

I nod, decide not to pursue it. It's both too bizarre and too awful to think about, so I change the subject. "John Hill says a few weeks of hard winter are coming."

David smiles coyly, and I know what's next. Despite everything, David will always find a way to tease me mercilessly about certain things.

I'm an idiot for bringing up John Hill.

"And how is young Grace?" he says.

Feeling myself reddening, I pour all my focus into the cutting of my potato. "Fine," I say.

When I look up again, expecting to see that jackal's smile of his and be tortured with more questions meant to embarrass me, I'm surprised to see he's not focused on me at all . . . but on the room. His cheer has vanished, and I almost want to mention Grace again, if only to lift his spirits. If chiding me helps, let me help.

"Quiet in here," he says.

It's true. There's the scrape of cutlery against dishes, and nothing else.

No arguing.

No laughing.

No teasing.

Not even a belch or a fart, nor the ensuing giggles. I glance around at the nearby tables, see morose faces intent on their food.

I don't know if it's my frayed nerves, my lack of nourishment, or my exhaustion, but as I look around the room, I see not only boys, but flitting *shadows*. They slip from boy to boy, dashing in and out of corners, resting in laps, on tables, over shoulders.

I blink and rub my eyes. Why am I cursed with seeing things? Phantoms and prancing shadows? I want to whimper from the rising terror that scrambles up my spine, bit-by-bit, like a fat spider trying to reach my tired mind and slip inside, take over.

When I remove my knuckles from my eyes, I notice Simon, three tables over, watching me. Next to him is that nefarious Jonah. His other new friends, Terrence and Samuel, sit across from him, showing me their backs.

I offer a small wave. But Simon, instead of waving back, does the oddest thing.

He sticks out his tongue.

It's unusually long, and blackened.

I turn away, refocus on what remains of my meal, which now looks less like food and more like garbage—rotten greens, moldy potato. I don't feel well. I don't feel that things are *right*. Something is wrong, and Basil's death, I think, is not the root of it, but the result of it.

Something is wrong with *me*.

"What's happening," I say, not meaning to speak the words aloud.

David hears me, however, and nods. "I don't know, friend. But if this was a dancing girl, I'd say we've only seen the skirts of it. The kicking legs are soon to come."

I set down my fork and look at him, feel the world climb back to a sense of normality. David's eyes are wide with feigned innocence. "And what would you know of dancing girls?"

He chuckles at that, and the sound is elixir to my soul. "Hey, you're the saint, remember? I'm the rapscallion. And proud of it."

He jams a fork of potato in his mouth, then makes a face. He speaks through a mouthful of mush. "Are the eyes supposed to be crunchy?"

We stare at each other for a second, then both burst into laughter.

It's the only human sound in the room.

30

The small library is my favorite place in the orphanage.

The room was originally built as part of the chapel, the walls built from the same bluish gray stone. Heavy oak crossbeams detail the high, vaulted ceiling. There's one window, above my reach, that in the daytime hours filters the sun, turns it crimson and blue, the colors of the image painted onto the glass: a guardian angel wearing a royal blue cloak, bold white wings unfurled, looking down from a blood-red sky. At night, the glass turns pure black, an empty mirror.

The floor is constructed with the same smooth stone as the foyer, giving the library a medieval feel. At each end of the oval-shaped room are two heavy wooden doors, crafted from dark oak and bolted through with rough, black iron studs. One door leads to the chapel, the other to the hallway where the priests' rooms are settled. The walls are covered in high shelves the same dark wood as the doors and filled with hundreds of tomes. Some of the shelving cases are designated for use by all, including the boys. Most, however, are exclusive to the priests and, when part of my private lessons, to myself as well.

The only thing about the library I dislike is the painting that hangs between two of the bookcases—an artist's depiction of hell splayed across a huge canvas. It has an elaborate, gold-painted frame that is almost disgustingly lavish given the image within, which is dark, graphic, and cruel.

In the painting, which Andrew once informed me was done by one of the founding priests of St. Vincent's, is an elaborate tableau of human suffering, demons, and a bleak, flaming landscape. The humans, naked and corpse-like, as if on the brink of starvation, are being poked into a lake of flames by the demons, who hold spears, swords, and daggers. The demons are spike-tailed, black-skinned devils, but their faces are almost angelic, a conflicting depiction that makes them seem even more obscene than if they had horns at their temples, wild yellow eyes, gnashing teeth.

I've had more nightmares about that painting than I can count, although mostly when I was younger and more susceptible to such things. I never told Andrew about them, fearing he'd restrict my usage of this part of the library, where only priests are allowed, and I would never forgive myself for having that access rescinded.

Still, it's a horrible, loathsome thing. I've tried, over the years, to find out more about the priest who painted it, but Andrew is either uninformed or uninterested in that part of the orphanage's history, and has little to say.

Sitting here now, the painting has a certain power over my mood, my thoughts. I have to force my eyes to turn away, force myself to focus on my lessons.

I take a moment to study Andrew, who sits across from me, quiet and pensive. We're stationed in our usual places at one of the stout study tables, the same one we sit at every time during my daily tutoring, my training for priesthood.

Sensing his aloofness and distracted nature, I debate if now might be the right time to reveal my decision.

When he looks up at me, however, his eyes once again focused and alert, I simply lower my gaze to the book in front of me and keep my mouth shut tight, my revelations to myself. I'm not ready. Especially not with things being so tumultuous, with the death of poor Basil and the strangeness surrounding some of the boys. No, it feels trite. Unimportant. Plus, I know it will break his heart, and I'd rather wait until things are better, when whatever is infecting our orphanage, and its inhabitants, has withdrawn back into the dark from where it came.

The book open on the table is in Latin, a language I've learned slowly over many years of study. I can read most of it, and speak a lot of it, but for some reason have trouble writing it. When I try, the words stop holding meaning, the structure of the sentences fall apart in my mind. Luckily, there is little need for that aspect. As a priest, reading and speaking the old language is enough, and even that, in my opinion, is an archaic trait of the priesthood that is more about tradition than knowledge, more about rite than helping others grow closer to God. So much of religion is ceremony that I sometimes wonder if priests like Poole have become so entwined with the process that they've forgotten the spirit behind it. The idea saddens me, but also emboldens my decision not to pursue the cloth.

I certainly have no desire to become a priest—or person—such as Poole. I don't want to be a disciple of protocol. Perhaps, as a normal man, I might continue to grow in my spiritual life, even if I'm not able to wear the garments, or be empowered to speak the proper blessings. I will pray, however, for myself, for Grace, and for the life we choose to live. That will be enough.

"*Credis in Deum Patrem omnipotentum, Creatorem caeli et terrae?*"

"*Credo.* Good," Andrew says, concentrating on my words, waiting for the next mistake.

"*Credis in Jesum Christum Filium ejus unicum, Dominum nostrum, natum, et pasum?*"

"*Credo . . .*"

"*Credis et in Spiritum Sanctum, santam Ecclesiam Catholicam . . . Sanctorum communionem, remissionem pecatorum, carnis res . . .*" I read the word again, but the pronunciation won't come. I'm tired, and after the events of the last twenty-four hours, incredibly distracted. I can't stop thinking about Basil, about Ben being dragged away . . .

"*Carnis resurrectionem, et vitam aeternam?*" Andrew says.

Without warning, I find myself enraged at Andrew for

correcting me, for being here reading this stupid dead language, for not saving Basil's life. I slam the book closed. "Maybe you should read the damn thing."

"Peter!"

I sit back, scowling. The outburst is completely unlike me. Well, unlike me as I am today, at least. As a child, I was constantly pushing back on my lessons, many times flustering Andrew in the process. Now I just feel foolish. Like a sulking child. But I don't care. It's silly to be learning Latin given all that's happened, and especially ridiculous given I'll never be using it.

I cross my arms, hold myself tight.

"It's a stupid language," I mumble, and a second wave of foolishness sweeps over me.

Andrew almost smiles. I'm sure part of him is amused by my outburst, but I know he's also concerned for me, for the others. Everything that's happened these last few days has been hard on him, as well. I drop my arms, force myself to soften.

"I'm sorry, Andrew. I'm acting out, I suppose."

"It's all right, Peter. Today hasn't been easy." He thinks a moment, studying me. "Still, you're doing very well, you know. You're nearly ready."

"Except for the whole Latin part," I say, but try to keep my tone light.

He laughs at this, nods. "There is work to be done, no doubt. But like I said, it's been a trying day, and I know you're hungry and tired and upset, as we all are." He leans forward, brows furrowed. "If you want to talk about Basil, we can talk about it. I know you loved him. I did, as well. What happened . . ." he shakes his head. "Was horrible. It defies reason."

I uncross my arms, let out a breath. "I'm fine, Father. It's horrible, like you say. And sad. But . . . there's more."

Not now. Not yet.

I won't tell him yet.

"Oh?" he says, and sits back in his chair, waiting.

I hesitate, choose my words with care.

"It's like there's a dark seed buried inside me, something I can't extract with any amount of prayer. I can feel it growing, Andrew. I can feel it taking root, and it frightens me. When I recall what happened to Basil, or to the boys being taken away to that hideous pit . . . I feel that black seed *swelling*, pulsing like a second heart inside my chest. It feeds me dark, terrible thoughts. It makes me feel . . . I don't know. Evil."

For a moment, Andrew says nothing. He runs a finger across his unshaven chin, a thing he does often when thinking on a problem. I give him whatever time he needs. It's not an easy thing to share, and I'm interested—hopeful—for his prognosis.

Finally, he takes a breath, folds his arms on the table, and finds my eyes with his own.

"First of all," he says evenly, "be careful you don't confuse evil with despair. One reason tragedy exists is to teach us how to help others, help others learn how to find a way through their own dark time, through a journey of growth. As a priest, you must always be in the light, Peter. You must find courage inside yourself when you feel there is none. It is in these darkest moments that you will discover your true self. When you do that, when you discover this new *you* through life's most difficult trials, only then will you find salvation. Only then will you lead others to that same salvation, guide them safely along their own dark paths. Do you understand?"

I nod because I understand most of what he's trying to tell me. I also nod because I can't keep my eyes open. I'm hungry, I'm exhausted; my body and mind desperately crave sleep.

Andrew stands, sensing my obvious weariness. "That's enough for tonight. Why don't you go on to bed. Check on the others for me, will you?"

"Yes, of course."

And I will. I am beginning to feel that it's expected of me, now. Not by the priests, but by the other children. In many ways, I am the only one they have to truly look out for them.

I will not let them down.

As I make my way back through the gloom of the orphanage toward the dorm, there is a conflicting storm brewing within me. An inner struggle between light and dark, each vying for authority, for command.

I climb the gloomy stairs, enter the long, unlit hallway. Wary of shadows.

I step faster.

Ahead, I focus on the thin bar of light beneath the closed dormitory doors. As I get closer, I hear muted voices, and take comfort in the idea of being back with the other orphans. I place a hand on the cool handle and pause, thinking about my conversation with Andrew, the struggle between light and dark. If embracing the light makes me a man of faith, what would embracing the dark make me?

The answer is simple.

Just a man.

I push inward on the heavy door. Orange lantern light floods through the opening. Someone calls out my name, and I smile.

Let the darkness come.

PART THREE
THE STORM

31

I'm choking.

The smoke is thick and black. The heat all around is so intense that it feels as if my skin is being cooked, my insides boiled.

No one is screaming because everyone is dead. My mother. My father.

I should have climbed out my own bedroom window when I had the chance, but I had to see Mother's face one more time.

Now I sit with her corpse, her heavy, limp head cradled in my lap, in order to say goodbye. I stroke her hair; tell her I love her . . .

But I take too much time.

When I finally leave her (gently resting her head on the wood-planked floor) and stand up, it's into a cloud of heated, swirling gray ash. I instinctively inhale, and the hot smoke burns my throat like acid.

Hacking, I drop back to the floor and begin to crawl. My vision is blurred with tears, the air opaque. I don't know if I'm going toward the front door or deeper into the house. In mere minutes, the entire structure has gone up in flames.

With reaching hands I grip a doorframe. I crawl through to more smoke and even more intense heat. Not the front door, then. Not escape. No, this is my parents' room. Still, there's hope. There is a large window in here that's easily opened. Mother always joked about the devil crawling through it at night to darken her dreams.

I keep crawling forward until I find the wall, place my hands on it, begin moving down toward the window. I know I'm in the right place because my parents' bed is behind me, and the window is set in the wall next to it.

I don't want to stand again, so I lift my hands as I move on my knees along the wall. Searching for the window frame, for the glass, for fresh air.

I search further and further . . . until I reach the corner of the room.

I've passed it.

Impossible!

I'm crying now, and it's getting harder to breathe. The flames must have seen me come in here because they've followed me—giddy and murderous—through the open door. As they climb the walls I hear their laughter.

Taunting me. Mocking me.

They leap to the bed in a furious arc and begin to feast on the handmade quilt, the cotton sheets. The stuffed mattress.

The back of my shirt catches fire and I jump to my feet, holding my breath, slapping the wooden wall in search of a window I cannot find. That, perhaps, no longer exists.

My hair is on fire. My scalp burns and sizzles. I begin to scream as I smell myself cook—my eyeballs pop and liquify, my charred skin peels away. I collapse, and the fire eats me to the bones. . . .

When I wake, my breathing is fast, my throat bone dry. I've kicked my bedding completely off my cot and I'm drenched in sweat. I take long, deep breaths, relishing the cool air. The *life* of it.

The dormitory is dark, but the silver moonlight coming through the windows give the room a soft, hazy glow.

"Bad dream?"

I gasp, twist over in my bed to see Simon right next to me.

Standing over my bed.

He looks down at me, head cocked slightly to one side. His face is a deep shadow. An abyss.

I swallow and nod. "The usual," I say.

My history of nightmares is well-known by the others; they are something I've been afflicted with since the day my parents died. It was a serious concern for the priests when I first arrived, but gradually my night terrors became accepted, and now not even the other orphans pay it much mind when I wake up screaming, clutching at my throat, or cursing at a nighttime visitor whose face I can never recall.

His cool hand touches my forehead, then strokes my damp hair. "You want a glass of water? I'll fetch it for you."

I would like nothing more . . . but I have no intent to ask anything of Simon. He isn't the friend I remember. Truthfully, he sickens me. The touch of his cold hand on my head makes my skin crawl. "I'm fine," I say, trying to keep the repulsion from my voice. "Go back to bed."

Simon takes a step backward, and the void of his face brightens when struck by moonlight. What my mother used to call the light of the dead.

"You've always been good to me, Peter," he says. His voice is not a whisper, but he speaks quietly, the words meant only for me. "I won't forget that."

I don't know what to say, so I say nothing.

Simon turns to the window, stares out into the night.

My breath catches when I see a shadow cross his face, as if something broke the flow of moonlight through the window. Something passing by outside—quickly, silently, in the night.

I want to speak, to yell in alarm, to question what I think I saw . . . but the words won't come. I'm frozen. I'm terrified.

Simon, perhaps sensing my fear, turns and smiles down at me.

His teeth are silver, his eyes black buttons.

"Goodnight, Peter," he says. "Sweet dreams."

32

Andrew sits just behind, and to the left of, the altar. On the altar's opposite side, also seated, are Father White and Brother Johnson. Poole's chair, next to Andrew, is currently empty. Poole himself stands at the small lectern, contemplating the upturned faces of the orphans.

"As believers in God," he intones solemnly, "we do not fear Death's sting. Like birth, it is but part of life, a gift from Jesus Christ, and the beginning of our eternal . . ."

Andrew's mind drifts. He's scattered, exhausted. His thoughts are fragmented, stormy, his attention frail. Anxious and seeking distraction, he shifts his eyes to the altar. They'd covered it with a red tapestry, one that had previously hung in the foyer but was moved, many years ago, to storage when the upper story and stairwell were added on. The retired decoration was large, old, and dusty. It apparently depicted The Last Supper, or possibly a hunting scene; it was hard to say, the once-vibrant colors having long-since faded to blurs. In addition, mice and insects had been at the tapestry while it sat in storage, and the fabric was now badly frayed. It should have been thrown out long ago, Andrew thinks, along with the rest of the artifacts stored in the church's oversized closet of spiritual junk.

The altar needed to be covered, however, so the antiquated wall-hanging came in handy, after all.

Despite the servants' best efforts, supervised by Poole himself, they simply could not get *all* the blood out of the altar's light-toned wood, or the porous floorboards. Even after several hours of scrubbing and washing, the stains still looked ghastly, a sharp reminder of what lay there only a day ago; of what was hung from the cross that still loomed over his shoulder—a symbol of man's salvation now degraded to a glorified meat hook. He shudders at the thought, uncrosses and re-crosses his legs, and tries to focus on Poole's sermon.

"... saddens me that young Basil did not come to me with his problems. Or to Father White, or Father Francis. We are all here for you children. We will listen and we will help you if you have feelings of despair, if you need guidance ..."

As if drawn to it, Andrew's eyes slide to the altar once more and a sick feeling stabs his guts. His nose twitches at the stink of dust and mildew radiating from the rodent-chewed fabric, and he abhors the way it congeals on the floor, misshapen and ridiculous looking. His eyes twitch higher, and he feels a fresh wave of despair, of deep-seated remorse, at what rests atop the blood-stained altar and the ancient cloth which hides it from view.

Basil's coffin.

The child's corpse tucked snugly within.

And now Andrew thinks he can smell other things, as well: the thick planks of knotted pine Johnson used to construct the box and—yes, another aroma, one that lies beneath the woody smell of pine, the mildewed rot of the tapestry—the body itself, of course. The decomposing corpse bloated with gases, the eyes sunken, the flesh cold.

"... praying on the matter, we have decided to bury Basil in the church graveyard. Although what he did is a crime against God, against nature ... he was also just a child. An innocent. Confused and haunted by grief. Who are we to judge a child? Does a shepherd blame a lamb for wandering near a dangerous wood? No, he gathers the lamb and returns him to the pasture. The burial ..."

Yes, yes, Andrew smells the boy well now. It's a putrid, awful smell. He adjusts himself in the hard chair, leans away from the altar, casually puts a hand over his mouth, his nose, as if pondering Poole's words. He shifts his legs yet again—clumsily so, growing agitated—and nearly kicks the heavy candelabra to the side of him, one of two that bookend the pastoral chairs. The tall, heavy candelabras stand sentry on either side of Basil's coffin, holding aloft melting candles burning bright, liquid black smoke curling from the wicks.

Finally, Andrew leans forward, puts both feet flat on the floor, and commands his body to stop fidgeting. He curses softly under his breath, tries to rein in his thoughts and discomforts, his anxiety. He looks out at the boys, wondering if they are watching him, judging him, mocking his obvious irritation.

But no . . . all eyes are on Poole. The children are more rapt at this speech about their friend's ugly death than they've been at any sermon Andrew has yet attended. He takes a deep breath, begins to feel better. His eyes travel over the boys, and he notices Simon and Jonah are sitting near the back, further away than they should be. He frowns. They must have moved . . .

What was that?

Andrew's attention is drawn to the double-doors that lead out of the chapel toward the foyer. They're closed, but the morning light coming from the foyer illuminates the seam, fills the wide gap where the two doors meet. A vertical string of silver.

A shadow passes by, causing the light to pulse.

There!

And again . . . perhaps . . . multiple shadows? Children?

That silver string of light darkens, becomes light again, flickering from some mysterious movement . . .

Now it goes dark again . . . and stays that way.

Someone is standing outside those doors.

Andrew's brow furrows. *Who could it be? One of the kitchen staff? But why? Perhaps they are curious? After all, it's not every day a boy is murdered at St. Vincent's.*

And there it was . . . *murder.* The word emerging from a sealed box in his mind, a black thing lifting the lid and crawling out into his consciousness.

Murder, then. *Not* suicide.

Is that what he believes? And if this is the truth of the matter . . . what needs to be done?

No, impossible. Pull yourself together!

He pulls his thoughts back to the present, to the issue at hand. If there are boys missing . . . but no. That can't be. Therefore, it's impossible for anyone to be outside the chapel. The kitchen staff are clearing breakfast, preparing for lunch. They'd have no business in the foyer. And if all the boys are accounted for . . .

Andrew's thoughts freeze.

Aren't they?

Feeling ever more anxious, Andrew looks around the chapel with renewed focus—studying faces, reciting names in his head.

Now, however, his mind plays a new trick. With each face he identifies comes a different thought, a new question: *Am I looking at a murderer?*

He looks more closely at each youthful visage, no longer searching for boredom, or mischief, but something far worse.

Violence. Hatred.

Evil.

Then he stops, cursing himself. *Stop it, you fool! Just find out who's missing, if anyone.*

He starts again, back to the beginning, and counts heads.

". . . and so, we pray for his eternal soul," Poole says, finishing his sermon. "Now, who would like to say a few words about their friend? Who wants to speak about Basil? A fond memory, perhaps. Hmm?"

None of the boys speak, nor stand. Andrew coughs lightly, nervously. Poole's question throws him off his count, but he thinks a few might be missing. He needs to be sure, but now his eyes shift once more between the children and the double-doors. The shadow has gone, but he watches for the light to break again, hoping to confirm someone is indeed outside those doors.

Doing . . . what?

He thinks of Ben and Bartholomew in the hole. He wonders if they're alive, or frozen. Stuck fast to the dirt like dead tree roots, needing to be pried from the cold earth, peeled free.

More coffins will be needed . . .

Andrew shakes the thought away. His mind is hysterical and strained. He must pray on these matters. For himself. For strength. He must get some sleep!

"I'll speak."

Andrew's eyes snap up and, for a moment, his troubles wash away. He smiles. A delicate warmth melts away the black ice which had been forming in his chest. It's Peter, of course. The kind, courteous boy he raised. The boy who will, one day, stand by his side as a priest.

Secretly, Andrew hopes that—if God wills it—he and Peter might someday oversee things here at St. Vincent's. It is a pleasant idea.

The first thing I'll do, he thinks, smiling as Peter approaches the front, *is fill in that awful pit. The days of medieval torture tactics will be over.*

As Peter steps up to the lectern, Poole pats him on the shoulder and steps aside. Andrew sits up, eager. For a moment, he forgets the stench of the coffin, the decay of Basil's corpse. He focuses only on Peter.

And in doing so, forgets about counting heads, and no longer watches for shadows, which have indeed returned, now standing just outside the chapel doors.

33

I don't know why I say anything.

I have nothing in mind, nothing planned.

But no one else is going to talk, and someone *should* talk. That's how I feel, anyway. Oddly, even though other boys have passed away during my stay at the orphanage, right now the last funeral I can think on clearly is that of my parents. I was so young I barely recall what happened that day. I retain pieces: feelings more than sights. I remember being with men I didn't know and being scared of them. Those same men took me to a graveyard where a priest spoke over two piles of dirt. It was very cold. I was shivering most of the time.

I remember feeling sad that I hadn't said goodbye. That I hadn't seen their bodies.

From what I was told, there wasn't much to see.

And then, after it was over, I was taken away. More strange faces. Hard voices.

I distinctly remember the sensation of being unwanted.

Two days later I was at St. Vincent's, being shown to my cot by Andrew, who seemed so old at the time, a proper adult, but I realize now how young he must have been. As the years went on, he seemed to grow younger as I grew older. A strange bending of perspective that eventually led to us becoming friends. The idea that we might be *true* friends—a priest and an orphan—strikes me as strange. I don't know if it makes him seem young, or me feel old.

Poole grips my shoulder, too tight, and I nod, focusing on Basil, on what I should say.

My mind races to find words.

But then I do.

"I knew Basil for about three years," I start, skimming over the faces of my brothers. "Since the day he first arrived here at St. Vincent's."

I glance around the room, trying to avoid eye contact. It's unnerving to have them all watching me. A few are smiling, a few look sad. Some are sneering, as if angry with me, or disgusted. I take a breath and stare at a point along the back wall, avoiding all expressions, pleasant or otherwise.

"He was so skinny when he first came here, all skin and bones." I give a little laugh, even though there is nothing humorous about it. "He'd been . . . well, when they found him, as you all know, he'd been nearly starved to death. Just a scared little kid, abandoned, like many of us." Someone coughs and I notice some of the boys shifting around. I must be boring them. I make a mental note to hurry through the rest. "Anyway, I remember him once telling me about some of the awful things he had to eat while living on the street. The things he needed to do to survive . . ."

Poole's throat clears to my left, and I turn to see him with raised eyebrows. "Sorry," I whisper, and turn back to focus on that spot in the back of the room.

"The point I'm making, I guess, is that he was tough. A survivor. But he was also kind. He wasn't the healthiest kid in the world. Always seemed to have a cough, or a snotty nose . . ."

A few kids laugh at this, and I'm careful to not look at Poole.

"Anyway, he was my friend. He was our friend, and our brother."

I'm not sure what else to say. I sense the weight of his body behind me, lying in his coffin, waiting for the earth. I scan the faces once again, and notice, distractedly, a few heads put together in the back of the room. I assume that whatever they're discussing has nothing to do with Basil, and feel a rush of anger.

Then there's a *knocking* on the chapel doors. I become flustered. Do the others hear it, as well? Is it my imagination? I wait, listen . . .

I look down at the worn lectern, annoyed and depressed. I finish my thoughts in a flurry. "He always prayed to the saints at mealtimes," I say, my eyes still cast down. "I know they are waiting to greet his arrival in heaven."

I nod at Poole that I'm finished and leave the podium, rush back to my seat. I avoid looking at anyone, anything. When I sit, I catch Andrew's eye. He smiles at me, and I feel a little better. Still, I keep my head down. I want this to be over.

Poole steps back into his place. He does not bother asking if anyone else wants to speak. He knows there's no point. "God is always here to watch over us, children. To protect us." His eyes roam the room and I keep my head lowered to avoid his gaze. Finally, he closes his eyes. I follow suit, eager for the darkness, for the completion of this horrid ceremony.

"Let us pray."

Within my own inner darkness, I imagine Basil's face. I focus on the sound of his laughter. I meditate on the gift of his existence and pray for his eternal soul.

A heavy knocking on the chapel doors disrupts my thoughts.

It sounds like a hundred angry fists, lost souls pounding for entry.

I open my eyes to chaos, and don't see my attacker until it's too late.

34

Andrew jumps to his feet when he hears the banging on the doors.

Johnson, always eager to confront mischief, is already striding down the aisle toward the disrupting sound.

Despite the noise, Poole continues to pray, the raising of his voice the only indication he's even heard the pounding. Boys are shifting in their seats, all eyes open now, watching Johnson as he huffs toward the rear of the chapel.

He reaches the doors and pushes against them.

". . . and so Holy Father, bless us all . . ."

"It's locked!" Johnson yells, cutting off Poole's blessing as if it were the mumblings of a beggar during a building fire.

Andrew watches, a slow panic rising inside him, as Johnson pushes against the doors again and again.

They don't budge.

Johnson hammers against them, howling in a rage. "Open these doors you bastards!"

Andrew recoils at the language, and instinctively looks to Poole, who seems to have finally abandoned his prayer.

Laughter comes from the foyer. Laughter that stands *just* on the other side of the double-doors. In that moment Andrew realizes—despite never having finished an official count—that his instincts about the number of boys seated for the service were correct.

Some are definitely missing.

Half the boys are now standing, watching Johnson in a sort of glee as he bludgeons the heavy doors with his fists.

Simon, however, has his back to the doors, as if they hold no interest for him. He stands stoic, in the middle of the aisle, facing Poole. He has one arm extended, as if reaching.

The flesh on his forearm is cut badly. Crimson stripes from wrist to elbow.

In the other hand he holds a large knife.

"Father, come see what I've done," he says. "Will you help me?"

Astonishingly, it's Father White who reaches the boy first. He kneels down before him, clutching the wounded arm, inspecting the damage.

Too late, Andrew sees the look in Simon's eyes change. He no longer looks afraid, or worried.

He looks angry.

Before Andrew can call out a warning, Johnson's bashing and cursing rises to a fever pitch. Andrew, his focus darting between Simon with his bloody arm and Johnson's attack on the chapel doors, hardly notices as two boys run up the aisle and past Father Poole, laughing.

He turns just in time to see them push over one of the large candelabras.

"Boys!" he says, but now there is movement all around him. "Boys," he repeats, no longer sure who he's addressing.

A guttural, wet scream splits the air, and Andrew's attention is drawn quickly back to Simon and Father White. Simon has thrust his knife into White's throat. The old man's eyes are wide as boiled eggs. Blood sprays in an arc as he twists away from Simon's grasp and falls backward to the floor.

"No," Andrew says. "No . . ." He's speaking so quietly that it's impossible for anyone to hear him. He knows he needs to speak louder, to yell, to shout orders. And yet finds himself numb, choking on his words. As he takes a step forward, knowing that he must help Father White—must get the knife out of the priest's *throat*—he stops in his tracks, mouth agape.

"Oh God." What he sees is not possible. A nightmare.

Many of the boys are up and moving now. They move with

purpose, and each of them brandishes a weapon, objects they had somehow—until now—kept hidden. Andrew's eyes dart around the chapel, spotting flashes of metal held tight in small fists. Samuel grips a mason's chisel. Jonah holds a knife, similar to Simon's, and is stabbing another boy in the back as he crawls away, shrieking in terror and agony. Terrence has hold of one of the younger children, five-year-old Marcus, and is beating his head with an iron candlestick. Andrew, in a shocked daze of connection between the impossible and the real world—now forever shattered—recognizes it as having come from the library.

"Stop!" he roars, but no one listens. No one cares. All the boys are screaming, from fear or rage he does not know. Most of the boys are fleeing, defending themselves, fighting back, and the rest are *attacking*. Viciously. Bodies are suddenly moving everywhere at once in a hellish tableau of chaos and murder.

He smells smoke and takes his eyes off the children. He turns around to see flames licking up one of the large tapestries hanging at the head of the chapel. There are two such tapestries, one hanging on either side of the large wooden cross. The one behind him is a deep violet, bears a gold-stitched crucifix. The other is red, embroidered with the likeness of St. Vincent feeding a fawn.

It is the red one which now burns.

Seconds later, that old, dusty tapestry covering the altar also catches.

It burns like dry kindling.

Two more children run by him. They push past him without thought, without fear, and shove over the second candelabra, its arms also filled with burning candles. It crashes into the altar; the candles jump free and flare against the pine box of Basil's coffin.

Andrew tries to reach for one of the kids. "Please stop!" he yells frantically. The face that turns to him is not one he recognizes, which doesn't seem possible. Before he can focus on recalling the name, he feels a stabbing pain in his arm. The boys laugh and leave him, running headlong into the fray. He holds up his arm and sees blood running from his palm, the cut so deep that it flows like spilled wine.

He goes white at the sight of it. Trembling, he slaps his opposite hand over the cut, hoping to staunch the flow. He moans as blood squeezes between clamped fingers, runs down his forearm.

There's a *crash*, and he spins to face the chapel.

Boys are fleeing those who wield the weapons. Many congregate behind Johnson at the barred doors. He notices little Thomas hiding beneath a bench, eyes wide with terror and confusion. Some of the boys fight viciously, tearing at each other. Punching, clawing. Pulling the other's hair. Biting.

Three boys with weapons fall on another against a far wall—pale-haired Aaron, who was always willing to lend a hand with the younger ones. They're assaulting him mercilessly with simple kitchen knives, stolen from the dining hall. Aaron screams and writhes beneath them, but the other three don't slow, don't stop. They stab him again and again.

"No . . ." Andrew moans, feeling faint. "Get away . . ."

But the children are now in full panic, the fervor growing as the room fills with screams, grows thick with smoke.

Poole is screaming at any children close at hand, demanding they *STOP!* Andrew watches, sickened, as two larger boys rush at Poole and push him backward into the altar, now fully aflame.

Basil's coffin rocks but does not fall. It blazes atop the table as if it is not an altar at all, but a funeral pyre.

Pressed back against this mass of flame, Poole's cassock catches fire. Andrew yanks the remaining tapestry from the wall and runs to Poole, throws the violet fabric over his burning body. He stumbles and they both crash to the ground.

There's an ear-piercing shriek and something punches hard into the side of Andrew's head. A bright light flashes behind his eyes. The sound of the chaos distorts. His vision goes blurry.

Now he's being kicked. Punched. He and Poole both. There's more screaming. He flips over, tries to defend himself, sees nothing but snarling faces. Bloodied weapons clutched in the grips of children, rising and falling against his body.

He doesn't know what's happened, has no idea how this came to pass.

He only knows this is the end.

35

"Open these doors you little shits!"

Johnson bangs his fists against the doors with every ounce of strength he's got. Flitting shadows dance through the cracks. He hears the laughter of at least two boys on the other side, the sound only inches away.

When I get out of here, I'm going to scrape the skin off their bones.

Worse than the fear, he can feel hot *panic* rising in his belly, spreading to his limbs, his mind. The nerve-shredding terror of being *trapped*.

It is something he's been afraid of his entire life, ever since childhood, when his mother would lock him inside the closet of their small apartment whenever he'd misbehave. She'd throw him inside, shove a chair beneath the handle, tell him through the thick wood that every minute he wailed and cried and banged his fists against the door was another minute he'd be left inside.

He'd try hard to be quiet, to stop the whimpering, the sniffling. Then he'd hear her nearby, as if she were purposely being sneaky, staying close so she could *listen*, like a spider with one bent leg poised upon a string of sticky web, waiting for it to shiver.

"I *hear* you!"

And then he'd start wailing all over again, knowing he was only making it worse for himself. But he was only a tyke, no more than four years old. Most of the time he hadn't even known what he'd done wrong.

Usually, he would be let out after a few hours. Other times, he'd be pushed inside during the day, then be let out at night. A couple times he slept there until morning.

It was terrifying.

In hindsight, as an older boy, he knew that what he'd hear in the closet was nothing but mice or rats in the walls or under the floorboards. But as a child, he'd hear the scratching at the wood around him and think it was ghosts or ghouls coming to get him. A few times he'd feel the skitter of paws run across his splayed fingers and he'd shriek for mercy. He'd try to stay on his feet all night but grew so tired after a while that he'd be forced to sit and lean, trembling, beneath the shelves of detritus that shared the closet space with him.

Once he'd woken in the dark to feel something crawling in his hair.

Something *big*.

He'd shrieked and wailed, begged his mother to let him out. Yelled that something was *in there* with him. Something that he knew, deep in his heart, wanted to *nibble* at him, gnaw at his cheeks and earlobes, sink tiny teeth into his eyeballs while he slept.

His fear of enclosed spaces, of being *entombed*, was the primary reason he'd chosen a life sentence of servitude to the church, to Poole, versus another five or six years in prison. Once they'd buried him in that box as punishment—the worst possible thing he could have imagined—he knew he'd never survive. Or, if he did, that he'd lose his sanity, a fate worse than any death.

And now, incredibly, *unfathomably*, these little pricks have locked him in again.

He will not stand for it.

"Let me out of here you goddamn brats!" he roars, slamming his shoulder into the doors again and again.

Must be something jammed between the handles. Something long and heavy. A shovel, perhaps, he thinks, panting, ignoring the pain in his hands, in the shoulder as he rams it into the doors. *Well, I can break a shovel! See if I can't!*

It's only when he smells the smoke and hears the heightened screams that he finally widens his focus, turns some of his attention back to the room.

"Oh dear Jesus."

He stares in horror as the front of the chapel burns. Some boys are running. Other boys attacking. Father White lies like a rag doll in the aisle, fresh blood pumping from a wound in his neck, his eyes wide and empty, staring at the ceiling, at nothing. Johnson takes a step forward, uncertain where to start.

I've got to get out of here, he thinks, but now the thought is more distant, the panic of being locked in defused by the chaos of what's happening all around him.

Then he notices the cluster of fallen bodies near the small podium. Poole and Andrew on the ground, being beaten, kicked.

If Poole dies . . .

He can't think it. Won't think it.

"NOOO!" he bellows, and begins to run away from the doors, from freedom, and toward the front of the chapel. Toward Poole. "Out of my way, ya cunts!" he yells at anyone standing between him and Poole—whether they be a child pleading for help or a child rushing at him with a damned kitchen knife. He sees one boy has stuck rusted nails between the fingers of his fist, is running from child to child, punching at kids. He turns to Johnson and punches into his belly. The pain is instant and searing.

Tyson, he thinks absently. *That's young Tyson. He's the one with the singing voice, who loves to sing the hymns. And now that fucker has gutted me.*

Johnson grabs Tyson by the throat and, without hesitation, drives the opposite fist into the boy's face. There's a gratifying *crack* beneath his knuckles. The boy goes limp and Johnson lets him go. He slumps to the floor, his handful of nails scattering like dropped change. Johnson steps over the body and continues forward.

As he nears the first child attacking the priests, he grabs

the back of a shirt and whips the boy backward and out of the scrum, causing the others to look up at him, faces sweaty and gleeful. There's a *screeching* to his right and he turns in time to see Frankie—the potbellied Italian who always seems to be laughing about something—leap at him from one of the benches. His thin arms wrap around Johnson's neck, his fingers clenching handfuls of long hair as he bares snarling teeth and bites into his cheek.

Johnson screams in pain, grips the boy hard by the shoulders and yanks him away. He sees blood and flesh stuck to Frankie's mouth. Thinking of his own face, what the insane child has done to it, Johnson goes mad with rage and horror, his reason flung from his conscious mind like a wind-blown leaf. Without thought of consequence, he grips the boy at the waist and swings him down like a club, slamming the child's head against the corner of the nearest bench. Frankie's neck snaps so dramatically that his head dangles from his shoulders like a broken toy. Johnson grunts and drops the corpse, turns back to the fray.

36

The whole room has simply . . . *erupted.*

I have hardly a moment to register the outburst when a bony, but iron-strong, arm wraps around my neck from behind.

All around me is screaming and crying, loud fists banging on the doors, which must have been somehow locked, or blockaded. But all of my sensory focus is now solely on the taut forearm crushed against my throat. A mouth is speaking near my ear, puffing hot breath against my neck as it speaks in a language I don't understand. The words nothing but constant, harsh whispers that sound to me like gibberish, or madness.

I can't breathe, and the pain of my throat being squeezed shut is too much to bear.

Suddenly, the arm on my neck loosens, then disappears. I spin around, expecting to see the face of my attacker, but find myself staring at Byron's back, his arm driving repeatedly into the shrieking face of another boy trapped beneath him.

"Byron!"

He looks up at me, and I can see that he's terrified beyond reason.

"Let him go!" I have to yell for him to hear me because now everyone is yelling. There are horrible shrieks of pain, cries for help, for mercy. Of rage.

When I take in the entirety of the chapel it seems to be nothing but writhing bodies, fire, and blood. "What's wrong with all of you!" I scream.

"Peter!"

I turn toward the voice and see David fighting his way toward me. He holds Thomas in his arms. Poor little Thomas, only six years old. He clutches David around the neck with such ferocity that it makes me think again of my own attacker. I look back over the edge of the bench, expecting to see a body, but whoever it was is gone. I want to ask Byron but he's already running to help David, now kicking at an older boy—Terrence, I think—who swings wildly at him with a stout iron carpenter's hammer. Byron leaps at the boy and takes him to the ground, and I run to David.

"What is this? What's happening?" I say, but he only looks at me, shakes his head.

His eyes dart to something behind me.

"Look out!"

I spin in time to see Jonah's snarling face. He's swinging a wooden mallet.

I raise my arms to block the blow, but feel it punch my temple.

Thomas is shrieking in David's arms.

The sound of his cries is the last thing I hear.

Johnson lifts Poole, gives Andrew a glance to make sure he's not dead. Having witnessed Johnson's strength and ferocity, the boys attacking Andrew and Poole have scattered like rats.

Flames rage around them.

"Father! Are you all right?"

Poole nods, his face white as a sheet, his lip bloodied. "Get me out of here."

Andrew stands, looks at Johnson with wild eyes. "Go! I've got to save who I can!"

Johnson begins to fight his way back up the aisle. The room is so filled with smoke that it's difficult to see anything clearly. Bodies run haphazardly through thick haze, shadows writhe in a heavy mist. It's impossible to see faces, to know who is attacking who.

Just need to get out of here . . .

He reaches the doors, where a group of kids are now clamoring, banging on the doors, screaming for escape.

"Stay close, Father!" Johnson screams, then starts driving through the throng, lifting bodies and tossing them aside. He has no time for discernment or delicacy, he must get those doors open. Reaching the front, he leans Poole against one of the walls.

This time, he takes a few steps back, gets a short run going, and lowers his shoulder as his bulk smashes into the heavy wood.

They hold, but he hears something crack on the opposite side. He can almost visualize a shovel or hoe (*or both*) jammed through the door handles, their wooden shafts already splintered. He once again takes two steps back, then throws himself with abandon directly at the seam between the two doors—the weak spot—where the added tension of the doors wanting to pull apart will aid his cause.

This time there's an audible *CRACK*.

The doors fly open.

Johnson stumbles through and into the foyer, the fresh cold air a balm for his scorched throat and lungs. Behind him, Poole shuffles through, and with him a mass exodus of sprinting, screaming, terrified children. Johnson knows he should be stopping them, separating those who were revolting—who were *killing*—from those who were victims. But he's too tired, too confused, too overwhelmed.

"Father . . ." he says, hoping Poole can guide him, tell him what to do next.

But Poole has his arms raised above his head, face lifted toward the foyer's ceiling. Toward, Johnson supposes, God Himself. Poole prays loudly, the words flowing like water through a broken dam, crazed as a manic street preacher, as children stream past on either side.

What the hell are you praying for, old man? Johnson wonders.

But cannot even begin to imagine.

37

I wake on a cold stone floor.

There's a sharp pain in my skull and a dull throb in my brain, pressing against the backs of my eyes, blurring my vision. I turn my head slowly and see Father Andrew kneeling nearby, focused on something other than me.

We are in the foyer, outside the chapel.

"Hey, you're alive," says a voice I recognize.

I push an elbow beneath me. The room swims for a moment, then refocuses. I look to my right and see David. He's holding Thomas's hand. Behind him are the twins, looking scared, but not terrified. I think that's good, that perhaps it means the danger is behind us. Surely the priests have secured the boys who attacked the others. They must have them locked up somewhere.

I sit up the rest of the way, and now Andrew notices me. He does not smile, there is no relief in his expression. He looks like a different man. His face is stretched and bloodless. His eyes wide and haunted. "Peter," he says, and it's only then I see a little of the old Andrew return.

He walks over to me and helps me stand. After a moment of dizziness, things stabilize, and I take a look around the foyer. Around me are small pockets of children, most of them talking quietly; some are crying.

Behind me is the chapel. Smoke seeps from the open doorway, but I don't hear the crackles of flame nor feel the heat of fire.

Andrew grips my elbow, turns me gently so he can speak to both David and me simultaneously. "I want you two to take all the boys here up to the dormitory. Close the doors behind you and find a way to secure them. Push furniture in front of them if you must."

Secure them? This makes no sense. I try desperately to clear my head, organize my thoughts. "I don't understand, Andrew," I say. "What happened?"

Andrew lets out a breath. "I don't really know, Peter. All I know is a handful of boys came to the chapel this morning armed with . . . well, anything they could get their hands on. One or two boys locked us in, using farm tools, and some others tried to burn the . . ." Andrew's words trail off, his gaze grows distant. "God, it's awful. Just awful."

I turn back toward the chapel doors, notice the remains of a shovel and a hoe, both shattered in half, lying lifeless on the floor.

"I don't know why they did it," he continues, "but they killed many of the other children. I don't know how many yet, I have to bring them all out of the chapel. There are also many wounded."

"Let us help you," I say, my body refueled by adrenaline and anger.

"No," he says. "Get these boys to safety."

"You keep saying that . . ." I say, still not understanding.

David puts a hand on my shoulder. "They're still around, Peter. When the doors opened, everyone took off in different directions, but we don't know who is safe and who is dangerous. I saw a few faces, but it was chaos in there. They could be anywhere." He lowers his voice. "They could be *here*."

I study the other boys in the foyer, looking for murderers. For evil in their eyes.

I see none. I see nothing but frightened children. Some badly cut. Most soot-stained in varying degrees. All of them needing protection. "Okay, fine. But then I'm coming back to help you."

Andrew does not respond with affirmation or denial, but simply turns away, heading back for the chapel. "Go! Go now!" he says, and disappears through the doors.

"They killed White," David whispers.

I turn on him, shocked. "What? Who?"

David looks away for a moment, as if not able to meet my eye as he tells me. "It was Simon who did it," he says. "Simon cut his throat."

I don't believe it. I *can't* believe it. "No . . ." I say, the despair surging fresh in my blood.

"Afraid so," he replies, and then he does meet my eye. "He's one of *them*."

We make it halfway down the hall before we're attacked.

They come from the first classroom just as we begin walking by. Four of them, all with weapons. All screaming.

They look insane.

"Run!" David yells, and scoops down to pick up Thomas.

The other kids from the foyer are all ahead of me, most of them already inside the dormitory. I volunteered to take up the rear, so I'm the first one they grab.

I feel the tug on my arm and instinctively turn and kick out randomly, connecting—by blind luck—with the gut of Auguste, who doubles over and drops awkwardly to the floor, cursing loudly in French. Something metal jumps free from his hand, skids to the wall. I don't bother to look at the object meant for my back, or my skull, and follow the others in a sprint.

Just ahead of me are the twins, Jon and Finn. In front of them are a cluster of five or six kids. David, carrying Thomas, leads our straggling group.

All of us run for our lives.

Two smaller boys, Harry and George, begin to stagger and slow, trying desperately to keep up with the rest, but the boys chasing us are older, faster.

The dormitory doors are wide open. Panicked faces from

inside beckon us to hurry. They can't be more than twenty feet away, but it seems like twenty miles.

"Run!" I yell at Harry as I catch up to him and George. They're both too big for me to carry, and the murderous screams behind us feel only inches away. I'm terrified. I don't want to die.

George, who had a birthday only last week, trips. He hits the floor in a heap. I spare a look back and see two of the pursuers fall on him like wolves. Flashes of metal. Pumping arms. His screams are horrible.

I trip next.

I fall hard, hitting the floor with such force it feels I've dropped a hundred feet instead of five. My breath shoots out of me. I scramble to my hands and knees when a body crashes down onto my back, flattening me to the floor. Something hard and sharp is stabbed into my shoulder and I scream. I manage to twist partly around, panicked with the need to fight back—to survive—but whoever is on me is heavy, their knees planted on my back, my arm. I wait for a second thrust of the knife, perhaps to my head or neck. A killing stroke.

Then I hear a *thump* and the body is gone. Hands are pulling at me desperately, trying to get me off the ground, to *stand*. I look up to see Byron. There's a spray of fresh blood on his face.

"Get up, Peter." He says it almost calmly, but his eyes are behind me, on those who still pursue us. I scramble to my feet, take a fleeting second to notice the meat hammer in his hand dripping blood, a clump of black hair mashed into its prongs.

Byron, who has now saved my life twice this day, is already running. I don't hesitate to follow.

David is at the doors. He's got one closed and stands holding the other, waving his hand at me and the boys in front of me, as I bring up the rear once more. "Hurry! They're coming!"

The boys running ahead slip through the door. Byron is through. Just me now.

I lunge through the opening and David slams it behind me, leans his weight against the doors. He turns and yells to me, to anyone. "Bar it!"

I look around frantically, then spot the iron cross on the floor by the wall, the same one which had hung over these doors for so many years. The one which had inexplicably fallen the night of the visitor, the night this all started.

I grab the cross, run back to David, and slide it neatly between the arched, twisted iron handles of the two doors. I'm reminded of the broken shovel I saw in the foyer, knowing this cross is not nearly as fragile. It won't be broken.

Almost immediately, bodies slam into the doors from the other side. Whoever is out there is shrieking like mad; making horrible, guttural, animal sounds. They punch and kick and push at the entry, but the doors hardly move thanks to the tightly wedged cross, barely fitting in the gap of each handle, the short arm hooking neatly over one grip, making it impossible to dislodge.

We all stare at the doors as the pounding slows, slows . . . then eventually stops.

There are voices. Whispers.

Finally, footsteps trail away, away . . .

And silence.

I look at the survivors we have with us. A rough count puts us at fifteen, give or take.

Minus those who fell.

I look for Byron, locate him sitting on a cot, bloody mallet between his legs, head bowed.

"Where's Jonathan?" Finnegan asks.

David and I look at each other, each asking the other the same question.

Finnegan tugs my sleeve. There's a strange look of humor on his face, as if we're playing a joke on him. "Where's my mate? Where's Jonathan?"

Once again, I look around the room, praying to see the boy's head, his smile, maybe waving a hand from behind a cot, laughing at how he got us. Got us good.

"He was right next to me," Finn says, the humorous look turning slowly to confusion, then alarm. "He was right next to me . . ."

I shake my head. "I don't know . . . I fell . . ."

Finnegan looks to the doors. The large, shining cross wedged in their handles.

"He can't still be out there," he says, voice breaking. He walks toward the doors, but David drops to a knee in front of him, puts a hand on his shoulder. Finnegan looks at David crossly, but warily, as if still unsure whether we're all playing a cruel joke.

"We need to go get him," he says.

"No, Finn. We can't," David replies, looking to me for help.

"But he's out there!" Finnegan yells abruptly, realizing the worst has happened.

The others are watching the scene now, all eyes on the doors. On Finnegan.

Obviously, we all realize that they're not biological siblings—not even related—but we also know, deep down, what we're seeing: a twin who has lost his other half.

"Finnegan," I say, and he spins on me, eyes red and wet with fresh tears.

"We need to go back!" he screams, his young, high-pitched voice breaking. "We need to get Jonathan! We need to get my friend!"

He runs for the doors, but David catches him, holds him tight as Finnegan fights against him, wailing and shrieking and calling out the name again and again.

"Jonathan!" he yells. "Jonathan, please! Jonathan!"

Beyond the doors, there is nothing but silence.

38

Johnson runs through the snow, now shin-deep after the early morning's heavy fall. Fat slumbering flakes drift down all around him, and he knows the storm that's coming won't be as peaceful, or as restrained.

It won't be looking to drown us slowly, it'll arrive howling and thrashing, eager to kill.

It doesn't matter.

By nightfall, he'll be gone.

After he got Poole settled in his chamber and treated the worst of his wounds, Poole told him to get to the town, find the sheriff.

Bring help.

Johnson doesn't know what the hell happened, or which of the children have lost their damn minds and which ones are still sane, and he doesn't care. All that matters is one cold fact: the boys have lost control. Turned into murdering savages. Killed Father White in cold blood. Tried to kill Poole and Andrew, and himself.

Not to mention the dead children.

When Johnson passed through the foyer on his way out, he saw Andrew laying a bedsheet over a small body. It was lain neatly at the end of a row. Johnson didn't count the shrouds, didn't have time and, frankly, didn't give a damn. Dead was dead. But he figured at least six or seven lay there, blood soaking through the clean linens.

Whole place stank of smoke and death.

He was therefore glad for his orders. It was time to run.

As he approaches the barn, he begins to wonder what the place will be like when he returns. If any will survive. Will it be a tomb he comes back to, with Sheriff Baker and deputies in tow? Or will those remaining somehow survive?

And then, a different thought creeps into his mind.

What if I don't come back at all?

Now, there's a thought. Of course, he'll be a fugitive. An outlaw. A wanted man.

Or . . . maybe not. Maybe there is another way.

What if he comes back the next morning and finds nothing but bodies? The murdering kids long gone?

He could burn the place. Burn it to the ground.

With so many charred corpses beneath the rubble . . . it would simply be assumed he was one of them.

Yes, or that you were the one who did the killing.

"Damn it to hell," he says, fighting through the last few feet of snow to reach the barn. He needs to get the horses tethered, needs to get to town. No more big plans. Get the sheriff, get back here, save who can be saved.

He unclasps the barn door, pulls it wide.

The inside of the barn is dark, musty, and oddly welcoming. An animal warmth. The smell of shit and hair and muscle. A good smell. A wholesome smell.

He reaches for the lantern hung by the door, finds the wooden matches on a nearby shelf and brings it to light. He walks past the wagon, the lamplight a halo shield, pushing back the dark.

A good hiding place, this, he thinks. But he's not overly worried. The snow was clean when he walked through it. No tracks. Wherever the little bastards are holing up, it isn't in the barn. *At least not the ones who done the killing. But there might be others.*

The thought gives him pause, and he stops, looks around and behind him. Studies the shadows. *And why can't I hear the animals?*

And what's that stench?

He hurries the last few steps to the stalls that hold the horses. No large heads protrude, no large brown eyes watch him, hoping he's bringing oats or an apple to feast on. He reaches the stall's opening, thrusts the lantern into the dark.

He cries out, surprising himself with the outburst; this new horror is too much. Too much.

Both horses lie in their respective stalls, butchered, the underlying hay soaked red with their blood. Johnson opens one of the stall doors and steps inside, holds the lantern near the body.

There must be a hundred cuts . . . a thousand.

It seemed every inch of the beast has been sliced, cut, or stabbed. Covering his mouth and nose with a sleeve, he staggers to the next stall, finds the same has been done to the other. A blood-stained scythe lies in the dirt, but there is no sign of other weapons. He assumes they must have cleaned and held onto the ones they could. Hidden them in pant legs and shirt sleeves, waist bands and socks. Pulled out at a signal, when they were all gathered.

Organized.

"Damn them," he says, his voice shaking with anger and fear.

He leaves the stalls and hurries back toward the main doors of the barn. He must tell Poole. They need to figure out a plan before the snowfall gets worse, before they're all trapped here. As he approaches the square of daylight, he slows, staring at the expanse of gray sky, the blanket of new-fallen snow. The landscape, framed neatly by the open doors, seems to almost be waiting for him. To welcome him into the light. It was almost . . . inviting.

I could make it to the Hill farm, he thinks. *I could go now and be there before dark. Before the storm loses its temper and buries us all.*

He blows out the lantern, sets it on the ground of the entryway. He doesn't bother closing the doors as he steps out into the brisk day, a tiny creature beneath an overarching pale sky. Wind tugging his face, he looks in the direction of the Hill farm, of the city beyond. The road has vanished beneath the snow cover, but he knows the way.

I'll tell Poole, then I'll go. Get my good boots on. A hat. Then I'll go. I'll get help.

Decided, he starts plodding his way back toward the orphanage.

When he hears a voice.

"Help!"

It's faint. Very faint. As if the wind itself is calling, pleading . . .

He spins around, confused. He sees nothing but snow.

He looks toward the shed but sees no one. The doors to the orphanage are likewise empty, open wide and barren.

"Help us!"

And suddenly, it clicks.

Oh my dear sweet Jesus.

The *hole.*

The *children.*

He forgot, and that's the truth. With the ceremony, and the horror of what happened, he simply forgot about the two boys out here in the cold, going on nearly a full day now.

He shuffles through the snow in the direction of the hole, flakes obscuring his vision. He can't locate it. The whole damn yard is covered in at least a foot of snow, maybe more, and the wind is picking up now, the flakes no longer drifting downward, but shooting sideways past his eyes. His cheeks and ears feel the burn of the storm's breath.

"Boys!" he yells. "Boys! Talk to me so I can hear ya!"

For a few seconds, there's nothing but the sound of wind.

Then: "We're here! We need help!"

Johnson takes a few strides forward, spins to look at the barn, the fence separating the road from the field, trying to get his bearings.

Straight ahead, it should be straight ahead.

He stumbles forward, trips and drops to a knee. Listens.

"Boys? Yell louder!"

"Here!" cries a buried voice. "It's Ben, Brother Johnson! There's something wrong with Ben!"

Bartholomew.

Johnson takes three more giant strides, then his leg sinks to just below his knee. His foot hits wood. "Boys!"

Now the voice is clear, muffled only by a couple feet of snow. Right below him.

"Johnson! Get us out of here! We're freezing! Ben is sick. I think . . ."

Johnson begins scooping away snow. He finds the rope, the outline of the door.

". . . I think he's dying!"

"I'm coming!" He finds the iron handle of the trapdoor and yanks it upward. A pitch-black square opens within the thick white blanket. He leans down on hands and knees, sticks his face near the opening, looks for signs of life. "Boys?"

"Johnson? Can you see us? We're here!"

Johnson leans lower, his head now level with the wooden platform. He sees nothing but darkness and hard-packed dirt.

"Bartholomew?"

The response is a whisper, so close to his ear he can feel the cold breath on his neck.

"I'm here."

Something strong grips the cloth of his chest and yanks him down through the opening, into the cold dark.

The view from the orphanage is bleak and colorless. A blur of new snow continues to fall on the empty yard.

The wind whistles and whispers, sings its own secret song.

Leafless trees beg and crack, succumb to the will of the on-coming storm.

The sun is a blind eye, a cold disc of white in a forlorn sky.

Of life, there is no sign.

39

David and I manage to calm most of the kids down.

Finnegan was the hardest.

In the end, he just sat on his cot, cross-legged, staring at the door. Willing his friend to materialize. The rest of the kids are shaken, but not to the point of hysteria. Some, I can tell, even find it exciting. As if it were a game, all this murder.

Once everyone is relatively ordered, we make an official head count.

Fourteen boys.

"So we're missing . . . what?"

"Eighteen," I say, mentally trying to categorize names and faces into groups.

Who's dead? Who's alive?

Who's still out there, hiding, plotting murder?

Ben and Bartholomew, I realize with a pang of guilt, are still in the hole. They've missed it all. Are there others, outliers, hiding? Has anyone tried to run away? Impossible to know. But important.

"Where's Poole right now?" David whispers to me, agitated and probably as frightened as I am. "Or Andrew? Where are the damn adults?"

I shake my head. Adults . . . or what's left of them. "If White is definitely dead, then we have one very big problem."

"Okay, what?"

"That the adults are badly outnumbered. Which means it might be on us to fix this."

"Oh, to hell with that," David says, his frustration boiling over. "I'm just a kid. And so are you." He points to the room. "And so are they. Let the priests figure out this mess."

The priests. I promised Andrew I'd return, and I must go help him . . . but I'm disordered, confused. Who can I trust? What if there are more boys in the hallway, or downstairs? Are they *all* in on it? Are the rest of us nothing but lambs waiting for slaughter?

"Who do we know for sure is, you know . . . dangerous?" I ask, ignoring David's protests for now. I make a point to keep my voice low. I don't want to frighten the others.

David thinks. "Simon, obviously. Sorry. And, well . . . Terrence. Samuel, for certain. Who attacked you in the hall? I didn't bother to turn around, carrying Thomas . . ."

"I'm pretty sure there were four of them," I say, thinking of the faces. It happened so fast. "I kicked one," I add lamely. "Auguste."

"Auguste? The Frenchy? Jesus . . ."

I nod. "Byron clocked the one who jumped me with a meat hammer, might have killed him. The same kid who stabbed me in the shoulder."

The wound hurt but, upon inspection by David, it proved to be superficial. Byron took a look and shrugged, noting only that it had likely been done with a table knife. The idea of being stabbed with cutlery made me numb with sick fear, but I tried my best to keep a brave face.

"Anyway," I continue, "I didn't get a good look at the others. But no one you mentioned was among them, which puts their numbers near ten, I guess. Plus, we know Jonah is on their side. That one was always plotting with . . ."

I stop, seeing a new light on all this. A black spark.

"What?" David asks, looking worried.

". . . with Bartholomew," I say.

It hits me then. It's as if a key is turned in my head, unlocking something I *somehow* knew, deep in my heart, to be true.

I recall the strange events of that night. The violence, the screams, the laughter. The gunshot and then, moments later, the doors blasting open, as if a horde were bursting through.

The fallen cross.

Yes, I'm absolutely sure of it now. *He* is behind all of this.

The dead man.

Somehow, that man—his arrival, his bizarre death—is the root of everything that's happened since: the strange gatherings, the personality changes. Rebellion.

Murder.

But there's more. I recall David's story of the dead grass. The sense of a pervading, continuing rot which the dead man left behind. A poison . . .

And now another name drifts into my head. The change in him the most dramatic of all. The quiet one, now the schemer. The silent one, now the voice.

One boy at the center of it all.

Bartholomew.

I need to talk to Andrew. I need to sort out what it all means.

David doesn't seem to notice my distracted thoughts, but simply nods at my mention of the boy's name. "What about him? I mean, I agree he's likely involved, given how he was part of that group. But Peter, he was stuck in the hole the entire time we were fighting for our lives down there."

"That's what worries me," I say. The wound on my back stings, and my stomach gurgles, empty and queasy. I feel lightheaded. I sit down on a nearby cot.

David sits next to me. "I don't follow."

"This whole time, he's been in the hole . . . with Ben."

I stand, shaking. Something inside of me stirs, then settles into place. As if some lost, inner piece of me, floating through the ether of my mind all these years, has only now found its destination. Locked into place like a final puzzle piece.

The mystery of who I am—who I *really* am—feels solved. The answer to a question I've been wrestling with my entire life, like

Jacob and the Angel. With the realization comes a wonderful sense of peace. Of certainty. Resolve.

A strength I have never felt swells up from deep inside me. A hidden flower that now blooms, to replace my beating heart.

"I need to go," I say, knowing what must be done. "I need to find Andrew."

David looks at me as if I've gone mad. And perhaps I have.

"They're still out there, Pete. Hell, for all you know, they're waiting on the other side of that door."

Obviously eavesdropping, Byron stands from his place at a nearby cot. "I'll go with you."

David eyes the mallet in Byron's grip and shudders. "You're both out of your minds."

"I need to know what's going on," I say, determined. "We need help. Locking ourselves in here isn't going to solve anything."

After a moment of consideration, he finally relents. "All right," he says. "But I'm going with you."

I put a hand on his shoulder. "I don't think so. Watch the others. Protect them."

He looks to me, then Byron, his face conflicted. "Fine, I'll play mother hen. But be careful, yeah? Try to remember, they're just kids. They're just like us."

I offer a reassuring smile, even though I know, in my heart, that he's wrong.

They're not kids. They're not orphans.

And they're not the children we know.

Not anymore.

40

"The slumbering giant awakens."

Johnson is facedown in the dirt. His head feels foggy and his mouth is bleeding. He slides a hand to the cold earth where his head landed, feels a smooth hard stone the size of a baby's skull. He spits blood into the dirt and pushes himself up off the ground. His fingers sink into the earth and for a moment his mind is flooded with grim imagery:

... screaming while being buried alive, clawing through the mud, seeking air, seeking light ... In a coffin, dirt hitting the top as he yells out that I'M ALIVE, DAMN YOU, I'M ALIVE ... Inside a closet, his mother talking to him through the door. "I can HEAR you. I hear you in there. That's more time! More time for you, Teddy." And he claws at the door but it's not a door it's dirt and it crumbles beneath his fingers because this is not a closet and this is not his childhood. This is a grave. He's buried in the ground, trapped deep down where the sun doesn't reach and the bugs and worms crawl into his hair, crawl over his digging hands, climb mercilessly into his eyes, his mouth, seeking life, seeking flesh.

"Stop!"

The images vanish like the snuffing of a candle. He's breathing heavy, hunched over on all fours, staring at the dirt at the bottom of the hole. His stomach boils and he wants to vomit, but holds it in, focuses on deep breaths. His skin is tingling, as if his limbs are asleep, and his mind feels untethered, no longer part of his body. If feels as though his entire being is in the hands of another, some awesome *power*, his body tied to his spirit by nothing but a flimsy thread of black yarn.

He raises his face slowly, looks through strands of clotted

hair. His head throbs. A bloody string of drool slips from his bottom lip. He sees Bartholomew, standing against the far wall, hands folded neatly in front of him, ankles crossed. His face a pale blur in the darkness.

Near Bartholomew, huddled into the near corner, knees drawn up to his chin, perceptibly shaking, is Ben. He looks so small in the thick shadows. Johnson can't see either of them clearly, the light from above is dim—darker, he realizes, than the early-afternoon light he was walking in when first going for the horses. The day has grown late.

The horses. Cut up. Butchered.

He shakes his head, grunts, and forces himself to his feet. The hole seems much smaller with him inside of it. He looks up toward the opening, gauging the distance. Were he to jump he could almost touch the open trapdoor with his fingertips.

Almost.

"What is this?" His words are thick, groggy. Slurry. "How long have I been down here?"

Bartholomew takes a step forward, and Johnson— inexplicably—fights off the urge to take a step *back*.

Something's wrong with him. Something is very off about this boy.

He looks over to Ben, as if for answers, but the child simply cowers. Johnson wonders if Ben's mind is broken, or if he's simply so frozen he can't think straight.

"I must have slipped," Johnson mumbles, answering his own question. A *sane* answer to how he got down here.

No, something pulled at me. Something seized me, yanked me down here.

It whispered in my ear . . . what?

I'm here . . . and then: Join us.

And whatever grabbed me . . . was strong.

"Impossible," he murmurs. He studies his dirty hands, then glances up once more at the open trapdoor—snow flurrying past, a charcoal sky above—then back to Ben in the corner. His eyes rove everywhere, everywhere except at the skinny boy now walking toward him.

Here, in the dark beneath the earth, Johnson is stunned to realize he's *frightened* of the child. He feels it in his bones, in his guts.

Pure, naked terror.

What's wrong with me?

He takes a sideways step toward Ben, away from Bartholomew, who pauses, eyebrows raised in curiosity. Johnson ignores him for now, tries to study the other boy more clearly through the gloom. "Ben? Are you okay?"

Ben's only response is to lower his forehead into the arms crossed over his knees; to shrink away even more than he already has. To hide inside himself.

"Ben's a little peaked right now, Brother Johnson."

Now Johnson turns, finally, to face Bartholomew. He's relieved at what he sees, what he feels. *Just a boy*, he thinks, almost grinning at his own fear, his stupidity. *Just another brat that needs dealing with.* He takes a step toward Bartholomew—in the confined space, he hopes it will intimidate the boy. He badly wants to wipe that little smirk off his face, wants to see fear in his big brown eyes. "What's wrong with him? Tell me."

But Bartholomew does not step backward, or frown in discomfort, or look in any way *afraid*. Instead, he puts a thoughtful finger to his chin. A doctor discussing a patient. "I'd say he's suffering from indecision. I think he's having a hard time deciding what to do."

Ben begins breathing more heavily. More rapidly.

Johnson looks at the boy huddled in the corner. "That true, Ben? What's wrong? Decide what?"

Bartholomew's eyes widen with feigned bemusement. "Well, right now, for example, he's trying to decide whether to kill you . . ." He gives Ben a sad, parental look. "Or whether to die."

Johnson says nothing—his mind drawing nothing but hollow

words and empty ideas, as if he's flipping a deck of poker cards looking for an ace, but the faces are all blank. He can't think. Can't respond. Instead, he simply looks around the dark hole, as if the answers will come seeping through the mud walls like worms.

There are voices in the air. Overhead. Surprised, he spins and looks up toward the opening. There are shadows now, their movement breaking up the dying light.

"Brother Johnson?"

His head snaps back to Bartholomew, who now wears a quizzical expression. Johnson's mouth works, but no sound comes out. His lips are quivering, as if he might start blubbering in front of this brat. There's a loud *KNOCK* from above. He gasps in fear, twists his head once more to observe the trapdoor, the flittering shadows. Tears sting his eyes, and a sob escapes his throat.

"Are you okay, Brother Johnson?" Bartholomew asks, gesturing toward the cold dirt floor. "Perhaps you should sit down."

His brain is stabbed with heat, sharp and painful, as if he's been rammed through the forehead with a red-hot needle. He sees a flash of white and he screams. Grimacing, he clutches the sides of his head. His legs give out and he crumples to the dirt like a ragdoll. Whimpering uncontrollably now, he shuffles himself backward, leans his back against the moist, frigid wall.

Dear God in heaven, help me. Let me THINK.

Bartholomew approaches him. The voices from above grow louder.

There's laughter.

"I've been whispering to him, Brother Johnson. Ben, I mean. While you were inside having fun with the others—and I heard it was a *lot* of fun—I was out here. Whispering. I think . . ." He turns his head, looks into the corner where Ben is huddled, then back to Johnson. "I think I frightened him. He hasn't been saying much. I don't think he liked what I told him."

He takes a step closer to the large man, now sitting, much like Ben, pressed against the wall, knees drawn up. He bends, puts his hands on his knees, as if addressing a small, lost child.

"Shall I whisper some things to you, Brother Johnson?"

"Get the fuck away from me," Johnson says, and then—in his tortured mind—the boy is not a boy, but a serpent. A black-headed snake, darting red tongue flicking at his face. *Flick flick flick.* No! Now he's a goat, horned and dark as death. Johnson blinks. Now he sees a beautiful woman, smiling, buck naked from head to toe, her skin slick with blood.

Johnson moans, closes his eyes tight.

When he opens them, Bartholomew is a boy once more. A pale, bone-thin sapling of a child. Weak and malnourished, doe-eyed and insolent.

Must have hit my head on that rock harder than I thought, he thinks. *There's something very wrong with me . . . something broken in my head. Not thinking straight. I need help, yes, I need medical attention. I need to get OUT OF HERE.*

Bartholomew pokes Johnson in the head. "You awake?"

Johnson slaps at the hand and sobs. "Get away!"

"Here's an interesting fact," Bartholomew says, pulling his hand away with lightning speed, undaunted, and wholly unconcerned about Johnson's wrath. His body moves hypnotically side to side, his face wavers, slides and drifts, as if he's underwater. Johnson rubs his eyes roughly, mixing blood and mud into his sockets, desperate to cease the visions. "Before you came into Poole's service, you were a troubled man. You were . . . a *married* man, am I right?"

"Shut up," Johnson says, but without much heat. His eyes are closed tight, his jaw is clenched. He mumbles whatever prayers he can remember. The bleeding crack in his head screams and burns like fire.

"Yes, married. And you had a beautiful baby boy. Isn't that nice? Do you remember him, Teddy?" Bartholomew pauses.

"Oh, do you mind if I call you that? It's familiar, I know. Maybe I should stick to Brother Johnson, hmm? We're not exactly friends. Not yet." Bartholomew winks, then continues jovially, as if recounting a favorite joke. "Anyway, one night you were very drunk. I mean, you were *very* drunk, and you hit your wife while she was holding sweet, tiny baby William. I like that name, by the way. It's . . . comforting, isn't it?"

"How do you . . ." Johnson swallows, the pain of buried memories tightening his throat. "Please stop."

"You hit her so hard that she fell backward down a flight of steps. More than ten and less than twenty, am I right? You know, the ones leading from your shitty hovel to the front door of the building you shared with the other pathetic, wretched people who lived there. She fell down the stairs, and then she didn't move. William, also, didn't move. Or cry. Or . . . much of anything, I suppose. Remember?"

Johnson nods. He weeps into his knees. "Yes," he says.

"Because his head was cracked open like an egg. His brains spilling out like broken yolk. And the mother—your wife—had broken her bloody neck!" Bartholomew stands up straight, eyes wide with appreciation. "That must have been some blow, Brother Johnson. Quite the strike, I'd say."

Johnson remembers it all. His family destroyed. The police taking him. The neighbors screaming. *It was an accident!* he'd cried, cried and cried until his voice was raw. *An accident!*

Something drops from the trapdoor, lands with a *thunk* in the dirt at Bartholomew's feet. He bends over and picks it up.

It's a claw hammer.

"So!" Bartholomew wiggles the hammer in front of Johnson's eyes, then pulls it back. "Here we are. And we have much to do." Bartholomew walks over to Ben, whose face is no longer buried, but now watches them both with wide, white eyes.

Bartholomew drops the hammer at Ben's feet. "I'm going to give each of you the same choice. Ben here, if he chooses, can pick up this hammer and beat your skull with it. Beat it against your thick head until it's nothing but broken bone and red mush. Like William's was, now that I think about it. And here's the kicker . . . Brother Johnson, are you listening? Believe me when I say this: You won't lift a hand to stop him. You'll sit right where you're sitting now, and you'll *take* it. You'll feel every blow, hear every crunch of breaking bone as your vision grows dim and blood pumps out your ears and nose, and then you will hear the beating of your heart slowing, slowing, until you slump over . . . and die."

Bartholomew picks the hammer up once more. Johnson notes, in some distant, distracted part of his mind, that Ben never moved an inch to take it.

"Or . . . *you* take Ben's life. And you live." Bartholomew seems to loom larger, his voice impossibly sonorous in the underground pit. "But you no longer live for Poole, *brother.*" He spits this last word like an insult and smiles widely. Too widely. "You live for *me.* You live for *us.*"

The voices above hoot and laugh. Sticks and feet clamor against the wood through the snow. The sound grows—more insistent, faster, louder. The chaotic rhythm fills the hole, clouds Johnson's mind. Guilt and hate and rage and deep, deep fear flood through him like icy water. Something inside his chest, in his very soul, becomes *dislodged*—an almost tactile sense of loss—and then it slides out and away, through his flesh, into the muck, into the abyss that lies beyond, that eternal darkness that waits to consume that which we lose, which we give away, which is taken.

"Lastly," Bartholomew continues, "if both of you refuse, and because I personally believe in free will, then the ones you hear above will come down here . . . and they'll kill you both. Chop you up like kindling and feed your guts to the earth."

Scurrying like a spider, Bartholomew skitters to Johnson on all fours, grabs a fistful of hair, and raises his head. His black, swirling eyes bore into Johnson's own, dissolving all thought, all purity. "Did you see the horses, Brother Johnson?" His voice is almost a hiss. A barely audible suggestion. "We'll do the same to you, Teddy. We'll carve you up and bury your bones in this fucking pit." Bartholomew turns and spits. "Which is no more than what you deserve."

Johnson, weary and confused, his body cold and numb, shakes his head. "No . . ." he says, disgusted at the simpering sound of his own voice.

Bartholomew lets go of Johnson's hair, stands straight, and takes a step back. His mouth is no longer smirking, but serious, composed. When he speaks again, his tone is clipped and direct, the voice of someone used to giving orders.

"Then do what needs doing."

There's a howling wind rushing through Johnson's mind. It fills him, consumes him. A screeching black storm made up of a thousand insects festers in his head, their clattering jaws and tapping legs so loud as to deafen out all thought, all rational decisions. All hope.

He's surprised to feel himself standing.

His dull eyes shift toward the small boy in the corner, and the boy looks back.

The pounding above crescendos. Incredibly loud, impossibly fast. Bartholomew is still speaking—talking rapidly, spitting out indecipherable, guttural sounds, the words foreign. Meaningless. The old part of Johnson's brain doesn't understand them but, in a new way, he *does* understand.

He understands many things now.

His past returning. Reprisal for the things he's done.

What waits for him behind the curtain of life. What waits for them all.

"I've never been baptized," he mumbles, but Bartholomew ignores him, still spitting strange words, his eyes turned to whites.

Johnson finds himself kneeling in front of Ben. He doesn't recall walking, but he's here. He's here now.

The insects crawl through his mind, his ears, his nose, his mouth. They scream their song, buzzing louder, louder. A deafening, pulsing chaos.

Ben is also screaming. Kicking and thrashing. Punching wildly.

"NO! Johnson are you MAD! Get away from me, you bastard! Get away from me!"

With a quick movement, Johnson grabs the boy's head between his strong hands. He pulls his body toward him with a hard, decisive jerk. Ben screams, but Johnson can't hear it. Can't hear the begging and the tears. Can't feel shame or remorse or guilt or indecision.

"Don't hurt me!" Ben cries, begs, muffled against his arm. "Oh Jesus, please don't hurt me."

But, for Johnson, there is nothing but the storm inside his head. Nothing but the pounding terror of death crawling toward him on hands and knees, a serpent's head on an insect body, long and deformed.

He won't let it take him.

He won't go beyond the veil. Not yet.

"Don't worry, boy," he mumbles, an unfelt tear sliding down his filthy cheek. "I'll make it quick."

Ben is able to shriek out one final thing before Johnson's mind snaps and he lets himself fall into that wonderful, warm abyss, that thought-dulling void: "You can't, Johnson, you can't! You'll be damned!"

He leans in, presses a muscled forearm against the boy's throat. He wraps the other arm around the head. Holds him tight.

Then, he squeezes.

Johnson does not feel horror.

He feels relief.

He feels reborn.

The child's cries become strangled, gagging chokes.

Johnson puts his mouth close to the small head entwined within his arms, whispers his dark secret into the dying child's ear.

"I'm already damned."

PART FOUR
SACRIFICE

41

I find Andrew on his knees in prayer.

He's lined up the bodies (*my God so many bodies*) along the wall of the chapel. Somehow, he's managed to procure enough linens to cover all of them, although I notice a few rough blankets, most likely taken from the priests' beds.

At the end lies Father White, the obvious grown man among the row of children, who will never have need of a blanket again.

I look around furtively, waiting for murderous brothers to spring from hallways or spill from a doorway, screaming, knives raised, eyes filled with madness and murder.

So far, however, there's been no sign. Byron and I made it out of the dorm without problem. Byron stayed close to me the entire time, never letting go of the bloodied hammer. I carry no weapon, which is my choice. I could never hurt another boy, a brother orphan. Not with a weapon, at least. I'd fight to survive, and I would use fists and feet if needed to defend myself, but not to kill. Not to permanently harm another.

Once we left the dorm, and David sealed the door behind us, we walked brusquely, soundlessly, down the long hallway. Our eyes never left the open and closed doors on both sides of the corridor: the washroom, the cloakroom, the classrooms. We passed each without incident, without a second attack. My heart was beating so hard I believed I felt it bumping against my ribs, pushing me to go *faster, faster*.

When we reached the balcony overlooking the foyer, we saw Andrew and the bodies. We stayed there a few moments, inspecting corners and shadows from above, making sure no one waited to spring out at us once we descended the stairs.

The whole thing is terrifying, and I'm grateful that Byron is with me. He's violent and vicious, but he's loyal, and even though I am no warrior, I'm glad to have one with me. I don't wish anyone harm but, given what I've seen already this day, I am not so naïve to think the murderers care a whit for my pacifism.

They'd stab me through the heart while I prayed for their forgiveness.

But such is the nature of faith.

As we approached Andrew, I was fearful of startling him, and made a point to call his name as we came down the stairs. He stayed where he was, crouched over a corpse, offering a few last words to God, a whispered "amen" before standing and turning to greet us.

My first impression was that he looked ten years older than the man I knew, the man I'd ridden to the Hill farm and back with only a day ago.

My second impression was that he looked scared.

"Peter." His eyes flick to Byron, noting, I'm sure, the bloody mallet, but he says nothing other than: "Hello, Byron. Are you hurt?"

"No, Father."

Andrew nods. His eyes glance around the room. "I don't think it's safe here. I don't know where the . . . where the *others* are. They might be outside, I suppose. They're hiding . . ."

There's something in Andrew's voice that gives me pause. A shakiness I've never heard before. His eyes shift wildly, and I wonder if I appear as trapped and fearful as he does.

I hope not.

"Peter, tell me. What's happening in the dormitory? How are the others?" he asks, his determination, his lucidity and command, obvious. I shake away my previous concerns. This is Andrew, after all. The very best of us.

"We count fourteen, Andrew," I say. "That includes me and David, and of course Byron here."

Andrew nods, doing the numbers in his head.

"How many?" I ask.

He looks at me, not understanding at first. Then he sees my eyes lingering on the white shapes lining the floor behind him. "Oh . . ." He lets out a held, shaky breath. "Nine boys. And Father White . . . those poor children."

He covers his face with both hands for a moment, sniffs loudly.

"Andrew?"

When he removes his hands, his eyes are watery, he looks ill.

"Are you okay?" I ask.

"I'll be fine, Peter. This is all just a shock."

I nod, and share a quick look with Byron, who seems more unsettled every second we stand here talking. Exposed. "What about the other priests, Andrew? Where are Poole and Johnson? It would help if the children could see a priest, an adult."

"Poole is resting in his chamber," he says. "His leg was badly wounded and it's difficult for him to walk. I told him to lock the door and I pray he did. I don't know where Brother Johnson is. I looked in his room, in the kitchen, but he's not there. I don't know where he is . . ."

"What about those kitchen folks?" Byron says, pointing toward the dining hall with the bloodied hammer.

I notice Andrew staring sickly at the weapon. He swallows, then replies. "Gone."

"Huh?" Byron says, and I share his confusion.

"Do you think they went to get help?" I ask. "Maybe with Brother Johnson?"

Andrew's face goes slack, his expression vacant. Part of me wants to take his hand and sit him down. Get him some tea, or some wine, until the shock wears off. The other part of me wants to shake him, tell him to *keep it together.* He's the only adult we have right now, and we need him. I certainly don't want to be alone with this. I can't do it alone.

"Father?" I say, more sharply than is polite, or friendly, but I do get his attention. His eyes focus once more, and he seems to have, temporarily at least, found his wits.

"I'm sorry." He takes a deep breath, lets it out. "Okay. We need a plan, yes? Peter, I think you should go to the Hill farm. Tell John what's happened. Get as much help as you can, as quickly as you can, and come back. Do you feel up to that? You're the only one who knows the way."

I have a flash of Grace's face in my mind, then quickly push it away, feeling ashamed. I instead focus on the road I'd need to take through the increasingly heavy snow. I mentally tick off the landmarks that would still be visible despite the snowfall. I'm sure I can do it. Regardless, I'm confident the horses will know the way.

"Okay," I say. Suddenly, I'm eager to be off, to get help. To take action. I want to tell Andrew what I know, what I *believe*, but I don't see what good it would do except to frighten Byron. Right now, getting help is the best idea. What comes after that, will come.

"Good." Andrew turns to Byron. "I want you to go into the chapel and help out the two boys resting in there. One has a badly twisted ankle and will need assistance getting to the dorm. The other, Paul, has a bad cut to the eye. I'm sorry to say he'll lose it, despite my best efforts. Both of them are together. I wanted them in there in case. Well . . ."

"In case the others returned," Byron says, nodding. "They could bar the doors. Smart." Byron's clinical, emotionless tone is a restorative tonic amidst all the fear and turmoil.

"Thank you," Andrew replies, smiling genuinely for the first time since we arrived. "Can you get them both safely to the dormitory?"

I notice, once again, Andrew's eyes flick to the mallet.

"Yes, Father," Byron says. "I think the upstairs is clear. At least we didn't see anyone whilst coming to you. My guess is they're all together somewhere, regrouping. Maybe the barn, maybe the storage room, maybe someplace we haven't thought of."

He shrugs as if the idea of ten boys hiding somewhere plotting murder is the most natural thing in the world, and I want to hug him for being stalwart. His bravery is contagious, and I make a note to myself to show the same trait around the others, as best I'm able, anyway. It may bring comfort.

"Then go, please, and thank you. Peter, I'll help you saddle one of the horses so you can ride to the farm. Then I'll come back and meet up with the other boys in the dormitory."

Without so much as a glance back, Byron heads for the chapel. Andrew and I begin walking for the front doors, when he turns back. "And Byron?"

Byron stops at the chapel entrance. From across the large foyer, I see him not as some great protector, but as the child he is. A brave, but frightened, little boy.

"When you get them safe, stay put." Then, to me: "Are the doors secured?"

"Yes, Father."

"Good," Andrew says, then raises his voice toward Byron once more. "And whatever you do, don't open them for anyone but Peter or myself." Byron nods a final time, then disappears into the chapel.

Andrew's hand clutches at my sleeve. His eyes are haunted.

"I don't know who we can trust anymore," he says quietly, and I nod, knowing exactly how he feels.

42

A few minutes later, they find the horses.

Andrew is staggered by the brutality of it; still reeling from the events in the chapel, all that death . . . and now this. *Butchered*, he thinks, for there's no other way to describe what had been done to the animals.

Peter, badly shaken, stumbles away from the stalls. He leans a hand against a wall and vomits whatever meager sustenance may still reside in his stomach. The sound of flies fills the air with the humming tune of death.

Finally, Andrew backs away, walks over to Peter. "Are you okay?" he asks. Peter wipes his mouth and nods, his face deathly pale in the barn's dim light. Together, they walk back toward the main doors—and it's only now that Andrew realizes how strange it was to have found them already open.

Perhaps Brother Johnson was here? Or, I suppose, whoever did that to those poor animals. I'll need to be more careful—more wary—if I'm to get through this alive, if I'm to help the children get through it. I can't withstand any more death, please God, no more.

"Andrew?" Peter's voice is steady, eager. His eyes are fixed on the horizon, as if judging its cruelty. "Perhaps I can walk to the farm."

Peter's bravery gives Andrew hope, but he is already shaking his head, having already thought of the option and dismissed it. Even if the boy wasn't undernourished, it would be too much of a challenge. Too large of a risk. "No, it's getting late, and dark," he says with a heavy sigh. "Maybe if it was morning, but now . . . you could easily get lost if the storm gets much worse. I think the odds would be stacked against you."

Nothing to do about it now, and we must get back to the dorm,
he thinks. *Figure out a way to reach help. Perhaps Johnson will
return . . .*

Andrew readies to close the doors when Peter speaks again,
his voice firm in the shadowy recesses of the barn, as if he'd been
building up the will to ask the question. "Father, what happened
the other night? To the man brought by the sheriff. The one who
died."

Andrew turns, studies Peter's face. "What are you concerned
about?"

But Andrew knows, because he's been thinking the same
thing. And Peter is no fool, not to mention a priest-in-training.
He can make the connection as easy as anyone.

There was an infestation, he thinks. But keeps that thought to
himself.

For now.

Peter looks at the ground, gathers his thoughts. "It's just . . .
this all started that night." He looks up to meet Andrew's eye.
"That man. There was something wrong with him, wasn't there?
Besides being hurt, I mean."

The two of them stand just inside the partially open doors of
the barn. The dying daylight, reflected off the silver-toned snow,
casts Peter in an eerie light. A hazy glow that makes Andrew
think of a halo, a nimbus effect causing the boy to appear insub-
stantial, as if Andrew is being visited by a spirit.

The light has another unsettling consequence. The way it
glints off Peter's eyes. As if the boy is fevered, or raving. Perhaps
suffering from delirium.

"His soul was poisoned, if that's what you're asking," Andrew
says finally, cautiously. "I won't go into the details of his troubles,
Peter. It won't help us through this."

"Father, please. Tell me who he was. Why did the sheriff
bring him?"

Andrew sighs. Peter has always been good at getting him to

talk, to give him information he should not be giving. It is his love for the boy that weakens him. But that's what love is, ultimately. A form of blessed weakness.

"Okay," he says, debating what he should say, what he should not. "I'll tell you what I can. The man was the sheriff's brother. He brought him because, well, he'd been shot. He was dying, and the sheriff hoped Father Poole could save him. Due to his medical training in the war . . ."

"Shot?" Peter says, wide-eyed.

Andrew nods. "That's right. But Poole couldn't save him. We tried, but the man died."

Peter thinks on this a moment, as if debating its truth. "But there were two bodies. One left in the wagon, the other buried here."

Curse the curiosity of a child, Andrew thinks. Too tired to think of a good excuse, a good lie, he does what is easiest. Under the circumstances, what could it matter?

He tells the truth.

"That was one of the deputies. Paul—the man who was shot— was quite fevered, Peter. Raving, in fact. He managed to kill one of the deputies before we could subdue him. It was tragic, awful."

"He was insane?"

Andrew does not immediately answer, but instead looks out toward the snow-covered landscape, the dimming sky. "Perhaps."

"Andrew, tell me the truth about one thing," Peter says, and Andrew finds himself forced to look directly at the boy, to meet his questioning stare. "Was the man possessed?"

"Possessed?" Andrew tries to imitate shock, but fails. He looks at the ground, toes some old hay into the hard earth with the tip of one boot. "I don't know, is the answer. God help me, I don't know. When they found him, he and some others had been performing a . . . well, a ritual of some kind. They killed a young girl, Peter. That's why he'd been shot by the sheriff's men. I don't know if that means he was possessed by devils, or simply insane, like you suggest." Andrew sighs heavily, studying the heavy carpet of snow, the swirling flakes falling, falling . . . "He was evil. That much I can say with assurance."

Now it is Peter's turn to study the ground, the drifting snowflakes.

What's he thinking about? Andrew wonders, but waits, knowing it will come in time. Peter is stubborn as a mule when it comes to questions needing answers, and Andrew knows he will not let this go until he is satisfied.

"When the man died," he says warily, as if even he isn't sure he wants the answers he is seeking, "something strange happened inside the dormitory. The doors were thrown open, as if by a strong wind. And the cross . . . it fell to the floor. It was as if . . ."

Andrew waits, trying to temper his own apprehension.

"As if something *entered* that room, Father," Peter says, his eyes no longer delirious, or frightened, or feverish. They look at Andrew steadily. Cold. Assured. "As if something had come inside . . . and settled there."

Andrew feels sick to his stomach. His muscles turn watery, and he has to fight off a wave of lightheadedness.

It's not possible . . .

He recalls Paul Baker's tattooed body. The impossibility of the wound, surely fatal in any other man.

The words he said to Poole.

WE ARE MANY.

He recalls that, for a moment, both priests were convinced the man was possessed. They spoke the rites . . . the holy water . . .

"Andrew, what if what was inside that man," Peter asks, speaking with more urgency now, knowing he's on to something dark, something impossible, "if what harbored inside him was somehow . . . released?"

"Enough!" Andrew winces at the sharpness of his tone, but he's shaken, upset. He wants to hear no more of this. The boy is scared, in shock, surely desperate for answers as to why his friends could do something so horrible.

He takes a few steps away, deeper into the dark of the barn. He breathes deeply.

When he speaks again, he tries to soften his tone, but the sharp edge still remains, albeit lessened. "Look, Peter, I know you're confused. And I know you're frightened. But we need to focus. These children that are doing this, they're . . . angry. They're desperate. They're filled with hate. But they are just *boys*, Peter. The same ones you've known most of your life. They're nothing but flesh and blood. Do you understand?"

Peter stares back at him, a thin shadow standing before the backdrop of framed daylight. Only the whites of his eyes are clearly visible—wide and frantic. Zealous.

But then, finally, he turns away, and his face catches the light, showing the confusion written there, reminding Andrew how young he is. That he's nothing but a scared child. "I understand, Father. I'm sorry," he says.

Andrew sighs with relief. This is not something he will entertain. He won't.

He can't.

"That's fine, that's good. Now, let's get back to the dormitory. I'm anxious to check on the children."

Andrew walks past Peter, out into the dying day. His boots kick through thick snow. He grabs the door to push it closed, then snatches back his hand, as if the wood is covered in burning thorns.

He ducks back behind the door, grips Peter's wrist tightly.

"What is it?" Peter asks, trying to look through the gap of the door's hinge, to see what has drawn Andrew's attention.

"No, stay back," Andrew says, whispering.

But Peter already has an eye to the crack between the hinged door and the barn. "I see them. They're going inside."

Andrew releases a held breath. His heart races. "Let me see."

Peter moves over and Andrew puts his own eye to the crack. He watches as the last boy enters the orphanage. He isn't able to tell how many there were, having only seen the tail-end of the group. But at least two, maybe three.

Maybe more.

"What do we do?"

Andrew looks at the sky, as if hoping the answer is written above. "We'll wait a few minutes, then we'll follow. We must get inside and make sure the other children are safe."

"What if that's where they're going?"

"I don't know," Andrew replies.

"And what of Poole? Or Johnson?"

"Peter, I don't *know*." Andrew takes a deep breath. He needs to control his fear if he's to help the orphans. "I'm sorry," he says, and turns to Peter, a sad smile on his face. "Pray for them," he says. "And pray for us." Andrew puts a hand on Peter's shoulder. "Now we know how Daniel felt, readying himself for the lion's den."

Peter smiles. "That turned out okay."

"That it did, son. Okay . . . let's go."

Andrew and Peter begin their walk through the accumulating snow, back toward the orphanage. They have gone only a few steps when Peter grips Andrew's arm.

"What is it?"

Peter is looking away, toward the fields.

"Ben and Bartholomew," he says. "They must still be in there."

Andrew tries to recall who he saw walking into the orphanage. Was one of them Bartholomew? He looks at the tracks the others made, a blurry gray line running through the sheet of white, a jagged line cutting from the hole's trapdoor to the front doors of the orphanage.

"I think that's where they *were*, Peter. But let's check, anyway. Quickly."

They jog toward the hole. Andrew looks everywhere—at the

doors, the fields, back to the barn. He doesn't want to be surprised again.

Despite his faith, he has no wish to die anytime soon.

They reach the wood platform. The snow all around has been trampled away by many, many feet.

"What happened here?" Peter asks, but Andrew has no answer. Instead, he kneels down, lifts up the closed trapdoor. He looks down into the dark pit.

And sees nothing.

"Hello!" He yells, just loudly enough to stir any bodies that may remain below, but not loud enough to alarm the ones inside. "Anyone there?"

They wait for a response, but the darkness is absolute and quiet as death.

"It must have been why they were here, to pull out the boys," Peter says, and Andrew agrees. He finds it hard to believe Ben would cast his lot with murderers, but much has surprised him recently, and he is in no position to make assumptions on the natures of the children he loves so dearly. Or, at least, those he once did.

"Well, there's no one here now. Come on, we best get inside, and hope we don't run into the others."

Peter bends down, begins to raise the trapdoor in order to seal the black pit.

He pauses.

"What is it?" Andrew asks, turning to leave.

After a moment, Peter lets the door close. "Nothing," he says. "I thought I saw something, in the shadows. But I was wrong."

Andrew nods, knowing it doesn't matter if he was wrong or not. If someone was down there, they weren't moving, and they weren't calling for help.

Not anymore.

43

Sullen and servile, Johnson watches as Bartholomew tries to open the thick wooden door.

He could have told the boy that Poole likely threw the iron bolt into place, but since leaving the hole it's been hard for him to find the right *words*. The buzzing in his head is so loud—that black cloud of insects (he now imagines them as fat, black flies) swarming behind his eyes, between his ears—cancels out everything else: all thought, all memories. Although his sight and hearing are, mostly, intact, speaking seems impossible. Like lifting giant bags of sand from deep water.

"Brother Johnson . . ." Bartholomew says. An order.

He knows what he must do. The instructions come to him from the flies. They are as clear and commanding as the voice of God.

Bartholomew steps aside as Johnson takes a step back, then kicks his boot at the spot where the bolt rests on the opposite side. The clasp housing the bolt blasts from the frame. The door bursts inward with a shower of splinters and an old man's scream from within.

The boys flow into the room as a slick line, an eager serpent slithering through a hole in a broken wall, as if smelling a digestible infant asleep on the other side.

Poole lies in his bed, the very one Paul Baker died upon only a few nights prior. As Johnson enters, the priest is perched up on one elbow, eyes wide with fear and indignation. "What is this? Get out!"

Johnson doesn't want to look at Poole. Doesn't want to see the betrayal on his face, the shock, the disappointment. Instead, he walks straight to a far corner and slumps down into it, head hanging on a loose neck, hair covering his features. The swarm in his head intensifies. He presses his hands onto his eyes to keep the bugs from escaping.

"Johnson? Johnson!" Poole screeches. "What are you doing?"

But Johnson doesn't reply. Even though he can hear the words, he doesn't allow himself to *feel* the words. He focuses instead on the noise inside his head. The instructions.

He loses himself to the swarm, lets his body go slack.

"How are we feeling, Father Poole?" Bartholomew says. There are snickers from the other boys, seven in all. The lion's share of the rebels. The totality of what evil has brought to the small orphanage.

And yet, there is another.

But, like Johnson, each of the boys has their own instruction. Their own tasks to perform.

"Your leg looks rather angry, Father Poole," Bartholomew says, tutting. "That wound is deep."

Despite himself, despite the swarm, Johnson dares to lift his eyes. He wants to see this . . . this *command* over Jeremiah Poole. He wants to see the man humiliated, the way he has humiliated Johnson for so many years.

Your dog is sick, master. The thought flows through the noise and he grins, loving the sound of his own inner voice mingling with the swarm. It feels glorious. *Your dog is sick. It's been bitten by a bat, or a rat, or a boy.* Johnson shows teeth. *Yes, bitten by a boy, and now it's sick. Now it's rabid.*

The swarm sings: *Lyssa! Rabere! Rabhas!*

Poole begins to pray. Johnson watches him from the floor; watches as he presses his cross to his lips, eyes closed. Murmuring nonsense to a deaf, uncaring god.

Bartholomew laughs, then turns and catches Johnson's eye. Something passes between them. Instruction.

Still, Johnson does not move. Not yet.

"Enough, Father. You're boring us, and we have much to discuss."

Poole's eyes snap open, lock on Bartholomew. Filled with hate.

"Are you so weak, demon? That you infest the innocent?"

Johnson looks from face to face. A few of the boys are frowning now. Not so confident. Not so cheerful. Simon, seemingly unfazed, studies the drawers of Poole's dresser.

Bartholomew sits at the foot of Poole's bed. Unbothered.

"Why not ME!" Poole screams, holding the cross on his neck aloft, aiming it like a weapon at Bartholomew. "Why not infest someone who deserves your scorn and your hate? You coward! You spiteful trickster!"

"Enough!" Bartholomew snaps, and slaps a hand down on Poole's thigh, where the bandage wraps the wound. Johnson sees him *squeeze*, sees the blood spill from the cloth, run down the skinny white leg and into the sheets.

Poole shrieks in agony until, finally, Bartholomew releases his hand, wipes it on the bed. "I need you quiet, Father. I need you supple. I need to tell you things. I need to whisper things to you." He grins. "Think of it as a type of communion."

Poole's face, pale and stricken, turns to stare directly at Johnson, who feels caught in the old man's eyes. Trapped. "Johnson . . . for God's sake, help me."

The swarm swells—the sound it makes is *deafening*. There is a mad, insane clamoring in his head, a division of his mind, his reason torn apart by a million legs, ingested by thousands of black mouths. He shuts his eyes and moans, presses his hands to his ears.

Listen!

LISTEN!

Johnson nods, and obeys.

From one heartbeat to the next, the intensifying sound of the swarm becomes muted, soft and warm. He lowers his hands. He has pissed himself but does not know it, would not care if he did. He smiles, keeps his eyes closed, falls into the dark warmth.

"I'm sorry, Father, but Brother Johnson is with *us* now. That must be disappointing, given how much you've done for him. But your God is weak, is he not? We are so much stronger." Bartholomew's voice is distant, dreamlike. "You have no idea how strong we are."

Johnson hears the creak of metal, the rustle of sheets. A few boys begin murmuring in a dull rhythm. Something hits his face, falls into his lap.

He opens his eyes to see a stained, brown sack.

Bartholomew, ignoring Poole for the moment, turns his back on the priest and stares at Johnson instead. His eyes are gleeful and cunning, and he holds a brightly lit lantern. "Brother Johnson, please pay attention. That hood in your lap was left behind by a dead man, thrown into a corner and forgotten. Can you believe it? And now it's yours, Johnson. Aren't you lucky? Aren't you thankful?"

Johnson looks down at the sack. His thick, trembling fingers clutch it, feel the stiffness of dried, dark stains, the coarseness of the weave. *Thankful* . . . he thinks, not knowing what to do with the word, so he leaves it.

"Put it over your head, Teddy."

Johnson's eyes lift to Bartholomew in surprise. The boy is now kneeling beside him, black eyes intent, wide irises flickering in the lamplight. "Put it on now."

Johnson doesn't hesitate. He finds the sack's opening with his fingers, then lifts it and slides it down over his head. The stench is intense and instant. His tongue flicks out, tastes the sour fabric. He grimaces and studies the room from within his mask. The weave is loose, and it's as if he's peering through a veil. He can see shapes. Bodies. There is sight, but no clarity.

He glories in it.

"Let me show you something, Father Poole," Bartholomew is saying. "Let me show you an example of our strength, so that you do not doubt."

"May God rebuke thee! May he cast you back to Hell!" Poole shrieks.

"Keep praying, Father. Keep praying. But please, watch while you do so."

Something cold and syrupy-thick spills onto Johnson's head, onto the mask, from above. It seeps through the cloth, instantly soaks his hair, slides across his scalp, leaks down his temples, into his eyes. It reaches his lips. He opens his mouth and licks his top lip, wanting to taste it. It's bitter.

The boys are all murmuring louder. Their chant mixes with the sound of the swarm and Johnson is blinking away the oil and he badly wants to stay inside this dark place forever because it feels *safe*, like a mother's womb, like a lover's embrace.

"Watch now," Bartholomew says.

Johnson sees the dark, distorted shape of Bartholomew stand. The light in his hand diminishes, then grows bright. It fills his eyes!

Pain explodes as the lantern smashes into his head. The oil catches rapidly and blazes against his skin. In a matter of seconds, the fire eats away his hair, his eyes, his lips.

Johnson screams! He leaps to his feet, slaps his head. The flesh of his fingers and palms becomes singed, the skin blisters and burns. He pulls his hands away, still screaming, panic and fear and pain bursting through every nerve, boiling his blood.

He runs, directionless, wanting to be anywhere but with this pain—desperate to get away from the flames.

He slams face-first into a wall and is knocked backward. Sharp edges and hard blows begin punching his back, his hips, his arms. He is spinning, knocking into unseen objects and shrieking in desperation, crying out madly from the pain.

Everyone around him is also screaming, but these are screams of laughter, of hysterical joy. God, there are so many voices!

And the swarm swells like a mighty host behind his scalded eyes and it begins to *sing*—a jubilant, buzzing chorus made of a thousand shrieking voices, rising to a maddening crescendo as he burns.

44

I knock lightly at the dormitory doors, holding my breath. I can't quit looking behind me toward the long, empty hallway. I wonder what happened to the bodies of those who fell on our mad run only hours ago. George. Jonathan.

Andrew stands beside me, looking apprehensive.

After our return from the barn, he insisted on going to the chapel once more. I waited at the bottom of the stairs, too terrified to go with him and wanting an escape route—either up the stairs or out the front doors—if attacked.

When Andrew re-entered the foyer, he carried a heavy-looking crozier, the top hooked into a flat spiral, the design supported by heavy knobs welded into the staff. It's taller than Andrew and appears to be made of iron, or some dark metal, although the top—that strange spiral—is painted dull gold. A good weapon for a priest, I suppose, if that's his intention.

Standing at the barred doors, waiting for the blasted kids to answer, I'm glad he has it.

Finally, a voice comes from the other side.

"Who is it?"

David.

"It's me and Andrew. Open the damn . . ." I sense Andrew turn his head toward me, and steady my voice. "Open the doors, please." I finish.

Several muffled voices talk at once. The sound of metal sliding away. One of the doors is pulled open, and David stands there. Behind him are several boys, including Byron.

All of them are armed.

I push through and Andrew follows.

"Anyone ch-ch-chasing you?" Timothy asks. He's got a folding ruler in his hands.

"Where did you get that?" I ask, slightly amused.

He looks abashed, turns to David, who answers for him.

"We raided the classroom for, uh . . ." He looks to Andrew, who raises his eyebrows but says nothing. "Well, weapons. To defend ourselves."

"A smart idea, David," Andrew says. "As you can see, I raided the priest's cabinet." He holds forth the crozier, and a few of the boys nod, some wide-eyed, as if seeing something holy in our crummy dormitory is somehow awe-inspiring. Andrew reaches into a pouch of his cassock and pulls out a glass vial, covered in spun silver, a cork stopper at the top. Part of the silver is woven into a cross.

Holy water.

"No offense, Father," David says. "But what's water good for against knives and hammers?"

Andrew inspects the bottle a moment, as if considering. "Well," he says, smiling at all the boys in turn. "Can't hurt, right?" I'm not surprised to see a few of us nodding.

"Did you gather anything else?" Andrew asks, tucking the blessed water away. "Besides the ruler, I mean."

David shakes his head. "Some pencils. A globe stand that might make a good head-knocker if push comes to shove. Harry found a letter opener, I think."

David leans in closer, lowers his voice. "Honestly, the place I really want to raid is the kitchen. These kids are hungry. Starving. We haven't eaten since breakfast, and that wasn't much to begin with. Even for this place."

I agree, and for the first time since the horrid memorial service I realize how hungry I am.

You get used to it after a while: the hunger. It becomes part of you. Familiar. You only really notice it after you've had a decent meal, and then time passes, and your body wants more. But there's nothing more to be had. Most of the time, though, it's there, inside you, festering and gnawing at your guts. Hearing David talk about food makes the craving inside me heighten its attack. It feels like my stomach is being folded in half, then wrung like wet laundry.

I realize now why he whispered about raiding the kitchen, and focused on finding weapons, lame and useless as they may be. If he can keep the boys' minds on danger, and on defending themselves, they'll likely forget they're starving. At least for a while.

"Maybe we can try later," Andrew says. "Besides that, how is everyone here? Anyone badly injured?"

"We're all good, Father," Byron says. "Scrapes and bruises. A few cuts. David's been keeping everyone tightened up. The little ones are resting, the older ones ready to do what needs doing."

David looks to the floor, likely embarrassed at the mild praise. "Just doing my best. I'm no guardian." Then he lifts his head, stares accusingly at Andrew. "You adults are supposed to be protecting us. You're the priests here. We're just a bunch of kids, despite what Peter thinks."

"Hey," I say, but Andrew interjects.

"I realize that, David, and I'm here now. You've done a fine job, and now I'll do my best. As for Poole, or Johnson . . . I don't know."

Timothy steps forward. "We saw the kitchen staff ru-ru-running for the hills," he says in his broken way, but loudly, proud of his report. "They were heading west, the th-th-three of 'em."

Andrew nods. "Maybe they'll get help," he says, but he sounds defeated, knowing it's a fabricated idea. The kitchen help, made up primarily of former prisoners and social outcasts, are likely fleeing to their meager homes, the penance they were paying not worth additional effort, or risk of harm.

"They'll be drunk by midnight," Byron says, "Likely toasting our demise."

No one speaks, or argues. We all know it's a lot closer to the truth than Andrew's idealized suggestion that they're bringing back help. Sometimes you just know the kind of person someone is, especially when they're lowly and selfish. You find they rarely disappoint.

"It's not the worst idea," David says, catching my eye with a significant look I don't fully understand. "Walking out of here, I mean."

Andrew is shaking his head. "No, Peter and I discussed this. It's already dark outside, the wind picking up. The snow will make it hard to see clearly, not to mention we'll have a good amount of buildup by morning. No path, no light . . . No, it's too risky."

"Then we take the horses," he says, pressing the issue.

"The horses are dead," I say. "Slaughtered."

Andrew gives me a surprised look at revealing the information, but then lowers his eyes and sighs, as if realizing, perhaps, this is not the time to withhold hard truths. "Look, you boys keep thinking," he says. "I want to go check on the others."

He walks away, kneels next to the cot of one of the younger kids, leaving David and me alone. I start to leave, but David grips my arm.

"Peter?" He speaks in a low voice, eyes shifting left and right. "*We* could go," he says. "You and me. We'd make it to the farm easy."

My poor stomach, already hungry and twisted with worry, now sinks. I'd hoped David had come around. Taken on more of a guardian role with the children, gained a sense of responsibility. It seems I was wrong.

"And leave the others to die?" I say, my tone quiet but sharp. He winces, and his eyes grow stormy in a way I've come to know well.

"Don't play Saint Peter with me. Not now. Not during . . . all this *shit*." He grips my elbow hard. "I want to live, Peter. I know you do, too. For yourself, for the lovely Grace waiting at the farm. You know the way, you've done that route a slew of times. I know we could make it."

"I don't agree. And even if I did, I'll never leave the others. They'll die without us."

"You're being selfish," he says, disgust on his face.

"How is helping them selfish?"

"Because it's for *you*," he says, poking me hard in the chest. "You buy into all the shit Andrew shovels at you, and it blinds you. Makes you think you're something you're not."

"Which is what?" I say, angry, but also uncertain.

"We're not their parents, Peter. We're not bloody *priests*." Tears well in his eyes, and some of my displeasure melts into compassion. I know he's scared. I am, as well.

But.

"I understand that," I say, trying to soothe him, but also wanting to instill a sense of honor into his bones. "But they *need* us. Andrew needs us. Together, we can keep everyone safe through the night. Then, in the morning, maybe you or I can go. When we have the light with us. But not both of us, and not in the dark. Look at them, David. Most of the older kids are with Bartholomew and the others. There's no one here but . . . children. Byron and Timothy are the only ones who could really fight if it came to it."

"And Andrew," David says, but I can tell he's giving up. The thought brings me no pleasure. "God, this is a nightmare."

"Besides," I say, deciding to take the risk of letting David know my thoughts on what's happened. Even if it means he thinks me insane. "I'm not sure what we're dealing with is completely . . . natural."

David looks at me skeptically. I expected no less. "What do you mean?"

I push forward, hoping he'll see my logic, my reasoning. See what Andrew did not . . . or at least did not want to. "Look, I wanted to tell you this before, but I thought . . . David, there's something dark at work here. Something evil. I don't know . . ." I look him in the eye, decide to trust him with this guarded secret. This uncanny belief. "I think those other boys are *possessed*, David. I think there are demons inside those boys, filling them with all this murderous hate. That man who died? I was talking to Andrew . . ."

"Wait wait wait . . . just wait a second," he says, looking at me as if I've grown a second head. As if I'm mad. "You think the reason those bastards are doing this is because they're *possessed*? Like, what, by the devil?"

I nod, but my face reddens. "I do."

"Jesus Christ, Pete. Had I known you were that far gone . . ." he says, shaking his head, ". . . good Christ."

"Stop it," I say, angry and embarrassed. Annoyed and sullen that he can't see what I see. "There is evil in this world we can't comprehend, David. The entire mountain of religion is built upon that fact. And that man who died here? That man was *possessed*. Andrew basically admitted as much. He'd been practicing the occult. Sacrificed a small girl, him and others . . ."

"Okay then, if this man released demons into the children, why are only half the kids acting nuts? Why not the priests? Hm? What about you? What about me?"

It's a point I've thought of, but I have no good answer for him, or myself. "Some wills are stronger than others, perhaps. Or, maybe some are more susceptible to possession." I shrug, knowing how lame it all sounds. "I don't expect to understand the ways of evil . . ."

"Jesus Christ. Look here, you want to see evil, Peter?" David says, thrusting both his hands up into my face, turning them so I have no choice but to stare at the backs of his scarred fingers, the broken, bent knuckle, the thick webbed tissue along the top of his hands and wrists where Poole strapped him when we were younger. In David's case, he would strap him until he bled. It happened more than once. "There, Peter. *There's* your fucking evil."

He grabs me roughly and pulls me aside, far from where anyone can overhear. "Those other kids? They're not *evil*, Pete. Not the way you think. They're just *mad*. They're broken. They're sick of this place. They're sick of the shit they've had to endure all these years. They're sick of being starved, of being bullied and beaten. Hell man, if it wasn't for you, I'd probably join them."

I can't help it, my mouth drops open. "You don't mean that."

"Don't I?" he snaps. "Do you know what's in my heart, Peter? Do you? Because I sure as hell don't," he hisses, his words choked by barely restrained tears.

He takes a deep breath, lets it out. His face softens, the rage seeping away like an early tide, leaving nothing but sorrow in its wake.

I don't know what to say. I'm filled with a deep, impenetrable sadness at all the things he must be feeling. The conflict. The hate. It makes me want to weep for him. I study his features, wishing—wishing more than anything—there was something I could do to take away the pain swirling inside him.

I place a hand on his shoulder. "Okay, okay. I hear you. But look, if we're going to beat whatever we're facing here, it needs to be you and me, little brother. You and me. Staying together is the only way we get through this."

David doesn't meet my eye, and I see the struggle inside him abating, worming back into his core to hide away, and I'm grateful.

I want to help him, but I also need him.

"I can't do it alone," I say.

Finally, he nods once. Then turns his back to me and walks away.

I watch him go, relieved at winning him to my side, at least for now. I take a moment to study those who reside in our tenuous fortress, then once more inspect the barred doors. My eyes rest on the slanted iron cross, our only defense against those who wish us harm.

I wonder if my decision to stay—to ask David to stay—is the right one, or if it will even matter in the end. As I ponder this troubled future, David lies down in his bunk and closes his eyes. He must be exhausted beyond measure.

Then a sudden, unbidden thought comes to me; one that slips through my defenses and burrows deep into my mind, whispering a horrid prophecy:

You've killed him.

45

The voice is distant and muffled. As if spoken through layers of webbing.

"Wake up, Brother Johnson. Wake up now. We've much work to do this night."

Johnson has no desire to wake up. He does not want to open his eyes, to return to the horror of his reality. The swamp of guilt for the things he's done.

The things he will do.

"I'm not asking, Teddy. WAKE. UP."

"You've killed him! You're mad!"

Poole? Yes . . . Father Poole. And the other one . . . the boy.

But not a boy. Not anymore.

The command could not be ignored. Gingerly, slowly, Johnson opens his eyes.

Or . . . eye, it seems.

The other eyelid refuses to move.

He sees a slanted floor and several sets of feet. The underside of a bed. His vision is . . . *distorted*. He realizes he's lying on his side, and that there's something very wrong with him.

"Killed him? No, Father," the boy says. Then: "Go on, Johnson. Show him. Show him our strength."

The buzzing in his brain, blessedly absent for a few moments, comes back on him tenfold. He winces at the intensity of it, and in doing so feels—no, *hears*—his face.

It crinkles like paper, there's a stench he can't place . . . and he's oddly numb.

Regardless, the instructions come through the swarm, and he obeys.

Johnson pushes himself up. First to an elbow, then to a sitting position. The room straightens, and he looks up into the faces of several boys. Bartholomew stares down at him, his eyes wide and so dark as to appear black, the pupils impossibly large. The others—Samuel, Jonah, Terrence among them—all watch closely. Some look guarded.

A few look afraid.

Good.

"Go on, Teddy. *Stand.*"

Johnson does, fascinated at how he towers over all these children. The very ones he now serves. He looks down at Poole, the once great dictator, now nothing but a weak old man, bedridden with a damaged leg. The priest looks up at him in horror, tinged with disgust.

Curious, Johnson raises his hands to gently feel his new face. Whatever damage was done, it does not hurt. Instead, it *tingles,* as if there is an enormous amount of pain waiting for him, waiting to be released, just on the other side of some thin neural membrane currently blocking it from his mind. A membrane he knows (somehow, deep inside, he *knows*) could easily be popped. Removed.

And all that pain would rush in. It would consume him.

It might even kill him.

Still, he's curious. He touches his cheeks, his nose, his chin. In some places, he feels tight, hot skin, and despite the membrane it hurts—just a little—at the pressure of his fingertips. Like being poked with a fine needle. In other places, he feels fabric, as if his face is part flesh, and part the cloth he was wearing when . . . when . . .

OH GOD.

Moaning, he frantically moves his hands higher. Groping now. He touches his eyes. The one he can open feels normal, unobstructed. Working.

The other is gone. A hollow of gnarled flesh. A lump of gristle. He moans louder, his tongue thick and useless in his mouth.

"Take it easy, Teddy." Bartholomew is watching him carefully. "You're fine," he adds, smiling as naturally as any young, innocent boy. "In fact, I think you're much improved. Don't you think, lads? Much improved."

The others laugh. The ones who were afraid now smile. The others murmur mocking agreement.

Johnson ignores them. He moves his hand atop his head. There are brittle patches of hair, but mostly what he feels is that same combination of taut skin and coarse, burned fabric. His scalp is wrinkled and hot. In places it feels cracked, and there's moisture there. Blood, most likely.

He lowers his hands to his sides. He closes his eye and lets out a large, held breath.

I want no more of this, a dying part of him thinks.

He opens his mind to the swarm, and the swarm consumes him greedily, taking away the guilt, the doubt, the pain.

It feels like heaven.

When he opens his eye once more, his vision is steady.

Bartholomew smiles with satisfaction, then turns his attention to Poole. "You see, Father? How can you possibly fight us?"

Poole tears his eyes from Johnson, focuses once more on the child sitting at the foot of his bed. "What do you want?"

Bartholomew shrugs. "What does anyone want? I want to *live.* I want to take. To kill. I want to breathe foul air. To laugh. To be *free.* You have kept us prisoners here, Father. Punished us. Hurt us." Bartholomew's sardonic smile slips away. For the first time, Johnson senses a flare of anger in the boy.

It terrifies him.

"But no more."

"Let's stick him with this." Simon lifts a treasure discovered within Poole's dresser drawers. An ornate dagger in a sheath of jeweled metal. He frees it from the sheath, which he tosses to the floor. Johnson recognizes the blade: a Chinese, silver-handled knife that Poole treasures, a gift from an archbishop given decades ago for his service in the war. The handle is intricately carved and subtly molded with a grip. The blade is razor-sharp, slightly curved.

Johnson has always thought of it as a gutting knife.

Bartholomew holds out his hand and Simon, albeit with mild reluctance, places it handle-first onto his palm. "And the sheath."

Simon bends and scoops it up, hands it over. Bartholomew sheaths and unsheathes it a few times, the sliding sound of metal on metal the only noise in the room. "This may come in handy, Simon. Thank you for the gift, Father."

Bartholomew sets the sheathed blade in his lap, studies Poole's face. "But it's not for you, I don't think. No . . . I have something else prepared for you."

"You children need to pray." Poole's voice is strained, weary. Delusional. "You need to ask forgiveness."

"Interesting you say that, Father Poole," Bartholomew says. "It reminds me of a story. Shall I tell it to you?"

Poole groans, lets his head fall to the side, his fire vanquished.

"Wonderful," Bartholomew continues, as if Poole has given him nothing but enthusiastic acquiescence. "It goes like this:

"Once there was a little boy named Jeremiah. He was very small and frail. Sickly, I'd say. Do you agree, Poole?"

Poole says nothing, but Johnson sees fear in the man's eyes. *Recognition.*

"Regardless, sickly Jeremiah was always difficult. Always suffering from some ailment or another, needing an ointment or medicine for this or that. A troublesome little boy for your poor mother, who raised you alone, am I right? Your father having died young, when you were just a baby. So sad."

Bartholomew pats Poole's hand. A boy snickers.

"But all those doctors . . ." Bartholomew tuts. "Quite expensive. Especially with no income from Father—God rest his soul— and almost nothing from Mother, who worked as a maid, I believe? Is that about right? I feel sick, you know, thinking how much money she had to make to continually heal you, to keep your pathetic little body alive."

Bartholomew looks around the room. A magician making sure the audience is paying attention. When his eyes fall on Johnson, he winks.

"But. But but but . . . there's a dark secret to this story, isn't there Jeremiah?"

Poole turns his head enough to look sidelong at Bartholomew. His eyes are wide, filled with fear and horror. His mouth moves, but no sound comes out.

Johnson thinks he's mumbling the word "no," over and over again.

"Yes, very dark. You see, it's a wonder how Mother was able to pay for all those expensive doctors. How was she able to buy you medicine, Father? To cure your delicate innards again and again? On a maid's pittance? Oh, wait. I remember . . ."

He leans close to Poole, relishing the moment.

"She was a *whore*. Mother was a prostitute, wasn't she Father Poole? She did what she had to do, but you . . . you *resented* her for it, didn't you?" Bartholomew's smile twists into a snarl. "You self-righteous, ungrateful ass!"

Bartholomew lets out a breath, then the smile returns. "To be fair, it didn't help that she did her business right there in your dumpy, shitty little house. As a matter of fact, she'd fuck strange men on the same bed where she'd once slept with your dead father. What do they call that? Oh, right. A marriage bed. Well, that was shot to hell, wasn't it?"

He laughs and all the boys laugh with him. Silent tears spill from Poole's eyes onto the thin pillow.

Johnson feels nothing. He only listens to the noise in his head. It comforts him.

"But the worst part? The worst part was that you could *hear* them, couldn't you, Jeremiah? Sure, you could. And it disgusted you. Upset your childish, Sunday School moralities. I bet it made your sickly skin crawl to hear the bumping and thumping and groaning and moaning of all that rabid sex, the slapping flesh. All those strangers *giving* it to old Mom. She must have been quite the dish, your mother, I'll give you that. What, for all the fucking she did."

"Shut up, damn you. Shut up!" Poole snaps, agitated, now weeping openly.

Bartholomew gently puts a hand on Poole's chest. His smile wavers, and for a moment Johnson thinks the boy's face flickers, becomes indistinct, as if covered in gray mold. But then the face returns, and he's just a boy again. Or what was one.

"Finally, there was the night you could take it no longer," he says quietly. "Do you remember, Father? The night you decided that you didn't want to hear the sounds from Mother's bedroom anymore. It was too horrible. Your imagination was going *wild*, wasn't it? And so, you decided that you didn't want to imagine it anymore. You wanted to *see*.

"So that night, you crept from your room and down the hall, quiet as a spider. You stood outside your mother's room, listening to all that groaning and thrashing and whatnot. You knew they'd never notice if you turned the knob and opened the door . . . just a crack. And so, you did. And you *saw*, didn't you, Jeremiah? You *watched*."

Bartholomew's voice grows quiet, so he is almost whispering into Poole's turned face. "And what did you do next? You ran!" Bartholomew yells this and all the boys laugh. A few of them jump, enjoying the scare. "You ran back to your room and jumped into your bed, pulled the ratty old blanket over your head and you *prayed*, Father Poole, oh my Lord how you prayed and prayed to your feeble God, to take the memory away, to erase the vision from your mind forever, so you would never again feel the horrible *shame* of it all! Feel that burning *hate* for your mother which you felt in that moment. Do you remember, Father?"

Bartholomew, laughing along with the others, lets the moment settle. Then, when the room is quiet, he whispers into Poole's ear like a lover, like a serpent.

"Do you remember what you prayed for?"

Bartholomew grips Poole by the chin, twists his head so their eyes meet.

"I do. I remember it like it was yesterday," he says, the words oily and hateful. "You told God to take your eyes, didn't you? You told him to take your eyes, because you never wanted to see anything like that ever again." Bartholomew sits back, hands resting in his lap. He shakes his head. "Such a horrible thing for a child to ask for. Nay, to *pray* for. But as I've told you—your God is weak. You still have your eyes, obviously."

Bartholomew stands. He slides the dagger into the waistband of his pants, and steps away from the bed. "But my god? My god is not weak, Father Poole."

For a moment, he stares away into space, into nothing.

"Teddy," he says, finally, and the swarm inside Johnson's head *screams*. "Fulfill the Father's childhood wish, will you?

"Take his eyes."

Johnson looks from the boy to Poole. Despair and rage and pain fight for dominance within him when, suddenly, a million voices shriek the *command* which bellows through his mind, fills his blood, takes over his body.

He runs his tongue over crisp, flaky lips, and steps toward Poole's bed.

The old priest stares up in terror. "NO!" he screams. "Johnson, stop this!"

Johnson bends over the bed, places his giant hands on either side of the frail head, and presses his thumbs against the priest's eyelids.

"Forgive me, Father . . ." he mumbles, the words as garbled and incoherent as his mind.

"NO! No no no no . . ."

Then Poole shrieks, an animal wail of absolute pain and despair, as Johnson shoves his thumbs deeper and deeper into his skull.

The swarm sings its pleasure.

46

I wake in the dark.

I don't recall having gone to sleep, and figure I must have accidentally dozed off. Not wise, given the circumstances. But David and Andrew are here, so I know things are under control. The children are safe, taken care of.

Still, it's odd that all the dormitory lamps have been extinguished. We should be keeping watch, staying vigilant. I need to get up. Speak with Andrew. Find out what's going on, how long I've been sleeping.

"Peter. You're awake."

I look to the voice at the foot of my bed. A man sits there. A heavy, remorseful shadow.

I recognize him instantly.

"Dad?"

The moonlight through the window catches part of his face. He looks whole, healthy. Young. He's smiling at me.

"Hello, Son."

I look around the room to see if the others notice my father's presence. I want to shake them all out of their cots and yell, "Look fellas! Look here! It's my dad!"

I'm no orphan! I'd say, boastful. *I'm not alone.*

"Do you remember . . ." Dad shifts his weight on my thin cot.

I sit up fully, rest my back against the wall. I feel the chill air seeping through the nearby window, hear the whistle and moan of the hard wind.

The storm, I realize absently, has arrived.

"Remember what?"

My father looks down, as if thinking. He laughs a little. It's good to see him happy, to see him smiling. Like it was before. "The first time we went hunting," he says, "you were ... what? Seven years old? A skinny thing. I gave you the gun and let go of the dog. The pheasants burst from the bushes like sparks from a fire."

He looks up, dreamy-eyed. It's one of the few nice memories we shared.

"You fired the gun and nearly fell on your ass." He laughs, and I laugh with him.

"The sky was so blue," I say.

Dad nods. "You killed your first pheasant that day."

I don't reply to this. I don't remember killing a pheasant. I fired, but missed. Dad was angry. He yanked the gun from me. He said ...

"I hear you want to be a priest," he says, and I forget about the day we spent hunting. I wonder how he knows about this. I wonder if my mother knows. "It makes me happy, Peter. Really. We're both happy for you. Proud of you."

He leans toward me and the moonlight through the window catches his face fully. He looks as I remember him, but he's also ... *distorted*. Smeared. I close my eyes and open them. There he is, normal again. His face moonlit, but dappled with shadow. His eyes black pools.

"You were always wise beyond your years," he says, but his lips do not move.

I try to see into the dark hollows of his eyes, but they're endless. I know that if I stare hard enough, I'll fall into them and keep falling, forever.

"You're a dream," I say. "You're dead. You shot yourself, and then you burned."

He doesn't reply to this, but when his face catches the light again, the youthful skin is dark and flaky. His eyes white and lidless. His lips charred black.

"When I watched your mother die, I knew at that *very* moment that I was going to Hell," he says. "It was like . . . like something *opened* up beneath me. A vast, cold abyss. And I knew—I fucking *knew*—right then, that no matter what I did with my life, no matter how hard I tried to set things right . . ."

He shuffles closer, grunting, his breath raspy, his movements jagged. I smell smoke and burned flesh. A blackened hand rests on my knee, staining my white blanket like charcoal.

"I would have always been standing over that chasm, Peter. That deep, terrible darkness."

"Dad . . ."

"There would be no escaping it," he says wearily. "Not ever. It would lie below every step I took, hiding under every bed in which I slept. Waiting. Waiting for my soul to untether from my body and fall, fall into that eternal chasm, to what lay beyond."

He turns to look at me with his lidless white eyes and the moon-silver teeth and charred skin, he pushes closer and I shrink back, away from him, disgusted and afraid. His breath reeks like the grave. Like spoiled meat.

"So I gave the darkness what it wanted," he says. "I fed it my soul."

Despite his appearance, part of me badly wants to reach out to him. To hug him and hold him one more time. I miss him so much. But I know that's impossible, so instead I beg, like the child I once was, for something I know in my heart I can never have.

"But didn't you love me?" I ask. "Didn't you want to stay . . . for *me?*"

My father doesn't answer. He seems confused now, looking around the room like a dog catching a scent, as if hearing sounds that I do not, or cannot, hear. When he looks at me again, he seems lost. "At the time," he says, "I thought, just for a moment, of taking you with me." His burned hand reaches for my face, and instinctually I pull away. He doesn't seem to notice. "I saw you there, you know. Saw you watching. If I had taken some time and considered . . . hell, I think so. Yes, I'm sure of it. I should have taken you with me. First you, then me. How's that sound? But at the time, I couldn't think . . ."

He slaps his head hard. His voice has turned to gravel, the sound of scraping brick. It makes my skin crawl. When he takes my hand, I want to scream. It's ice cold. And now his face changes, becomes misshapen. The eyes bulge and leak. The lips flake away and his teeth grimace and shine. His body shivers as the tissue falls away from the bones on his hands. I see pale skull where a patch of skin has rubbed away.

"When you become a priest, Peter," he says in that horrible voice, "will you visit my grave? Will you bless the ground, and pray for my eternal soul?" His garbled words become phlegmy and guttural as he liquifies; the sound of his voice leaks out, molten and slippery. "Pray for my soul, Peter, because I suffer. I'm in the dark, Son. It's so dark!"

"Dad," I say, voice shaking, my skin clammy, my stomach in knots. "I miss you."

"Pray for me, Peter . . ."

". . . I miss you and Mom so much . . ."

"Will you bless the ground? Will you pray for my soul? Will you forgive me?"

"Dad, please don't."

But he's looking down at his knees, and he's crying. Sobbing in great, heaving gulps. His body decomposing, falling apart at my feet. He reaches down and lifts the shotgun from between his legs.

"I'll see you soon, won't I, Peter? Yes, I think I'll see you very soon."

"Dad!"

He puts the gun between his bared teeth, turns his back to me and pulls the trigger.

"NO!"

The back of his black head explodes. A hot spray of flesh and bone and brain splatters me in a wash of gore.

I wake up to a room filled with light.

47

Peter wakes up screaming, and David groans.

They've been cooped up for hours, and despite leaving all the lanterns lit, including the two wall sconces, most of the kids are asleep. It's late, and they haven't heard a murmur from beyond the doors since Peter and Andrew entered.

A couple of the kids needed to use the privy but going through the lobby and outside seemed like a bad idea. Luckily (or unluckily if your cot is nearby) there are a few bedpans for overnight use if the little ones don't want to make the walk to the outhouse.

Of course, everyone missed both lunch and dinner. David swears he can hear stomachs growling all around the room. His included. Some complained of hunger pains, but most know the drill by now. Hunger is part of life at St. Vincent's, and complaining certainly won't change anything.

To make things worse, the storm is building in strength. The windows rattle incessantly, and the snow blurs past with such density it makes David feel as if *they* are moving, as if the whole orphanage has lifted from the earth and is now flying through the sky, carried on the shoulders of the storm.

Unable to sleep, or even rest his eyes, David sits cross-legged on his cot. He looks across the room at Peter, who now stares wildly around, as if in fear of fleeing spirits.

"You okay?"

Peter turns to David, wipes his brow, and swivels his feet to the floor. Hands on knees. Breathing heavy. For a moment, David wonders if he's going to cry, but then the moment passes, and Peter looks like Peter again. Unafraid. In control. Saintly.

"I'm okay," he says.

Peter stands, stretches. He looks at the clock on his small bedside dresser. David watches him, curious. In the wavering orange light of the lanterns, Peter looks older. His face appears lined, as if he's aged twenty years in the last twenty hours.

A few cots over, Father Andrew is comforting Timothy, a hand around his shoulder as the red-haired boy whimpers about being afraid, about being hungry. About everything.

David wonders if he should be talking to some of the younger boys. Checking in with them. *They must be scared.*

But then his heart hardens, and he looks inward. *We're all scared. I'm fucking scared. Who's comforting me?*

Knowing he's being selfish and hating himself for it, he sighs and swings off his cot. He'll talk to Peter and Andrew, see what they should do next. Waiting it out until morning seems the best idea. Things will be better in the light of a new day.

Who knows? Maybe they'll leave this horrid room in the morning and this nightmare will be over. The others will have departed. Run away.

If they haven't already.

His spirits are buoyed by the idea. Yes, he's sure they're gone. They just need to wait until morning, maybe even find some breakfast . . .

KNOCK KNOCK KNOCK.

All eyes turn to the double-doors, still held closed by the metal cross wedged into the handles. David and Peter look at each other, terrified, hoping the other will deal with it. Will take charge.

A few boys cry out in fear. David notices James hide beneath his blanket.

Byron is already approaching the doors.

"Byron!" Peter snaps.

Byron turns, looks at Peter patiently. "Just gonna have a listen."

Andrew leaves Timothy's side and starts toward the doors,

the strange staff gripped tight in his hand, ready to bless or destroy as needed.

David stands, falls in next to Andrew. Peter does the same.

When they reach the doors, Byron has an ear pressed against the wood.

His head jerks back when the sound comes again, louder now.

KNOCK! KNOCK! KNOCK!

They all look at each other, each waiting for another to make the decision of what to do next. Finally, Andrew steps forward, gently moves Byron aside.

"Who's there?" he says into the thin black seam between the doors. He listens carefully.

David hears someone whispering from the other side, but can't make it out.

"And you're alone?" Andrew says.

Again, a whispered reply. As if whoever's out there doesn't want to be overheard.

David hears movement behind him, turns to see some of the boys are now standing nearby, staggered, waiting to find out what fresh horror has arrived to greet them. He sees James, Finnegan, Harry, and Timothy—all of them watching warily. Many of the boys are still asleep. Seeing their scared faces in the pale lantern light, David feels a pang of protectiveness sweep through him. It feels sudden, this rush of concern. Like a door has been flung open inside his heart. The guilt of his conversation with Peter springs forward like a trap, stunning him with shame. But he's made the decision to stay, and that will have to be enough. He never claimed to be perfect, and he's here now, for whatever that's worth.

He's here.

I won't have them hurt, he thinks, wishing he had a weapon.

Instead, he curls his fingers into fists.

"Who is it?" he asks.

Andrew, who has been leaning over in order to hear the mysterious guest, stands up straight. He gives Peter and David a quick look. "It's okay, I think. Be ready, I'm going to open the doors."

"Father!" hisses Harry, but Andrew ignores him and slides the cross free.

"It's okay," he says again, and pulls one of the doors toward him, exposing a wedge of black so dense David wonders for a moment if anything at all still exists outside this room or if it's all vanished into some endless void, one that they're dropping through forever, unaware that they're already lost.

But then a slim, pale boy slips through. There are long scratches on his cheek and forehead. His eyes are wide and frightened, but when the door closes behind him and Andrew quickly replaces the cross barrier, he smiles at them.

"Jonathan?" Peter says.

David is bumped to the side as Finnegan rushes to his friend, yelping with unabashed joy. Jonathan laughs and they clutch each other in a tight hug. David sees tears spill from Finnegan's tightly closed eyes and looks away, letting the two friends have their moment in relative privacy.

After a few moments, they let each other go, each studying the other eagerly. Those who are awake watch the reunion with shocked, happy faces, their despair momentarily forgotten.

"What happened?" Finnegan says excitedly. "One moment you were there, and then you were gone. We thought they'd gotten you!"

Jonathan, smiling grandly, shakes his head. "Nah, I fought them off, Finn. Slipped right through 'em and ran like the devil. Ended up hiding in the dining hall, underneath one of the tables. They come through a few times, one or two of 'em, calling out like. But I lay still, didn't move."

He looks around now at Peter, Andrew and the others. "Glad to see you lot are okay."

Andrew puts a hand on the boy's head. "You're hurt."

"Nah, it's nothing, Father. Scratches is all."

And then they're gone, Finnegan and Jonathan, the twins. They're talking too fast for anyone else to understand, and walking toward their old cots, side by side, as if nothing happened, as if nothing else matters.

"Jonathan," Peter calls out, and the boy turns impatiently. "What about the others? Did you see them? Earlier, we thought we heard screaming, but it's hard to know with the wind. Are they still out there?"

Jonathan's cheer is swallowed by fear or, possibly, shame. He looks around at all the faces, all the sleeping boys. "Well, I don't know for sure, Peter, but yeah, they're still here. I heard 'em when I snuck through the foyer, down by the priest's rooms. I heard voices."

David steps forward, sensing the boy is holding something back. "Voices?"

Jonathan looks at David, almost guardedly. He exchanges a glance with Finnegan before dropping his eyes to the floor. "I can't be a hundred percent sure," he says.

"What is it, Jonathan?" Andrew says patiently. Coaxing. "It's important we know as much as we can if we're all to get through this. You can tell us anything. This is a safe place."

Jonathan nods. "Like I said, there were voices. Other kids. And Poole, screaming. Like they was hurting him. I heard one of 'em, Bartholomew I think, talking. Right when I snuck by. He was talking to someone. I heard it clear."

They all look at him, waiting. Letting him get it out in his own way.

"He was talking to Brother Johnson," Jonathan says. "And not in a bad way, but like they were telling him stuff. Like . . ."

Jonathan trails off, looks at Finnegan, who nods. *Go on.*

"Like what?" Peter says softly, and David feels his skin tingle with dread.

"Well, you know," he says, wringing his hands. "Like he was one of 'em."

48

The chapel is charred. It reeks of smoke, and decay.

Basil's coffin lies on its side where it fell, forgotten. The wood is scorched black and there are gaps where his corpse lies visible. The linen wrapped around the body is completely burned away, the exposed skin beneath a mixture of pale white and blood red, where the flesh had been licked by fire.

Johnson is transfixed by the sight of it.

He's been told to carry Father Poole from his bed into the chapel, which the boys have made their makeshift headquarters. A rallying point.

Poole now lies atop the altar from which Basil's coffin was so rudely dismissed, knocked down in the tumult to rot and stink on the chapel floor.

Johnson is surprised, as much as he is still capable of thinking or feeling anything, that Poole is alive. Alive, and very much alert. Babbling prayers in a thick tongue, motioning in the air with his long pale fingers. He can't walk, or at least not well. Johnson figures he could hobble if he needed to, but not far, and not fast.

He can't see, of course.

Johnson tilts his head away from Poole and back toward Basil's coffin. Through the hazy sound of the flies infesting his mind, he recalls when he first found him in the chapel, hung by the cross. He remembers how light the body was when he took it down.

"Teddy, are you listening?"

Johnson grunts as the swarm intensifies.

He wants to laugh, because it doesn't hurt like it used to. Not the way it did at first. His brain is dulled now. Numb. Whatever the bugs are doing in there, building a nest to house their multitude, or biting and piercing him as punishment for not obeying, or thinking stray thoughts, it doesn't affect him like it did before.

He hardly cares.

He still obeys, however. He listens to the instructions when they come. He lets the waves of noise rush through him, push him and torture him, because he can *stand* it now.

He can stand it quite well.

In a dark, secret closet of his mind, a place where the flies can't enter, a piece of him hides. Like the closet from his childhood, except now, instead of fearing the dark, he welcomes it. The dark means safety. It means that there is a thread of will that remains to him. A thread of *sanity*.

That part of him hiding in the dark closet, in the form of the child he once was, who hears the swarming insects outside the thin door, wonders if perhaps this new immunity is part of their plan. Or if Bartholomew and his minions know that the closet, and the hiding child within, even exists.

He thinks not.

Bartholomew, he notices, is watching him strangely, his eyes critical. Johnson swallows hard and, momentarily, absorbs the swarm, and leaves the child be. Hidden. Waiting.

"I'm listening," he mumbles, not sure if the words are understandable through his burned lips and engorged tongue.

Bartholomew holds his eyes on him a beat longer, then nods. "Good."

The rest of the boys sit together on the smoke-blackened benches. Bartholomew stands at the front, preaching darkness. The candelabras have been straightened, relit. Johnson stands to the side, the body of a moaning, babbling Poole a bizarre centerpiece behind the place where Bartholomew stands. "When the time is right," he says, orating loudly and clearly, like a Sunday pastor delivering a fiery sermon of redemption, "we will leave this place. There are other places we can go that are not far, where we can travel easily. Where we can stop and rest. Feed."

"The Hill farm for one. We all know about that," Simon says, his voice happy and sane, as if they're not discussing murder at all, but a friendly afternoon visit. "And those kitchen folks have cabins nearby, don't they, Johnson?"

Johnson says nothing, but the children don't care. They ignore him and Poole, these former adults who have been turned into playthings.

"Exactly right, Simon," Bartholomew says. He studies each of the faces in the room, his followers. "But we'll live here for a while, I think. Thankfully there are plenty of supplies, enough to get us through the storm and the worst of the winter."

"Aren't as many mouths to feed as before," Samuel yells, and the others laugh.

Bartholomew smiles. "But when the time is right," he continues, raising his voice, demanding their attention. "We *will* leave. There is much we have to do."

"The city?" Jonah asks, tapping a butcher knife against his chin, the blade crusted with dried blood.

"Yes," Bartholomew says. "The city. But!" He raises a finger and, from one moment to the next, Johnson doesn't think the boys look like boys at all.

They look like animals. Eager and vicious. Hungry.

Like wolves, Johnson thinks, ignoring the stabs of pain the swarm delivers. *They look like fucking wolves.*

Bartholomew turns around and glares at Johnson once more. When he speaks, he looks directly into Johnson's ruined face, even though the words are meant for all of them.

"But first, we have a lot to do here," he says quietly, showing teeth as he grins.

The boys stand, almost as one.

Their laughter is gone, the good humor has vanished. They're all about the business of death now, and God help those who stand in their path.

"Before the sun rises, we will finish our work."

49

The argument started soon after Jonathan's arrival.

It was sparked by the news that Brother Johnson is, quite possibly, helping the others.

Andrew did not take the news well. He wants to immediately leave the relative safety of the dorm, sneak down and see if Poole is okay, then try to discover if there is any truth to the rumor about Johnson.

David and I, for once, are on the same side. We both know it is a terrible idea. And, from David's perspective, a selfish one.

"You can't leave!" David says, too loudly for my taste. I don't want him waking the ones who have managed to sleep.

We've taken our discussion to the farthest end of the room, as far from the beds as we can. At the opposite end, Jonathan and Finnegan have taken over watch at the barred doors.

"You're the only adult we have left. The only priest," David pleads, desperate to keep Andrew from abandoning us. "If Peter wants to be responsible for a dozen kids, that's up to him, but it's not fair to force it on us."

"David, please try to understand, I need to check on Father Poole. I can't just leave him down there if he's in danger."

"We're in danger, damn you!" David snaps.

Andrew turns a shade of red and I see he's getting heated. I don't see him angry often, but I know when it's building, and know to leave well enough alone when it is.

He's not a good priest when he's angry.

"And what should we do, David?" he says, his voice almost as loud as David's, both failing in their efforts to keep their voices down. "Sit up here cowering until spring?"

David's anger slips away like a hat blown off in the wind. He looks at Andrew with surprised, blinking eyes. "You said until morning," he says softly.

I nod along. Both because it's true and, in my opinion, the correct move.

Leaving is madness.

They could be anywhere.

"I'm sorry, David," Andrew replies, gripping his crozier like a talisman, as if it will do any good against knives and other weapons, against Brother Johnson. "I don't mean to snap at you. It's just . . . boys, I can't let them hurt Poole. I can't stand by and do nothing if Johnson is . . . God help us . . . *helping* them. That would alter our chances . . . well, it would change things dramatically for the worse."

"Yeah, no shit," Byron says, then bows his head. "Sorry, Father." Andrew ignores the curse. I'm not even sure he heard it.

I take a moment to study the small leadership group remaining to St. Vincent's Orphanage. Me, a sixteen-year-old priest-in-training, who would rather read strange fictions and kiss a lovely farmgirl than wear a cassock and serve God.

David, a rascal if there ever was one. A street rat turned orphan turned leader of children. I know for a fact he is out of his moral depth, fighting against his instincts for survival at every turn. If it weren't for the storm, I doubt he'd still be standing beside me through this . . . Or would he? I wonder now if I've made the right assessment about him. He's full of surprises, my friend.

Then there's Byron, the stocky brawler whose fierce devotion to me would be embarrassing if it wasn't so touching. Not to mention comforting, given the level of violence we've been put up against. Not only does he seem calm, he also seems perfectly fit into his element. War suits him.

And, last in our circle, Father Andrew Francis. My friend and mentor. My surrogate father. It's fascinating to watch the conflict broiling within him, the struggle between defending and attacking.

Between praying for deliverance and taking to the halls with his crozier to battle the demons at our doors with holy fury.

We are conflicted, we four. Our flipped assumptions and twisting devotions swirl within us with the same voracity and ferociousness as the storm beating and howling outside the windows.

I like to hope that, ultimately, these tests of character will strengthen us, versus weaken; that these storms of conflict, of struggle, will brighten our inner light and make us beacons to those in need, and not darken our minds, hurl us into madness and despair, lead us to defeat and certain death.

I'd like to hope a lot of things.

"Andrew," I say. "If you go, and something happens to you . . ."

"Then you do what you're already doing," he answers, and I can see the argument is lost. "You keep those doors barred, you stay here until daylight. Then you find a way to the Hill farm, one of you anyway, and you bring help. I'm sorry, men."

He leans the crozier against a wall carefully, puts a hand on each of our shoulders, looks into our eyes. "I *am* sorry. About all of this. I know you are scared. And I know how unfair all of this is, but I need you two to *lead* while I am gone. I need you to stop being boys, and become the men I know you already are, inside and out. Not everyone gets a choice as to when they are forced to grow up, but this moment, this day, is yours. You must meet the challenge."

He releases us, grips his crozier once more, and smiles. It breaks my heart.

"You are God's instruments now. Be strong. Be compassionate. Be brave. The Lord will give you strength."

I don't look at David, but at the ground. I nod, wipe away a lone tear.

I know how this will end.

For his part, David says nothing, but I can feel the answer

in his posture; I sense his defeat, his acquiescence to Andrew's wish.

"Besides," Andrew says lightly. "Peter's basically a priest. It was only a matter of his final assessment, and then a brief ceremony. A ceremony that was already being planned, I might add."

I look up, startled. For the briefest of moments, the danger is forgotten. "What?"

"Peter? A priest?" Byron says, and taps my arm with a fist. "Attaboy, Peter."

"I'd already spoken to Poole about it," Andrew says. He speaks to all of us, but I know he's also speaking directly to me. Likely wondering how I will react. "It was all worked out."

I stare at him, see the obvious joy in his eyes.

I wonder if he can see the betrayal in mine.

"I was going to tell you in a week or so, Peter, once we'd gotten you better versed on some of the Latin. Now you know why I was pushing you so hard lately." He laughs.

Even David looks pleasantly astonished. "How about that," he says, and puts an arm around my shoulders. He's never done that before. "Saint Peter for real."

"Only a matter of some pomp and the Ordination. A few simple words," Andrew says, pride shining on me, a light that exposes my every shadow, my every deceit. "Anyway," he says. "There will be time for all that. I promise. But right now . . ."

Andrew's words are cut off. He's staring past me, toward the far end of the room, suddenly transfixed. Blood drains from his face. His jaw drops open.

I turn, unable to imagine what could cause such a reaction, and see Jonathan standing a few feet behind us. He looks at each of us in turn, a look of shame on his face I don't quite understand . . . until I do.

He's holding the cross.

I look past him, to the far end of the room, past the rows

of beds, the sleeping boys, the flickering lamps. To the double-doors.

Unobstructed.

"I'm sorry," he says, but I sense humor in his tone. A maliciousness I've never heard from his lips.

"Jonathan?" Finnegan, apparently having left his sentinel duties long enough for this to happen, is now catching up. He walks up to stand next to Jonathan, a look of confusion on his face. When he sees the cross, he stares at his friend as if he's turned bright blue—more confused than afraid. "What are you doing?"

Jonathan looks at Finnegan sadly, but again I see deceit below the surface of his mask. "I'm sorry, Finn, I really am. I love you. You know that, right?"

He smiles. It's a wicked, foul thing.

And then he turns, and he runs—screaming at the top of his lungs—toward the doors.

"Come in!" he yells, triumphant as a trumpet blast. "Come in! Come in!"

Beds are stirring.

Byron steps in front of me.

David grips my arm. "Oh no," he says.

Then the doors burst open, and death pours in.

50

For a long moment, I'm frozen.

Unable to move.

To think.

I stand in sickened horror as the doors fly open. I see the other boys in the darkened hallway, a horde of shadows. The first one through is Brother Johnson, striding in front like a vanguard of pure evil.

It comes off him in black waves.

Despite the shock and horror, a cohesive thought works itself into my brain:

What happened to him?

His face is a nightmare. His heavy mop of hair has burned away, revealing a red, bleeding scalp. Some sort of blackened fabric is melted into his face, covering his mouth and nose.

One eye is missing, or burned shut, as the flesh looks to have melted over the socket. The other is open wide, showing the white, roving the room like a mad predator.

He's the most terrifying thing I've ever seen. My naked fear keeps me from acting.

When I do, when the spell is broken, it's too late. Much too late.

Like a swarm of locusts, the others come charging in behind him. They're screaming, weapons raised, faces distorted with hate and violence. The orange lamplight gives the scene a hellish hue, shadows become red-faced demons as they flood my vision, and still they come.

In a blink the room is chaos.

I watch in shock as three of the others fall on the bed nearest the doors. A sleeping child shrieks in terror and pain, waking to find his body being bludgeoned and stabbed. They tear at him like dogs.

Other boys are doing similar at the other beds. It appears strategic.

They're going for the sleepers.

In the next heartbeat, those of us who are armed, who are conscious, begin to fight back. James runs directly at one boy, raising a piece of wood I can't identify, but Johnson reaches out like a viper and snags him by the arm. He lifts him like a doll and hurls him at a nearby wall. Even with all the screaming, I still hear the sharp crackle of breaking bones. James falls to the floor, lifeless, and never moves again.

Byron and Andrew sprint forward, joining the fray. Byron takes a boy down with a mallet to the head, and Andrew is yelling commands to *STOP! GO BACK! GO BACK! LEAVE THEM ALONE!* while swinging the crozier, beating the others away from defenseless children as one would fight a wild animal mauling an infant.

David gives a loud yell, a battle cry, and runs directly at Johnson. He has no weapon but his hands and his raw shout of defiance. Johnson turns at the last second, catches David at the chest and lifts him, then hurls him crashing through a window like a stone.

My last glimpse of my friend is his body shattering glass before disappearing into the night. The wind buffets through the opening, charges into the room like an angry spirit. Flurries of snow rush through the broken window, gleefully filling the air of the dorm, swirling around the combatants—the murderers and the dying alike.

All of this happens in a matter of seconds.

And now time restarts.

I must force myself into action. I must defend who I'm able. No matter what comes.

As if released from an unseen hold, I move.

I run first to the cots nearest me, gather those children who have not yet been harmed, pull them from their beds, yell at them to run to the far end of the room, away from the attackers. The poor things cry and wail, and some take more convincing than others, but there's little time so I'm pushing them, screaming at them to *MOVE! RUN!*

I'm reaching for a child just as I'm knocked hard by a body and thrown to the ground. Two boys I can't recognize in the dim light are clutched in snarling combat, tearing at each other, screaming into each other's face as they tug and punch and kick, each trying to best the other.

I roll onto my side and find myself looking beneath one of the beds. Lying on the other side of the cot, blood boiling from his mouth, is Andrew.

I cry out, then scramble beneath the bed to reach him, yelling his name.

He turns his head toward me; his eyes are pained and scared. Blood flows from his mouth in a weak stream. His staff lays on the floor between us.

"Andrew!" I grip my father's pale hand. It's icy cold. "What's wrong with you . . ." I frantically study his body for injury.

And then I see his stomach.

Someone—I don't know who, and can't begin to imagine the strength needed to do such a thing—has plunged the length of the heavy iron cross through his gut, deeply enough that I wonder if it might have gone through him completely.

I bury my head against his chest. "Father!"

He puts a hand to the side of my head, raises my face to see him.

With his final breaths, he speaks to me.

All around us is horror and death and pain, but for a few moments, it's only me and Andrew, together for the last time. I pray that I'm hidden from view beneath the cot; and with Andrew almost dead, bleeding out, run through, perhaps they'll leave us this peace.

"Peter . . ."

I force myself to meet his eyes. "I'm here."

He swallows with a bitter grimace.

When his voice comes again, it's impossibly clear, impossibly strong.

"Are you resolved to exercise the ministry of the word . . ." He takes a breath, eyes locked on mine with almost preternatural determination. ". . . preaching the gospel and explaining the Catholic faith?"

In this instant, my life rushes past me.

Within this split second of time, I see my real father, a shotgun pressed to his face, the room around him alive with flames. I see my childhood at the orphanage, the disciplinary moments with Poole and the other priests, my battles of will with Johnson, my study sessions and many conversations with Andrew. My friendship with the children, with David and the others I've come to think of as my family. My brothers.

I think of Grace. Of my deep love for her. Of our hidden letters, our secret love. Her warmth, her goodness. I think of our future together.

A future that will never come.

"I am," I say. Tears sting my eyes.

It's decided. I've decided.

I'm sorry, Grace.

"Are you resolved to consecrate your life to God . . . for the salvation of his people, and to unite yourself to Christ?"

"I am, with the help of God," I say, and feel something shift inside me. A rush of strength flows through my body, coursing from my heart to my limbs. A growing warmth that clears my mind like an elixir.

Andrew moves his hand into his pocket, pulls out the small jar of holy water.

"Help me . . ." he says.

I press his fingers around the bottle with my own, pull free the cork stopper. He puts a thumb on the opening and tilts it until water trickles out. I stopper it for him once more, then take it from his dying hand.

He moves his thumb to my forehead. With a shaking finger he makes the mark of the cross. "May God, who has begun the good work within you . . . bring it to fulfillment."

It's done.

Only now do I notice a single witness to this bloody ceremony. Hiding under the bed beyond Andrew is Finnegan, wide-eyed and watching. Listening.

Andrew's eyes roll wildly away from me. He blinks rapidly and coughs a spray of blood.

"There is light . . ." he says, then his head rolls to me a final time. He looks almost relaxed. In a strange way I can't fathom . . . *content*. His eyes are bright, as if in wonder.

"There is light all around you . . ." he says weakly, then closes his eyes.

My father is gone.

After a brief moment, I slide out from under the bed. I grip the crozier.

Pushing gently against Andrew's body, I'm able to squeeze out and stand, still holding the staff. I tuck the holy water into my pocket.

To my left, a small group huddles against the far wall. Byron stands in front of them, fighting off anyone who dares come too close. A few of the others dance around him, jeering, mocking. All around me are blood-soaked beds, blood-spattered bodies.

For the first time since the attack, I spot Bartholomew. He stands calmly to the side of the open doors, watching the scene play out. For a brief moment, our eyes meet, and he looks surprised. Then he smiles. The shadows blacken his teeth.

There is movement in my peripheral vision. I turn in time to see a boy rushing at me, a knife bared in his grip.

Jonah.

I raise the staff defensively and thrust it at his chest. He stops, hops to the left, and I follow, stabbing forward again. He laughs.

"Time to die, Saint Peter," he says.

Then he winces in pain, looks to the floor. I follow his eyes and see Finnegan, half-crawled from his hiding place. At some point, he's picked up a bloodied knife.

And stabbed it through Jonah's foot.

"Leave us alone!" he yells, then scrambles back beneath the bed.

Without thinking, I drop the crozier and spin back toward Andrew's body. I grip the top of the cross sticking out of his midsection.

Forgive me.

I yank on the cross with both hands. It slides out deceptively easy, almost knocking me off balance. I spin back toward Jonah, already swinging. He has a split second to look surprised before the point of the cross's arm strikes his temple. There's a sickening *thunk* and I feel the metal sink into his skull.

Jonah collapses to the ground, convulses once, then goes still.

Beside me, someone has snatched up Andrew's crozier. I turn to see Timothy, eyes blazing. Blood is sprayed across his face, his clothes. When he speaks, he does not stutter.

"I'm with you, Peter," he says.

I nod, step into the middle of the room. Byron, having laid down his tormentors, leaves those he'd been guarding to stand beside me. The three of us now form a weak blockade against the young, defenseless ones gathered behind us. The fighting has slowed, but there are small battles going on around the room as boys try to kill or survive.

Enough.

I raise the blood-slick cross above my head, feel the cool rivulets of a stolen life slide down my wrist.

"STOP!" I scream. "Stop in the name of Our Lord! Stop in the name of Jesus Christ!"

To my surprise, the attackers slow, as if tired.

Then stop.

Two of ours who'd been in combat with the others take the momentary distraction to scramble away, hurrying to relative safety. All of the others have turned toward me.

I take another step forward, still holding the cross aloft. My hand shakes. I have no idea what I'm doing, have no concept of power or command. I only know that my path has been chosen, and my mission is clear: save who can be saved. Whatever it takes.

But who remains?

Behind me, there are now barely a handful of children. A few of them, like Thomas, not even big enough to hold a shovel, much less fight. A few make their way, wounded, to a distant wall or corner. Otherwise, there is only Timothy, Byron, and me.

Even so, were it not for Johnson, I think we could take them. We are at least equal to the five or six remaining boys who stand across from us, hands fisted with metal, eyes wide with murderous rage.

For now, though, the battle has paused.

I do an accounting of those we face: Simon, Terrence, Samuel, Aubrey.

Little Jonathan.

Bartholomew.

Johnson.

Slowly, Bartholomew steps to the front of his group, all of them blood-soaked and panting. Johnson, seemingly back on whatever leash they have him tethered to, simply stands to the side, eye aimed at nothing.

I study the swirling shadows dancing around them. I can *sense* the depths of their evil, know that what I only considered before is the truth.

I am not looking into the faces of boys, of orphans. Of children.

I am looking at the possessed.

I am looking at demons.

Keeping the cross raised above my head, I take a few tentative steps forward. Bartholomew raises a hand toward his followers, staying them. He also steps forward, as if he and I have silently agreed to a parlay.

When he nears, I press the heavy cross toward him. In the grip of my outstretched arm, the bloodied iron is only inches from his black eyes.

"In the name of Jesus Christ," I say, not knowing the right words, not knowing anything. I muster all my confidence, all the supposed power bestowed in me by Andrew, and forge ahead. I search for the light. "Be gone, demons!" I say, my voice rising. "Torture us no longer. I command you to leave in the name of the Lord God, Jesus Christ, and the Holy Spirit."

My arm trembles, as does my voice, but I force strength into both of them.

I will not fail.

Bartholomew says nothing for a moment, as if pondering. His eyes stay fixed on mine, black and empty. For a moment, as he breathes this close to me, he appears almost normal.

It's hard not to see him as nothing more than another skinny orphan. If anything, he looks tired.

"I fear, good Peter," he says, "that you've misjudged us."

Finnegan comes to life behind me. "That's Father Peter!" he yells defiantly. "He's a priest now. I heard it, I heard Andrew give him the words!"

There's a noticeable stirring among the boys. *All* the boys.

I notice Johnson shift his body at Finnegan's words. He looks at me directly, that one gruesome eye focused on me with a devil's interest.

"Well then, it sounds like congratulations are in order. By the looks of it," Bartholomew says, looking at the carnage around us, "we're going to need some new priests around here."

Simon snickers, and a few others are grinning now. I begin to feel uneasy.

"But I wonder . . ." Bartholomew says, eyeing me ruefully. "Is it what *you* wanted, Peter?" He lets his words linger as he studies my face. "No, I don't think it is," he says finally. "Sad, really. Smart boy like you. Nothing but another bootlicker."

"Stay back," I say, but my resolve is wavering.

"Put down the cross, you fool," Bartholomew says roughly, his voice a snarl. "You're embarrassing yourself. We're nothing but flesh and blood, Peter. Like you."

"Stay back," I repeat, and am astounded that they do.

For now.

"You don't believe me?" Bartholomew says, slowly stepping closer, knowing there's nothing I can do to stop him. "You don't think I can be merciful?" He turns and motions to one of his followers. "Close those doors and bar them. I don't want anyone leaving."

The boy nods. He runs to the doors and jams his own weapon—a long iron candlestick—through the handles.

Bartholomew turns back to me, lip curled. "Let me prove it to you," he says, then spits out a final word, as if he'd tasted something rotten. "Priest."

51

David opens his eyes but forces himself to lie still. He doesn't want to move, doesn't want to breathe. He's afraid that if he does, the miracle will evaporate. The pain will come. The damage—the injury—will be made clear.

Because I have to be injured. Right?

And yet.

He looks around slowly. The wind drives against his face, snowflakes cling to his eyelashes. He feels the cold on his back, his legs . . . and realizes.

"Thank God for snow!" he shouts, a gust of hard wind dissolving his words.

He pushes his hands into the deep snowbank, the one he luckily landed in after being thrown—with shocking, brutal power—through the window by Johnson. He's fallen over twenty feet and landed in a drift he assumes is at least three, maybe four feet deep. A newly formed bank curled up along the side of the orphanage. Standing up, buried in snow past his knees, he experimentally bends one leg, then the other. He lifts his arms, flexes his fingers.

There's a nasty cut on one forearm, which he assumes has something to do with being thrown through a closed window, but otherwise . . .

"I'm fine," he says in disbelief, and begins the slow, careful process of walking.

He looks around, shocked at how completely the storm has covered the land surrounding their home, and still the flurries whip around his face, fill the air with fresh cover. He steps out of the drift into snow no deeper than a foot and knows his fate could have been much worse.

From above, he hears screams, the sounds of children in pain, likely dying. He turns to stare up at the orange-lit windows. The sounds seem distant, quickly whisked away by the brutish, icy wind, a wind which carries its own screams, its own threat of pain. The longer he stands still, the more he feels it.

I must get back. I must help them!

He pushes himself from a cautious walk to a shuffling jog, and finally to a run. When he reaches the front doors, he prays they're not bolted, and pushes on one of the large handles.

It opens with ease.

He stumbles into the foyer, the howling wind at his back. The screams from the dormitory are louder now. Horrible.

I need a weapon.

He starts running for the kitchen, but stops short when he sees a dull, flickering glow of candlelight coming through the open doors of the chapel. He steps cautiously forward, wondering if there are more of the others inside, waiting. He pokes his head around the doorframe, studies the interior. He sees no orphans and is about to turn away when something moans from the front, something splayed across the altar. Realizing, David gasps.

"Father?"

David steps into the chapel tentatively, eyes flitting anxiously from shadow to shadow.

Father Poole lies, unmoving, atop the altar. He's turned onto his side, his back to David.

He's breathing, I can see him breathing.

"Father Poole? It's David."

The priest's voice is weak, tentative. "David?" The old man lifts his head. "Are you . . . with *them?*"

David walks slowly—carefully—forward. Luckily, the chapel is not large, and there are few places to hide. It stinks like burned wood and smoke and blood, but there is no one else visible.

"No," he says. His heart is beating, he wants to run, to help the others, but there's something about Poole's frailty, the ee-riness of the chapel, that holds him. "I was in the dorm with Father Francis, Peter, and the others. I've got to get back."

David is close to the front of the chapel now, only a few feet from Poole's body.

"I think they're being killed, Father."

"Most assuredly, my boy. Come closer. I need help." Poole groans and begins the process of shifting his body, trying to turn himself over. "We have much to do."

David looks at the low-burning candles on the candelabras. There's a vacuous feeling to the room, as if all the life and hope has been sucked out of it, *burned* out of it. He has no desire to stay, not for another second. "I'm sorry, but I have to get back, Father. I have to help."

"You will, my son, you will." Poole finally gets himself into a sitting position upon the altar. His voice is phlegmy, rattling like a loose wagon wheel.

David gets no closer.

"But first," Poole says, shifting his body, turning himself around toward his visitor. "There's something we must do. And I'm sorry . . ."

Poole lifts his eyeless, blood-crusted face to stare into David's, and it's all the boy can do to keep from screaming. "But I'm afraid I'll need your eyes."

52

Bartholomew has us corralled near the back of the dorm, or whatever constitutes the furthest point from the doors, the only exit. The only means of escape. Two boys stand near the doors, both armed with knives, the sharp steel dangling loosely from their hands. At the ready.

We've been forced to sit on the floor, and they've taken what weapons we had, if you could even call them weapons. Sticks and pencils. Byron's meat hammer. The cross that killed Andrew.

The crozier is held loosely by Samuel, who stands watch next to our small cadre. These kids I'm already thinking of as the survivors. I pray we continue to wear the moniker.

I've done my best to calm those who need calming. And, since the attack ended, I've also been able to do a proper accounting.

There are six of us left alive. Six of us still sane.

Byron. Timothy. And three younger boys: Harry. Thomas. Finnegan.

Me.

I have to assume Poole, like Andrew, is dead. Father White, I know, is wrapped in a shroud along the outer wall of the chapel, along with the other victims of that massacre.

There's no one left but us.

"Now listen to me carefully," Bartholomew is saying, pacing before us like a teacher delivering a complex lecture. "If you swear yourselves to me, I promise you will not be harmed. You can continue on, with us. The first thing we're going to do, once the sun comes up, is make a big, hearty breakfast. Doesn't that sound pleasant? We have all the food, and we're a much smaller number now, and best of all . . ."

He looks at each of the faces sitting beneath his gaze. He ends on mine, holds there.

"No priests."

He walks over, lifts a foot, and puts it on my chest. I sense Byron shift next to me, but I stay still and hope he will, as well. The slightest rebellion now and they'll tear us apart like snared rabbits.

"Do you see my mercy, Peter? Do you still think me . . . what? A demon? Possessed? Do you still believe you can cast me away with your cross and bad Latin?"

He gives a little push with his foot and I rock back, catching myself from falling with a hand to the floor behind me.

"Now," he continues, pacing once more, "who will take me up on this offer of mercy?"

I hear shuffling behind me, the sound of someone standing. I close my eyes, feel the sour pit of my stomach roil. A bitter taste fills my throat. Despair threatens to overwhelm me even before I hear the words.

"I will," someone says. "I want to live."

A boy steps past me. Byron curses under his breath. I open my eyes and see Bartholomew embracing young Harry, only eight years old and terrified. Part of me is relieved. One less to die. One less I'm responsible for saving.

I wish him well.

"Good," Bartholomew says. "Who else?"

No one moves, and I see a sharp flare of anger, of disappointment, cross Bartholomew's face. A flash of dark eyes, the grim set of his mouth.

"I think," he says slowly, "that you lot have put a heavy load of confidence in Saint Peter, here. Excuse me, I apologize. *Father* Peter. Even so, and I hate to say it, brothers, but I think Peter is steering you all wrong."

He turns his back to us, folds his hands behind him. "Brother Johnson," he says, and the giant—who since the end of the onslaught has been leaning against a wall, head down, as if bored with it all—looks up.

Bartholomew turns back, and when I see his face I know once more that I am right. That is no child's face, no young boy's expression. It is not the visage of Bartholomew I see in the dim, winking orange light, but a wrinkled mass of black flesh with deep-set red eyes, a mouth filled with too many teeth.

"Come over here, Johnson. Come over here and kill Peter."

Johnson pushes off the wall, begins walking toward us in shambling steps.

Bartholomew addresses the others in the room, his voice filled with mockery and hate. "Some of you may want to look away for this bit," he says, then turns back to me.

His smile has returned, along with his child's mask.

"It won't be pleasant."

53

The root cellar below the kitchen is about the worst place David can think of being sent. It's dark, damp, cobweb-strewn, scary, pungent, and disgusting.

And the second trip is no better than the first.

He wants to leave Poole, run back up the stairs to the dormitory, jump into the fight to save his friends from whoever, or whatever (if you believe Peter) those *others* are. Children or demons, he thinks, it is the same difference to him. Either way, they want him dead. Along with Peter, Andrew, and the others.

He *has* to get back.

But Poole has convinced him that the best way to save them is to do what he says, to help him exact revenge on *all* of them.

"An eye for an eye," he said, and cackled like a fairy tale witch. David almost broke and ran then. Almost. But a decade of discipline and punishment, of following orders, has been ingrained deeply into him. Poole scorched his will onto David's mind, cut it into his soul. He does not think Poole can punish him for disobedience, not anymore, but it hardly matters.

He can't disobey even if he wants to.

So he's gone to the root cellar, and gotten the things Poole had asked for:

Four barrels of kerosene oil. A lantern. A hatchet.

"They're heavy, but you're strong," he said, his face so close that David had to force himself not to stare into those red pits that were once the priest's eyes. "And don't forget the hatchet! It's on the woodpile in the boiler room. While you're there, feed the furnace. No point in everyone freezing to death. Now go."

He brought two barrels the first trip, huffing as he made it back to the foyer, his arms burning with the strain. On the second, he returned with the second pair. He plucked the lantern from the dining hall, and the wood hatchet was stuck into his belt. The hatchet being the one thing he grabbed that made sense.

At least he can defend himself now.

I pray you're okay, Peter. Curse me for listening to this old fool!

Poole has somehow managed to stumble to the chapel doors on his own. He's waiting there when David returns the second time. "Put three of them in the center of the foyer, so you can see them easily from the balcony. Put them close to the doors."

"Well, which is it?" David snaps, using a tone he would never have imagined using in a million years toward the head priest, the very one who scarred his hands and back when he was younger, punishment for indiscretions he can't even remember.

And by God it feels good.

"You want them in the center or by the doors?" he says, more softly now.

Poole hesitates a moment, as if debating whether to chide the boy's tone, then simply waves a hand impatiently. "Just do it."

David sighs and splits the difference, putting all three barrels in a clump. "Okay, Father. They're down."

"Good. Do you have the hatchet?"

David pulls it from his belt and grips it, feeling its heft and balance. He thinks he hears muffled screams, and impatience runs through him like wildfire. "Yes. Father, we need to hurry . . ."

"Don't sass me, boy," he spits, his voice like a whip. "I let it go once."

David swallows. *Got to hand it to him, he's still a mean old bastard even without the eyes.* "Yes, Father," he says, and waits.

Poole nods. "Break the spigot off one of the barrels. If it won't break with the butt of that hatchet, then chop into the wood."

David looks down at the barrels, the dark red wood, the dark iron spigots near the base. "But . . ." he starts, but Poole cuts him off.

"Do it! As you say, we must hurry!"

David nods dumbly, spins the hatchet in his hand so the blunt end faces downward, and chops hard at the spigot.

It pops off clean, and kerosene oil burbles from the new hole, begins puddling onto the floor. Satisfied, he walks over to Poole. "It's done."

Poole reaches out, finds David, and pats his arm. "Excellent." Poole grabs one of David's hands and slaps a tin case into it. "Use my matches to strike your lantern. You'll need to bring the lantern and the last barrel, along with the hatchet. Can you manage?"

"Yes, Father," David says, disgusted at the pride he feels carrying out the man's wishes.

Poole pats David's cheek, smiling. His skin is rough as sandpaper, and David tries not to recoil at his touch. "Good boy. I'll tell you the rest as we go. Now, grab your things, and let me take your elbow so you can lead me."

"Okay, but where are we going?"

"Where you've wanted to go this entire time, my son," he says, clenching David's arm in a fierce, painful grip.

"Take me to the others."

54

Johnson pushes Bartholomew roughly aside in his eagerness to get his hands on me.

Once again, like an idiot, I'm frozen to the ground. My mouth hangs open as my brain screams commands to my useless body:

GET UP! FIGHT! RUN! SURVIVE!

SAVE THEM!

"I . . . wait . . ."

Johnson reaches for me and my mind goes blank. All I can think to do is scream, and I'm about to do so when Andrew's crozier smashes into the side of the big man's scorched, hideous face. His head knocks to the side, and he appears momentarily dazed. I turn my head to see Byron gripping the staff like a Mongolian warrior bracing for an onslaught of cavalry.

Samuel, who he somehow wrested it from, looks dazed as well, his lip bloodied. Byron must have knocked him in the teeth before he grabbed the weapon.

The action jars me from my wretched stupidity and in a burst I find my feet.

Is this the moment? Our last stand?

So be it.

I'm ready to fight.

"Stop!" Bartholomew yells, and whether he's addressing my group or his own or Johnson, I have no clue. All I know is everyone stops, at least for a moment. "Johnson, how fucking stupid are you? You oafish, dumb ox," he says, and his fiery eyes meet mine. "I've changed my mind. Kill Byron instead. I want Peter to watch his friend die."

Byron roars and swings the staff once more, but this time

Johnson is ready and catches it neatly. He rips it from Byron's grip and throws it aside. Before Byron can retreat, Johnson reaches out with his big hands and grips his head, yanks the stout boy toward him.

Byron screams as Johnson drops to a knee, wraps an arm around the child's throat and begins to squeeze. Over Byron's reddening face, Johnson looks at me with that one hideous eye, as if the pleasure of his kill is reflected in my face, and he is eager to study it.

"Peter, do something!" Finnegan yells.

Yes! I must! But what? I have no weapon, no bloody cross, no hammer, no knife.

I don't have the strength to pull Byron free, and we are outnumbered.

The others laugh and yell. They prod Johnson onward, scream words of encouragement as Byron's life is slowly taken.

"Johnson! Stop!" I say, trying for my most commanding—most priestly, most adult—voice.

But he only adds pressure. Byron's eyelids flutter, his face turns red as a turnip. His legs weaken, which only increases the pressure on his throat.

I don't know how, or why, the thought comes to me. I only know that it does.

I think of it when I remember the vial of holy water in my pocket.

I pull the vial free and yank out the stopper. My mind is blank, chaotic, completely overrun with panic and fear and a mad desperation. My actions seem not my own.

I throw the water at Johnson's face.

His eye opens wide, as if in shock. Water drips down the burnt skin, glistens on the bloodied fabric melted into his face.

The practiced words of baptism spill from my mouth like oil.

"Theodore Johnson, dost thou believe in Jesus Christ, His only begotten Son, our Lord, who was born and suffered for us?"

Finnegan tugs at my elbow. "Peter, what are you doing?" he hisses.

Amazingly, I notice Johnson's hold on Byron loosen. The boy gasps in a short, tight breath. Johnson gives me the faintest of nods.

"Enough! Kill that boy!" Bartholomew screams, and I turn on him.

"Quiet, demon!" I shout the command, can almost feel my heart bursting with inner light. With strength. "You are in the presence of God!"

I notice a few of the others take a step back. Bartholomew's mouth clamps shut.

I put my focus back on Johnson, gently place a hand on the arm tucked against Byron's throat, willing it to let go. I speak quickly, confidently. "Do you believe in the Holy Ghost, the Holy Catholic Church, the Communion of Saints, the forgiveness of sins, the resurrection of the flesh, and life everlasting?"

Johnson tries to speak, but nothing comes from his mouth but a gurgle, followed by a squeak I can't decipher.

I take it as a yes.

"Theodore Johnson, I baptize you in the name of the Father and of the Son and of the Holy Spirit." I step closer and make the mark of the cross over him. I dare not touch his flesh, but I place a gentle hand on his shoulder, my eyes locked onto his own.

I hardly notice when Byron squirms free and steps away, scurries behind me.

A swollen tear leaves the giant's eye, and I rush the words. "By the blood of Jesus Christ your sins are washed away." I let out a large breath I did not know I was holding. The light leaves my body, and I realize the enormity of what's occurred. I tremble, but force myself to carry on, to finish it. Breathless, and as astonished as anyone that this somehow worked, I complete the ritual. "May God the Father bless you and keep you."

And it's done.

There's a *quiet* to the room. A stillness. As if we've all been frozen in time and place.

Even the howling wind of the storm seems oddly muffled. Johnson continues to stare at me in a sort of wonder. His head tilts, as if listening for something. In a thick, rough voice he whispers something odd.

"No more flies."

I nod, though I don't understand. Even worse, I have no idea what's to come next. Then I hear David.

"Peter!" His voice comes from the hallway.

And with it, a sound reminiscent of distant thunder.

"You still alive in there?" he yells, his voice muffled by the closed doors.

David . . . alive?

All this horror has turned bizarre, and everyone seems equally stunned at the turn of events. I look at Byron, who stares at me questioningly, then shrugs, all the while rubbing his sore neck.

"I'm here!" I yell, loudly as I can, waiting for Johnson to grab me or a boy to run me through or Bartholomew to leap at me. But none of this happens. "There are several of us!"

The rolling thunder gets closer, closer.

There's a thump at the doors.

Finally, the moment breaks, and Bartholomew hisses at Simon, who stands beside him. "Simon! Go!"

Simon nods and runs toward the doors, Terrence following right behind.

David, run! I think, but then he yells out again, and I'm thrown back into confusion.

"Peter!" From the nearness of his voice, he must be just outside the doors. The two boys who've been guarding the entrance pull the long candlestick from the handles, prepare to pull the doors open.

When David's voice comes again, it's further away.

A sick worry stirs my stomach.

I have the sudden, overwhelming sense that something very bad is about to happen.

"I'm sorry!" he says.

And the doors are pulled wide.

55

Having run at a dead sprint back down the length of the hallway—doing his best not to slip in the trail of oil he's spilled rolling the cursed barrel from the balcony to the dormitory—David reaches Poole just as he hears the doors opening, followed immediately by angry voices.

Poole thrusts the lit lantern into his hands.

"Now, you fool!"

David grabs the lantern and spins.

The long hallway is dark, but instead of terminating at the shadowed wall of the dormitory entrance, it ends at a lantern-lit room. He sees a handful of faces looking back at him—some with confusion, some with pure hate.

Two of the others are running toward him fast, fleet as shadows and sinister as death.

David holds the handle of the lantern lightly in his fingers, swings it back, then brings it forward, as if tossing a horseshoe at a peg.

"Peter!" he screams as the lantern is lofted into the air, the two would-be attackers already midway down the hall.

"Get down!"

There's a flare of light at the far end of the hallway. It floats upward, like the fireflies I would sometimes chase at night, back in the fields outside my childhood home.

Then the light smashes to the ground and a trail of fire rips down the middle of the hallway, heading right toward us. It's only then I notice the barrel resting at the foot of the entrance.

The trail of flame touches the barrel and there's an ear-shattering explosion. The two bodies nearest the door are blown into bright pieces. I spin, hold my arms wide, and lunge to the floor, catching two or three of the little ones in my grasp as I fall.

There's a monstrous roar and the sounds of children shrieking as a cloud of burning air climbs my legs then my back, neck, and head. I squeeze my eyes closed as it engulfs me.

The barrel explodes and a rolling wave of flame erupts from the source. In a flash, the fire fills the hallway, pushes like a giant orange fist toward the spot where David and Poole stand.

"Jesus Christ!" David yells, and grabs Poole. He throws both of their bodies to the side, out of the open mouth of the hallway, and against the wall at the top of the stairs. Fire belches out into the air above the foyer like a dragon's furious breath.

David doesn't even realize he's screaming.

Poole curses. "Let go of me!" he shrieks, and takes three quick steps toward the hallway, which is now on fire. David reaches out, grapples for a sleeve.

"Father! There's fire!" he yells.

"Of course there's fire! Now we need to finish the job and ignite the barrels in the foyer! The whole place must burn, David!"

"But the others," David says, and Poole's eyeless face frowns.

"Their reward will be in heaven, my son."

David knows he must try and help any survivors. He takes a step toward Poole, ready to fight him if needed, and grabs his robe in two fists. The old priest screams and pulls back, so that they both stand once more in the mouth of the burning hallway. "Damn you!" David screams, but then sees something moving—moving *fast*—from the corner of his eye.

He turns to see a child, covered in flame, running toward them like an earth-bound phoenix. He lets go of Poole and stares.

Impossible!

When it's within a few feet, it scurries up a wall then leaps through a licking river of flame. Through the veil of fire David sees the deadly snarl on its face, the long knife held tight in one burning hand.

It flies at him.

Simon, David thinks, connecting the last remnants of flesh on the thing's grinning face with the boy he once knew.

Instinctively, David drops to the floor.

The heat of Simon's body passes over him and collides with Father Poole, who shrieks in pain and terror as Simon's propulsion knocks them both backward and over the banister.

David spins, follows the path of the two bodies—both consumed in fire—as they fall through the murky darkness of the great foyer. They appear to him as two entwined souls falling forever through the great pit, cursed to feel their earthly flesh burn for eternity.

In the earthly realm, however, they meet an end, as the tangled bodies of Poole and Simon crash to the stone floor.

Into the barrels of kerosene.

"Oh shit." David falls flat to the floor, covering his head with his arms as the pool of oil catches and the barrels, simultaneously, combust.

The ensuing explosion blasts the front doors of St. Vincent's free of their hinges and flings them through the air, out into the night, where they land, burning, in the deepening snow. The shrouded bodies of the dead, so carefully laid out beside the chapel, are blown apart like tissue. A roiling ball of flame shoots upward, singeing David's unprotected clothes and hair as he screams, falling back and away.

After a moment he stands, choking on the growing smoke rising upward, filling the air. He looks toward the stairs, but they already crackle like kindling as the fire climbs them toward the balcony. He looks back toward the hallway, still aflame, but sees no safe path to the dorm.

Everything is burning.

"No no no no no!" He looks around, desperate for some route of escape.

His eyes trail upward, where a short, knotted rope hangs from a hatch in the ceiling.

I'll never reach it, he thinks, eyeing the distance to the rope as at least four or five feet above his head. He takes a half-step backward, reaches behind him, and rests a hand on the warming banister.

The banister!

"Now or never, David. Time's a-wasting!"

Not wanting to overthink it, and ignoring the ever-growing flames surrounding him—the intensifying heat, the choking, billowing smoke—he places both hands atop the banister then climbs up and onto his knees, balancing precariously, the growling lake of fire beneath him waiting hungrily for his inevitable fall.

In a quick motion, he sets his feet on the wood railing then releases his hands, momentarily standing erect on the narrow strip of curved wood.

He eyes the rope, knowing he'll only have one chance.

And leaps.

56

Johnson can't explain it. Can't understand it.

One moment, his head is bursting with the swarm, an infinite number of angry flies battering the inside of his skull, countless black legs pressing against the backs of his eyes, crawling through the deepest reaches of his ear canals, climbing up the back of his throat. So loud, so dense, so heavy . . . he can do nothing, *think* nothing but for the instructions.

The command to *kill* is simple. Direct.

He wants nothing more than to comply.

He doesn't see the boy swing the staff. He's focused on Peter, the one who needs to die. The one they say is a priest.

And that word . . . *priest* . . . it cuts through the swarm, like a sword slashing through mist. It's there, then gone. It means something. Someone who once gave him instruction.

He ignores the thought, the swarm *makes* him ignore it, grows deafeningly loud, shutting out all else.

And then the boy hits him, hits him *hard*. For a moment, the sound of the flies grows distant and a ringing takes its place; the reverberation of a struck bell that never wavers, never ceases. He's confused. Unsure of himself.

Then more instructions. More commands.

Kill the other one.

Frustrated and angry at the conflicting voices, the confusion, he swats away the second attack, grabs the child, and begins to crush him.

His head ROARS with the sound of the gleeful swarm, buzzing and growing fat on his sin, crowding every inch of space inside his mind, devouring his thoughts.

He can think of nothing but squeezing the life out of the child, like he did the other . . .

But then something cold hits his face, and from one second to the next . . .

Everything changes.

The sound is gone.

The swarm is gone.

His head is clear of the flies, of the instructions. His eye focuses on a face. The boy.

Peter.

The priest.

As the boy-priest speaks the words of baptism, he can almost feel his body being submerged in cool water. The sun shining on his skin as he's raised up, renewed. Reborn yet again, but this time in mercy.

All the evil he's done comes back to him, fills him like smoke, and then . . .

It's blown away.

He's free. An empty vessel with only his soul—a new soul born of light—resting inside. He looks at the boy in astonishment. He doesn't even remember letting the other one go, but he's gone, and his arms are empty. They are *his*. His mind . . . is *his*.

Johnson wants to thank the boy. Tell him what he's done. That he's *saved* him. But he can only mumble three words, the most important words:

"No more flies."

And, briefly, there is peace.

Then, chaos.

Johnson stands and turns, ready to defend the children he's been hell-bent on destroying. He sees the doors pulled open, the distant light of the tossed lantern, the rush of flame and the waiting oil barrel. He turns and sees Peter dive down, away, grabbing children to bury beneath his own body.

The explosion rocks the room and a gust of burning air hits him.

He sets his feet, stands in front of the few remaining children. Wanting to make himself large as he can, he spreads his arms wide, lifts his head high, the black robe and the flesh of his body the only thing he can offer, the last thing he can offer.

His eye goes wide as the flames roll toward him, blasting the boys who stood closest to the entrance into bits, burning corpses and blowing the flimsy cots into the air as it crosses the room in seconds, a raging bull of fire, and slams into the shield of flesh that is Johnson's body, who stays on his feet until he can think no more, and his body no longer has a master.

And, by doing so, saves the lives of the children huddled on the floor behind him.

57

The trapdoor opens so easily beneath David's weight that he almost—*almost*—loses his grip on the coarse knot from which he dangles.

A rickety ladder spills out, almost clubbing him in the head. He manages to avoid it and grip the rungs. He climbs into the attic, flames licking at his heels.

He reaches the cool dark, the ladder already burning beneath him.

Now, he must decide.

And he has to do it quickly.

The high crawlspace goes two ways: south, toward the dormitory (where gray smoke is already filling the air of the attic space), or east, over the chapel, which leads to another access door at the end of the residence hallway. If he drops down there, he'll land directly in front of the orphanage's rear doors, a service entrance used primarily by the staff. And through those doors . . .

Escape.

Freedom.

Life.

David looks one way, toward the smoke-filled attic, where death almost certainly awaits, and then the other, toward salvation.

They're all dead, he thinks. *There's no way they could have lived through that explosion. Damn you, Poole.*

He sighs heavily, having decided.

Then, hunching over to avoid the cross beams, he starts to run.

58

When the blast of heat subsides, I open my eyes.

Two bodies squirm beneath mine, and I roll off them, take in my surroundings.

The dorm is ablaze. The beds roast like bonfires and flames carpet the floor, lick up the walls. Half the windows are blown out, and the circulating wind of the storm is twisting and curling the fire burning inside. Flames are dancing.

I see no way out.

I get to my knees, notice the bodies lying next to me. Everyone here seems intact and, for the most part, unharmed. I don't know if there are others within the flames, but I think I see shadows moving in that forest of heat. I wonder if the blast killed them all, or if some remain to do us harm.

The bodies I landed atop are Timothy and Finnegan. Byron, it seems, had pushed Thomas to the ground and covered him, and they both seem well, if shaken. I look around and see Harry, who, despite his servility to Bartholomew, didn't survive after all. He's sitting awkwardly, back braced against a wall. His face is blackened, his eyes emptied, leaking down his charred cheeks like cream. I imagine him standing in shock as the flames approached, watching as they tore his flesh and slapped his small body into the wall like a bug.

I want to cry, to scream. To mourn. But there are still five of us. I must save who I can.

But how?

I stand slowly. The heat is intense, but for now the fire seems to be staying away from us. There is only one exit, however, and traversing the room is impossible. We would be dead before we made it halfway, even with the greatest of luck.

Byron steps beside me. He speaks as quietly as he can, not wanting to alarm the others, but it's hard to hear over the sound of the fire. "Any ideas?"

I shake my head.

I'm still working my tired brain for a solution when a loud thumping comes from above our heads. I look up toward the sound and see, in the corner, positioned near the far wall, a hatch in the ceiling.

Something is banging against it. Once. Twice.

And then it pops downward. A ladder unfolds from above like a miracle.

Then David's head appears, upside down, from the ceiling. He's smiling like a madman, and I can't help but cry out in a rush of joy at seeing his face again.

"Peter!" he yells. "Bring them! Hurry!"

I grab the others by their sleeves, their collars, and begin pushing them toward the ladder.

"Go! Go!"

There isn't much time.

I take one last look back at the dormitory, the room where I've spent a majority of the last ten years of my life. The flames have reached the ceiling. They ripple across it like water, blackening the white plaster.

Time to go.

I follow the others, all but pushing them along. "Hurry!" I yell.

One by one, they start up the rickety ladder.

At the top, David is grabbing hands, pulling them to what I hope is safety.

I try not to think of the flames on the ceiling.

Now Byron is climbing, and I'm right behind him, bringing up the rear. Everyone else, I have to assume, is dead.

I reach the top. The air turns immediately cooler, but is still dense with smoke. David has gathered the others, and they all look at me as I emerge and stand in the crawlspace. It's dark, but the flames coming through the hatch offer just enough light to see our way.

I've only been in the attic once, a long-ago day when Andrew sent me up looking for candles. But that was on the other side of the building, by the chapel, and I have no idea where this will lead, if anywhere.

Thankfully, David seems confident, and the realization strikes me that he must have reached us from *somewhere*, so we simply need to get back to where he started, and pray it was free of fire.

"Is that . . . *everyone?*" he says. It takes me a moment to realize what he's asking, and it hurts my heart to see the surprise in his eyes. When they first attacked, there were so many of us. He has no idea how many have been lost.

But I can't think of that now, so I only nod. "I'm the last."

"Okay," he says, recovering. "Follow me. Stay close and try not to breathe too much of this smoke. Cover your mouth with your shirt or sleeve or something. Right, let's go."

We begin moving forward, but make it no more than a dozen steps when the floor in front of us snaps like a breaking tree, followed immediately by a loud, rustling noise. David stops, steps quickly backward, right into Thomas.

"What . . ." I say, but don't have time to finish my thought before, only a few feet in front of us, the entire width of the attic floor collapses downward in a shower of sparks and black smoke. Flames immediately shoot up through the gap, gulping the new air, pressing toward the rooftop, hungry and deadly and unstoppable.

David's head jerks around and our eyes meet. He doesn't say anything, but he doesn't need to. I can read his look easily.

He's telling me that he's sorry.

59

I don't know what to do. Don't know what to tell the others, how to comfort them. I only know we can't stay here, in this attic crawlspace filling with smoke and fire.

There *must* be another way.

"We need to go back down!" I yell above the increasingly loud crackle of burning wood; the sounds of hungry fire and the occasional *BANG* or *POP* of furniture being consumed from down below. I don't bother looking to David for confirmation, the smoke is too severe and I'm beginning to feel the first plucks of panic on my nerves. I turn around, take two steps.

And stop.

Oh no.

Bartholomew stands in the crawlspace, a hunched shadow blocking our way to the trapdoor, as if he's Cerberus guarding the gates to Hades. The hatch, still open, glows from below in pulsing reds and oranges; rising cat tails of smoke curling, twisting up from behind him. He smiles, showing black teeth. His eyes are red as embers.

"Hello Peter," he says, and raises an ornate, silver knife in his hand. He points it at my heart. "Appears you boys are in quite the pickle."

I take a step forward, trying to peel my eyes away from the blade, from his horrid eyes. "Move out of the way, Bartholomew." I try to sound commanding again, but the gift of divine authority is as fleeting as it is unreliable.

Something to hone, I imagine. Over time. That voice of one who is certain of things, who knows what's right. Who knows what's best. In the end, I revert to the boy I am. A pugnacious child. A cheap imitation of a savior. "I said move, goddamn it!" I take another step toward him, and it does me good to see him flinch. "Move or I'll move you, you murdering bastard!"

Bartholomew's eyes go wide in mock surprise, and he laughs. Composing himself, now it's he who takes a half-step forward.

I feel a hand pressing me gently from behind.

Byron speaks calmly, but the words only increase my panic. "It's getting too hot, Peter. Let me do it," he says, trying to move around me.

I shift, blocking his path.

We're running out of room, and we're running out of time.

"Come, Peter," Bartholomew says, and he's not laughing anymore. He's snarling. His feet are balanced, and he's lowered the knife to his side, taunting me.

Daring me.

"Come and find your God!"

I spring forward, hoping to catch him off guard. I run right at him—two steps, three—and start to grab for the knife with one hand and his throat with the other. For a moment, I think I have him. He wavers. His eyes widen.

Then he bows neatly, so quick I can barely trace his movement.

I reach for his knife hand, and find air.

I reach for a throat, but he is gone, tucked down low.

Thrusting upward.

The pain is a hundredfold what I could have ever imagined. The sharp blade slides easily into my stomach. I can feel it puncturing through tissue, through my insides, as he drives it deeper.

His hot breath slithers into my ear like poison.

"You were right, you know. About me, about us," he says, and I feel the blade slide out of my body. My hand instinctively goes to the wound, and blood escapes like warm water between my fingers. He talks quickly, joyfully. "You think you're holy, that you're strengthened by the divine, but you're *nothing*. You're a pathetic little boy playing dress up." He kisses my cheek, and I can almost feel the burning hate of his smile next to my ear. "And now, Peter, it's time to die. But first, you're going to watch me kill every last one them."

He pulls away from me and, with a gasping breath, I drop to my knees.

"Peter!"

I don't know who screams my name. My ears are rushing with sound, as if a hole has been blown open in my mind and a black ocean is now pouring through, filling me with death.

"God help me," I say, and manage to turn my head as Bartholomew steps past me, unconcerned, knife at his side, dripping with my blood.

The remains of my brothers are huddled together. Byron and David have put themselves in front of the younger ones, shoulder to shoulder. I know they'll fight, but they won't survive.

None of them will survive.

I look at Bartholomew's back as he steps away and I see black smoke rising from his body that has nothing to do with this earthly blaze. It is the evil inside of him smoldering. The demon's stench leaking through his flesh.

My thinking goes fuzzy, and the roaring in my ears goes silent. Instead, all I hear is the pounding of my heart. The throbbing beat fills my head. I visualize it pushing more blood through me, out of me. Saving me. Killing me.

I find myself travelling.

I am no longer in this attic.

I'm home. In our family cabin. I'm at the table with my mother and father, who are laughing. Laughing at something silly I've done with my food. I don't know what it is, I'm only an infant, but I love that they're happy. I love that they're laughing.

Then I'm gone, and I'm walking through a field with Andrew.

A memory that's only a few days old. He's telling me about priesthood. About what it means to live for something other than yourself.

He tells me I have a choice.

This life of the flesh, which is over in the blink of an eye, or your eternal life with God.

We stop walking. I smell the rough wheat, the sweetness of the tall grass. A golden sun sits on the horizon and Andrew is alive and happy. Radiant.

When he speaks to me, his voice is strong, resonant.

If you can sacrifice this life for the other, then you will know more joy than you can possibly imagine. A joy that will last for eternity.

I want to hug him, to tell him that I'll always love him as a son loves his father.

Tell him I miss him. Tell him that I tried.

I'm not a fool. I know no amount of words or blessings can save me, no more than they can transform me into something more than I am. But priest or not, blessed or not, I must do what I feel is right. I must believe in something. Even if it's only myself.

"Come on!" David yells, and I'm thrust back into the narrow, smoke-filled attic.

"Help me, Father," I whisper. "Give me strength."

I put a hand on the attic floor and slowly push myself upward. My insides cry out, but there is strength in my legs, and there is strength in my arms, up my back and across my shoulders. The hand not holding my wound is curled into a tight fist.

David sees me rise but keeps it to himself. His eyes flick from Bartholomew to me.

I am light. I say it again and again. A mantra. *I am light. I am light.*

There is light all around me.

There is light inside me.

I raise a hand so David can see it clearly. I turn it, fingers straight up and flattened, then motion it to one side. I pray

David understands. Still, he says nothing, but I see a flicker of comprehension in his eyes. I notice him grip the shirt of Timothy behind him.

"Demon!" I cry out, and am gratified when Bartholomew spins. I relish the shock in his face, take courage from the fear in his eyes.

"Your time here is done," I say, and charge.

This time, he truly is caught off guard.

He tries to move aside, but is kicked from behind, throwing him off balance.

I don't see if David has pulled the others out of the way. There's no time for me to know for sure. As I leave my feet, I can only hope.

I throw out my arms and lower my shoulder, ramming it square into his stomach. I hear his breath come out of him as I propel us both backward through the smoky air and down, down through the opening of the ceiling. Into the flames.

For a moment, we are falling, and there is no sound, no pain. His arm is wrapped tight around my back, as if holding on for safety.

We land with a massive, bone-crunching impact, his body beneath mine. But we do not hit the floor, landing instead atop the sloping iron at the foot of a metal-framed cot. I hear the snap of Bartholomew's back as he connects with it, my weight crushing down atop him.

We both collapse off the bed and thump down to the floor. I roll onto my back, panting for breath, staring at a gaping hole in the ceiling high above.

There are flames surrounding me on all sides, and the wound in my gut sends lightning streaks of pain through my body. Yet I am able to turn my head, to see Bartholomew crumpled beside me. His eyes are wide with shock, but I swear they are his own.

Here, then, is nothing but a boy. Broken, dying. His mouth opens and closes, as if gulping desperately for air. He is bent unnaturally, his legs lifeless and limp, twisted at the hip to lie nearly perpendicular to his torso.

I'm surprised he's still breathing, but he is.

And he's staring right at me.

When he speaks, there's no menace in his voice. No mockery. No command. Only the voice of a frightened child. A little boy, terrified of death, like all of us.

"I think . . ." he says, having gained some control of his breathing, "I think my back is broken."

I press a hand to my bleeding stomach, but I keep my eyes on his. I'll stay with him now, in his final moments, if that's what he needs. There's little else I can do.

"I'm sorry," I say, and I mean it. I'm sorry for everything, for all the horror and death that has taken place. I'm sorry I couldn't save everyone. That I can't save him.

He closes his eyes. His face is peaceful, if saddened. "I don't want to die."

I study him as he slips away, his breath labored. I can't help wondering.

"Is it finished?" I ask, even though I'm unsure whether I really want to know the answer.

Bartholomew's eyes spring open, locking onto mine, and for a split second there's something *else* there staring back at me. Something unfathomable.

And then, it's gone. And there's nothing left before me but Bartholomew. He lets out a heavy sigh, and his body seems to deflate.

"Yes," he says. "For now."

I don't know what else to say, so I simply stay with him. I reach out my free hand and place it on his head. He begins to weep, and I can hear the rasping of each breath as his body fights to function. "Forgive me," he rasps at the end. Then he grips my hand tight, his words barely audible. "Absolve me, Peter."

I nod, then close my eyes and say the words that, in this

religion of men, take away the sins of those who ask it. I do this as a vessel of God, as a servant of the spirit, in order to cleanse the light we all carry and release the weight of our doings—both good and evil—from that infinite space inside each one of us.

When I remove my hand from his head, his eyes are open and still, his charred lips pressed into the floorboards. He does not move again.

In the next moment, hands grip me hard beneath my shoulders and I'm being pulled away, backward through patches of flame. The last thing I see of Bartholomew is the fire catching in his hair.

60

The escape is a blur.

David pulls me free from the worst of the flames, back toward the far end of the dormitory where the ladder still hangs like a wooden tongue from the smoke-filled attic hatch.

After I fell through, they all made their way back down. David wrapped himself in the blanket of one of the few unburned cots and fought his way toward me, pulled me out of the worst of it.

He's screaming something in my ear.

"The snow, Peter! It'll break our fall. Trust me on this!"

I'm lifted to my feet as the whole world burns. The heat is unbearable. I can't see, can't breathe. Ahead of me is an empty square of roiling smoke and snowfall, a window completely smashed clear of glass. I watch in a daze as Byron hops on the sill, takes a last look back, then leaps.

"There's a decent buildup right below this window! If we're lucky, we'll only break our legs!" He's still yelling and pulling me through the smoke. I don't know how he has the breath or the energy, I only know I am grateful.

"You first!" he says, and half lifts, half shoves me into the window frame.

I look down.

It's a long drop. Twenty feet, give or take.

"Let your legs crumple when you hit, try to fall into snow so you don't hit the ground, you know, *too* hard."

At the open window, the cold air hits my face like a hard slap, and my breath goes out of me. From nearby, there is a flash of faces watching me anxiously, all of them eager to escape. I want to say something, to encourage them, but then I'm pushed from behind, and I fall into the night.

Once more I'm falling, not into fire this time, but toward earth.

Byron, the crazy fool, has his arms extended, as if he's going to catch me.

Halfway down, I do David's advice one better. I let my body go limp, turn to face the stars, and let my arms float out from my sides.

When I hit, there's no pain.

I don't know if it's because I'm safe, or because I'm dead.

61

I'm dragged away from my landing spot. Once released, I plop down into the snow on my rear, watch as David helps the last of the survivors out the window. Byron is admirably trying to build up as much snow as he can where he and I and a few others have already landed, fluffing it like a pillow. When he feels it's good enough, he yells up at David, who pitches Finnegan out the window. Then Thomas, followed quickly by Timothy, who gives a mighty bellow as he leaps. I can't help but smile at his bravery.

Finally, David jumps, and ironically is the only one injured, badly twisting an ankle.

Byron does the best he can wrapping a ripped sheet around my waist, pressing my wound, tying it so tight I can hardly take a deep breath. But the pain subsides, as does the blood loss.

"Can you walk?" David asks while he helps me up. He looks at my stomach—a place I've avoided looking since Byron patched me up—then back to my face.

"I can walk," I say, not knowing if it's the truth, but also knowing there's no other option.

I won't die here.

"Can you?" I ask.

He laughs, puts an arm through mine to steady me. "A hundred miles if necessary," he says, and I believe him.

The five of us who remain walk a safe distance from the orphanage, then up a gentle rise, before turning back to watch St. Vincent's consumed by fire.

To watch our childhood burn. For me, a second time.

It's cold, but not as bad as I would have thought. The snowfall has lightened, and the wind, though strong, is not unbearable.

David stands next to me as I lean against the bark of a leafless tree. The trees on the rise are far enough away from the fire to live another season. To live a hundred more seasons.

"That place," he says, and leans his back against the tree, his shoulder pressed to mine. "That was *my* hell."

I look at him, see his orange-lit profile as he watches—with what I would swear is pleasure—as the orphanage burns.

The fire is strong enough that, even from a distance, the heat is intense. The marauding flames reach high into the night sky, the rising smoke erasing the field of stars. The blaze appears to me as a giant hand reaching upward, pointing toward the heavens in a final rebuke. Or, possibly, a promise. A vow to one day return.

We can't help ourselves. We stay and watch for what feels an eternity. We watch until the giant, accusatory hand becomes nothing but burning wood. A wall collapses inward, and soon the entire roof follows.

We've seen enough.

"We need to go," I say, hoping David doesn't register the fear and pain in my voice.

David nods. His eyes flick to my stomach, then back to my face. "Okay, yeah. The farm?"

"I think so. It'll be light soon, and I know the way. The storm has lessened, I think we can make it. Timothy may need to be carried at some point."

"I can walk," he grumbles, and is already stumbling forward through the snow. "Which way, Father?"

It takes me a moment to realize he's referring to me.

Andrew, I can see you smiling at all of this.

I'm so sorry.

"East," I say, and begin walking. My hand grips a bunched knot of Byron's torn shirt, pressed firmly against my torn skin. I don't think the bleeding has worsened, and for now my wits feel relatively clear.

I am light, I think.

David comes up next to me, presumably in case I falter, or fall; but as he limps by my side, a set grimace on his face, I take reassurance from his presence.

The fire at our back lights the way ahead.

The others follow in our tracks.

62

Grace sits down to breakfast after pouring fresh coffee for her father.

She eyes the biscuits and eggs hungrily, but takes the time to fold her hands and offer up a prayer of thanks. When the blessing is complete, she digs in with vigor.

John watches her thoughtfully.

"What?" she says, wiping at her chin for loose crumbs.

"Nothing, nothing. Just admiring your appetite."

She gives a wry smirk, then pops another piece of buttered biscuit into her mouth, making him laugh.

Outside the window, the day is breaking, and she'll soon be at chores. She's excited to wade through the fresh snow. She loved falling asleep to the careless creaking of their strong house in the hard wind of the storm, the knowledge that she would wake to a gorgeous new world of white, the crisp dry air of a clear day after a good snowfall.

She studies the sky through the window, amazed at how clear and blue it is, like the shell of a robin's egg. She wonders if she can convince her papa to walk with her, up the nearby hill with the toboggan he built last winter.

Grace takes a sip of coffee, debating whether the snow will be too soft for good sledding, when she glances once more out the kitchen window.

A dark shape emerges atop a distant rise. A gentle crest, now covered in snow, dotted along its ridge with blanketed pines, is soon marred by multiple figures, each of them slogging through at its center, aiming for their home.

"Papa?"

John Hill sees his daughter's concerned stare and turns his body to face out the window. He squints into the brightening day, trying to make out the shapes.

And then he knows.

"Grace!" he says, standing so abruptly his chair nearly falls backward. "Get your coat and boots and follow me. Hurry now."

She stands, shaken and frightened. She steps up to the window, puts a finger on the chilled glass, as if it will bring her closer to the distant shadows.

Then Grace, like her father, makes out the shapes for what they are.

"Oh my God," she says.

And then she's moving.

The front door is open, her father already running through the deep snow. "And get blankets! As many as you can carry!"

Grace does.

Her father reaches the boys first.

An older boy, seeing his approach, staggers, then drops the sleeping child he's been carrying in his arms—for who knows how long—into the thick snow. As the smaller boy hits the ground, the older one drops to his knees. Head hanging limply to his chest.

Two younger-looking boys stand on either side of the tallest one. They each have an arm looped around his waist, as if to keep him from falling. His feet drag through the snow. Grace sees them as she approaches and has only a moment to wonder how they managed to get him so far in that condition.

Her father is at odds, seemingly not knowing which boy to go to first, but it doesn't matter. They're done. Spent. Having found their way, they all collapse into the snow.

Grace arrives like a flurry of warmth and energy. She begins draping blankets over them all, one by one. Her father removes his coat and wraps it around the smallest one, bundling him.

The tall one, who the other two carried along on sheer willpower, also collapses.

Grace knows.

She doesn't say, but she knows.

She runs to him, already crying, and rolls Peter over so she can see his face.

The first thing that catches her eye is the dark red stain in the snow, followed by the blood-soaked wound in his stomach. So much blood has spilled that it's crusted nearly the length of one pant leg, pooled into the waistband where, in the freezing temperature, it's crystallized along his skin like red ice.

"Peter?"

His face is pale as the snow, his lips gray. But his eyes open, bright blue, and he shifts them to look at her. His throat clutches, as if he means to speak, but only air comes from his mouth. A soft, cold gust. The breath of the dying.

"I'm gonna carry the little one inside, I'll be back," John says. He lifts the wrapped boy in his arms, runs as best he can toward the house.

Grace looks around at the others.

They all look back at her openly. Plainly. One of them, an older one who looks Peter's age, says her name. It's not a question.

"Yes," she replies.

She does not know them. Does not know their faces.

Peter has told her names, so many names, but right now she can't remember them. Can't remember a single one. But these are the ones he's lived with. These are the ones he told her stories about. She feels a kinship to them, to these half-frozen, exhausted strangers.

The other two boys huddle together, under blankets now, shivering.

Their eyes are not on her, nor the home in the near distance, with promises of warmth and food and shelter.

Their eyes are on Peter.

The older one gets to his knees, crawls closer. He takes one of Peter's hands in his own. Tears spill down his face, dotting the snow silver.

"Peter? It's David. Look, Peter. It's Grace. She's right here. We made it." He sniffles, rubs at his face. He looks at Grace for a moment, then back down to his friend. "Please stay, Peter. Please stay with me."

Peter's eyes shift to look at the older boy—David, he said—then his eyes move up, focus on the bright, depthless sky overhead.

Grace grips his other hand, hoping he can feel her. She bends down and kisses his cheek. It's icy, but she lingers there, letting her lips heat his skin before sitting back up.

When she does, his eyes are locked on hers.

He looks happy.

He swallows, then speaks. His voice a raspy whisper, a dry leaf skimming across a frozen lake. "Grace," he says.

She squeezes his hand harder, tries to rub warmth into his fingers.

"Grace, do you see them?"

She opens her mouth, but doesn't know how to respond. She looks to David, but he only shakes his head sadly, as if it doesn't matter anymore.

And maybe it doesn't. But she still wants to know. She feels that it's somehow important, so she says, "Who, Peter? See who?"

With surprising strength, or purely by power of will, Peter lifts his head. He looks all around the empty landscape, his eyes darting from place to place. "There," he says. "And there."

He looks back at her, amused. He smiles weakly, teeth red with blood. "You can't see them, but they're here. They're all around us, Grace, and I saved them. I saved them all."

Grace watches her father's return from the house. She wills him to move faster, to help her get Peter inside. Get him to shelter. Care for his wound. Heal him . . .

Peter's fingers suddenly tighten around hers and she turns back to look into his face, into his eyes. He's still smiling, but it grows weak now, and she knows, right then, that there's no nursing him back to health, that no amount of warmth or medicine will cure him, will keep him here, with her.

With the knowing, her heart slows. She feels the anxiety drain from her body. The need, the desire to help him, to hold him, slips through her like a dream that dies upon waking.

"I love you," she says.

"They're all around us, Grace . . . they're waiting for me."

David buries his head into Peter's shoulder, weeping. Through wrenching tears, he lifts his face and whispers something into his ear.

"Yes, Peter," Grace says, and lowers her own face close to his. "You saved them, and it's okay. It's okay now."

Peter's head settles back into the new snow. A soft exhale escapes his lips. His eyes lose their focus and turn upward to stare, forever, into the blue open sky.

ACKNOWLEDGMENTS

My thanks to the following people for helping to bring this story to life in all its forms:

Paul Miller at Earthling Publications, who first published the novel.

My ever-patient, hard-working agent, Elizabeth Copps.

My wonderful editor, Kristin Temple.

Thanks to Nadia Saward at Orbit UK, Kelly Lonesome, Chris Scheina, Jakub Nemecek at Gnom Press, and Jose Angel De Dios García at Dilatando Mentes Editorial.

Sadie Hartmann, for the tweet.

Stephen King, for the retweet.

Richard Chizmar, for the assist.

Andy Davidson, for the intro.

Glenn Chadbourne, for the original artwork.

Brendan Deneen, for getting this story to the screen.

To my early readers, who offered great advice and input: Paul Tremblay, Eileen Simard, Laird Barron, Thomas Joyce, John Foster, Douglas Wynne, John McFarland, Bill Breedlove, Logan England, Jake Marley.

If I missed anyone, give me hell and I'll get you next time.

Thanks to everyone who reads this book. I'm forever grateful.

Lastly, all my love to Stephanie, as always, for everything.